W9-BQU-462

USA TODAY BESTSELLING AUTHOR

JASMINE CRESSWELL

THE
DAUGHTER

MIRA

ISBN 0-7783-2371-4

THE DAUGHTER

Copyright © 1998 by Jasmine Cresswell.

www.MIRABooks.com

Printed in U.S.A.

Prologue

Maggie Slade realized three things simultaneously: Cobra was drunk, he was angry, and he was going to rape her. She pummeled his chest in a vain attempt to push him away, and he laughed, apparently pleased and stimulated by her resistance. She willed her body to go limp, trying not to gag when he clamped his mouth over hers and stuck his tongue halfway down her throat.

Think! she ordered herself. *You can get away from him if you don't panic.*

Cobra had her pinned to a half-finished wall in a house on the construction site where he worked, but he was so confident of his strength that he wasn't expending much effort to keep her there. Instead of holding her by the hair or the throat, he was trying to unzip the fly of his jeans, leaving her with a few precious inches of wriggle room. But how to take advantage of that? Oh, God! Why had she smoked that stupid joint? Her brain felt as mushy as her knees.

It's now or never, Maggie decided. And she'd better get it right the first time because stupid dickhead Cobra wasn't likely to give her a second chance. Yanking on his long hair, she thrust upward with her knee as hard and fast as she could, catching him full in the groin. His eyes crossed and for a split second he made no sound. Then he doubled over, howling in drunken rage, spewing obscenities.

Maggie didn't hang around to listen. She ducked backward through a gap in the wall and ran through the house, heading for the door. Construction debris littered the floor, and a couple of times she almost fell over empty paint cans that were difficult to see by the faint light of the moon. The sound of Cobra's lumbering footsteps spurred her on and she finally found the side door where they'd come in. It was open! She dashed out into the sharp cold of the Colorado night, slamming the door shut behind her.

Let it be self-locking. Please, God, keep the stupid jerk penned up inside for an extra couple of seconds.

Running across the sandy front yard, she drew in shuddering gulps of fresh air, but her stomach still churned, threatening to send back the pizza she'd consumed earlier. Where could she hide? How in the world was she going to get home? Cobra was so angry that if he caught her, he'd beat her up for sure. She could be hurt badly enough to end up in the hospital, and then there would be no hope of keeping tonight a secret from Mom.

Maggie pulled a face into the darkness. Sometimes life really sucked. Her mother was gonna be madder than a nest of hornets if she discovered that Maggie had snuck out to meet Cobra. Mom disapproved of him and the Red Raiders—said they were all losers with overactive hormones and underactive brain cells—and she'd flat out forbidden Maggie to see Cobra again. Maggie knew she'd be grounded for the rest of the year if her mother ever found out what had happened tonight. She *had* to get home before Mom noticed she was missing!

Maggie jerked her head from side to side, searching for some sign of help, but the area was deserted. The house where Cobra had taken her stood in a row of similarly empty, half-finished houses, and there were no trees to provide cover, no people to help. Nowhere to hide.

"I'm gonna kill you, bitch. First, I'm gonna do you real good, then I'm gonna kill you."

Cobra's voice sounded behind her, way too close. She heard the sound of smashing glass and realized he was coming out through a window. What for? Was he too drunk to find the door?

Maggie didn't waste a second telling herself that Cobra didn't mean what he said. Propelled by terror, she ran to where Cobra had parked his Harley. She took a running leap onto the bike and turned on the ignition. An eternity passed before the engine roared to life, a vibrating beast only a fraction less terrifying than Cobra.

The beer and the blow to his groin must have slowed Cobra's reactions or he would have pulled her off the bike long before she could get it in gear and set it moving. As it was, she had a precious few seconds to put her scant mechanical knowledge to the test while he clambered through the window. When he realized that Maggie was taking off on his Harley, Cobra let out a bellow of rage loud enough to attract the attention of anybody alive and breathing within a two-mile radius.

Gunning the engine, Maggie set off down the dirt road, half-blind with terror, sweat drying on her skin in an ice-cold sheen. The bike swerved toward the ditch. She steered it back onto the middle of the road and it swayed, threatening to topple her, before swooping toward the ditch again. She gritted her teeth, shifted gears and rode doggedly on, teetering and swerving but managing to keep the Harley upright.

By the time she hit a paved road, her terror had faded slightly. Thank God it was late and there wasn't much traffic. Her luck held, and she teetered another six or seven miles closer to home before she encountered a truck coming from the opposite direction. She managed, just barely, to avoid crashing into the truck head-on, but the near miss brought her to a screeching halt in the middle of the highway. No way she could control Cobra's Harley in traffic. Guiding the bike over to the side of the road, she cut the engine and stood, straddling the bike, her whole body shuddering.

Without the spur of an immediate threat from Cobra, she couldn't bring herself to drive the Harley any farther. Leaving it by a clump of scrub oak, she started trudging toward Pineview, the subdivision where she lived. If she walked fast, she would be home in less than forty minutes.

Earlier in the evening, when he'd still seemed hand-some and just wild enough to be exciting, Cobra had persuaded her to share a joint. Maggie hadn't wanted to admit that she'd never smoked pot before, so she'd forced the smoke into her lungs, trying to look cool. By the time the joint was finished, she'd had a mild buzz, but she hadn't felt out of control. Now, she wondered if she'd been higher than she realized. Either the joint or her narrow escape had left her legs feeling like over-stretched rubber and the edges of her mind fuzzy, so that her thoughts kept slipping away before she could grab hold of them.

Maybe it was just as well she couldn't think straight, Maggie reflected gloomily. She had a sinking suspicion that when she finally got home and looked back on what had happened, she'd realize that she'd behaved like a total retard. The only thing more solid than the muscles in Cobra's arms was the lump of concrete he called his brain. Right now, she couldn't remember why she'd ever found him exciting.

It seemed a lot longer than forty minutes before she finally turned off the main road and crossed between the stone pillars that marked the entrance to the Pineview subdivision, but her watch said it was barely 2:00—only a little more than an hour since Cobra had tried to rape her. Jeez, it was good to be home! In Maggie's opinion, the suburb of Pineview housed the most terminally bor-ing collection of people in the entire universe, but tonight the neat, tree-lined streets looked like a real safe haven. Fortunately, her old fogy neighbors were all tucked into bed by eleven, so there was nobody to see her walking home, nobody to report back to her mother that wild Maggie Slade had been roaming the neighborhood at 2:00 a.m.

She congratulated herself too soon. Just as she turned the corner onto Blue Spruce Way, she heard the sound of a car approaching. She swung around and saw a couple in a maroon Buick. The Jacksons! Just her luck that they should be out tonight of all nights. Mrs. Jackson was a major pill and the biggest gossip in the neighborhood. Maggie absolutely did not want Mrs. Jackson to see her.

Maggie happened to be walking right past her friend Tiffany's house, so she dodged behind the clump of aspens that held pride of place in Tiffany's front yard. Fortunately, Mr. and Mrs. Jackson looked like they were yelling at each other—they usually were—and they drove past without noticing her. Maggie's spirits lifted. All right! Only seconds now, and she'd be home. Maybe this night wasn't going to turn out to be a total disaster after all.

She'd learned her lesson, she decided, edging out from behind the trees as the Jacksons' Buick disappeared around the corner. No more cutting class to hang out with the Red Raiders. Maybe she'd work a bit harder in physics class and improve her grade some. Then she could at least *think* about applying to the Air Force Academy like Ms. Dowd, her dorky old counselor, kept suggesting.

Her dad would be real proud if she went to the Academy. Except that he'd probably never know she'd been accepted. Mom insisted Dad was in heaven, looking out for both of them, but Maggie wasn't at all sure that she believed in heaven, although she wished she could. Sometimes, when Father Tobias jabbered on at mass, preaching a sermon that was even more boring than usual, she'd try to picture her dad sitting on a cloud and playing a harp. Dad had liked really cool music, not dorky classical stuff, so the image always made her smile, and sometimes she could almost feel her father smiling right along with her. That was about as close as she got to believing her dad was still around and looking out for her.

The familiar outlines of her house took shape against the darkness. Finally. She didn't want to get caught now, at the very last minute, so she edged around the house, keeping to the shadows, the route familiar after a half-dozen other nighttime escapades. She eased herself into the window well in the backyard, pushed up the basement window and jumped down into the rec room.

She was greeted by a warm, comforting silence and stood for a moment, enjoying the familiar surroundings. Boy, was it ever good to be home! Heady with relief, Maggie crossed the carpeted floor and crept upstairs. The basement door always creaked, but she'd left it open on purpose. She slipped around it noiselessly, keeping her back pressed to the wall as she headed for her bedroom.

She was halfway up the stairs when she heard a tiny creak that came from the kitchen. Was it her mother? No, the sound was too faint, almost furtive. If Mom had come down for a drink or something, she would have switched on the light.

Maybe the gerbil had escaped from his cage again. Gosh, she hoped not. Mom always got really torqued when Howard was on the loose. Maggie listened intently as the sound came again, and the back of her neck pricked. Someone—not the gerbil—was hurrying across the kitchen and the sounds she'd heard were creaking floorboards. Was it a burglar? Holding her breath, she braced herself against the banister and leaned over so that she could see into the kitchen.

The angle was wrong for her to see more than a small section by the window, but just as she debated going downstairs for a better look, she heard the unmistakable sound of the back door opening and a key turning in the lock. The intruder had left the kitchen.

Maggie's alarm was instantly replaced by fury. Someone—no prize for guessing who—had just used a key to let himself out of the house. There could only be one person who'd be slinking out of the back door at this hour of the night, using a key. Her mom's boyfriend. And there was no mystery as to why he'd been creeping around so secretly. He had no idea Maggie was out of the house, so he'd been afraid of waking her. When she was sneaking back *into* the house, her mother's boyfriend had been sneaking *out!* It would make a funny scene in a movie, but Maggie wasn't laughing. Far from it. She felt hot and sweaty with anger.

She scowled, the ache of hurt spreading from her stomach all the way to her fingers and her toes. She hated the fact that her mother was having an affair. How could she be so disloyal to Dad's memory? Dad had been a real live hero who'd flown combat missions all over the world before he came to the Air Force Academy as an instructor. Then his plane had crashed on a training flight, killing the entire crew. Mom had been devastated, or so she claimed, but Dad hadn't even been dead for two years, and she was already seeing someone else.

As if *seeing* was all that was going on between Mom and her boyfriend, Maggie thought scornfully. Mom must be having sex with the guy. Why else would he come to her so late at night? She'd seen them kissing once, when she'd come home unexpectedly from a ski trip. They'd been tangled up together on the sofa in the living room, and their hands had been all over each other. It had been disgusting, a real gross-out. But lately, Maggie had started to be even more worried. Why did this guy only come to the house at night? Why was Mom keeping their affair such a big secret unless he was married?

Maggie glared into the darkness, waiting for the sound of a car engine to start up. When no sound came, she shrugged, pretending an indifference she didn't feel. So Mr. Stupid Meathead had walked here. Which meant that he was a neighbor.

Mom's having sex with one of the neighbors.

Maggie felt her mouth twist downward. More than likely Mr. Stupid Meathead was the father of one of the kids she went to school with. She hated even to think about that possibility, it was so gross. She stomped along the upstairs hallway toward her room, angry enough that she didn't care if her mother heard her. So what if she'd snuck out of the house to meet Cobra? So what if she'd smoked a joint? Her mother was doing something just as bad. Worse. This secret lover thing with Mr. Meathead had gone on for months now, and Maggie was tired of the pretense and the evasions, not to mention the outright lies her mother kept telling.

Maggie sniffed and used the heel of her hand to scrub away a few tears. Dammit, she wasn't going to start bawling just because her mom was having an affair. But tomorrow, after school, when Mom got home from work, Maggie was going to demand some answers. She was fifteen years old, nearly sixteen, not a baby anymore, and she had every right to know if her mother was fooling around with one of the neighbors. She would demand to know who Mr. Stupid Meathead was. So that she could kick him in the balls, maybe, just like she'd kicked Cobra.

"Maggie..." The sound of her mother calling her name stopped Maggie in her tracks. Her mother must have heard her footsteps. Should she answer? On the point of sauntering into her mother's bedroom, she changed her mind and decided to play it safe. She dashed into her own bedroom, pulled off her sneakers, shucked her jeans and sweater, and only then—left wearing her typical sleeping outfit of T-shirt and panties—walked back along the short corridor to her mother's bedroom.

She opted for the casual, innocent approach. "Mom?" She stuck her head around the half-open door of the master bedroom and yawned to convey the message that she'd been disturbed in the midst of deep, blameless sleep. She strolled farther into the room. "Mom, did you call me? What's up?"

Her mother didn't reply. An acrid smell hung in the air, and Maggie felt a sudden twitch of fear. What was going on? The room was in darkness and she reached clumsily for the light switch.

Rowena Slade lay in the center of the king-size bed she'd once shared with Maggie's father. Her eyes were closed and she was holding a pillow to her stomach. The pillow was stained with red.

"Mom! *Mom?*" Mouth bone-dry, legs shaking, Maggie ran to the bed. The fear she'd felt when Cobra attacked her was nothing in comparison to the terror that gripped her now. She leaned across the bed and lifted up the pillow her mother was clutching. Blood jetted out from her mother's abdomen, hitting her in the chest. Maggie screamed and pushed the pillow back down on her mother's stomach. "Oh my God! Mom, what happened? What should I do?"

Her mother's eyes flickered open, then closed again. She groaned faintly.

Maggie was crying so hard she could barely catch her breath. "Mom, please tell me what to do. I don't know what to do. You have to tell me, Mom."

Rowena Slade opened her eyes. Her gaze wavered for a moment, then focused on Maggie. For a moment, Maggie was sure she saw her mother smile.

Rowena held her daughter's gaze. "Love you... Mags. You're...the greatest..." Her words slurred into silence. Her eyes closed again.

"No, Mom, please don't shut your eyes! Wake up, I

need you! I love you so much, Mom." Maggie grabbed
the hem of the sheet and swiped at her eyes. As she disturbed the sheet, something fell out of the folds. A gun.
Maggie picked it up and stared at it in disbelief. "He
shot you! Oh, Mom, I'm sorry, so sorry. Oh my god, I
should've been here."

Her mother made a tiny gesture with one hand.
"Not…your…fault…"

Maggie suddenly realized that she was wasting precious, life-giving seconds. She put the gun on the nightstand. Then, unable to bear the sight of it, she swiped
at it angrily, knocking it onto the floor.

"I'll call the paramedics," she said, trying to hold her
mother's hand and dial 911 at the same time. The op-
erator came on the line and Maggie sobbed into the receiver, "My mother's been shot. You have to send the
paramedics. She's bleeding and I can't stop the bleeding." Her hands were so slippery that she dropped the
phone and it bounced on the bed, the edge of the mouth-
piece just catching her mother's chest.

Rowena groaned and Maggie turned, horrified by her
carelessness. "Mom, I'm so sorry. I didn't mean to hurt
you—oh my gosh, I'm so sorry, Mom."

"'S'okay…. You didn't mean…" Her mother's
voice faded.

"Miss, miss! Are you there? I need your address,
miss."

Maggie scrabbled to pick up the phone. "You have
to come real fast. My mom's bleeding something awful.
She's losing consciousness." The tears choked her. "We
live in the Pineview subdivision, 4141 Pinon Way. You

have to send the paramedics right away. My mom's hurt really badly."

She hung up the phone and cradled her mother's head in the crook of her arm. Rowena's face was white, her lips blue as Arctic ice. She's dead, Maggie thought in stark terror, and the whole of her insides seemed to freeze. Sobbing, she took her mother's hands and pressed them to her face. She felt the lightest of pressures from Rowena's hand and realized that her mother was still alive.

Thank you, God! Thank you.

Rowena's lips twitched and she made a harsh sound deep in her throat. Maggie realized her mother was trying to say something, but she couldn't bear to see her struggling and she pressed her fingertips against Rowena's mouth.

"Don't talk," she said. "We'll talk later." She stroked her mother's face, fingers trembling. "It's okay. Everything's going to be fine, you'll see. The paramedics will soon be here and they'll fix you right up."

Rowena's eyes opened again. She stared straight at Maggie and spoke, her voice clear and strong. "I love you, Maggie."

Her eyes closed.

When the paramedics arrived, Maggie was still sitting on the bed, her mother's body clutched in her arms. She heard the ring of the doorbell, followed by knocking and pounding, but she couldn't figure out how to move without causing blood to spill out of her mother again, so she just stayed where she was. Or maybe you didn't bleed after you were dead. The paramedics banged and pounded some more. Then the phone rang, but she couldn't reach the phone, either, so she ignored it.

Finally, after a lot of noise and shouting, a bunch of people crowded into the bedroom. She stared at them, but her eyes were misted over and she couldn't see too well. They spoke to her, but their words didn't make any sense and she was too weary to figure out what they were telling her.

One of the men knelt beside the bed and pressed a stethoscope to her mom's chest. Then he got up and shook his head. Maggie watched him because she had to look somewhere and her mind had gone blank.

A woman came up to the bed and said something. Maggie heard what she said, but when she tried to answer, she realized she'd already forgotten the question. She switched her gaze from the man with the stethoscope to the woman, who had black skin and blond hair cropped close to her head. Maggie wondered how often the woman had to dye her hair to keep it such a sunny shade of yellow.

"She's in shock," a tall, gray-haired man said.

Maggie swiveled around and stared at him. She licked her lips. "My mother's dead," she said finally.

The woman reached out and touched Maggie gently on the arm. "Honey, maybe you'd like to come into another room with me. Just while the paramedics take care of your mother."

A few thoughts were beginning to creep into the emptiness of Maggie's mind. "They can't take care of her. She's dead."

The body in her arms felt cold and Maggie's muscles had cramped from staying so long in one position. She stared down at the alien face nestled against her chest, suddenly repelled by the strangeness of the body that had once been her mom.

From the corner of her eye, she noticed the gray-haired man exchange a glance with the woman. They nodded to each other and the man unwrapped Maggie's arms from around her mother's body while the woman half pushed and half lifted Maggie off the bed.

"I'm Detective Washington," she said. "But you can call me Janette. Your name's Maggie Slade, isn't it?"

Maggie nodded. She tried to turn so that she could see what the paramedics were doing with her mother's body, but Janette put her arm around Maggie's waist and propelled her toward the bedroom door. Maggie didn't have the energy to protest. Janette wanted her out of the bedroom. It was easier to go than to stay.

They made their way into the kitchen. Maggie sat down at the table and saw that her hands were covered in her mother's blood. Nausea spewed up from her stomach so fast that she only just reached the guest bathroom in time to throw up.

Exhausted, she leaned against the sink. For a while, it seemed that her stomach was never going to stop heaving even though it was empty. When the nausea finally ended, she turned around to find Janette waiting for her outside the half-open door.

"You okay, honey?"

No, she was quite definitely not okay. She was tearing apart inside. "I have to wash my hands," Maggie said.

"I'll wait here," Janette said.

Maggie didn't care what Janette did. She washed her face and hands with scads of scented soap and oodles of hot water, then she scrubbed her arms and her neck and every piece of exposed skin she could find, but she couldn't get rid of the smell of blood, or the feeling of stickiness.

The numbness of shock was passing, leaving so much pain in its wake that Maggie didn't know where to put herself. Her body felt brittle, the various parts not properly connected. She wanted to cry, but the tears seemed jammed into a huge lump that was stuck in her throat, too big to swallow—so big that even breathing was difficult. She stared into the mirror, watching herself sway. Boy, breathing was complicated, once you started to think about it.

Janette suddenly grabbed Maggie's head and pushed it down toward her knees. "Whoa, girl. For a moment there, we nearly lost you. Let's go back into the kitchen, honey. You look like you could use a cup of tea."

Maggie didn't want tea—she didn't want anything— but she followed Janette into the kitchen and obediently drank the hot, sweet brew when it was put in front of her. The lump in her throat shrank just a little as she swallowed the tea, but even so, she couldn't get any words out of her mouth.

She was glad that Janette sat across the table from her, holding her hand. Maggie hoped they could sit there for a long time. If she didn't speak and didn't move, maybe she wouldn't have to think about what had happened to her mother.

The gray-haired man came into the kitchen. Behind him, in the hall leading to the front door, Maggie glimpsed the paramedics pushing a stretcher. They were taking her mother's body from the house, she realized, transferring it to wherever paramedics took dead bodies.

She couldn't stand to think of her mom lying alone in the morgue, wrapped up in plastic, her body congealing from icy chill into frozen morbidity. Maggie felt a great burst of pain rise inside her, like a scream that couldn't come out. She wrapped her arms across her tummy, holding in the pain, suppressing the scream.

It's not fair, she thought in a wave of raging self-pity. *Why is this happening to me? First Dad and now Mom. It's not fair that they're both dead.*

If she'd been home like she should have been, then her mother probably wouldn't be dead. If she'd been home instead of out fooling around with the Cobra and the stupid Red Raiders, she would have been able to protect her mother—save her from Mr. Stupid Meathead and his gun. Guilt washed over Maggie in a suffocating wave. She hung her head and stared down at her feet, wriggling her bare toes against the cold kitchen floor. She had snuck out of the house against all the rules, and her mother had died.

The gray-haired man came and sat at the table, drawing up a chair between Maggie and Janette. "My name is Tom Garda," he said. "I'm a detective sergeant with the South County Police Department. I know how upset you must be, Maggie, but I need to ask you a few questions about what happened here tonight."

Janette made a gesture of protest. "Tom, give the kid a break. She's not in any state to answer your questions right now."

Tom's mouth narrowed angrily. "Christ, Janette, Rowena Slade was shot in her bed at point-blank range. There's no sign of a break-in, and there's only one other person in the house. I think we're entitled to ask that person a couple of questions before we all go home to catch up on our beauty sleep."

"She's a juvenile, don't forget."

"That's why you're here," Tom said curtly. "Maggie, you don't have to answer these questions, but would you like to tell me what happened here tonight?"

She didn't like Tom much, Maggie decided. He had a real mean expression, as if he was angry with her. She shook her head. "I don't want to talk about it."

"Why not?" Tom asked.

"Because my mother's dead," she said, her voice trembling. Stupid, dorky question. Stupid, dorky man.

"Do you know how that happened?" Tom asked. "How did your mother die, Maggie?"

"She was shot." Maggie kept her voice cold because otherwise she'd start screaming and never be able to stop.

"Yes, we saw that she'd been shot," Tom said. "I guess it was an accident. Was it an accident, Maggie?"

"I don't know," she said. "I wasn't there when he shot her."

Tom looked startled and Janette let out a little hiss of breath before leaning forward to take Maggie's hand again. "Do you know who shot your mother, Maggie?" she asked. "Was it a man? Someone you know?"

Maggie shook her head. "Not exactly. Just that it must have been her boyfriend."

Tom interrupted before Janette could say anything else. "Who is your mom's boyfriend, Maggie?"

She opened her mouth, then shut it again without answering. Now that her mother was dead, it seemed sort of disgusting to admit to this man that her mom had been having an affair. No way she was going to admit that she didn't know the man's name because she suspected he was married.

Maggie scuffed her toes across the wooden floor, drawing a semicircle. "I don't know if Mom has… had…a boyfriend," she said at last.

Tom leaned forward until his face was only inches from hers. "But a moment ago you said it must be your mother's boyfriend who shot her."

"I guess I made a mistake."

"So your mother didn't have a boyfriend? Is that what you're saying?"

"I don't know…. We didn't talk about it much. My mom loved my dad, that's all I know."

"So if you aren't even sure that your mom had a boyfriend, Maggie, why did you say that he was the person who shot your mother?"

Tom sounded as if he thought she was stupid. Maybe he was right. At the moment, Maggie felt pretty stupid. "I heard him creeping around in the kitchen," she said. "And then I heard him leave. He opened the back door and locked it behind him. So it must have been Mom's boyfriend because nobody else has a key."

Janette and Tom exchanged incredulous glances

again. So much for telling the truth, Maggie thought tiredly. "You heard him in the kitchen when he was leaving," Tom said, stroking his chin. "What time was that?"

"Around two. A bit after."

"A bit after two." Tom wrote busily in the notebook he'd pulled out from his jacket pocket. "Did you happen to hear your mom's boyfriend arrive, Maggie?"

"No."

"Why was that?"

She hesitated. "I was asleep, I guess." She shifted her gaze, uneasy with the lie, but unwilling to risk another attempt at telling the truth. Tom was a police officer, and she'd committed several crimes this evening. She'd drunk beer even though she was underage, she'd smoked pot, and Cobra would probably save his own ass by claiming that she'd stolen his Harley.

Tom leaned back in his chair. "So you don't know for sure that your mother has a boyfriend, and you don't have any idea who he is. But he may have arrived some time tonight, because you think you heard him go out of the back door and lock it behind him."

Maggie knew that the detective didn't believe her, but she didn't care. The kitchen walls were closing in on her, the air too hot and heavy to breathe. She wanted to get outside. She wanted to be alone. She wanted to cry. She wanted it to be yesterday so that her mother was alive again and Maggie could promise never, ever to sneak out at night. She was deeply ashamed that she'd spent the last night of her mother's life hanging out with Cobra.

A young man came into the kitchen, his dark hair tousled and his jeans dusty, as if he'd been crawling around on the floor. Maggie vaguely remembered seeing him arrive at the same time as she and Janette had gone into the kitchen. He looked at her once, sharply, as he held up a plastic bag with a gun inside it.

"I thought you'd want to see this, Sarge," he said.

Even from where she was sitting, Maggie could see that there was blood smeared all over the handle of the gun. She remembered the blood spurting from her mother's abdomen, and she pressed her hand to her mouth, fighting a renewed attack of nausea.

The detective turned swiftly, and his breath came out in a low but audible hiss. "Yeah. Where did you find that?"

The young guy thrust his hands through his hair. "I found it shoved down behind the nightstand. Might have been a clumsy attempt to hide it since there's no sign of a struggle."

"Prints?" Tom asked tersely.

"Beauties," the young man replied.

"You're new, aren't you?" Tom said. "What's your name?"

"Sean McLeod."

"Good work, Sean, but don't screw up now. I don't have to tell you that you've gotta preserve the integrity of the evidence."

"Yessir."

At that moment, Maggie heard angry voices at the front door. There was a scuffle and then Tiffany's dad came into the kitchen. He was wearing sweatpants and a robe, and his hair was all rumpled. He reminded Maggie of the way her dad used to look on Sunday mornings. She was so happy to see a familiar face that she ran straight to him, bursting into tears as she ran.

Mr. Albers put his arms around her and hugged her. He patted her hair awkwardly. "Maggie, sweetheart, I'm real sorry, honey. We heard the news. We can't believe it…." Maggie tried to stop crying, but tears were bursting out of her in great coughing, choking waves. Mr. Albers hugged her tighter. "It's okay, honey. We're going to take care of you. I just found out what all the commotion was about and so I came over to take you back to our house. Tiffany and her mom are making up a bed for you in Tiffie's room right now."

Maggie clung to him, weak from grief and exhausted by her burst of sobbing. "Thank you," she mumbled.

"It's our pleasure, honey. Come on, grab a jacket and some shoes and let's go. Tiffie can lend you anything else you need."

"Not so fast," Tom said, stepping forward. "I still have a lot of questions to ask her."

"You don't have a damn thing to ask that can't wait until tomorrow," Mr. Albers said, sounding really angry. "Come on, Maggie. Let's go up to your room and find your shoes. Tiffie and her mother are both waiting for you."

"Before Maggie can leave this house, I'm going to need the clothes she's wearing," Tom said.

Mr. Albers stared at the detective in amazement. "What for?"

"To check for forensic evidence," Tom said.

"What kind of forensic evidence?" Mr. Albers demanded.

"Powder residue," Tom said curtly. "Evidence that would show whether or not the person wearing those clothes had fired a gun."

Maggie was too tired to understand what the grownups were talking about, but Tiffany's dad sounded outraged. "You can't possibly suspect this…this *child* of shooting her own mother! You've got to be joking, Sergeant!"

"No, sir. I don't joke about murder. Testing Maggie's clothes could also demonstrate that she was not the person who fired the shots that killed Mrs. Slade."

Maggie blinked. The stupefying realization dawned on her that Tom, whose last name she'd already forgotten, suspected her of shooting her own mother. The idea was so silly that she simply stared at him in disbelief for a second or two. He returned her gaze, his eyes hard and disapproving. She felt a swift flash of anger before sinking back into numbness. Who cared what dumb old Detective Tom thought? He was turning out to be Mr. Stupid Meathead II.

Tiffany's dad kept his arm around her shoulders while he talked to the detective. "The only reason I'm going to agree to let Maggie give you her clothes is because I'm one hundred percent positive they'll prove that she had nothing whatsoever to do with this tragedy."

"If that's what you th—"

"We appreciate the cooperation," Janette said, interrupting her colleague. "Maggie, honey, would you like me to come upstairs with you?"

Maggie nodded. She didn't want to have to pass by the door to her mother's bedroom again. She looked down at her T-shirt and saw it was covered with blood, just like the sheets and pillows on her mom's bed. Just like the handle of the gun. Only the presence of Tiffany's dad and Detective Tom Whoosit prevented her from stripping off the bloody clothes right there in the kitchen.

When they got upstairs, Janette helped her find clean underwear as well as sweatpants and a thick sweater. Maggie didn't even care that the police were taking her T-shirt and panties away because they suspected her of murder. She just wanted the bloodstained clothes out of her sight forever.

"Mr. Albers, I understand why you're so anxious to get Maggie away from here," Janette said to Tiffany's father when they came downstairs again. "But we do need to know your address and phone number so that we can be in touch with you tomorrow. We need Maggie's help if we're going to find out who's responsible for the death of her mother."

Mr. Albers gave his address and phone number. "Don't you call us," he said to Janette. "We'll call you. My wife plans to give Maggie a strong sleeping pill, and I hope to God the poor kid can get a few hours' rest. She looks like she's going to keel over any minute. You people are so used to dealing with crooks and thugs, you don't seem to realize what she's facing. The poor kid's an orphan. Two parents lost in two years. That's a tragedy, not something to question her about."

"We want to find the person who's responsible for

this murder every bit as much as you do," Janette said. "Here's my card, Mr. Albers. I'll wait for your call." She turned to Maggie, smiling kindly. "Take care, Maggie. Try to get some sleep, okay?"

"Okay," Maggie said, although she couldn't imagine how in the world anyone expected her to sleep. She didn't think she'd be able to sleep ever again.

The gray-haired detective didn't smile and he didn't look sympathetic. "If you haven't been in touch by 2:00 p.m. tomorrow, Mr. Albers, I'll be calling at your house to speak with Maggie."

"Fine, you do that. In the meantime, I'm going to call my lawyer."

"That's your right. Good night, Mr. Albers. Maggie." Tom nodded briefly and turned to go back upstairs. The young man with the gun had disappeared ages ago.

Janette followed the sergeant into the master bedroom. "What's eating at you, Tom? You could ease up on the kid just a bit, couldn't you? I mean, we don't *know* that she did it."

"Don't we?" Tom held up the bloody pillow, thrusting it toward Janette. "There was a woman killed here tonight—shot to death while she was sleeping. There was only one other person in the house when it happened. And that's the kid you're asking me to ease up on."

"It could have been suicide. Or maybe the kid really did hear her mom's boyfriend—"

"Yeah, and Mrs. Slade *might* have been shot by a little green man who'd just arrived from Mars." Tom tossed the pillow back onto the bed. "I'm sick to death of middle-class kids with too much money who think they can get away with anything, up to and including murder."

Janette shook her head. "You're angry because the jury wouldn't convict Nathan Brookings of rape last week just because he was handsome and spoke real nice and quiet. Don't take out your anger on Maggie Slade, Tom. We don't know she killed her mother."

"What about her call to 911? You heard her apologizing to her mom for hurting her. And what about her pathetic attempt to throw the blame onto a mysterious intruder?" Tom snorted. "Ten bucks says she's guilty as sin."

Silently, Janette turned away.

She didn't take the bet.

One

St. Petersburg, Florida
May, 1997—

Detective Sergeant Sean McLeod was not in a good mood. Unfortunately, that was nothing new. He'd been in a bad mood for most of the past year, so he was getting used to the feeling. He finished his beer, crumpled the empty can and tossed it toward the trash. It missed, which figured. He stared at the fridge, wondering if it was worth the effort of walking over, opening the door and getting another beer.

His mother picked up the empty can while he was still searching for the energy to haul his ass out of the chair. "We recycle here," she said, not complaining, just stating a fact. She took a sponge and wiped up the drops of beer that had trickled out of the can onto her decorative tile floor. "This gray bin is for cans and glass, and the blue basket's for papers."

"Okay, I'll remember. Mom, for God's sake, stop cleaning." Sean pushed back his chair and grabbed the sponge from her hand, throwing it into the sink. "You'll wash the pattern off the damn tiles if you keep scrubbing at them like that."

"I just want to keep them looking new. They're so pretty."

She sounded apologetic, as though she were the person at fault, not him, and Sean felt instant—inevitable—guilt for his flash of temper. Guilt was about the only emotion he did well these days. His parents had lived in the same row house in Chicago for forty years, and this condo in Florida was their dream home, bought with a lifetime of hard work and scrimping. He had no right to begrudge his mother the pleasure of caring for her shiny new kitchen and fancy tile floors any more than he should feel irritated because his father spent all morning, every morning, rearranging his power tools on a workbench set up in a corner of the two-car garage.

He tried to make amends. "Everything looks great, Mom. They'll be asking you to do *Lifestyles of the Rich and Famous* any day now."

"Go on with you." She laughed, but he could see she was pleased.

His father called from the living room. "Shirl, *20/20*'s starting. Come and sit down."

"I won't be a minute. I'm just unloading the dinner dishes."

"I'll do the dishes." Sean turned her gently toward the living room. "You go watch your TV show. You don't want to miss the opening."

"Well, thank you, dear. If you're sure you know where everything goes…"

"I'm a detective, remember? I'll find out where everything goes."

He could see that the mention of his job made her nervous, as if she expected him to break down in front of her eyes. She gave him an uncertain smile, then untied her apron and hung it on the hook behind the kitchen door, squirting lotion onto her hands from the bottle on the counter as she went through into the living room. "The salad bowl goes on the top shelf of the cupboard to the left of the sink."

"Fine. I'll take care of it."

"Everything okay in there?" he heard his father ask as his mother went into the living room. Ron McLeod was getting hard of hearing and tended to talk loudly even when he thought he was whispering.

"Shush, Ron, don't talk so loud. Everything's fine."

"Yeah, sure it is," Ron snorted. "Sean's been like a bear with a thorn in his paw ever since he got here."

His mother made more shushing sounds. "A few more days and he'll be fine," she said.

"Not if he sits around drinking beer and pacing the goshdarn condo all night long." His father's voice boomed over the opening credits for *20/20*. "I tell you, Shirl, he may be our son, but he's driving me crazy."

"He just needs time to unwind. He's lost two partners in the space of a year, remember. And been in the hospital twice—"

"He should have had the smarts to quit while he was ahead."

"I think he would have if he hadn't realized Lynn was having an affair."

"You're not trying to tell me he cares about losing Lynn, are you? When the two of them were married, he hardly spent a night at home. Personally, I don't blame the girl for divorcing him. He's a workaholic. Lives, breathes, eats and sleeps that darn job of his."

Ever the peacemaker, his mother didn't respond directly, although Sean guessed she agreed with her husband. "Whatever his feelings toward Lynn, it was real hard for him to say goodbye to Heather. She's such a sweet little thing and you know how much he loves her."

When the dishwasher was empty, he went to the phone and called his brother. Damned if he was going to sit around all night remembering that it was six months until Thanksgiving, which—thanks to Lynn's latest victory in court—was the next chance he'd get to spend time with Heather.

If Don was home, he would answer the phone on the first ring. His brother maintained that you never knew what kind of a business deal might be waiting for you and kept a phone in all fourteen rooms of his waterfront penthouse just so he'd never miss out on a hot opportunity. He rarely screened his incoming calls. If the call turned out to be from one of his ex-wives or somebody else he didn't want to talk to, he simply hung up as soon as they started speaking. No self-doubt and residual guilt about failed marriages for Don. His brother was confident that his ex-wives—all three of them—were scheming bitches. He was equally confident that he'd been a model husband. His marriages had failed because his bitchy wives hadn't tried hard enough to make them work. End of story.

After this past weekend in Atlanta with Lynn and her new surgeon husband, Sean was beginning to think Don's attitude toward ex-wives had a lot of merit.

"Hello, this is Donald McLeod." His brother, third generation American, managed to sound as if he'd just stepped off a plane from Glasgow. He'd discovered that a Scottish accent created an image of trustworthiness that helped to sell cars, so he now spoke with a brogue that was thicker than a bowl of cold porridge.

"This is Sean. Is your offer to hit some of the high spots in Ybor City still open?"

"Well, hell, it most surely is. You wouldna believe what a collection of fine young women you can find in Ybor City on a Friday night."

"So drive one of your fancy cars over here and let's get going. I'm in the mood to drown my sorrows. And lose the fake accent while you're driving over, will you?"

"And what fake accent wuid you be referrin' to, may I ask?"

"Don, if you want to live to see forty—"

"Okay, I'll be right over." The phone clicked. Whatever else you could fault Don for, you couldn't complain that he demanded long explanations or that he had trouble making up his mind.

Sean took a shower and cleaned his teeth so that he could sober up some before he started the night's serious drinking. With Don, it was guaranteed that they'd be going to a bar where there were lots of available women, a good DJ and a decent-sized dance floor. If Don remained true to form, he would circle the dance floor once and have his bedmate for the night picked out before the bartender could serve their first drinks.

In the past, back in prehistoric times when Sean had believed that men and women could have honest, meaningful relationships, he'd always tried to convince his brother that sex was more rewarding if you talked to a woman before you screwed her. Since his divorce, he'd come around to his brother's view. If a woman was willing and curved in the right places, you knew everything about her that was important. Tonight, he planned to walk around the dance floor right behind his brother and pick out a bedmate strictly on the basis of the length of her legs and the size of her tits.

His mother had insisted on doing his laundry when he arrived from Atlanta, and she'd ironed and starched everything, including his boxers. Sean found a pair of Dockers, almost unrecognizable with knife-edge pleats, and shook out the starched folds of a forest green linen shirt, wincing when the cloth around the buttons crackled as he fastened them. He'd forgotten what it felt like to put on a shirt that was almost stiff enough to stand by itself. He hoped the women in Ybor City would be impressed by his mother's efforts to spruce him up.

Slapping cologne onto his cheeks—another postdivorce innovation—Sean went out onto the patio to wait for his brother. The day had been hot—this far south, spring was already a memory—but the night had cooled off just enough to be pleasant. He was admiring the view of the full moon reflected in the tiny artificial lake when Don arrived.

His brother breezed in, all smiles, wearing pastel clothes that looked right out of *Miami Vice*. If you didn't know Don was the most successful used car dealer in central Florida, you'd think he ought to be.

"Hi, Sean. Dad. Mom, you're looking gorgeous. Who did that great new hairstyle for you?" Don planted a hearty kiss on his mother's cheek. "I brought you and Dad some chocolates," he said. "Enjoy them while you watch your show."

"You shouldn't keep bringing us presents," Shirley said. But she smiled as she looked at the box. "Oh, Don! Belgian truffles, my favorites!"

"Only the best for my favorite lady." Don gave his father a hearty clap on the back. "What about those Cubbies, Dad? Incredible game yesterday, wasn't it?"

"They're going to win the Pennant," Ron said. "You mark my words. This is the year the Cubs will go all the way."

"Let's hope you're right. That'd be something for the record books, wouldn't it?" Don leaned over the back of the sofa and helped himself to one of the chocolates. "Come and watch the game at my place next time. The team looks even better on a big screen."

"That'd be nice—"

"Then we'll do it. It's a date." Don licked chocolate from his fingers and made his way to the front door, his arm looped around Sean's shoulders. "Okay, folks, you be good while we're gone now. Lock the door after us."

Shirley looked up from her chocolates. "When will you be home, Sean? Do you have the key I gave you?"

"Right here." He held up the key, attached to a plastic pink flamingo. He wasn't quite sure if his mother considered the key chain a joke.

"Sean may decide to spend the night at my place, so don't wait up," Don said. "Oops, there's Barbara Walters coming back on. We won't interrupt your program anymore. Coming, Sean? Bye, folks."

Less than three minutes after arriving, he was out the front door.

Sean laughed, genuinely amused for the first time in days. "Dammit, Don, you haven't changed since high school! How the hell do you get away with it?"

"Get away with what?" Don whistled a few bars of "Loch Lomond" as he unlocked the doors of his rebuilt 1956 T-bird.

"Blowing off our parents while leaving them convinced that you're the most dutiful, caring son this side of sainthood?"

"Hey, I love Mom and Dad." Don looked genuinely hurt. "They're great people."

"Yeah, right. Just not people you want to spend any time with." Sean buckled his seat belt, one of the remodeled T-bird's few concessions to modern safety regulations.

Don reversed out of the parking lot at a reckless speed. "It's nothing personal," he said. "But old people are boring. You should have stayed at my place, and then I'd have been able to show you some real action." He zoomed down the street and onto the entrance ramp for the highway, heading for Tampa on the other side of the bay. "What do you think of my new baby?" he asked. "She's a beauty, isn't she?"

Sean didn't make the mistake of assuming his brother was talking about a human being; Don's deepest emotions were reserved for his cars. Sean admired the T-bird, then they talked about V-8 engines, the success of Don's four dealerships and the sins of Japanese car manufacturers until they turned off the highway for Ybor City, an area of Tampa that housed the clubs, bars and cafés that passed for exciting nightlife on the sleepy west coast of Florida.

Don was obviously no stranger to Ybor City. He negotiated the narrow streets without hesitation, and when they got to a pedestrians-only area, he turned into a parking garage set well back from the road behind a small playhouse. He tossed the car keys to an attendant who greeted him by name and strode out onto the crowded sidewalk without bothering to pick up a parking ticket.

A group of young girls walked by, tanned legs gleaming in the light of the streetlamps. Don sighed appreciatively as they passed, pivoting to stare after them. "I tell you, Sean, there's nothing like living in a tropical climate. I don't know why you insist on freezing your ass off in a place like Denver. Is this a great place to live, or what?"

"It's usually quite warm in Denver, even in winter." Sean clamped his hand on his brother's collar and turned him face forward again. "Quit drooling, Don. They're high school kids."

"So?"

"So you'd better watch out or you'll wake up one morning and find yourself facing charges of statutory rape. Every time you get rid of a wife, you start looking for a younger model to replace her."

"Not this time." Don looked smug as he pushed open the door to a bar. "I've found me the perfect woman," he said, raising his voice to be heard over the tidal wave of rock music and human voices. "She's gorgeous. I've brought you here so you can meet her."

"Is she legally an adult?" Sean asked dryly.

"She's twenty-nine years old," Don said huffily as they squeezed their way through the crowded nightclub. "And for your information, she not only has a great body, she's smart, too. Real intelligent." He looked momentarily bashful. "She means a lot to me, Sean."

Sean gave his brother a friendly thump. "She can't be that intelligent if she's willing to date you."

"She went to college and she has a degree in political science," Don said. "Besides, she isn't dating me. Not exactly." For the first time, he looked less than a hundred percent sure of himself.

Sean grimaced. "What does *not exactly* mean? Is she married?"

"No. She's divorced."

Warning flags went up. "Let me guess. She's in the middle of this divorce, and it's getting real messy, so she's wondering if you could help her out with the legal fees."

"No, you're wrong. Her marriage was over a couple of years ago, before she came to Florida. Her husband's right out of the picture, and she hasn't asked me for a dime."

Sean grinned. "Wow! That must be a first among your lady friends."

"She doesn't seem interested in money at all."

Clever woman, Sean thought cynically, then forced himself to snap out of his acid mood. He was giving Lynn far too much power over his emotions. Other men had custody battles with their ex-wives and didn't end up suspecting every female on the planet of ulterior motives. He had no justification for condemning Don's new girlfriend sight unseen.

His brother edged expertly around the writhing mass of bodies on the dance floor. "Seriously, you'll like her. She's not just cute, she's a nice woman, a real lady, you know what I mean?"

"You met her here?"

"Yes, she's a waitress." Don peered through the crowd, seeking his true love of the moment.

Sean shook his head, marveling at his brother's odd combination of street smarts and country-boy naiveté. Hadn't his brother stopped to wonder why this woman, who was pretty and a real lady—not to mention a college graduate with a degree in political science—was working as a waitress in a nightclub? You didn't need to be a detective to smell something fishy about that story. When he negotiated a business deal, Don never believed anything that wasn't signed, notarized and approved by a clutch of high-priced lawyers. And yet he'd been through three damaging divorces and still believed just about anything an attractive woman told him.

"How long have you known her?" Sean asked, smiling in acknowledgment when he caught the eye of a good-looking redhead who was sitting at the bar, sipping a drink decorated with a little paper umbrella.

"Six weeks. Her name's Maggie Stevens. There she is! God, isn't she a babe!" Don sounded reverent, a sure sign that he and Maggie weren't sleeping together.

Six weeks, and his brother hadn't persuaded the woman into his bed? That had to be a first. Sean tore his gaze from the redhead and looked in the direction his brother indicated. The waitress in question was tall, wearing the standard outfit of skintight shorts, halter top and white sneakers. He supposed you could call her pretty—if you liked women with teased blond hair, makeup thick enough for a third-rate hooker and false eyelashes long enough to swat flies. Still, she was obviously over the age of consent, and if Don was attracted to her, Sean wasn't about to voice any objections. More power to her if she was smart enough to play hard to get and keep Don interested.

"Go get her, man!" He gave his brother a high five. "Personally, I have my sights fixed firmly on that cute redhead."

Don glanced toward the bar and the woman with the umbrella drink. "Nice," he said. "Real nice. Your taste in women is improving, kiddo. If you wanna ask her back to my place, feel free. The guest suite is all yours. The Jacuzzi in there always makes 'em wild." The music stopped and he edged quickly toward the corner where they'd seen his waitress. "See you later. I gotta go talk with Maggie while I can. She's got a manager with a mean streak and you have to catch her on the run. It's a pain in the ass dating a woman who works nights."

Sean made his way to the bar. The redhead's name was Bree. She was originally from Texas, she'd been captain of the high school cheerleading squad, and her life's ambition was to work at Disney World as one of the show dancers. While waiting for her big chance, she was living with her married sister and working as a receptionist in a lawyer's office in Tampa and taking ballet lessons. She never stopped talking and rarely said anything interesting, but she had a lust-inducing body, and Sean reminded himself that he was here for the sex, not for the conversation.

She was a great dancer, supple and lithe and sensual, and she felt good in his arms after a week of watching Lynn fawn over her fancy new surgeon husband. He kissed Bree a couple of times just to stem the flow of words, and she returned his kisses with hot, open-mouthed enthusiasm. In his present mood, her obvious availability more than compensated for the fact that he'd already been forced to listen to a second-by-second account of her six failed interviews with the personnel department at Disney World.

Finally running out of steam, she locked her arms around Sean's neck and clung. "Now it's your turn to tell me all about you," she purred. "Where are you from?"

"Denver."

"Denver!" she exclaimed, sounding amazed, as if he'd claimed to live somewhere unbelievably exotic like Ulan Bator or Samarkand. "Wow, what a coincidence! I have a girlfriend who works in Aspen, and she says it's the greatest. But I don't like cold weather."

"Then you certainly wouldn't like living in Aspen." He didn't tell her that Aspen was hundreds of miles from Denver and several thousand feet higher, not to mention snowier and colder. Nor did he explain that Denver's winters were typically warm and dry, with a couple of snowstorms thrown in just for variety. In fifteen years, he'd never yet convinced his brother or his parents that Colorado wasn't buried year-round under a layer of permafrost, so there seemed no point in trying to correct Bree's misconceptions.

The music stopped, the laser lights flickered, and Bree broke free of his hold. "I'm thirsty," she said. "Aren't you?" He took her back to the bar, bought her a frozen strawberry daiquiri and ordered a beer for himself. Bree sipped her drink eagerly. "Mmm. This is just what I needed. I love Mexico, don't you?"

After an hour of following her conversational leaps, Sean didn't waste any time wondering what Mexico had to do with strawberry daiquiris. "I've never been there," he said.

"Oh, you should go. Cancún is wonderful. So's Acapulco, but the beaches are better in Cancún." Bree treated him to a detailed analysis of hotels she'd stayed at and meals she'd eaten in Mexico.

Sean tuned out the words and focused on her breasts, which were lush and bouncy enough to compensate for a lot of chatter about Mexico. Especially when she leaned forward and her nipples nearly spilled out of the satin vest she was wearing.

"Something tells me you have an exciting job," she said huskily. "What do you do for a living, Sean?"

Her left breast was about to pop. "I'm a cop," he said. And instantly regretted it.

"A cop!" She straightened, nipples retracting, and stared at him with wide, excited eyes. "Oh my," she breathed. "That's so cool. Are you carrying a gun, Sean?" She ran her hand down his chest, across his belt and straight down to his crotch. "Hmm…I guess I found your concealed weapon, Detective." She giggled. "It feels like it's a mighty fine one, too."

He felt a swift, hot rush of primitive desire. If they'd been alone, he'd have taken her to bed right there and then. But they weren't alone, and he had to go through all the mechanics of driving her back to Don's apartment before they could get to the satisfying part of tumbling onto a big bed in an air-conditioned room and pleasurably screwing their brains out.

In a minute, he'd go look for Don. They should have had the forethought to work out transportation details before they separated. But first things first. Sean slipped off the bar stool and stood in front of Bree, pulling her tight against his body, his hands kneading the soft curves of her bottom. "I'm staying with my brother," he said. "He has a great place, a penthouse apartment right on the water."

"Ooh, sounds lovely."

"There's a Jacuzzi and a stocked bar in the bathroom." He was laying it on thick, but it happened to be true. He lowered his voice to a suggestive murmur. "Would you like to come home with me so I can show you the view?"

Giggling, she wriggled against his crotch. "Which view would that be?"

He closed his teeth around the lobe of her ear. "Any view you'd care to see, honey."

The waitress Don was pursuing happened to choose that precise moment to walk up to the bar and place an order. "Two Coors' Light, one Heineken and two house zinfandel," she said to the bartender. Her glance flickered over Sean, registered the position of his hands on Bree's bottom, then flicked away again. Beneath the spiked lashes, he could have sworn he saw a flash of contempt.

Sean glared at her, tightening his hold on Bree. What right did Don's waitress have to be passing judgment? She *worked* in this place, for Chrissake, whereas he was just taking advantage of the facilities. Seen up close, her body was leaner and more athletic than he'd realized, and her legs were Vegas-showgirl quality. But she'd troweled makeup onto her face, which, combined with the bushy hairdo and fake lashes, made it difficult to imagine what she might look like underneath it all. If Don planned on taking her to bed tonight, he'd better be prepared for a shock in the morning, Sean thought acidly. Her face would be left behind on the pillow.

The drink order was ready. The waitress leaned across the bar, upper body muscles working, and slid the drinks onto her tray without spilling a drop. She added napkins and a bowl of pretzels, then took off, weaving her way through the tables at lightning speed. Sean watched her deliver the order to a table of kids wearing University of South Florida T-shirts. She smiled a lot, said something that made the kids all laugh, then went quickly to the next table, where two middle-aged men were sitting. Within seconds, she had them smiling and laughing, too.

Belatedly, Sean realized Bree was saying something to him. He turned, oddly reluctant to stop watching Don's waitress. There was something about her…. "I'm sorry, what did you say? I couldn't hear you over the noise."

"I said I need to find my girlfriend and tell her I'm going back to your apartment with you."

Jesus, had they reached that point already? Yeah, he guessed they had. Sean looked at Bree, and instead of seeing a sexy collection of female body parts as he had only a few minutes earlier, he saw a lonely young woman who had left her hometown in search of a dream she was probably never going to fulfill. His desire vanished, replaced by the deadly weariness that had dogged him ever since Arturo's death.

He stepped back, putting some space between their bodies, but keeping hold of Bree's hand. For the first time since they'd met, he felt a faint spark of intimacy, a moment of genuine caring. This was a woman who really needed to be protected from herself, Sean thought, or she would end up badly hurt. His years as a cop suggested it was useless to warn her, but he had to try.

"Bree, have you any idea how dangerous it is to go home with a man you've picked up in a bar? I could be a murderer or a psychopath. Or I might get off on beating women up. You're really putting yourself at risk when you accept invitations from men you don't know."

"But you're a policeman!" she protested, snatching her hand away and eyeing him with new wariness. "Of course I wouldn't go home with just anyone."

"I *told* you I was a policeman," Sean said grimly. "You have no way of knowing I told you the truth. Think about it, Bree. Is a murderer going to walk up to you and say, hey, come home with me, babe, I like to slice women into little pieces?"

Bree tossed her head angrily. "Are you saying you were lying?" she demanded. "You're not really a cop? Jeez, I hate it when men lie to me!"

"No, that's not what I meant…." Sean broke off. "Forget it. I'm sorry, Bree. You're a beautiful woman and a terrific dancer, but I guess…"

She walked away before he could even finish his apology. *Great job,* Sean told himself. *You got your message across real well.*

He watched the women gyrating on the dance floor and tried to think of one good reason why he would want to have sex with any of them. Unfortunately, he couldn't think of a reason, good or bad. No doubt the police psychiatrist would have a field day with that one.

You don't want to have sex because it's too life af-firming, and you blame yourself for the fact that Art is dead.

Yeah, he could hear the shrink tossing out some sort of crap along those lines.

He looked for his brother, but Don was nowhere to be seen. He occupied himself by observing Don's waitress, who seemed to be responsible for more tables than anyone else.

Don emerged from the men's room and made a bee-line for her. They exchanged a few moments of conversation and she made his brother laugh, too, but she didn't seem any more intimate with him than she had been with her other customers. Odd, Sean thought. She gave the impression that she was the friendliest little thing this side of a new puppy, but there was a remoteness to her—a watchfulness—that set all his cop instincts on full alert. What was her name? Don had told him. Sean tried to remember and couldn't.

He slumped against the bar, nursing his warm beer. No wonder they had the department psychologist on his ass every time he tried to go back to work, he thought grimly. His sex drive—or lack thereof—was his own business. But if he couldn't remember a name he'd been told only two hours earlier, he was obviously no use as a detective. His memory for details had once been his most valuable asset.

He pushed aside the constant, nagging fear that the bullet they'd scooped out of his skull had done permanent damage and ordered another beer. The doctors had sworn the bullet merely chipped bone and that his brain hadn't been touched. According to them, his memory lapses and mood swings were caused by psychological problems—survivor's guilt—because he was alive and Arturo Rodriguez was dead. Dead because Sean hadn't recognized the punk who approached Art and set up the meeting that ended Art's life.

Sean thought he'd coped okay with losing his partner. It was coming home from the hospital to find his wife in bed with the doctor who'd cut the bullet out of his skull that had sent his attitude all to hell. But even then, he'd handled things. Until his new partner had been shot and killed. Yeah, then he'd gone straight to pieces.

Sean shoved his beer away untouched, stomach roiling. Lynn had committed adultery and the courts had rewarded her by giving her custody of Heather. Okay, as Don would say. Life sucks. Get over it. He leaned back against the bar and fixed his gaze on his brother. The no-name waitress was laughing and joking with Don again, but she sashayed neatly out of reach when his brother tried to put his arm around her waist.

Sean didn't realize that he'd moved until he found himself hauling up a chair and sitting down next to his brother.

"Hi, Sean!" Don's good cheer sounded a little forced, as if he was frustrated at getting nowhere with his waitress. "Hey, I want you to meet a real nice lady. Sean, this is Maggie Stevens. Maggie, this is my brother, Sean. He's visiting from Denver."

For an instant, for a split second, it seemed to Sean that Maggie's entire body froze. Then she smiled at him with such casual friendliness that he wondered if he'd been mistaken. The psychologist kept telling him that he was oversensitized.

Maggie tossed her hair out of her eyes. "Hi, Sean, it's nice to meet you. Are you down here on vacation?"

"How did you guess?"

Her eyes twinkled. "You look as if you've still got some of that northern chill clinging to your bones. A few more days in the Florida sun and you'll feel more mellow."

Her manner carried no hint that she remembered seeing him earlier at the bar. Perhaps she didn't. Probably he'd imagined the scorn he read in her eyes back then. These days, along with all the other miscues and misjudgments he kept making, he often imagined hostility where none existed.

"You're right on all counts," he said. "I'm down here visiting my family and hoping to unwind a little. It's been a rough winter. How about you, Maggie? You don't sound like you're from the South."

"No, I'm not. I was raised in California. Sacramento." She shifted her tray from one hip to the other, drawing their attention to the narrowness of her waist and the magnificent curve of her bottom. Great move, Sean thought cynically. Especially if she didn't want him or Don to concentrate too hard on what she was actually saying.

"So what brought you to Florida?" he asked.

She gave a rueful laugh. "Well, I made the mistake of getting married right out of college, and my husband moved us to Michigan, way up north. Let me tell you, for a California girl, those winters were really something. All that lake-effect snow and dampness." She shuddered. "When Pete and I split up, I wanted to get back somewhere warm, so I came to Florida."

"How long have you been here?" Sean swirled his beer until it foamed. Don shot him a puzzled glance, and he realized he sounded as if he was conducting a police interrogation. He softened his next question with a smile. "Does it feel like home yet?"

"It's getting better. I've been here almost a year now

and I like the area a lot." She cleaned their table with the same sort of swift, economical movements he'd noticed before. "Did either of you want anything else to drink? Or maybe some nachos to munch on?"

"Sure. I'll have a diet Coke, please, Maggie." Don patted his stomach and grinned sheepishly. "Nothing to eat. I'm watching the old waistline here."

"I'll take an order of nachos," Sean said.

Maggie gave him another smile. "You'll enjoy them, I'm sure. The nachos here are good. You want anything to drink, Sean?"

"Club soda." Suddenly, he wanted to be sober.

"One diet Coke, one club soda, one order of nachos. I'll be right back." She was gone, leaving Don to follow her progress to the bar with an expression of dreamy-eyed infatuation.

"Isn't she wonderful?" he said.

"Sure." Sean leaned back in his chair. "Great boobs. Legs to die for. She may even have a face under all those layers of makeup."

Don swiveled around, looking hurt. "You didn't like her, did you? Jeez, what is it with you and women? Are you looking for another ballbreaker like Lynn or something? Because if you are, I got a news flash for you, buddy. There's a hell of a lot of women out there who don't make you eat dirt before they'll give it to you."

"Yeah, but Maggie Stevens isn't one of them. Give it up, Don. Can't you see she's never going to accept your invitations?"

"How do you know that?"

Sean gave a wry grin. "Let's say that after six years

of living with Lynn, I recognize a ballbreaker when I see one. Maggie Stevens might as well have a sign printed across her forehead. Back Off Or I'll Bite."

"Hell, she can bite me anytime." Don scowled, then shrugged. "So, what happened to the redhead?"

"She decided to take a rain check."

"You blew her off, you mean. She was damn near eating you up on the dance floor," Don snorted. "You need to work on your attitude, Sean. Trust me, sex doesn't always have to be meaningful. Sometimes it can just make you feel good, you know?"

"Yeah, I know." Maybe. Sometimes it seemed as if he'd forgotten what uncomplicated, mutually satisfying sex felt like.

Maggie came back, moving as fast as ever, although it was almost one in the morning and she must have been working for hours. She put down a basket piled high with nachos and deftly flipped the tabs on Sean's club soda and Don's diet Coke. She added napkins and a dish of jalapeño peppers, smiling all the while.

"Here you are, gentlemen. Enjoy your snack." Don paid with a fifty-dollar bill. "I'll be right back with your change," Maggie said.

Don's hand closed over hers. "Keep the change, honey."

"But your bill was only thirteen dollars—"

"That's okay, honey. You've been rushed off your feet all night and you deserve a little something for your trouble."

"Well, thanks."

Don patted her hand. "You're welcome." He cleared

his throat and avoided Sean's eyes. "Listen, Maggie, I know this great place down by the waterfront. Serves the greatest brunch in the city. How would you like me to come and pick you up at your place tomorrow, around noon…?"

"Gee, thanks, but I'm awfully busy…." She was already pivoting, ready to leave.

Don caught her wrist. "You've got to eat," he said. "It won't take more than an hour."

"Well, maybe I could spare an hour. Thanks, Don, I really appreciate the offer. Lunch with you would be fun."

For some reason that he couldn't pinpoint, Sean was convinced she'd only accepted the invitation because he was there. Her gaze met his, and he could have sworn he saw defiance in her eyes. She took the fifty-dollar bill Don had given her and tucked it deep down into the front of her halter, almost as if she wanted Sean to know that she was only accepting the invitation because Don was acting like he had money to burn.

"Don't bother to call and pick me up," she told Don. "I have a couple of errands to run tomorrow, so I'll meet you at the restaurant. How about twelve-thirty? Would that work for you?"

"Any time you say, honey." Don gave directions on how to get to the restaurant, and Maggie seemed to know the area he was describing because she didn't write anything down.

"I'll look forward to seeing you," she said. "Bye for now." She moved quickly to answer a summons from a nearby table, leaving Don staring rapturously into space.

The nachos had lost any appeal they might once have had. Sean snapped his fingers in front of his brother's nose. "Hey, Don! Anybody at home in there?"

"What?" Don came back to earth with a start. "I've never met a woman who's so easy to talk to," he said, following Maggie with his eyes. "She's got a cheerful word for everyone, you know? She's got so much class."

"Right." Sean wondered if he should try to inject at least a smidgen of reality into his brother's fantasy and then decided there were some battles that couldn't be won.

"I just know she's the one for me," Don said. "She's the woman I've been looking for all of my life."

Sean began to feel genuine alarm. "Hey, get serious here. Have you ever seen this woman in daylight? Have you even seen her outside of this club? You know nothing about her, and something's telling me she's trouble. Big trouble. There's something about her that's really getting to me."

Don got to his feet. "You know what your problem is? You've spent so long swimming around in sewers, chasing thieves and murderers, that you smell garbage even when you're in a garden."

"Could be," Sean said dryly. "But any gardener can tell you it's the manure that makes all the pretty flowers grow."

"What's that supposed to mean?" Don asked.

"Don't get so busy admiring the flowers that you step into a pile of sheep dung."

Don laughed. "Sean, my fine laddie, what am I going to do with you? Maggie is a wonderful woman, and I'm a grown man, so cease your worrying."

There was no arguing with Don when he adopted his fake Scottish accent. Sean accepted the inevitable and changed the subject. But if his brother planned to see Maggie again after tomorrow's brunch, Sean had every intention of finding out more about her. Maybe he was no good as a detective these days, but he could at least save his brother from making disastrous marriage number four.

Two

Sean McLeod. He was there again, sitting at the bar, nursing a beer. Maggie felt his gaze as unmistakably as she would have felt his touch. It scorched her skin and made her shiver. Why had he come? She was good at sizing up men—she had to be to survive—and she didn't think Sean was the type who'd find the Pink Parrot an entertaining place to hang out. But if he hadn't come back because he liked the liquor or the available women, then what was he doing here?

Possible answers didn't bode well for Maggie's peace of mind. She'd changed plenty in the fifteen years since he'd last seen her, and last night—after a couple of heart-stopping moments—she'd been reasonably confident that he didn't recognize her. Now she wasn't so sure.

Fear settled in her stomach, an icy weight that made her hands tremble and her legs turn leaden. She should have run yesterday while she still had the chance. That was easy to say now, of course. Hindsight always made mistakes appear patently obvious, but yesterday, when she'd been trying to decide what to do, things hadn't seemed quite so simple. In the first few weeks after she'd escaped from prison, she'd learned what it meant to be truly destitute. She'd survived by searching for scraps in the Dumpsters outside fast-food restaurants, and she'd sworn then that she would never again take the simple necessities of life for granted. With the memory of those days still sharp in her mind, she'd decided to delay her departure from Tampa for twenty-four hours so that she could clean out her bank accounts and pick up her paycheck.

The trouble was that she was tired of living on the run, tired of lying, tired of hiding, tired of the endless need to weigh the risk of discovery against the cost of running away. But weariness with her way of life was no excuse for stupidity and Detective Sean McLeod was the reward she'd earned for a truly lousy piece of decision making. For the sake of two thousand bucks, she'd risked her whole life.

Oh, God, he'd left the bar and was walking toward her. She couldn't afford another face-to-face encounter, so there was no choice but to run. Again. Drawing in a deep breath, Maggie dodged behind a group of tourists and headed for the locker room for her purse and car keys. She gripped the tray of drinks she was holding and focused all her attention on getting across the room without spilling anything. Right now, the most important thing was to appear calm. Criminals got caught because they behaved like criminals. She needed to act like a regular, normal citizen until she could get through that door into the locker room.

Damn Sean McLeod! It was years since she'd felt this terrified.

He cornered her when she was still twenty feet away from her goal. "Hello, Maggie."

Smile. Act as if you're pleased to see him. She could do this. She'd done much scarier things than facing down a cop who didn't recognize her.

"Well, hello yourself," she said, pretending surprise. "Where did you spring from?" She hoped her smile was bright and her voice casual despite the fact that her heart was pounding and her breath could only squeeze out of her lungs in short, choppy gasps. "How are you doing, Sean? Where's your brother? Don didn't mention that he was coming here tonight."

Sean didn't answer her smiles. "Don isn't here. One of his ex-wives wanted to see him about something, so I came alone. When Don goes to see his ex-wives, the conversation always seems to end up lasting all night." His eyes, the same vivid blue that she remembered, were about fifty years older and a hundred years more cynical than they'd been fifteen years ago.

Maggie ignored the pointed reference to Don's ex-wives and forced herself to chuckle, although the sound that came out was more like a despairing cackle. "Well, you don't look as if you're enjoying yourself too much now that you're here. Don't you like the music? Most people think our DJ's the best in town."

"I didn't come for the music." His gaze locked with hers, intense almost hypnotic. "Dance with me," he said.

An unfamiliar sensation shivered down her spine, fusing with the fear. She stared at him, wanting to deliver a polite brush-off, but her voice had frozen along with the rest of her body. Fortunately, one of the other waitresses saved her from making a complete fool of herself. Charlene bumped into her, swearing when the drinks on her tray spilled. "Maggie, what's with you? You need to bust some ass. Beau's lookin' this way and table six is gettin' real impatient."

The mundane reminder defrosted Maggie's vocal cords so that she could speak again. She apologized to Charlene, then forced herself to direct another smile at Sean. "Thanks for the invitation, but we're not allowed to dance with the customers. Strict rules, you know. And now I'd better get moving or I'll be fired. Beau—that's the manager—doesn't believe in paying his waitresses to stand around and chat."

"Come out with me when you get off work and we'll go someplace where you're free to dance. I'd like to spend some time with you. Just talking, if you don't want to dance."

Why was he persisting? She'd bet a hefty percentage of her hard-earned money that this tense, charismatic brother of Don's wasn't physically attracted to her. She'd hitched her way to Florida in trucks and trailers and she could spot every size, shape and variety of male sexual desire. Female, too, she thought wryly. Sean had loads of animal magnetism, but he wasn't directing any of it toward her. So if it wasn't sex, what reason could he have for wanting to spend time with her? The obvious answer was that he suspected something.

But what? Did she have genuine cause to be terrified or was she overreacting?

Maggie wanted so much to stay in Tampa that for one brief instant she was tempted to accept Sean's invitation and count on her acting ability to deflect any suspicions he had. This man might be the detective who'd found the gun that killed her mother, but she'd taught herself to be one of the world's very best liars, and the life she'd built for herself here was worth fighting to preserve. The city had become as close to a hometown as any place she'd known, and she didn't want to leave just because Sean McLeod *might* suspect something. Surely if he'd recognized her—if he had the faintest clue who she was—he'd have arrested her by now.

She discarded the tempting rationalization as soon as it formed in her mind. She hadn't made it this far by taking chances. Running had kept her safe for more than six years, and she'd be crazy to change her tactics. She'd broken her own rules by staying almost an entire year in Tampa. Sean McLeod was her wake-up call. He was the warning she needed, a reminder that putting down roots, however fragile, was a guaranteed way to get into big trouble.

The decision made, Maggie refused to waste time on regrets. Tampa was history, and so was her little apartment. She reached deep inside herself and found the courage to paste on another fake smile. "Thanks again, Sean, but I'm real busy for the next few days." She walked across to the bar and slid a fresh supply of napkins and pretzels onto her tray as if that was the reason she'd come over here in the first place. "Say hi to Don for me when you see him, will you? We had a great time at brunch this morning. He's a nice guy with a generous heart."

She deliberately slipped in the reminder that she'd met his brother first and that Sean was invading Don's territory. With any luck, Sean would take the hint that she was interested in his brother and accept her refusal without a second thought.

Sean failed to oblige her. "You and Don would never get along," he said.

He stopped abruptly as if he'd said more than he intended, and Maggie took advantage of the momentary pause to give him a final friendly wave before squeezing between two overweight conventioneers in Hawaiian shirts. She heaved a profound sigh of relief when she glanced over her shoulder and realized he'd stayed at the bar. She wished he would leave, but there was less than twenty minutes to closing, so she wasn't going to obsess about his presence anymore. Best if she did as little as possible to make her behavior tonight stand out in anyone's memory. Eighteen more minutes of Sean McLeod's eyes boring into the back of her neck. She could make it.

She was still trembling when she got back to her tables and took orders for a final round of drinks. While she waited for Carlos to make a margarita, she glanced surreptitiously toward the other end of the bar. Sean seemed to be making no move to leave. On the contrary, he caught her looking at him and tipped his hand to her in a mocking salute. She'd swung sharply away before she realized it would have been a lot smarter simply to smile and return his wave.

Oh, God, why didn't he just go home?

Far from leaving, Sean seemed galvanized into becoming the life of the party. He was a fantastic dancer, agile, sexy and oozing charisma, and the women were all over him. He tried out a sleek blonde, attracting a lot of admiring attention as they twisted around the laser-lit floor. Then, when the DJ announced the final selection, she saw him dancing with a stunning raven-haired beauty in an elegant black dress that clung much too tightly for underwear to be a possibility.

Maggie carried the drinks back to the table and politely said it was no trouble when they decided they needed nachos. She wove her way toward the counter to place her order, annoyed when she caught herself sneaking repeated glances at the dance floor. Sean and the raven-haired woman were locked together, swaying languidly, barely even pretending to dance. The woman's eyes were half-closed, her expression dreamy. Sean's eyes had the predatory gleam of a successful conquering male.

Emotion shivered down Maggie's spine, accompanied by a strange, tight feeling in the back of her throat. She saw pick ups—dozens of them—every time she came to work and she couldn't understand why she was reacting so strongly to this particular one. She wasn't even sure exactly what she was feeling. Some slightly sick form of terror masquerading as sexual attraction, she decided with wry self-mockery.

"Hey, Maggie, what's wrong with the nachos? You need to speed it up, girl. Your customers have less than ten minutes to eat."

"What?"

Betty Lou jiggled the basket of nachos. "You haven't picked up your order for table seven. What's wrong with it?"

"Nothing," Maggie said, feeling the muscles in her face grow tight with tension. "Sorry, Betty Lou. Could you stick 'em in the microwave for a minute and heat 'em up? I've been so busy tonight, I guess I just slowed down when I shouldn't have."

"Sure. But don't blame me if your table complains that they're soggy."

"I won't. Thanks a bunch."

The manager, a slimy creep with wandering hands, called her over as she made her way back upstairs. "Maggie, what's your problem? There were two tables waiting for you to take their orders and I had to ask Charlene to cover for you."

"Sorry, Beau. It's been a busy night."

"Gettin' above yourself, are you?" the manager asked. "Thinkin' that you don't need to worry about your job here anymore?"

What in the world was he talking about? How could he possibly know she was planning to run? "No, of course not, Beau—"

"I've seen how that McLeod guy comes on to you. I hope you're not teasin' yourself with the notion that you're gonna be the fourth Mrs. McLeod."

Sean had been married three times already? Only years of self-discipline prevented Maggie swiveling around to stare at him yet again. "I just went through a messy divorce last year," she reminded Beau, the lie so familiar that it almost felt true. "I'm not looking to become anyone's wife, certainly not Sean McLeod's. Good grief, I only just met the guy."

"Sean?" Beau snapped. "I thought his name was Don. That's what it says on all his car dealerships. Don McLeod—Home Of The Best Deal In Tampa."

Beau had been talking about Don. Of course he had, since Don was the man who'd been coming here four times a week for the past six weeks, openly pursuing her. Maggie quickly covered her embarrassing mistake. "Yeah, now you mention it, you're right. It's Don McLeod, not Sean. Guess that shows how interested I am in him, huh?"

The manager still looked suspicious. Maggie had realized a long time ago that like a lot of not very smart people promoted beyond the level of their abilities, he constantly worried his employees were trying to make a fool out of him. Recently, he'd shown far too much interest in Maggie. His instinct for self-preservation seemed to have kicked in and warned him that she was not exactly the woman she seemed. That was dangerous for her, and she had to distract him.

Despising herself for doing it, she yawned and stretched, moving in such a way that her breasts jiggled inside her halter. Beau's eyes gleamed just as she'd known they would. "Well, I guess I'd better go check on my tables," she said, uncomfortably aware that her ploy had worked much too well. Beau was the sort of man to pounce on any woman who offered him the least encouragement. "It's almost closing time."

Beau licked his lips. "Not so fast. I need to speak to

you after we close tonight. Let the other girls do the general cleanup tonight."

"Sure. My pleasure." It was easy to agree because she had no intention of following through. And by dawn, she'd be gone, safe from his sleazy advances.

"In my office, then. As soon as you've cleared your tables. Don't forget."

"I'll be there." *Don't you wish, buster.*

"You'd better be, if you want to keep your job." He turned and went back to his perch next to the DJ, where he had a view of the entire club.

Revolting, bug-eyed creep. Maggie waited until Beau's attention was claimed by a customer, then she made a quick, quiet dash for the locker room. She was good at inconspicuous exits, and none of the other waitresses noticed her disappearance. As for Sean, he was fully occupied on the dance floor. A nuclear explosion might have caught his attention although Maggie wouldn't have been willing to bet money on it. So much for Sean McLeod's brief reappearance in her life.

She collected her purse, tugged on a sweatshirt and was at the point of slipping out of the rear emergency exit when she realized that Beau had followed her into the locker room.

She'd been at work since five-thirty and she was exhausted, not to mention worried sick by the pressing need to get out of town. But she'd been tired and worried before and not gotten careless, so she couldn't explain how she managed to be stupid enough to get cornered by Beau, especially when he'd given her a red-flag warning that he was on the prowl for her.

She knew she was in big trouble when he crossed his arms and leaned against the emergency exit to the parking lot, barring her way out. Maggie looked quickly over her shoulder toward the door that led from the locker room back into the main section of the club. If she made a dash for it, would she get there before Beau caught her?

"I wouldn't try to run, Maggie Stevens. That would be a real bad mistake." There was an edge to the way he said her name that troubled her. "I thought we agreed to have a little chat after work?"

"I'm sorry. I guess I forgot." Maggie kept her response low-key. She'd found that sometimes you could ward off a sexual attack by behaving normally, as if you expected the man to conduct himself like a civilized human being instead of a brutal predator. She edged slowly and carefully toward the door that would give her passage back into the club. "It's awfully late, Beau. Could we maybe do this tomorrow? I could come in half an hour early if you still need to speak to me."

As she'd hoped, Beau was disarmed by her normal, everyday manner and he hesitated just long enough that she almost got away. But at the last moment, when she reached behind her to open the door, he grabbed her arms and dragged her back into the locker room. "How tired can you be? The night's still young. Why don't we have a drink?"

"Thanks, but I'm gonna take a rain check if you don't mind." She tried not to show her revulsion although her stomach churned. "It's been a long day, and I really do need to get some rest."

"What I want you for won't take long," he said, tightening his hold on her arms. "In fact, my wife always complains that it's over much too fast. Come on, let's go into my office where we can have some privacy."

"If you try to take me into your office, I'm going to scream."

"No, you aren't," he said softly. "You don't dare scream, Maggie Stevens. You're hiding too many secrets."

Why did he guess that she wouldn't scream? Why did he keep saying *Maggie Stevens* in that odd tone of voice? "Beau, that's crazy talk. I'm not hiding anything. Let me go home, please."

"I want to see how much money you made tonight, bouncing those tits at the customers." He snatched her purse and opened it, rummaging until he found her wallet. "Holy shit, you've got close to two hundred bucks in here!" He sounded genuinely surprised.

Resigned, Maggie waited for Beau to take the money, but he surprised her by shoving the bills back into her wallet before dragging her into his office and slamming the door shut behind them. He pinned her to the wall by placing his hands on either side of her head. "This is nice," he said. "Just you and me. It's real private in here."

"Beau, stop it. Let me out of here."

He didn't move, didn't even bother to lock the door to his office. "Look, babe, let's quit dickin' around and tell it like it is. You've got a cushy job here. More 'n likely you're taking home a thousand bucks a week in salary and tips, which must help you to enjoy a real nice lifestyle down here on the Florida Sun Coast."

"And your point is?" she asked wearily.

"My point is, you'd better make nice to me, babe, or you're goin' to lose the nice cushy job that supports your nice cushy lifestyle."

She knew she shouldn't protest or argue, but she couldn't help it. For some reason, the emotional controls she'd carefully put in place over the past six years weren't working tonight. "I do make nice to you, Beau," she said bitterly. "I bust my ass serving customers every night, and that's what I get paid for. It's *all* I get paid for."

"Yeah, well, that's a matter of opinion, honey. Speakin' as your employer, I'd like to see a little payback on that generous salary I'm givin' you. I'm owed."

She pushed his hand away from her breast. "I take care of twice as many customers each night as any other waitress in this place. I earn every cent of my salary, and the tips, too. I don't have to pay you off with sex on the side."

"Well, now, maybe you do and maybe you don't." He stopped smiling and pushed her back against the wall, one hand across her throat, the other reaching inside her sweatshirt and fondling her breasts.

Oh, God, not again, she thought. *How many times do I have to go through this same stupid scene?*

Beau grabbed her face so that she was forced to look at him. "Let's be real clear about what you owe me, sweetheart. You owe me everythin'."

"How do you figure that?"

"I'm keepin' quiet about you," he said. "Have been for the past month."

Her stomach lurched. "What have you been keeping quiet about?" she asked with false bravado. "My life's an open book, Beau."

He laughed at that. "Is it, sweetheart? Tell me, what do you think would happen if I dropped a word in the ear of our friendly local policeman about how I just discovered that the Maggie Stevens I employed in good faith more than ten months ago is not quite the honest, law-abidin' citizen she seems."

Maggie's mouth was bone-dry with fear. "I imagine they'd laugh at you."

"Would they? Your Social Security card is a fake, Maggie Stevens, or whatever your name is. Now what I'd like to know is why a citizen of this country would be usin' a fake Social Security card. Seems to me that isn't the action of an honest, law-abidin' person like you claim to be."

She had no choice but to brazen it out. She just needed to get out of here tonight and then Maggie Stevens would vanish from the face of the earth. "You're mistaken," she said coldly. "Of course my Social Security card isn't a fake. Get your hands off me. I'm walking out of here."

"We both know that's a lie, Maggie Stevens. You aren't goin' to walk anywhere till I say you can." This time, he said her name with deep mockery. "But if you're real accommodatin', I might be willing to keep the information about your Social Security card to myself. I guess you have your reasons for pretending to be somebody you're not, and I always like to give a pretty girl like you the benefit of the doubt. Providin' I'm rewarded for my generosity, of course."

She stopped pushing him away. "What do you want?" *As if she didn't know.*

"Well, now, darlin', that sounds a lot more accommodatin'. Here's the deal. You give me a piece of that tail you've been waggin' at me for the past ten months and I won't see any reason to talk to my friend, Sergeant Morelli, down at the local precinct. How's that for a real generous offer?"

Having sex with Beau wouldn't be the worst thing that had ever happened to her, Maggie thought bleakly, but it would come pretty high on the list. She didn't reply and he read her silence as consent. His mouth twisted into a triumphant leer and his nostrils flared in excitement. Like a bull on the charge, she thought sickly.

She closed her eyes as he took her in his arms, not cooperating but not resisting, either. Every time you thought there was no way you could sink any lower, you found there was a new level of degradation waiting to greet you. She turned her head sideways when Beau tried to kiss her, but she didn't scream, didn't run away, didn't kick him. Sometimes life just made it too hard to keep fighting.

Another shining first in the screwed-up saga of her existence, she thought, letting Beau take off her sweatshirt and throw it onto a nearby table. *Maggie trades her body in exchange for the chance to spend the rest of her life running and hiding. What a great deal—what a noble cause!*

He had her halter off now and his tongue was making wet, slobbery circles around her nipples. Memories of another night, another attempted rape, flooded her mind. Nausea welled up from Maggie's stomach and she started shivering. Her body convulsed, the shaking beyond her control.

Beau completely misread her reaction. "Yeah, baby, does that turn you on? There's lots more where that came from." His hands seemed to be all over her, contaminating every inch of her skin, sending filth in through her pores. She bit her lip and endured until he unzipped her shorts and reached clumsily inside. She swallowed bile.

"Please," she said, her palms pressed flat against the wall, her eyes open but staring blindly into the semidarkness. "Please don't do this, Beau."

For answer, he pushed her shorts down over her hips and reached for the crotch of her panties. She swallowed, choking back her screams. There must still be people in the building—lots of them—but she didn't dare cry out. If she accused Beau of sexual harassment, he'd defend himself by telling everyone that she'd given fake references and a false Social Security number when she applied for work.

He unzipped his pants and pulled out his penis. Maggie gagged. "Don't, Beau," she said. "Don't make me do this. Please."

Miraculously, the hideous licking at her breasts ceased and Beau's hands stopped groping. Astonished, she jerked her head up just in time to see Sean McLeod haul Beau away from her by the scruff of his neck. "You heard what the lady said, Beau. She asked you to stop."

"What the hell…?" Beau swung around, zipping his pants, fists clenching.

The punch he aimed never landed. Sean caught Beau's wrist and twisted his arm around behind his back, immobilizing him. "And she even said please," Sean continued as if he'd never been interrupted. "Time to open the door and let the lady out of here."

"Fuck off," Beau said. "And mind your own business."

"This is my business," Sean said. "The lady said no. That means you were planning to rape her and that's a crime."

"Rape her? Are you nuts?" Beau appeared genuinely horrified. "She was enjoying it, you stupid asshole. Don't you know women always say no until you persuade 'em to start saying yes?"

Maggie had no intention of listening to Beau expound on the sexual habits of womankind. She grabbed her sweatshirt and pulled it quickly over her head, not bothering to fasten her halter, then yanked her purse off the table where Beau had thrown it. "Thanks for the rescue," she said to Sean. "I really appreciate your help. I owe you one."

"You're welcome." Beau tried to move and Sean jerked hard on his arm just to remind him who was in charge. "What would you like me to do with him? Tie him up until the police get here?"

"There's no need to call the police," she said quickly. "I don't want to lay charges." She sent Beau a look of desperate entreaty.

Please, God, let him be smart enough to realize she

was offering him a deal, that if he kept quiet about her fake documentation, she'd keep quiet about his attempted rape.

She thought she saw him give a slight nod and she couldn't wait for anything more. She made a dash for the door, calling out her thanks as she ran. "I'm truly grateful, Sean. You'll never know how much." She pushed open the heavy door of the emergency exit and fled to the parking lot.

She was inside her car, about to start it, when the building door slammed open and Sean McLeod appeared.

Maggie stared at him across the empty parking lot, her heart pounding. For a split second, her hands hovered unmoving over the ignition. Then sanity returned. She turned the key, slammed the car into reverse and backed out of the parking lot at full speed. It didn't matter that she was giving Sean every reason in the world to be suspicious of her. Within a couple of hours, three at the most, she'd be on I-75, heading north to Georgia.

She took a circuitous route home—the precaution automatic even though she'd been out of the parking lot before Sean could have reached his car to follow her. Although she had a seemingly valid driver's license, she carefully drove a mile under the speed limit so as not to attract the attention of any passing police cars. She arrived home, light-headed with reaction to the stressful night, but with no other mishaps to slow down her escape.

Once back in her apartment, she packed with ferocious concentration because that way she had no spare energy to think, and leaving the only home she'd known since childhood didn't hurt quite so much. Her apartment was a small efficiency, sparsely furnished, but it had a tiny strip of balcony and a bathroom so clean and new that when she took a shower using scented soap and creamy lotion, she almost felt as if she'd finally scrubbed the smell of prison from her skin. She hated to leave that shiny new bathroom even more than the pristine kitchen.

Still, there was no time for regrets. A veteran of at least a dozen nighttime getaways, she knew exactly what to take with her and what to discard. Only her wig gave her pause. She pulled the ugly thing from her head about to thrust it into a big plastic garbage bag along with the toilet articles and food items that she didn't plan to take with her. Then she changed her mind. A neighbor might notice her leaving the building, and it seemed important that she should leave looking exactly like Maggie Stevens always looked.

Methodically, she emptied the fridge and swept cans and boxes from her kitchen cupboards into the trash bag. She'd find a Dumpster between here and the interstate, and the last debris of Maggie Stevens's life would vanish. She had a collection of fresh herbs growing on the kitchen windowsill, and just last week she'd bought a framed reproduction of Monet's famous water lilies and hung it over her bed. She'd never had a picture of her own choice hanging on her walls before, never watered a plant and watched it grow. It was amazingly difficult to take the picture and the herbs and stuff them into the trash bag. But when the landlord came to repossess the apartment because of Maggie Stevens's failure to pay the rent, she wanted him to be greeted by a place impersonal enough to offer no clues as to the likes and dislikes of the person who'd lived there.

She understood the rules of the game she'd chosen to play. When you were traveling with two suitcases and pretending to be on vacation, you couldn't afford to lug paintings and plants around with you. That was one of the reasons she'd been so grateful to earn a decent amount of money at the Pink Parrot. Life got expensive when you constantly abandoned clothing and possessions and lost your deposit for utilities and phone service. Plus this time, she would lose over six hundred bucks in security deposits on her apartment. She reckoned it cost her at least a thousand bucks in up-front expenses every time she ran from one hiding place to the next. And that wasn't counting the cost of lost wages.

At least she'd been smart enough to have a new identity waiting just for this sort of an emergency. Maggie Stevens would leave this apartment and check into a motel somewhere. Nobody would ever hear from her or see her again.

Christine Williamson would be arriving in Columbus, Ohio, sometime very soon.

Three

Sean was driving one of Don's least favorite cars, a dark green Pontiac sedan that happened to be great as an inconspicuous vehicle for tailing. It took him a couple of minutes to catch up with Maggie, but once he spotted her car, he was never in any danger of losing her. After he'd spent six months surveilling the gangs planning to impose L.A.'s efficient coke distribution system on Denver's amateur marketplace, sitting tight on Maggie Stevens's tail was pretty much child's play for him.

Circumstances made pursuing her especially easy. The Pink Parrot was located on the edge of Ybor City, in the middle of a one-way traffic system, so he didn't have to guess which route Maggie would take after she turned out of the club parking lot. She was driving a battered blue Chevy, old enough to be distinctive, noisy enough to be heard at a distance. As a final bonus, six blocks from the club, traffic filtered in from several surrounding side streets, providing sufficient cover so that he could stay out of sight without difficulty.

Still, he needed to concentrate since he had no familiarity with the Tampa Bay area and no idea where she might be heading. It wasn't until he was safely parked in a shadowy section of the lot outside her apartment building that Sean took the time to wonder exactly why he'd jumped into the car and pursued her with such single-minded determination.

What was he doing here? The cop in him was outraged by what he'd witnessed tonight. He wanted to march up to her apartment, haul Maggie down to the local precinct and insist that she file charges against her sleazeball boss, though he never for one minute expected that she would. Maggie Stevens was so anxious to avoid drawing attention to herself that she hadn't even screamed or struggled when her boss attacked her. Instead, she'd leaned back against the wall, submitting to Beau's onslaught with an expression of such utter despair that Sean's stomach knotted at the memory. Obviously, this wasn't a woman who would be willing to file charges. So what the hell did he hope to achieve by staring up at the lighted third-floor window, watching her shadow move back and forth behind the blinds?

No answers were immediately forthcoming, but he continued to watch and wait. His brother was talking about getting married to this woman and there were some big-time holes in her biography. Sean was outraged by Beau's sexual assault, but that didn't mean he'd decided Maggie was a saint. Far from it. He was convinced that she was not only working a scam, but that Don was the designated mark. Don was such a pushover where women were concerned that Sean felt the need to look out for his brother and find out exactly what Maggie was up to—and what she was hiding. Something that would make her mighty unsuitable as a candidate for the role of the fourth Mrs. Donald McLeod, he'd bet big money on it.

Maggie had opened a window as soon as she got home, and the predawn breeze moved the vertical slats from time to time, affording brief glimpses of her movements. She clearly wasn't settling down to unwind by watching a night owl show on TV and she didn't seem to be getting ready for bed. Was she doing laundry?

Sean sat up a little straighter. *Hot damn, she was packing!* Her boss's attack must have scared her off from whatever she'd been planning, and she was going to skip town.

He was about to jump out of the car and run upstairs to confront her when reason took over and he slumped down in the seat again. What rat was gnawing on his toes tonight? Where had he stashed his common sense? Even if Maggie was planning to leave town and start over somewhere else, he had no reason to interfere and no right—moral or legal—to be peering through her window like some pervert, watching her every move. He had no evidence that she'd committed a crime, or even that she was setting up a scam involving his brother. No evidence, that is, beyond the pricking of his thumbs. A pricking, according to all the experts, that wasn't worth a damn right now anyway.

Disgusted with himself, Sean stretched and yawned,

flexing his muscles. Time to go home and leave his three-times-married brother to take care of his own relationships. Tonight's moronic behavior would make a fine piece of evidence for the departmental psychologist, he thought grimly. Hell, another few nights like this one and he'd begin to wonder if maybe the little creep wasn't right. Maybe his mental faculties really had been shot to pieces by the bullet that plowed into Arturo's heart.

Sean was just about to start the car when he saw Maggie coming out of the apartment building, lugging two big suitcases. She was hurrying and didn't notice him parked under the cover of an overgrown Brazilian pepper tree. He debated driving away, but he didn't want to draw attention to his presence. He was all too aware that he'd behaved like an idiot and the best outcome he could hope for now was that he'd be able to slink away undetected. He shrank back against the seat, trying to hide in the shadows cast by the tree branches and hoping she wouldn't glance in his direction.

Maggie left her suitcases on the sidewalk and went back inside the building. She came out again, hauling two plastic trash bags, which were apparently so heavy that she had to drag them out onto the walkway. Instead of taking them to the Dumpster on the far side of the parking area, she hefted them over to the Chevy.

Sean felt a tingling sensation at the back of his neck. He forced himself to ignore it. The trashbags probably contained surplus possessions that wouldn't fit into her suitcases. He'd been a cop too long if he started to think "disposal of incriminating evidence" every time he saw a black garbage bag.

Maggie bent down to open the trunk. At first it jammed, and she gave the lock a quick thump as if this was a procedure she'd gone through many times before. Which she probably had, since the Chevy looked as if it was dying right where it sat. The first thump didn't work, so Maggie administered another and the lid flew open fast enough to catch her off guard. As she jumped back to avoid getting hit in the face, the latch hooked into her hair—and lifted a mass of yellow curls high into the air.

Sean was out of his car within seconds. Hell, he should have known that Maggie's unlikely profusion of curls was a wig. "Where are you going?" he demanded, striding across the lot. "Why are you running away, Maggie?"

She was untangling her wig from the latch when he spoke. She swung around at the sound of his voice, and her whole body stiffened when she recognized him. "It's none of your business," she said, freeing the wig and tossing it into the trunk. "More to the point, why are you stalking me?"

"Because I want to know why you're so scared," he said, realizing as he spoke that it was the simple truth. Don was only a small part of the reason he'd followed Maggie home tonight. "Is it Beau, or is there something else that frightens you?"

"You're imagining things, Sean. I'm not scared, just tired of working at the Pink Parrot, so I've decided to move on. No big deal. I'm going to try Orlando for a while, that's all."

She was lying, Sean decided, but he couldn't force her to confide in him if she chose not to. He looked at her in silence, acknowledging how attractive he found her. Without the garish wig, she was more than attractive; she was beautiful. She'd discarded her false eyelashes and washed the layers of makeup from her face, taking at least five years from her apparent age. Her natural hair was light brown and dead straight, probably too fine to hold a style, but he knew it would be soft and silky to his touch. The breeze blew several strands across her face into her mouth, and she pushed them away impatiently, looping them behind her ears.

Sean's stomach lurched. The simple gesture seemed poignantly familiar, as if he'd watched her make that same movement many times before. But if he'd ever met Maggie Stevens, surely he'd remember? She wasn't the sort of woman a man forgot. Her face was haunting and her body luscious—a dynamite combination.

Sean let out the breath he was holding. There was one thing he knew for certain about Maggie Stevens. She'd been real smart never to turn up at the Pink Parrot without her wig and makeup. Shorn of disguise, she was so beautiful and so obviously classy that she'd have stood out like an heirloom silver spoon on a picnic table of throwaway plastic cutlery.

She held his gaze for a brief moment, then abruptly busied herself lifting the garbage bags into the trunk of the Chevy, refusing his offer of help. She'd never answered his question, so he asked it again. "Why are you skipping town, Maggie? Is it because of what happened tonight?"

"I'm not *skipping*—"

"Right. This 4:00 a.m. departure is part of a carefully thought-out career plan."

She refused to rise to the bait. "Something like that."

He tried again. "Listen, if you're scared of Beau, you should file sexual assault charges against him, not run away. I'd be more than happy to back up your story about what happened tonight. You won't be the first woman Beau has hit on, and you won't be the last unless you show him that his behavior wasn't just sleazy, it was criminal."

"He already knows—"

"No, he's never been made to face the truth. And if you run, he learns the lesson that he can force himself on vulnerable, unwilling employees and there won't be any consequences."

Rolling her suitcases to the car, she sent him a look of mingled incredulity and pity. "I'm a bit too busy this week to take time out to save the world. But thanks for your offer to back up my story. Now, if you don't mind, I need to get going."

"I'm not asking you to save the world, Maggie. Just to help protect yourself and all the other women who work with you."

He felt her hesitation, but her answer was flip. "Sorry, Officer, but you're appealing to the wrong person. All that feminist crap about the sisterhood never really did much for me. I've learned it's a real dog-eat-dog world out there." The plastic bags filled the trunk so she loaded her suitcases onto the back seat of the car. "Goodbye, Sean."

"How do you know I'm a cop?" He shot out the question bullet fast.

She stared at him. "Your brother told me, of course."

Of course. What else? He almost reached out and grabbed her wrist to stop her leaving, but he drew back just in time. Jesus, he was truly losing it! "Goodbye," he said. "I think you're wrong not to file charges, but good luck in Orlando."

She looked at him, her expression momentarily both sad and vulnerable. "Thank you," she said. "I really did appreciate your help tonight, Sean. Beau would have raped me if you hadn't arrived when you did."

"And you'd have let him."

She turned away and got into the Chevy, her silence all the answer he needed. There was nothing more for them to say to each other, no place to go with the sexual attraction flickering between them. Feeling regret that he would most likely never see her again, Sean walked back to his own car. His initial interest in Maggie Stevens had been strictly on his brother's behalf, and once she left town, she would no longer be a threat to his brother's wallet or emotional well-being. If she was a scam artist, even if she had a criminal record, it wouldn't matter once she disappeared. Logically, he should be pleased to see the back of her. Unfortunately, not much about his life seemed logical these days, least of all his feelings. For some reason, Maggie had really gotten under his skin.

As he latched his seat belt, Sean heard the sound of her car starting, but he didn't look around even when he realized that her engine had cut out almost immediately. There was a thirty-second pause, then he heard her crank the engine again. The Chevy was having problems, which was no surprise given its age and junklike condition. Sean shrugged and drove out of the parking lot, leaving her to cope as best she could. Maggie Stevens had made it plain that she didn't want his help, and he had zero reason to persist in offering what wasn't wanted.

He switched on the radio and rolled down the car window. At this time of night, it was cool enough to drive without air-conditioning and he liked the feel of fresh air blowing across his face, the tang of salt and sea mingling with the city fumes. In the distance, he heard the noisy revving of the Chevy's engine. He ignored it.

When he reached the end of the street, there was still no sign of Maggie or her car. He made a right to access the highway and return to his brother's waterfront penthouse. Twenty feet from the on-ramp, he slammed on his brakes, swore long and hard, then did an illegal U-turn and drove back.

Maggie and the battered old car were still exactly where he'd left them, except that the hood was now up and she was leaning over the side, examining the car's innards. As he drove into the parking lot, Maggie straightened, sent one swift glance in his direction, then dropped her gaze and concentrated on wiping her oil-smeared fingers with a piece of clean rag.

Sean got out of the car. "Need some help?" he asked coolly.

"I guess I do." Gratitude and relief warred with hostility in her expression. "I've checked everything obvious. Do you think maybe it's the alternator?"

"Could be. Let me take a look." Sean had never been as good with car engines as his brother, but he didn't take too long to spot the problem. "The feed wire to your spark plugs has burned out. In addition to that, yes, your alternator looks like it's on the blink."

Panic flickered in Maggie's eyes before it was ruthlessly stamped out. She lifted her shoulders in a small shrug of resignation. "I guess those aren't things either of us can fix with a couple of twists of a wrench. But thanks for coming back to offer your help. I appreciate that."

"You're welcome." He took the piece of rag from her and wiped his hands. "What are you going to do now?"

"Call in professional help. At least I broke down close to home." Maggie smiled, and Sean wondered how he knew that it had damn near killed her to produce that seemingly perky grin. "Thanks again, but there's no point in your hanging around. I need to go back up to my apartment and call the towing service, and who knows how long they'll keep me waiting at this hour of the night?"

She did such a good job of conveying the impression of casual, not too serious frustration that if he hadn't been watching her really closely, he might not have noticed the betraying flicker of the muscle in her jaw and the way she had to work at keeping her hands hanging loosely at her sides. "What's got you so much on edge, Maggie?" he asked softly. "Why is it so important for you to leave town tonight?"

"I was nearly raped," she said shortly. "Is it surprising that I want to get away from here?"

"It's not surprising," he said. "Except that I have this gut feeling that the attack on you tonight is an *excuse* for you to run, not the reason."

"You're wrong," she said sharply. "Do you think that because I work in a nightclub, I should just brush off the fact that I was assaulted by a man who repulses me?"

"You know I don't think that. I'm the one who's been asking you to press charges, remember?"

"I guess you don't understand—"

"I understand better than you want me to," Sean broke in. "Here's what I believe happened tonight. I believe your boss threatened you, and whatever he used as a threat was powerful enough that you were willing to submit to his sexual advances to keep him quiet."

"Well, Detective, I'd say that you need to brush up on your detecting skills. How can you possibly leap to a crazy conclusion like that?"

Sean ignored the insult and counted off on his fingers. "You're the best waitress in the place and you could find yourself another job in a flash, so you don't have to pay Beau off with sex in order to keep your job. That means he has the power to coerce you. I doubt if you're an illegal alien, so he can't have threatened to call the INS. Do you have a drug problem, is that it? Has he seen you dealing and threatened to turn you in?"

"I hate and despise drugs," Maggie said, her voice low and intense. "I've seen up close the harm they can do, and I'd never use in a million years. You're making things much too complicated. Beau is the sort of man who turns violent when he's frustrated. I submitted to his attack because he cornered me and because I decided that I'd prefer to be raped rather than murdered. End of story."

"No, it's only the beginning. If what you've told me is what you really believe, then it's even more important for you to file charges."

"Enough, Sean. No more. I'm not going to file charges. Now, if you'll excuse me, I'm going upstairs to my apartment to call for a tow—"

"Don't go." Sean moved in front of her, blocking her path. "Have breakfast with me. It's almost five, too late to go to bed tonight. When we've eaten breakfast, I'll call Don and ask him to send over a tow truck. Your car will get serviced just as quickly that way, probably quicker in the long run." She hesitated, and he pressed his advantage. "It's going to be expensive to get this car up and running again, and you know Don will give you the lowest price of anyone in town. Isn't it worth waiting until seven, which is only a couple of hours from now? At least with Don you can have confidence that the job's been done properly."

She didn't disagree, which Sean considered was as good as conceding the point. "Where could we eat at this hour?" she asked. "I don't know anywhere that's open, and you've only just arrived in town."

He grinned, oddly lighthearted. "You're talking to a cop. Cops always know where to find food. Send us to Mars, and we'll know where the Martians are eating their roasted toody grubs within ten minutes of disembarking from the spaceship. I had all the best eating spots in Tampa located days ago."

She smiled. "I'm impressed."

"Hey, they didn't promote me to sergeant for nothing. You're talking to the state of Colorado's premier locator of gourmet doughnuts. So you'll come?"

"Well, all right. Thank you. I could use a cup of coffee right about now." She looked at him uncertainly. "You're being very kind."

"No, I'm being selfish. I hate to eat breakfast alone." He opened the door to the Pontiac on the passenger side and she slid into the seat, long legs flashing. He drove onto the highway, heading away from town and watching for the first roadside sign that advertised twenty-four-hour food service. Maggie realized what he was doing and laughed when he took an exit ramp that landed them in the midst of a travel plaza containing a Denny's, a McDonald's and a Burger King.

"So this is your special, inside scoop on Tampa's greatest place to eat breakfast?" she asked.

"Sure is." He grinned. "What were you expecting? A stall on the waterfront, surrounded by stevedores and crates of freshly caught fish?"

"Mmm. At the very least, after all your boasting."

"Sorry." He pushed open the door and waved her inside. "Welcome to Denny's, an exciting alternative to waterfront dining, recommended by cops, firefighters and other connoisseurs of fine dining."

She walked past him, still laughing, and tripped on a step that she didn't notice. "Oops," she said, toppling against Sean and quickly righting herself. "Sorry," she said, her voice a little breathless.

A wisp of her hair tickled his chin, and as he'd expected, it was soft and silky, the smell of shampoo oddly erotic. "Are you okay?" he asked. "No twisted ankles?"

"None. I'm fine. I should have watched where I was walking."

The restaurant wasn't full, but it was surprisingly crowded given that it wasn't yet 6:00 a.m. The hostess gave them the last of the booths in the nonsmoking section and poured coffee almost before they could sit down. Settling back with his giant plastic menu, Sean suddenly realized he was hungry and ordered an omelette with everything. Maggie changed her mind a couple of times, then settled on a blueberry muffin and a giant glass of orange juice.

When the waitress left with their order, Maggie took another sip of coffee. "Don tells me you've been living in Colorado ever since you finished college. I guess you must like it there."

"I love it," he said. "Although Denver's been growing so fast these past few years that I sometimes get nostalgic for the small and friendly town I used to know. We've acquired a lot of big-city crime to go along with our influx of new citizens."

She didn't seem to want to discuss crime and urban growth. "You went to the University of Colorado in Boulder?"

"Yes, and I had a great time. Even after my freshman year when I realized that I was going to have to do some work as well as go to parties."

Maggie laughed. "Yes, it's a real party school. I guess you'd expect that with so many out-of-state rich kids coming there for the skiing."

Sean looked at her, his interest piqued. "You sound as if you've been there. Is that where you went to school, too?"

"No, I've never been to Colorado—unfortunately. I grew up in Springfield, Illinois and went to school in state."

"I thought you were born in California."

"Yes, in Sacramento, but when my parents got divorced, my mom went home to Springfield so that she'd be closer to her family." She pulled a little face. "I always wanted to learn to ski and I would have loved to go to the University of Colorado, but my father remarried and started a whole new family. So with three more children to put through school, he wanted me to get a degree as cheaply as possible."

"I lived in the Chicago area, and my parents would never have been able to afford an out-of-state school, either," Sean said, thinking that her story sounded entirely credible—and yet he didn't quite believe it. "But I got an athletic scholarship, which helped a lot with expenses."

"Mmm, now let's see. What did you play? You're barely six feet tall…"

He sat up straighter. "Six feet and half an inch, actually."

Her eyes gleamed with amusement and he felt his mouth curve into an answering grin. "So you're over six feet," Maggie said. "Okay, but that extra half inch wouldn't make you tall enough for college basketball, so you must have played something else. Football, maybe?"

"Football," he agreed.

"Wow, I'm impressed."

"Don't be. My career was significantly lacking in glory. I'd been the big star on campus at my high school and I arrived in Boulder convinced I was about to become the next Joe Namath."

"What happened?" she asked. "Were you injured?"

"Nothing that tragic. I discovered that when you stacked me up against the best players from schools all over the country, I was nowhere near as good as I'd imagined. I made it to second-string quarterback in my junior year, and that was my supreme achievement. Once a month, when it didn't matter, the coaches would let me play in an actual game for about five minutes." He grinned, the memories no longer painful. "Hey, I've no regrets. Being on the football team was great for getting dates, I traveled a lot, and my parents didn't have to pay my tuition. Plus I never made it to the pros so I can still walk, sleep without painkillers, and I haven't had a dozen or so knee and shoulder operations like every pro you've ever heard about."

"It's great that you have such a down-to-earth perspective on what happened," Maggie said. "I once worked for a man who'd played for the Green Bay Packers back in the days when they were a pretty mediocre team. He only lasted one season, but he could never forget that he'd once been a professional football player. It was the highlight of his entire life, and he couldn't talk about anything else."

"It's sad when you see something like that," Sean agreed. "So now you know how I spent my college years. What about you? How did you spend your time in college?"

"I studied political science," Maggie said. "Like you, I had a scholarship, but it was offered by the Catholic church and required me to keep up a certain grade point average and meet some strict behavioral standards, so I had a pretty dreary time of it. All work and no play or I lost my financial support." She smiled, but her eyes were sad. "I guess college wasn't quite the same experience for me that it is for most people, although I'm always grateful for the way my professors worked so hard to give me a window out onto a larger world. I had a couple of great teachers who made a real difference in my life."

"Did you ever try to pursue a career that took advantage of your degree?" Sean asked.

She made some pleats in her paper napkin, then shook her head. "Maybe I didn't try hard enough, but what job needs an applicant with a degree in political science? Except maybe local government, and I could never work up any enthusiasm for that. Once I thought I might go on to law school…."

"Why didn't you?"

She shrugged. "Marriage intervened. And a messy divorce."

"Do you have kids?"

She shook her head. "No. And the way my marriage

ended, that's a good thing. What about you? I think Don told me you have a daughter."

"Yes, I do. She's five years old and her name's Heather, and you're damn lucky that I've trained myself to carry no more than three photos of her at any one time." He reached into his pocket and pulled out his wallet, opening it so that Maggie could see the pictures. She took them readily enough, but he had the strange impression that she was holding her breath, almost as if he'd done something to scare her.

The impression quickly passed. She studied the pictures carefully, with genuine interest. "She's a lovely child, Sean. You're very lucky."

"Yeah. In addition to being amazingly beautiful, you can probably tell from the pictures that she's also intelligent, talented, cute, funny—"

Maggie laughed. Her tension, if it had ever existed, seemed completely gone. "This is, of course, a totally unbiased assessment on your part."

"Of course. Well, a little understated, maybe, since I don't like to boast. Seriously, she's a great kid. I just wish I could see her more often."

"Divorce is always hard even when it's the best option for everyone."

"Maybe divorce was the best choice for me and Lynn. I'm not so sure about Heather."

Maggie pushed his wallet back across the table. "Wallowing in guilt might make you feel good, but it isn't going to do a thing to make life better for your daughter, is it? If you really think Heather's the one who's been shortchanged by the breakup of your marriage, you need to find constructive ways to make the new set of relationships work." She flushed. "Sorry to lecture, but in my line of work I meet so many men who are more interested in settling scores with their ex-wives than they are in finding ways to build a positive relationship with their kids."

Was that what he'd been doing? Sean wondered. Punishing Lynn by fighting her every step of the way in their various custody battles? He pocketed his wallet, relieved when the waitress returned with their breakfast orders and provided him with an excuse not to answer his own question.

Either he was even hungrier than he'd realized or the omelette was genuinely good. Sean took a few hungry bites, then leaned back and smiled at Maggie, deciding just to live in the moment for once and be glad that he was here, sharing the start of a new day with a sexy, beautiful woman.

"This muffin's really delicious," Maggie said, licking a crumb from the corner of her mouth.

Sean felt an unexpected flash of arousal, intense enough to make him hard. He looked at her across the table, and awareness shimmered between them. Whatever he was feeling, Maggie was feeling it, too.

"How's your omelette?" she asked quickly.

"My omelette's good." He smiled. "I told you I had a certified talent for finding great places to eat."

Maggie drank half her orange juice without coming up for air. "Gosh, I was more thirsty than I knew." She seemed determined not to acknowledge the sexually charged atmosphere that had sprung up out of nowhere and she seemed equally determined that he wouldn't mention it, either. She ate some more of her muffin, entertaining him with stories about the customers at the Pink Parrot that had him laughing out loud.

"Are any of those stories true?" he asked, putting down his fork and deciding, with regret, that he couldn't finish the hash browns.

"All of them," she said. Her eyes twinkled. "Well, more than half of them anyway."

He leaned across the table, not realizing he'd put his hand over hers until she looked down and he followed her gaze. He deliberately grazed his thumb across her knuckles and watched, fascinated, as color flashed briefly in her cheeks. "More coffee?" he asked.

"No more coffee, thanks, but some ice water would be great. But first I have to find the rest room." She disengaged her hand and glanced at her watch. "Good grief, we've been sitting here for almost an hour. We can call Don and ask about my car as soon as you've finished eating."

"I've finished," he said, thinking again how remarkably attractive she was without the wig and the makeup. Her eyes were a common enough shade of blue-gray, and yet there was something about them....

She stood up. "I'll be right back. Could you ask the waitress to put a slice of lime in my ice water?"

He raised an eyebrow. "I'll ask, but don't hold your breath. Do you want lemon if they don't have lime?"

"Please." She smiled at him. "Thanks, Sean. I'm so glad you suggested we should do this. It's been fun."

He watched her walk up to the hostess and get directions to the rest room. She gave him a tiny, intimate wave and a little smile before turning into the corridor that obviously housed the phones and the rest rooms.

The waitress came back and he requested ice water with lime for Maggie and another cup of coffee for himself. He yawned, feeling the caffeine circulate through his system, boosting his energy levels, even though his eyes were gritty from lack of sleep. It had been a while since he'd pulled an all-nighter, and he rather enjoyed the familiar sensations of being simultaneously strung out but sleepy.

The waitress came back with his bill. "You pay on the way out," she said. "Thank you, sir, and have a nice day."

He fished out his wallet again, found five bucks and left it under the salt shaker in the middle of the table for the waitress. The total bill, with tax, was just under eleven dollars, but he felt in the mood to tip generously. He watched the corridor leading to the rest rooms. A few people came and went, but Maggie didn't return.

Sean suddenly felt cold. He sat bolt upright on the fake leather seat of the booth, then he grabbed his wallet and shoved it into the back pocket of his jeans as he strode over to the corridor where he'd last seen Maggie. A woman came out of the rest room.

"Excuse me," Sean said, "but did you see a slim, tall woman with light brown hair and blue eyes in there?"

The woman stared at him, her gaze suspicious. "No," she said. "But I wasn't looking."

Sean found the waitress who'd served them. "Do me a big favor," he said. "Look in the rest room and see if my girlfriend's in there, would you?"

"Your girlfriend?" the waitress asked. "Is that the woman who was sitting at the table with you?"

"Yes," Sean said, trying not to sound impatient. "That's the one."

"Well, she can't be in the rest room," the waitress said, "because I saw her leave five minutes ago."

"Leave?" Sean repeated blankly. "What do you mean, leave?"

The waitress stared at him as if he was the one asking stupid questions. "I mean she got into her car and drove off," she said.

"Her car?" Sean gave a wild glance toward the parking lot and just managed to prevent himself giving a howl of rage. Jesus H. Christ! Maggie had stolen the friggin' car!

"Sorry," the waitress said. "I didn't realize she was stiffin' you."

"It's okay. Not your fault." He threw ten dollars and a pile of change on the cashier's desk as he ran outside, muttering curses that should have turned the air around him blue.

Don's sedan was nowhere to be seen. Sean patted the front pocket of his jeans. His car keys were gone, along with the spare key to his parents' condo and a key to Don's penthouse. Dammit, how could he have been such a prize idiot? He'd fallen for the oldest trick in the pickpocket's handbook. When they were coming into the restaurant, Maggie had pretended to trip. She'd bumped against him, filched his keys, then sat across the table from him and sweet-talked him into a state of appropriate gullibility before making off with her prize.

Don's car. Probably the only reason she'd agreed to have breakfast with him in the first place, Sean thought grimly. She'd planned to steal herself a set of new wheels. No wonder she'd been so nervous when he reached for his wallet to show her photos of Heather. She'd been on tenterhooks in case he realized that his keys were missing.

She'd played him for a sucker, but she wasn't going to get away with her theft, by God! He was going to track down Maggie Stevens if it took him the rest of his leave. And when he found her, if she was *real* lucky, all he'd do was murder her.

In the meantime, he needed to get home as fast as he could. Sean swallowed his pride and went back into the restaurant to call his brother and beg for rescue.

Four

Less than thirty-six hours after she ran out on Sean McLeod, Maggie reached her destination, the city of Columbus in central Ohio, home to one of the largest universities in the country. An ideal sort of town for her to get lost in, with plenty of bars and restaurants, and cheap student housing, where young women came and went without their neighbors paying much attention. As an added attraction, she'd never before set foot or wheel in the state of Ohio. No police department computer would be able to churn data and come up with a set of variables that linked Maggie Slade, alias Stevens, alias too-many-other-names-to-remember, with the state of Ohio.

She'd successfully run a thousand miles from Tampa, but Maggie's stomach knotted into a tight ball of nervous tension whenever she considered Sean's likely reaction to her disappearance. She'd spent each agonizing mile of her journey north feeling the imag-

ined heat of his pursuit. Still, in her more rational moments, she wondered why she was so fearful that he
would come after her. She was quite sure he hadn't realized she was an escaped convict, which probably
wasn't surprising given how much she'd changed over
the past fifteen years. These days, there was very little
left of the naive, terrified young girl Maggie Slade had
once been.

It was depressing to view herself through Sean
McLeod's eyes, but Maggie couldn't afford to waste
time on wistful daydreams about an attractive man who
was dangerous to know. She'd made too many mistakes during those final days in Florida, and she needed
to get a grip on her wayward emotions. She was now
Christine Williamson, and Christine would be smart to
stop worrying about Maggie's problems.

She slowed for road construction, wending her way
through the maze of orange cones. Her thoughts drifted
back in forbidden directions. She'd accepted Sean's invitation to breakfast for the simple reason that when her
Chevy broke down, she'd been flat out of other options.
She understood Beau all too well—she'd been dealing
with his type for years—and she'd known that he would
try to make trouble for her any way he could. His blackmail hadn't bought him the sex he wanted, so he was
quite likely to seek revenge by informing the cops that
Maggie Stevens's Social Security card was a fake.

With the threat of imminent disaster looming over
her, she'd been despairing when her car refused to start.
How quickly would Beau act? Had he already called the
police? The need to get out of town burned inside her

like molten steel overheating inside a furnace. If she didn't want her life to explode in her face, she had to be far away, with her identity as Christine Williamson securely established, before the police came looking for her. She could call a cab to take her to the bus station, but that meant there would be records, and the cab-driver might remember her. She didn't want to leave any clues as to where she'd gone, so how was she supposed to get herself and her belongings to the bus station?

Standing in the parking lot, analyzing and discarding plans, she'd realized at once that Sean's invitation provided her with a rare piece of good luck. So she went with him and then rewarded his kindness by lying through her teeth, filching his keys and stealing his brother's car. She might be attracted to Sean, but he was the enemy, and she couldn't afford to feel regret at deceiving him.

Ducking out of the restaurant through the emergency kitchen exit, she'd driven the Pontiac back to her apartment and collected her luggage from the broken-down Chevy. She'd disposed of the two trash bags in an overflowing Dumpster and driven to the bus station, where she'd stored her cases in a rented locker. Then she'd driven the Pontiac to the airport, left it in long-term parking and immediately sent the keys and the parking ticket to Don by Express Mail. Don was a laid-back kind of guy and might not file charges if his car was returned soon enough.

As for Sean, who was not in the least laid-back, she hoped he might be fooled into concluding that she'd caught a plane out of the city, but she wasn't counting on it. She just had to hope that he wasn't going to waste good vacation time tracking her down. With luck, he and Don would bitch and moan about her over a couple of beers and then forget her.

That was what her life had come down to, she thought, wallowing in a rare moment of self-pity: a hope that the most attractive man she'd met in years would never remember how and when he'd first met her.

She cut off the self-pity and mentally reviewed the final stages of her escape from Tampa, drawing some comfort from the knowledge that, in the end, she'd managed to get out of town without leaving any traces of where she'd gone. She'd taken a shuttle from the airport to a downtown hotel, then walked out onto the street and hailed a passing cab to take her to the bus station. She'd caught the first bus out of Tampa, not caring where it was going, and ended up in Atlanta. The middle-aged bus driver had been a morose man who'd seemed indifferent to his passengers and paid her no attention whatsoever.

In Atlanta, she'd switched to a bus going to Washington, D.C., and there, she'd finally caught a bus to where she really wanted to go: Columbus, Ohio. An hour earlier, on the other side of town, she'd paid a thousand dollars cash for the Hyundai she was now driving. The dealer had seemed halfway honest, and the paperwork wasn't an obvious forgery, but he'd accepted her cash payment with barely a blink, which wasn't a good sign. Still, given that a Hyundai had almost the lowest resale value of any model on the market, she was reasonably optimistic that she wasn't driving stolen property. Optimistic, but by no means certain. When you were an escaped criminal, it was hard to avoid committing new crimes. You were just too desperate to do otherwise.

The construction barriers ended in a stoplight. Maggie braked and stared out at the endless vista of minimalls on either side of the road. If she'd memorized the city map correctly, she was quite close to the university, and this looked like the sort of lower-middle income area where she could safely disappear. Now all she needed was a motel—big enough that the desk clerk wouldn't remember her, but small enough that the owners didn't bother with an elaborate computerized registration system.

She felt out her new name, trying it on for size, getting used to thinking of herself as Christine instead of Maggie. Christine Williamson was one of those neutral, middle-America names she preferred and much safer than Maggie Stevens, which had been too close to her real name for comfort. When you had to keep shedding identities, you tended to become attached to those few possessions you dared to keep, and Maggie had been absurdly grateful to spend the past year living with her real first name and initials. But that was another of those luxuries she couldn't afford to continue. These days, with computers able to configure searches using any number of variables, an escaped convict who stuck to the same two initials was laying down a trail of giant bread crumbs.

Thirty-year-old Christine Williamson had a Social Security card, a notarized copy of her birth certificate and a Pennsylvania driver's license, purchased at high cost to ensure that there would be no unpleasant surprises when they were used. Fortunately, Maggie had worked in Pittsburgh at one stage in her wanderings, and she knew enough about the city and surrounding suburbs to be able to fake a convincing conversation if she met anyone from Christine's supposed hometown.

The cost of the documents had been high, putting a real strain on her finances, but otherwise the purchase of Christine Williamson's identification had been easy. There were lots of advantages to working as a waitress, not the least that it put you in touch with the vast underground network of America's illegal immigrants. A dishwasher in New York—formerly a dentist who'd offended the drug cartel in his native Colombia—had shown Maggie how to avoid the attentions of the IRS. A busboy in Baltimore—a freedom fighter in his native Guatemala—had explained how she could use a fake Social Security card to acquire credit cards, a bank account, a driver's license—all the little pieces of plastic essential to modern living. The fact that she spoke decent Spanish, learned in jail, was a big help in getting herself accepted into the inner circle of illegals. And once you got inducted into their self-help network, you had access to the finest and best forged documents and stolen papers.

Maria, a fellow waitress who'd never been educated past the third grade but was smart as a whip, had drummed into Maggie that part of the secret to remaining safe from INS attention was never to use the same set of fake IDs for too long. In retrospect, Maggie realized just how valuable Maria's advice had been. Beau had taken ten months to discover that her Social Security card was a fake. If she'd left Tampa six months ago, before he got curious enough to start checking her out, the stress and near disasters of the past several days could have been avoided.

Once, when she was still in prison, Maggie had watched *The Great Escape* on television. The movie told the true story of dozens of Allied prisoners who'd escaped from a German prison camp during World War II. The prisoners had nearly all been caught in the end and most of them had been brutally shot, but the movie had taught Maggie several important lessons about life on the run. She'd learned that even in a police state, even during a world war, most of the escaped prisoners hadn't been recaptured because of the cleverness of the authorities or the efficiency of their checkpoints and barbed wire. Instead, the prisoners had been caught because of their own mistakes.

After more than six years on the run, Maggie knew that if she was ever caught, it wouldn't be because the FBI suddenly got extra smart or because the police computers finally started talking to each other more effectively. It would be because she made a dumb mistake. A dumb mistake like thinking she could create a home for herself as if she was a normal person. Or a fatally dumb mistake like feeling attracted to a cop who'd helped get her convicted of murder.

She was feeling sorry for herself again. Maggie blinked and blew her nose, then refocused her attention on the suburban scenery flashing by her car windows.

She turned into the courtyard of The Happy Traveler before she consciously registered that the motel was there and that the red neon sign advertised Vacancies.

Once inside, she found that her instincts hadn't failed her. The small lobby had cheap carpeting and a Formica counter that probably dated from the early seventies. But the place was clean, and the middle-aged man behind the desk muted the sound on his television as soon as she came in before greeting her politely. A respectable place, this one, not a motel that would attract the attention of cops on patrol.

"Evening, miss. It's been a nice day, hasn't it?"

"Good for driving," she agreed. "Do you have a room for tonight?"

"Just for one person?"

She nodded. "Yes, I'm traveling alone."

"Sorry, we got no singles left. But we got unit 106 downstairs and units 206 and 208 upstairs. Gotta charge you the double rate. Seventy-nine bucks a night, including tax, payment in advance, no checks. King-size bed in 106, two queens in the others. You don't have no pets, right? We don't allow pets in the rooms."

"No pets," she said. "And I'll take one of the upstairs units." She was tired, she realized, and not eager to drive around for the sake of saving a few bucks, even though her funds were getting frighteningly low. "I guess it doesn't matter which one."

"No difference from one room to the next," the clerk said, pushing a key across the counter. "You'll need to drive your car around to the back to find a parking space. There's a phone in the room, but you have to give me your credit card number if you want me to turn it on."

She smiled, picking up the key and slipping it into the pocket of her jeans before finding her wallet and extracting eighty dollars. "I've driven all the way from Buffalo, New York, today, so I don't think I'm going to be making any phone calls. I'm planning on going to bed real early." The lie about where she'd come from was as automatic as breathing. "Here you go. Three twenties and a ten." She counted out the bills.

"Sign here, please." The clerk pushed a register with tear-off receipts across the counter.

She scrawled the name Christine Williamson. He tore off the receipt and gave her a dollar change without bothering to glance at her signature.

"Have a good stay," he said, his head already swiveling back to the basketball game on TV.

As she'd expected, because she paid cash in advance, he hadn't asked for proof of her identity. With luck, he would forget everything about her long before she'd driven her car around to the parking lot at the rear of the motel. If he remembered anything at all, Maggie hoped it would be the totally false statement that she'd driven to Ohio from Buffalo.

Given the depleted state of her finances, finding a job was the major item on Maggie's agenda the next morning. But first, she had to change her appearance. A quick trip to the drugstore two miles down the road provided the necessary supplies, and by 9:00 a.m., she was a vividly unnatural redhead, with a bouffant style reminiscent of the 1960s at their worst. Always have one eye-catching feature, and the rest of you will go unnoticed. That was another of the rules she'd learned to live by.

Dressed in jeans and a T-shirt, she drove to the local public library and spent two hours in the reference section reading the local newspapers and scanning a couple of guidebooks to the city. Once familiarized with a few essential facts about the various neighborhoods, she was able to select the area where she planned to concentrate her job search.

German Village was her best bet, she decided, a section of town that seemed to be self-consciously quaint, full of bars and restaurants, and appealing to a wide cross section of locals. A couple of restaurants in the area were advertising for kitchen help, and one needed waitresses. Definitely worth a trip out to the area, Maggie concluded, since lots of bars and clubs never bothered to advertise their job vacancies in the paper, relying on word of mouth to fill the slots.

As she'd expected, there were more jobs available in German Village than had made it into the Help Wanted columns of the paper. She'd already filled out applications at two bars and was thinking of taking a lunch break when she stumbled across a successful-looking restaurant called the Buckeye Brewery. An excellent prospect, Maggie decided. It would likely be a decent place for tips even though Columbus wasn't the sort of city that attracted free-spending tourists and conventioneers like Tampa.

The moment she stepped inside the fake-oak entrance doors, Maggie saw that the Buckeye Brewery was basically the Pink Parrot transferred a thousand miles north and modified to suit Midwestern tastes. Instead of fake palm trees and gleaming turquoise walls, this bar had decorative beer steins and fake-oak ceiling beams, but the concept was identical: an environment in which men and women could pretend to enjoy themselves dancing and drinking while they overpaid for snack food and dealt with the serious business of securing themselves a date for the night.

The bar was open for lunch and there was a decent crowd of customers. Maggie waited for the bartender to pour two glasses of zinfandel before approaching him. "I just arrived in town and I'm looking for work as a waitress," she said. "I've got a lot of experience and my last two jobs have been in bars like this one. Do you know if you have any openings?"

The bartender gave her a cursory glance, then jerked his head over his shoulder while simultaneously taking care of another order. "Manager's office is back there. You can ask to fill out an application."

The door to the office the bartender had indicated was open, and a fiftyish woman with platinum blond hair stood behind the desk, talking on the phone. When Maggie hesitated, the woman beckoned her inside. She wore a black sweatshirt embellished with more gold paint and appliquéd crystals than Maggie had ever seen on one female bosom before, and since the bosom in question was of truly eye-popping proportions, there was plenty of room for adornment.

"So haul some ass," she roared into the phone, her voice gravelly with temper. "Hire a new driver! Stop pickin' your nose and drive the damn stuff over here yourself if you have to! Listen, Tommy, if I'd wanted to hear a bunch of dumbass excuses this morning, I could've stayed home and listened to my husband. Get the delivery here on time, okay?"

She hung up the phone and turned to Maggie. "You needed to see me?" she asked mildly, sounding perfectly good-tempered, despite her recent explosion.

"I'm looking for work," Maggie said. "The bartender said to come back here and fill out an application."

The woman moved to the side of the desk, revealing the rest of her outfit—a pair of black leggings covering surprisingly long and shapely legs, and a pair of gold high-heeled sandals. The overall effect of huge, decorated bosom and slender legs was startling, to say the least. "What sort of work are you looking for?" she asked, perching on the corner of her desk and setting one slender ankle swinging.

"I've got seven years' experience as a waitress—"

"Why are you lookin' for a job? You get fired from your last one?"

"No. I've just moved to Columbus—"

"Where did you live before?"

Her car had Ohio plates, but her driver's license was from Pennsylvania, so her story had holes in it big enough to drive a prison truck through, but she had no choice but to spin the best story she could and hope nobody would pick up on the inconsistencies. "I've come from Pittsburgh," she said. "My ex-husband's family is from there."

"Why did you leave?"

Maggie had the answer to that one all worked out. "Well, it's a long story…."

"I'm listenin'."

Maggie launched into her standard biography, one of the few things that remained constant from identity to identity. Heck, it was common enough to be a generic background for half the waitresses she'd worked with, so there was no reason to mess with it. "I'm from California. I met Pete—that's my ex—when he was stationed in San Diego with the Marine Corps." She shrugged, trying to appear simultaneously cynical and wounded. "Pete walked out on me a couple of years ago and I divorced him when I discovered he'd been cheating on me right from the start. Now he's gotten married again and I decided it was time for me to move on."

"Why?"

This was the oddest job interview she'd ever had. And, God knew, she'd had some weird ones. Fortunately, after years of living with the same lie, Maggie had the story of her nonexistent marriage fully fleshed out. "I'm an only child, but Pete—my ex—comes from one of those big families with four brothers and sisters and three dozen cousins all living in the same town, and it got so it was driving me nuts, you know? Every time I went to the grocery store, there was one of his cousins or a sister-in-law waiting to tell me the latest piece of gossip about Pete's new wife. It got so I'd hear the name Darlene and break out in a rash—"

"I didn't mean why did you leave Pittsburgh. I meant why did you come to Columbus, Ohio?"

Maggie gave what she hoped was a rueful, faintly

embarrassed smile. "Well, I didn't exactly plan on coming to Columbus. I was planning to head out west, back to California. I miss the sun, you know?" She paused for a split second, realizing that she had to be careful what she said next. Women were always harder to deceive than men, and this club manager looked as if she'd be an especially tough mark. "Pete got a real smart lawyer and he took everything in the divorce, so this was as far west as I could get. I need to save some money before I can move on. Serious money, you know? Like five thousand dollars, so I can put down a deposit on an apartment and everything when I get to California."

"You can't move in with your folks?"

"No." She gave another carefully calculated shrug. "My dad left home when I was fifteen, and my mother's new husband doesn't like reminders of her first marriage."

The woman showed no signs of sympathy at this hinted tale of woe. "So the bottom line is this. If I hire you, you're gonna turn around and move on lickety-split soon as I got you trained?"

"It'll take me the best part of a year to save the amount of money I need," Maggie said hastily. "I'm not going to be moving anyplace for at least a year. Five thousand bucks is a lot of cash when you've got living expenses to take care of, as well. I'm worth hiring even though I'm planning to move on. You won't have to train me because I've got lots of experience and I'll get right on the job."

The woman reached for the pack of cigarettes on her

desk, pulled one out but kept it in her mouth without lighting it. She toyed with a shiny gold lighter, flipping the cap back and forth. "You got yourself a place to stay here in Columbus?"

"Not yet." Maggie forced herself to meet the woman's gaze and give what appeared to be a frank, open smile. "First I have to get a job. That way I can get a place to live that's real close to where I'm working and maybe save some money by walking to work." It was always nice when you could actually tell the truth, she reflected wryly. It made a refreshing change.

The phone rang and the woman threw her unlit cigarette in the trash, snatching up the receiver as if it were either a lifesaver or a dangerous enemy. "Yes?" She waited while a voice spoke at the other end of the line, then roared with laughter. "I always enjoy a good laugh, Tommy. Thanks for that one. And if you don't have my order here within the next two hours, that's the last order you ever get from me."

She hung up the phone while the hapless Tommy was still spluttering excuses and stared thoughtfully across her desk toward Maggie. Then she turned and opened a drawer in the six-foot-high filing cabinet behind her. She pulled out a form and pushed it across the desk toward Maggie. "Here's an application," she said. "Fill it out for me, will you? You can sit at the credenza by the window. You got a pen?"

Maggie patted her purse. "In here, thanks." She walked to the small cabinet the woman had indicated and sat down, pulling out her pen.

She would fill out the application, but she very much

doubted if she would be offered a job here, and she was quite sure she wouldn't accept one if it was offered. There was something about the woman behind the desk that was making Maggie nervous, some quality in the way the woman watched her that set all Maggie's internal alarms ringing at maximum volume.

She worked quickly through the simple form and signed her name—Christine Williamson—to certify that all the statements she'd made on the application were true. Maggie wasn't in the mood to appreciate the irony. She walked back to her original position in front of the club manager's—owner's?—desk. "I've filled out the form," she said. "Since I don't have an address or phone number yet, I gave you my old address in Pittsburgh."

The woman skimmed the application. "You filled this out very fast, Christine Williamson, and you didn't make a single spelling mistake."

In future, she'd remember to insert at least one.

"Didn't I?" Maggie tried to sound pleased. "Well, I always did okay in school, but the questions on the form weren't exactly rocket science, you know?"

The woman tapped her long burgundy nails against the application. "What do your friends call you? Christine? Chris? Tina? Christy?"

Again, Maggie was prepared. "Pete's family all used to call me Chrissie," she said. "But since I'm kind of starting over, I think I'd like to be plain old Christine from now on."

The woman's gaze narrowed, and for a moment Maggie had the odd impression that she'd said something that gave her away. Panic stirred inside as the woman continued to stare at her. My God, what had she done? Surely there was nothing on that simple application form that could have betrayed her? Maggie was starting to sweat when the woman finally put down the paper and stretched out her hand across the desk.

"I'm Dorothy Respighi," she said, introducing herself. "And I'm the owner of this place. For new waitresses, I pay 2.75 an hour, you keep all your own tips, no splitting with the hostess and the busboys. If you stay for ninety days and work full-time, the company kicks in and pays your health care benefits. If you'd like the job, show me what you can do for the rest of the lunch shift. I'll watch, and if you're any good, you're hired."

"I need to wash my hands before I start," Maggie said, trying to make up her mind whether to go after the job or to leave well enough alone. Given the state of her finances, work was essential. On the other hand, she'd learned never to get involved in a situation where she didn't understand the other person's angle, and she had no idea what was going on behind Dorothy Respighi's heavily made-up features.

"Washroom's across the way," Dorothy said. "I'll take you over and introduce you to June—she's our lunchtime floor manager—soon as you're ready."

In the end, pride won out over caution. For some reason, Maggie felt a real need to impress Dorothy with the fact that she hadn't been lying when she claimed to be a good waitress. She was given two tables to take care of and did the best job that she could without knowing anything about the routines of the establishment.

At three o'clock, when the Buckeye was almost empty, Dorothy called her over. "Okay, you're hired. Daytime shift Monday to Friday, that's twenty-five hours, and eleven hours on Saturday, three to closing. That's thirty-six hours total, if you can hold up for an eleven-hour shift. The tips on Saturday night are usually pretty good."

"I can hold up."

"Okay. Be back here tomorrow at ten-thirty and I'll have someone show you the ropes. Wear jeans because we go for the casual look, but make sure they're clean with no rips or stains. We'll provide the red shirt and the pocket apron."

"Thanks. I'll be here." Maggie was almost to the door when Dorothy called her back. She turned. "Yes?"

"Just a warning. I always check references."

Maggie smiled. "Good. Then you'll find out I'm a great waitress even before I start work." She tipped her hand in a casual salute and hurried outside, unable to hold on to her smile. She was trembling, she realized as she unlocked the car door, shaking like a leaf. She got into the car and drove a few blocks, turning at random because she was so anxious to be out of sight of the Buckeye. She parked in the first place she found and cut the engine, leaning forward to rest her head on the steering wheel, trying to calm herself.

The pressures of her lifestyle caught up with her every now and again, subjecting her to a wave of terror so intense that she was powerless to fight it. There was no cure, except to let the fear wash over her in crashing waves that frothed and foamed with years of accumulated panic.

Today, like the other occasions, there was no rational cause for her terror. Dorothy's remark about references had precipitated the attack, but Maggie gave references whenever she applied for a job, so this was nothing new or unknown to worry about. On her application, as always, she'd given the phone numbers of real restaurants as references. She'd simply chosen two establishments where management had changed hands and where she was confident there were no records that went back further than a few months. Nothing, therefore, to reveal that Christine Williamson had never worked at the place in question.

It wasn't the fact that Dorothy would check her references that scared Maggie; it was the fact that Dorothy had sent an unequivocal signal that she expected to find something wrong with those references. And yet the woman had hired her. What was going on?

Maggie straightened, her trembling finally under control. Dorothy suspected something, heaven knew what or why. Maggie now had two choices. She could get the hell out of town and pick another city in which to start over. Or she could bluff it out and turn up at the Buckeye tomorrow.

Maggie went into a supermarket and bought a jar of instant coffee, some Granny Smith apples and a stick of aged cheddar cheese while she mulled over her options.

In the end, it was a photocopied flyer stuck on the public service notice board that made the decision for her. St. Anthony's Church announced that they would be holding a special high mass on Sunday, June 8, to celebrate the arrival in Columbus of the new arch-bishop, the Very Reverend Tobias Grunewald, formerly bishop of Phoenix, Arizona. The new archbishop would preach the sermon, and there would be a reception afterward in the parish hall. Everyone was welcome.

Maggie stood for a long time in front of the neon green notice and finally acknowledged that there wasn't a chance in hell that she was going to leave this city. She hadn't come to Columbus by chance or because she hadn't yet spent any time in the state of Ohio. She'd come here by deliberate choice, with a specific purpose in mind. After she'd survived nearly seven years of running, Beau's near rape had forced her to admit that bars, guards and a cell door weren't the only way to keep a person imprisoned. Until she could prove her innocence, she was as much a prisoner as the inmates still locked away behind steel bars in Cañon City. In fact, in some ways, she was worse off than they were because she was tormented by the constant evidence of freedom and normal living all around her.

She wasn't going to run anymore, she decided, pulling the notice from the board and stuffing it into her grocery sack. She was going to stand and fight. She wasn't going to leave Columbus until she'd seen the Very Reverend Tobias Grunewald, until recently, bishop of Phoenix, Arizona.

And, long ago, in 1982, the priest assigned to the parish church of St. Jude, in Colorado Springs. Father Tobias. She knew him well.

Five

"Son of a gun, there it is." Don halted his vintage Thunderbird on the fourth floor of Tampa airport's long-term parking garage, but he didn't get out. No way he was going to abandon his beloved in an airport parking lot even for a few seconds. He tossed the Pontiac's keys to Sean. "You want to look it over? There doesn't seem to be any damage."

"Yeah, okay." Sean checked the trunk of the Pontiac, which was empty, before unlocking the car and getting in. The interior had been recently vacuumed, but the car had been closed up for two days and it smelled hot and stale. Otherwise, it looked and felt exactly the same as it had when he'd last seen it two days ago.

He turned the key in the ignition and the engine grumbled to life. He'd noticed that the odometer read 999 when he parked at Denny's. It now read 1026, which meant Maggie had driven twenty-seven miles before abandoning the car here at the airport. Great, he congratulated himself. It sure was good to know that his photographic memory for facts and figures hadn't failed him despite a bullet to the head. He could add that snippet about the number of miles she'd traveled to everything else he already knew about Maggie Stevens and come up with enough useful information to cover the surface of a pin. Provided, of course, that it was a damn small pin.

He finished his inspection of the car's interior and poked his head out of the window to speak to his brother. "There's no visible damage. You want me to drive this back home or take it to the dealership?"

"Take it to the shop," Don said sourly. "I never did like that car anyway, so I may as well put it back on the lot as soon as it's been checked out."

"Okay. See you." Sean put the car in gear and headed for the exit, only realizing how ferocious his expression must be when the woman collecting parking fees seemed afraid to reach out and hand him his change. He switched on the radio and tried to shake loose from his frustration, but two days of brooding about Maggie Stevens hadn't improved his mood. Nor had a phone call from his ex-wife informing him that she was pregnant and that Heather was very excited at the prospect of having a new baby brother or sister to play with next September.

Lynn had always said that she wanted more children, so the news shouldn't have come as a shock, but it did. He could feel his daughter slipping away from him, becoming more entangled with her new family and more of a stranger to him as each day passed. His helplessness to change their situation gnawed at him. He couldn't even get satisfactorily angry with Lynn. Yeah, she'd been a bitch about visitation rights, but it was his obsession with his job that had driven her into the arms of the asshole neurosurgeon who was now her husband. Bad as it was to lose Heather, it was even more infuriating when he had absolutely nobody to blame except himself.

He handed the Pontiac over to one of the mechanics and wound his way through the showroom to Don's office. His brother was on the phone and waved him inside. Sean soon realized Don was talking to the police, informing the duty officer that his missing car had been returned, and he no longer wanted to press charges against Maggie Stevens.

Don hung up the phone, avoiding Sean's gaze. "Don't start," he warned. "Save your breath. I know everything you're going to say."

"Don, she stole one of your cars and God alone knows what else she was up to! At least let the cops try to find out something about her."

Don threw a stack of sales documents into a drawer and slammed it shut. "Sean, listen up. It's over and done with. Maggie Stevens screwed both of us, but there's nothing we can do about it. So forget her and move on."

"Maybe you don't care when your women fuck you over, but I sure as hell do!"

Don leaned across the desk. "Was Maggie Stevens one of your women, Sean? If so, it seems to me I'm the person who's been fucked, not you."

Sean drew in a tight, hard breath, then let it out slowly. "Maggie Stevens wasn't one of my women," he said curtly. "My only interest in her was making sure that she didn't fleece you. It still is."

"She's gone, Sean. She isn't going to fleece either one of us." Don walked over to the refrigerated bar, found two sodas and handed one to his brother. "Stop thinking like a cop for five seconds, okay? I was the one pursuing Maggie Stevens, not the other way around. She wasn't trying to set me up for any sort of scam."

Don was so naive that he didn't realize all the best con artists convinced their victims that they were the ones doing the chasing. But there was no point in trying to explain something his brother simply wasn't willing to believe.

When Sean didn't say anything, his brother gave him a light punch on the arm. "Let it go, kiddo. You don't have to save all the world just because you didn't manage to save your partner."

Sean fought back the hot denial that sprang instantly to his lips. He was sick and tired of everyone assuming that everything he did and didn't do was somehow connected to the fact that he'd allowed his partner to get shot.

"You're right, Don," he said, trying not to sound as weary as he felt. "I'm blowing this incident with Maggie Stevens way out of proportion." He took a swig of icy Dr. Pepper. "What do you say we forget about women for tonight? How about I treat you to dinner at this great steak restaurant I've found? We'll order up a couple of T-bones, bloodred, and we'll talk cars and sports all night."

"Jeez, I wish I could, but ex-wife number one wants me to have dinner with her." Don glanced at his watch. "Five-thirty already. Damn! If I had time, I'd come and eat with you first. Tara's always on a diet, so she's probably going to serve me three lettuce leaves and a pasta shell." He ran his hand through his thinning hair, looking gloomy. "God, I hate women's food."

"What time do you have to be there?"

"Seven." Don sighed. "One way and another, this sure has been a pisser of a day."

"Do you really need to go?"

Don shrugged. "Yeah, I guess I do. Tara says she found a can of chewing tobacco in Mike's backpack and she wants me to deal with the situation. As if I'm gonna do any good. Mike never speaks to me except to ask for money. Besides, what the hell are you supposed to say to a fourteen-year-old kid who's chewing tobacco?"

"You could tell him to quit because it's real stupid to put your health at risk for such a disgusting habit. Or, since all fourteen-year-olds think they're immortal and don't care about health risks, you could simply point out that girls hate boys who chew."

"As if he'll care about that any more than the health risks. He's not interested in girls."

"Not interested?" Sean finally found something to laugh about. "Hey, Don, wake up, man! It hasn't been that long since you were fourteen. Probably the only time Mike isn't thinking about girls is when he's asleep. And then he's dreaming about them. Give him a few pieces of manly advice on how to handle women and he might even listen to your lecture about the health hazards of tobacco."

Don grinned, then shook his head ruefully. "Hell, is that supposed to make me feel better? If my son relies on me for advice about how to handle women, he's gonna make a real horse's ass out of himself."

"Why should Mike escape the destiny of the rest of mankind?" Sean asked. "Maybe it's time for you to let him know about the cosmic rule that says men will always end up looking like dipshits when in the company of women."

Don shot him a shrewd and sympathetic glance. "You're cynical tonight. Maggie Stevens really got to you, didn't she?"

Sean crumpled his empty Dr. Pepper can and made a successful long shot into the trash. "Who's Maggie Stevens?" he asked.

Sean stirred the ice cubes in his bourbon and forced himself to keep his attention fixed on the dance floor. He reminded himself that he'd come to the Pink Parrot because it was the best place in the Tampa Bay area to find an attractive single woman and because he wanted to prove to himself that he'd gotten his strange obsession with Maggie Stevens out of his system. His presence here had nothing to do with some cockeyed notion of speaking to Beau and finding out what hold the manager had over Maggie.

By the time he'd snapped refusals at three lusciously curved women who approached and asked him to dance, he was ready to acknowledge defeat and take himself back to his parents' place, where he could brood in solitude and avoid inflicting his bad temper on the rest of the world. Time to face up to the fact that although he had a nearly photographic memory for the written word, he'd never been very good at putting names to faces, and that he probably was never going to find out why Maggie Stevens's features seemed so hauntingly familiar. He slid off the bar stool and made his way around the edge of the crowded dance floor, heading toward the exit.

He and Beau collided at the foot of the stairs leading to the balcony. Maybe he truly hadn't seen Beau. Or maybe his subconscious was willing him to take the precise path that he had. In any case, Beau recognized him instantly and ducked around him, anxious to move on.

Sean reached out and grabbed the manager's arm. "Not so fast. I want to talk to you."

"But I don't want to talk to you." Beau shoved past him. "Get out of here or I'll have you thrown out."

Sean sidestepped and blocked the manager's path. "I'm a cop," he said. "Detective Sergeant Sean McLeod." No need to add that he was a Denver cop on enforced sick leave, without a shred of authorization to question anybody in Tampa, Florida. Or anywhere else in the world for that matter. "If you're smart, Beau, you'll decide to answer my questions here instead of down at the station."

The bluff worked. Beau hesitated, then reluctantly led the way to his office. "I'm a busy man," he said, standing behind his desk and not inviting Sean to sit down. "And if you're gonna try and make somethin' of what you saw the other night... Well, I can tell you, Detective, you're barkin' up the wrong tree. Nothin' happened between me and Maggie Stevens that she didn't ask for. You were mighty fast with your fists, but you didn't see her strugglin' to get away, did you?"

"I know she didn't want to have sex with you," Sean said. "And I can think of a whole bunch of reasons why she might have decided not to struggle." Sean leaned across the desk, invading Beau's space, changing the balance of power. "How much do you weigh?" he asked.

Beau drew back, simultaneously sucking in his paunch as if Sean had touched upon a sensitive subject. "What the hell's that got to do with anythin'?"

"Well, I'm guessing you weigh in at somewhere around two hundred pounds, give or take a few. Maggie Stevens, on the other hand, weighs in maybe at— oh, let's say one twenty-five. Tops. So I'm wondering if those seventy-five extra pounds of yours might have something to do with why she was looking sick to her stomach, but not struggling to get away. The way you had her pressed up against the wall, she must have been unable to move, don't you agree?"

"How big I am had nothin' to do with why she wasn't strugglin'." Beau stopped abruptly, realizing that he wasn't helping himself. "Look, Detective, this isn't gonna get either of us anyplace we want to go. You know you haven't got a chance in hell of makin' a charge of sexual harassment stick, much less anythin' more serious."

"How do I know that?" Sean asked.

"Because Maggie won't testify," Beau said. "Hell, I'd be real surprised if she's still in town."

Sean let out a long, quiet breath. "Why did she run, Beau? What were you holding over her that had her so scared she was willing to let you rape her?"

"I never came close to raping her! She'd been showin' me every way she could that she'd be willin' to put out for me."

For ten seconds, Sean allowed himself to fantasize about beating Beau's repugnant features into a pulp. "Okay, why did Maggie Stevens indicate that she'd be willing to...put out for you?"

The manager looked sulky, and for a moment Sean thought he wouldn't answer. Then he shrugged. "Hell, what do I care? I'm not the one who's committed a crime here, so I've got no cause to keep my mouth shut. I found out she was using a stolen Social Security card, and I told her we run a clean shop here at the Pink Parrot and I'd have to let the police know what I'd discovered."

"She was using stolen ID?" Sean was startled. Criminals used stolen identification all the time, but they used it to steal cash from automatic teller machines or to buy goods and services with stolen checkbooks and credit cards. As a general rule, it was only illegal aliens who used stolen Social Security cards to get work. Did that mean Maggie Stevens was undocumented? Whatever he'd expected to learn about her from Beau, it wasn't that she was an illegal alien. "Are you sure?" he asked, unable to accept what he was hearing. Good grief, Maggie's citizenship was one of the few things he hadn't questioned about her.

"Yeah, I'm sure. Her Social Security card was stolen

all right. I got suspicious about a few things, then I realized the numbers on the card weren't right. They belonged to an older person than Maggie. So I asked a friend over at Immigration to run a computer check. Turns out the real Margaret Marie Stevens was a fifty-year-old who'd had her purse stolen when she was on vacation in Disney World. That was a year ago, right before Maggie Stevens turned up here lookin' for a job."

Beau squared his shoulders defiantly. "I didn't do anythin' wrong, nothin' at all. I let Maggie know that I'd found out her papers weren't legit, and she hasn't turned up for work since. So if you're lookin' to make an arrest, Detective, she's the person you need to go after, not me."

Self-righteous bastard, Sean thought in disgust. But at least now he knew how Beau had forced Maggie to submit to his sexual attack. Beau had threatened to reveal her undocumented status unless she cooperated. No wonder she'd stood against the wall, her face deathly pale, but making no move to repulse her manager's crude advances. The life of an illegal immigrant was never easy, and they were exploited at every turn.

"What made you suspect her papers weren't in order?"

"I told you already. The numbers weren't right."

"But why were you checking the numbers? Something must have made you curious."

Sean wasn't sure why he persisted, why the memory of Maggie's face still had the power to disturb him. He was haunted by the despair he'd seen in her eyes. And there was something about her eyes, and her mouth, too…. Something that tugged at his memory, an irritant that wouldn't let go. A totally infuriating sense of familiarity that simply wouldn't come into sharper focus.

Sean shook his head, bringing his attention back to Beau. "She looks American and she doesn't talk with an accent, so what was there to make you think she might be an illegal?"

"She was too smart and too good at her job," Beau said promptly. "Right away, the first week she started here, you could tell she had lots of experience and plenty of smarts. After a couple of months, I put her in charge of scheduling and she did great. Then I got her to take care of some of the orderin'—for beer coasters, paper napkins, stuff like that. She cottoned on in a flash, and we had better inventory control than we'd ever had before. She not only learned real fast, it was like she was hungry for somethin' to do beyond takin' orders for cheese puffs and makin' sure the customers didn't pinch her ass."

"And that was how you knew she was undocumented?"

"Sure." For once, Beau sounded as if he was telling the whole truth and nothing but the truth. "If she was here legally, she wouldn't have stuck it out for as long as she did. She'd have moved on, gotten herself a real career. With her looks and brains and no husband or kid holding her back, she ought to have been more ambitious. Hell, I must have seen a dozen businessmen handin' over their cards, offerin' her job interviews. Half of 'em probably just wanted to get her into bed, but some of 'em were legit."

Beau might not be a very nice man to work for, but he couldn't be totally stupid or the Pink Parrot wouldn't be such a successful nightclub, so Sean had to respect his assessment of Maggie's abilities. Anyway, they coincided with his own. "Maybe she had a drug problem," he suggested.

Beau shook his head. "No way. In my job, you soon learn to spot the employees who are shovin' their pay up their noses, and you get rid of them real quick if you want to keep a smooth-runnin' operation. People with drug problems turn into thieves, and I want to keep this place tickin' over real nice and easy. Maggie didn't have any drug or alcohol problems. She didn't even smoke, which most of the girls do. Fact is, I'm really sorry to lose her."

That was undoubtedly the truth, Sean thought sourly. Beau had probably hoped for months of free sex in exchange for keeping his mouth shut. The more he knew about Beau, the less he liked him, and he'd have been delighted to pin charges of sexual assault on him. Except that he and Beau both knew that there wasn't a chance in a billion of making such charges stick. And that left nothing much for Sean to do, except go home and quit brooding about how many days were left—twenty-three—before the departmental witch doctor was willing to check him out and declare him fit for duty again. Maybe.

"If you have any idea where Maggie's gone, you'd better tell me," Sean said, more to give himself an exit line than because he had any expectation that Beau would have something useful to impart. "After all, she's using stolen ID papers."

Beau shrugged. "How should I know where she's gone? I'm the last person she'd confide in."

"True. But that doesn't mean you didn't dig around and come up with a few interesting pieces of garbage. Come on, Beau. You might as well give up anything you've got on her because it's no use to you and that way you keep on my good side."

"Well now, Detective, I have to say that I don't see any real reason to keep on your good side."

"Think again. You don't want me to contact the INS and suggest they should pay a visit to the Pink Parrot, do you?"

Beau looked sick, as well he might. The INS was overworked, understaffed and underfunded. Most of the time, it suited everyone for the authorities to look the other way while illegal aliens took on the jobs that American citizens didn't want. A club like the Pink Parrot, in a state like Florida, would have a hard time operating at a profit without a generous supply of un-documented workers, and Beau understood exactly what would happen to his profits once the INS decided to start raiding the club on a regular basis. He and Sean both knew that there wasn't a dishwasher or busboy in the place whose papers would stand up to scrutiny.

He directed a look of undiluted loathing toward Sean, then walked over to a cabinet and pulled out a folder. "This is Maggie Stevens's personnel file," he said. "Take it. Everything I know about Maggie Stevens is in that file, and, believe me, there's not much there."

Sean tucked the folder under his arm. "Thanks, Beau," he said. "You have a real nice day, okay?"

Beau hadn't been exaggerating, Sean reflected as he spread the meager contents of Maggie Stevens's file across the bed in his parents' guest room. The file contained her original application for employment, a photocopy of her supposed Social Security card, a change-of-address form showing that she'd moved into her apartment on September 1 of the previous year. There was also a listing for her home phone number and a form she'd signed agreeing to be tested for the presence of illegal drugs in her system.

In addition, there was a reference letter from the manager of a restaurant in Dallas called the Sizzlin' Steer that said Maggie Stevens had worked for him from May 1995 to September 1996 and that she'd been an outstanding worker whose services he was sorry to lose. A scribbled notation on the letter indicated that Beau had called to check the reference and been told that the Sizzlin' Steer had changed owners and was now known as Piccolo Mondo. Nobody knew where the former manager was currently employed.

Sean was impressed that Beau had even bothered to make a long-distance call to check on Maggie's supposed reference. He knew from two years' experience with the fraud squad that most employers never took the time or the trouble. If Maggie was providing herself with fake references, she could safely gamble that nine out of ten places where she applied for a job would never bother to check up on any glowing letters of recommendation that she wrote for herself. He shuffled the pages back together again. Nothing in this skimpy file was ringing any bells or helping him to isolate what it was about Maggie Stevens that seemed so familiar.

The final item in the personnel file was a color photograph, posed against a plain background and clipped to the slender stack of health benefits documents. The HMO used by the Pink Parrot apparently required all enrolled members to present a photo ID when they went to the doctor or used other HMO services.

Sean tilted the lamp shade so that he could see the photo more clearly. It didn't do Maggie justice. She stared head-on with no smile, her eyes curiously blank and her profusion of yellow curls looking more obviously like a wig when viewed through the revealing eye of the camera.

Sean had spent plenty of time searching through mug shots, and there was a definite art to blocking out superficial changes so that you could recognize similarities in criminals who'd been fat and clean shaven five years ago and now were thin and bearded. Some cops had a real knack for recognizing criminals despite clever disguises. Unfortunately, Sean wasn't one of them, which was part of the reason Art had died. But staring at Maggie's picture, he felt a sudden lurch of his stomach, an unmistakable jolt of recognition, too powerful to be dismissed. He'd seen this woman's photo before. He'd stake big money on it.

In real life, Maggie's features were mobile, her eyes expressive, her body charged with energy. In the health insurance photo, all that energy had been drained out of her, and it was her very lifelessness that was triggering such a strong sensation of familiarity. For days, he'd been haunted by a feeling that he knew Maggie Stevens. Now he was sure of it. He'd seen this woman before, in another situation where she'd kept her face expressionless and her eyes carefully blank.

Experts at identification always looked at a person's ears because they were the feature that was most unique and changed the least. Maggie clearly knew that, since she'd arranged the wig so that not even her earlobes were visible. Sean fixed his attention on her other features, trying to bring the elusive memory into focus. Nothing clicked. Where the hell had he seen this woman's face before? In a police lineup? A mug shot? He visualized her with raven black hair, red hair, cropped hair. He stared at her eyes, imagining them changed by colored contact lenses or obscured by glasses. Still nothing. The harder he tried to grasp hold of the memory, the more it faded into stubborn obscurity.

He got up and paced the room, facing the fact that he might be inventing a memory that had never existed. The obnoxious prick who served as the departmental psychologist had subjected him to a battery of tests when he'd applied for return to duty after his physical injuries had healed. The psychologist had been able to find no measurable defect in his mental abilities—Sean still retained his amazing memory for facts and figures—but he'd announced that Sean was psychologically traumatized and put him on a further six weeks sick leave. Sean's judgment was impaired, the psychologist had said. Because of the circumstances of his partner's death, especially the fact that he'd failed to recognize Art's murderer when he'd spotted him earlier in the day, Sean had become prone to doubts about his own competence and excessively prone to seeing threats where none existed.

Sean forced himself to consider the possibility that his suspicions about Maggie Stevens were nothing more than an example of impaired judgment, overcompensation for the fact that he hadn't been suspicious enough when Art needed him. He looked at the photo again and shook his head. Damned be the shrink and his psychobabble. Maggie's behavior had aroused his suspicions, not some defective quirk of his own psyche.

Sean slammed his fist into the wall. He wasn't going to wallow in doubt and self-blame anymore. He recognized Maggie Stevens. He'd seen her picture before. The only question was where.

He heard the sound of his mother's footsteps, followed by a light tap on the door. He smothered a slightly impatient sigh and opened the door. "Hi, Mom. I thought you and Dad were in bed."

"I was." She tightened the belt of her cotton robe, and her gaze flicked briefly to the wall. "I heard you…moving around. I thought you might have a headache or something."

"No, I'm fine."

She gave him a worried look. Searching, no doubt, for signs that he was about to do something truly crazy as opposed to merely neurotic, like banging on the wall. Her expression of frazzled concern was all too familiar. Since he got out of the hospital, he'd seen it regularly on the faces of his friends as well as his colleagues.

"I was planning to make a cup of tea," she said, apparently satisfied that he wasn't going to go berserk in the next few minutes. "I'd welcome the company if you'd like to join me."

She spoke hesitantly, as if she expected a curt refusal, and Sean felt a wave of mingled love and guilt. Her gray hair was getting thin in places, and where she'd been lying down, flattening her usual careful style, he could see a tiny patch of pink scalp. He felt a tightening in his throat and bent down to give her a quick kiss on her soft, wrinkled cheek.

"What was that for?" she asked, sounding pleased as well as surprised. "Sean Michael, if you were twenty years younger, I'd know you'd been up to mischief for sure."

He grinned. "I'm too old to get up to mischief," he said. "That kiss was from the heart."

She looked flustered, but her reply was typical Mom. "Too old for mischief? At thirty-eight? Heavens to Betsy, child, when you get to my age, you'll realize that it takes a man until he's forty before he even starts to get smart."

"Women, of course, are born smart. At least according to you."

She smiled. "Let's just say we wise up a bit sooner than men."

He linked his hand with hers and followed her out into the corridor. "Some tea would be great," he said. "Is Dad asleep?"

"Asleep and snoring."

"Couldn't you get one of those strips to put over his nose? Or a special pillow?"

"I've tried. Nothing works." His mother shook her

head. "I've given up on finding a cure. I'll roll him over onto his side when I go back to bed and that should keep him quiet long enough for me to drop off."

There was exasperation in her voice, but there was affection, too, and Sean wondered if he'd ever be able to build a marriage that would carry him into his seventies with such a solid basis of love to counterbalance the rough, irritating edges of daily living. When he grew old, he wanted what his parents had, he realized. He wanted their contentment, their pleasurable routine, and the joy they'd found in building a spick-and-span new retirement home to replace the cozy, shabby home of his childhood.

"You really like it here in St. Pete, don't you, Mom? You and Dad are both having a great time being senior citizens."

"Yes, we are. We like our neighbors and this development's very well maintained. We were lucky in the choice we made." She poured boiling water from the instant hot tap into the teapot. "I love all these little luxuries," she said, gesturing to the tap. "Your dad and I were in grade school when the Depression started to bite really deep, and unless you lived through those times and the world war that followed after, you can't imagine how much fun we're having, indulging ourselves with all the treats that we couldn't afford when we were first married."

They carried their mugs onto the little patio, then sat in the spiffy new outdoor loungers and enjoyed the warm night. "For all the hardship you and Dad went through, it seems to me life was a lot simpler back then," Sean said, looking up at the sky."You knew government was good, almost everyone thought FDR was a great president, you respected the minister at your church, and if a teacher kept a student back after school, you didn't wonder if it was because of some horrible sexual perversion. We don't have any of that nowadays."

"You're right. I'm sure life was much simpler back then. But in some ways, that's just because we didn't have so much freedom to choose what we would do with our lives. For example, your father and I couldn't have gotten divorced even if we'd wanted to. We'd never have been able to pay for the lawyer, our parents would have disowned us, and the parish priest would have convinced us that we'd burn in hell forever. But you and Don…you've got four divorces between the two of you. Even though I'm glad people have more choices, sometimes I think they make divorce too easy these days."

"Maybe. Maybe for Heather's sake, Lynn and I should have tried harder. But we would never have made each other happy, Mom. Not like you and Dad. Lynn wanted me to turn myself into—" He broke off abruptly. "We wanted things from each other that we couldn't provide. Things we just didn't have inside of us, so we couldn't have given them to each other even if we wanted to."

"I know about the job offer from InterTech," his mother said softly. "Lynn was really upset when you turned them down. She loved the idea of telling all her friends that you were taking a job as a corporate security executive."

"Yeah, it sounds so much more upscale than saying I'm a cop, doesn't it?"

"Lynn's a snob, but there was more to it than that, Sean, and you know it. She had good reasons for wanting you to take the job at InterTech, as well as silly ones. She really loved the idea of having you home at a regular time each night so that you and Heather could spend more time together."

"So she divorced me and made sure Heather hardly ever gets to see me at all. Mom, we both know that what Lynn wanted was for me to take a job where I brought in a hundred thousand a year for her to spend." Sean swallowed a gulp of tea. "I guess she wanted money and I wanted...something else."

"Justice?" his mother suggested. "Law and order on the streets and in neighborhoods?"

He shrugged, embarrassed. "Something like that."

He heard the warmth in her voice, even though he wasn't looking at her. "You always were a sucker for lost causes, Sean."

"Yeah, I guess I was. But maybe when I'm forty, I'll wise up. According to your theory, I've got another eighteen months to get smart."

His mother spoke into the darkness. "I don't want you to wise up," she said. "I just wish you could get your happiness back. You worry me, Sean."

"There's nothing to worry about," he said. "Or there won't be once those assholes...sorry, once those morons in the department agree to let me get back to work. I don't understand why everyone's making so much damn fuss about a couple of bullets."

"It's not the bullets that worry me. It's the guilt you can't put aside because your partner died."

Sean finished his tea before he replied, "Art should never have been in that alley. But I've accepted that I'm not responsible for his decisions or his actions. It's insulting to his memory for me to act as if he didn't understand the risks he was running. He was a twenty-year veteran and he knew exactly what was at stake when he went under cover. It's not my fault that my supposedly infallible memory for details screwed up and missed a big one."

His mother didn't believe him any more than he believed himself, but she put the best face on it that she could. "Time heals," she said. "You'll forgive yourself in the end, Sean."

"I guess so." He stood up, realizing that to a certain extent, his mother was right. He was glad he'd spent this time with her, glad that they'd talked. And mentioning Art's name hadn't set off the explosion of guilt and pain that it would have done even a week earlier. He stretched and yawned, feeling a wave of welcome sleepiness. "What did you put in the tea, Mom? It was good, but I can barely keep my eyes open."

"I just added a teaspoon of honey to a regular herb blend," she said. "I'm glad you liked it."

They set their cups in the kitchen sink and passed through the living room en route to bed. "Good night," his mother said quietly, standing outside the door of the guest room. "Sleep well, Sean."

"Mmm, you, too." Sean kissed his mother on the forehead and walked into his room, his mind blurry with tiredness. Behind him, he heard his mother open her bedroom door. He heard the click of the door closing and then the sudden cessation of his father's snoring.

Sean grinned and stepped out of his jeans. He'd better get to sleep fast, before the snoring started up again. The contents of Maggie Stevens's personnel file were spread over his bed, and he shoved them into a haphazard pile, ready to dump onto the bedside table.

Her photograph ended up on top of the pile and he stared at it, transfixed. The blood rushed from his head and he sagged down on the bed. "Holy shit!"

Drowsiness had obviously let down some sort of barrier in his mind, and when he stopped trying to force the memories, they'd arrived in full flood. He picked up the faded Polaroid, then turned it around and around while the mental barriers that had prevented his seeing the truth became transparent.

He finally remembered where he'd seen a picture of Maggie Stevens. It had been about seven years ago, when the authorities circulated her mug shot to every police department in Colorado, announcing that she'd escaped from the women's prison in Cañon City and that she should be considered violent and dangerous. The bulletin warned that she'd shown great cunning by attaching herself to a squad of trusted prisoners being transported to a secure facility outside the main jail after a virulent epidemic of vomiting and diarrhea had been traced back to contamination in the prison water supply. She'd escaped with a group of four other women, all of whom had been recaptured within hours.

Only Maggie was still on the run when this bulletin was circulated, three months after her escape.

He also remembered her real name, which was Margaret Juliana Slade.

Sean wiped his sweating palms on his T-shirt. It had taken him much longer than it should have to recognize her. He'd been a cop for sixteen years, so he'd helped in the arrest and prosecution of more murderers than he cared to count. But he had plenty of reasons to remember Maggie Slade, not only because her trial had aroused a great deal of public interest, not even because the murder of Rowena Slade was the first homicide he'd ever worked on, but because the investigation into the death of Rowena Slade was the only one in his entire career of which he felt profoundly ashamed.

The memories poured in thick and fast. Now that he'd made the right mental connection, he was quite sure that Maggie Stevens and Margaret Juliana Slade were one and the same person. Despite the passage of fifteen years, despite the fact that she'd grown from a young girl into a mature woman, the similarities were there to be found by anyone who knew what to look for.

Sean drew a ragged breath. His instincts hadn't failed him after all. Maggie Stevens had been hiding secrets just as he'd suspected, and now he knew exactly what those secrets were.

She was an escaped convict, and she'd murdered her mother.

Six

It was more than a decade since Maggie had last seen Archbishop Tobias Grunewald, but he was still as handsome and dynamic as she remembered. Their first encounter had been sixteen years ago, when he was simply Father Tobias, the priest assigned to the parish of St. Jude in Colorado Springs. Their last encounter had taken place inside the walls of the women's prison in Cañon City, when he'd already been promoted to the rank of bishop. He was making a name for himself as a prelate who cared about juvenile offenders, and he'd taken a personal interest in Maggie's case, arranging for her to receive a scholarship to attend college by mail and videotape while serving her sentence.

He'd been no more than fifty at their last meeting, which meant that he was still only sixty, young to be an archbishop. Although his thick mane of hair had turned silver, far from making him appear old, the gray hairs seemed to emphasize his athletic posture and the youthful vigor of his movements. His manner was confident and his presence even more charismatic than Maggie remembered.

The local media loved the new archbishop, in part because of the contrast to his predecessor, who'd been frail, deaf and stern, rarely communicating with the public except to remind his flock that mothers who worked outside the home were the prime cause of America's problems. The press had only sought interviews with the previous archbishop when they wanted to pick a fight with Planned Parenthood or the ACLU, so it was a refreshing change to have a dynamic new incumbent who offered a message of hope, acceptance and love.

Although it sent chills of revulsion down her spine just to look at him, Maggie watched with compulsive attention as the archbishop moved to the chancel steps to deliver his sermon. True to his reputation, he kept away from high-flown rhetoric and concentrated on the practical. He told the congregation crowded into St. Anthony's that he had great hopes for all the good things Catholics in the diocese of Columbus could achieve with hard work and God's help. He expressed his pleasure at the warmth of the welcome he'd received from the people of Columbus, Catholic and non-Catholic alike, and he reminded his listeners that both his mother and his father had been born in Cincinnati, so he was almost a native son.

Having gotten his audience firmly on his side, the archbishop went straight to the meat of his sermon. He explained that he'd spent a lot of time over the past few years working with juveniles caught up in the criminal justice system, and that his experiences in Arizona suggested that justice had very little to do with what was going on within the nation's overworked and underfunded judicial system. Potentially good kids were getting thrown away. Vicious young criminals were cynically manipulating the courts. To help change this, the archbishop looked forward to starting a constructive dialogue with city officials and parishioners on ways in which local churches could help to keep at-risk kids out of trouble.

His audience stirred uneasily. For the most part, they were solidly middle class, and the concept of their churches getting actively involved in experimental programs for juvenile lawbreakers unsettled them. There was a murmur of relief when the archbishop explained that he considered education and home life the two magic keys that could turn young offenders into model citizens, and that he planned to do everything in his power to support the family and strengthen Catholic schools in the diocese.

Maggie had heard the archbishop preach many times before, when he'd been a humble parish priest and her mother had dragged her to weekly mass at St. Jude's. In those days, though, she hadn't paid him a lick of attention and she had no idea if he'd always been this powerful a sermonizer. Knowing him as well as she did, she was immune to his phony blandishments, but she was impressed by the slick way he played his audience. He avoided the mistake of talking too long, even though he was blessed with the gift of a wonderful speaking voice and could probably have recited classified ads and remained entertaining. Maggie wasn't in the least surprised when she looked around as he wound up for his grand finale and saw that he'd bewitched the entire congregation, including some local journalists who were trying to appear professionally detached but were clearly charmed and even inspired.

Just once, Archbishop Grunewald seemed to look in Maggie's direction, and for a split second she felt as if her gaze locked with his. The eye contact was dangerous—there was always the faint chance that he might recognize her—but she could no more have looked away than she could have flapped her hands and learned to fly. Then he tilted his head heavenward and the illusion of eye contact shattered. Holding his arms wide to embrace his listeners, he carried on with his impassioned summation.

At that moment, Maggie hated him with such fierce intensity that she could barely keep to her seat. She wanted to stand up on her chair and scream the truth for all the world to hear.

Liar! Fornicator!

Murderer!

Fortunately, her years behind bars had taught her how to keep her face expressionless and her body motionless even when she wanted to yell and tear her hair out at the savage injustice of life. So she kept to her seat with her head meekly bowed, and when the archbishop's sermon ended, she produced an appreciative smile and a nod of approval just like everyone else.

She'd planned to slip out of the church two minutes

before the end of the service, but the sight of Archbishop Grunewald pretending to be holy subverted her usual self-discipline and she hung around, tormenting herself by watching him give the final benediction. He sounded incredibly caring as he offered them all the blessing of God's love and peace. Caring and totally sincere.

Maggie pressed her knuckles against her mouth, fighting nausea. What a monster! How did he dare to profane his calling like this? She'd lost her faith in a benevolent God years ago, but at least she still respected priests and ministers who were true to the high standards imposed by their beliefs. Some of the prison chaplains she'd met were among the people she admired most in the world. The archbishop, on the other hand, exploited people's longing for moral certainties and spiritual guidance, and Maggie found his cynicism despicable.

Even though she knew she was taking a terrible risk, she let herself be swept along with the rest of the congregation as they spilled out of the church and into the parish hall, where trestle tables had been loaded with fruit punch and homemade goodies. She discovered there was a perverse, masochistic pleasure to be derived from circulating through the crowd and hearing everyone sing the archbishop's praises. The raw pain of watching her enemy at close quarters filled the vast emptiness left by the death of her mother.

"Isn't he great? Such an inspiring speaker!" *He's a great liar, that's for sure.*

"I hear he's truly wonderful with teenagers." *Mmm. But did you know he's even better with married women?*

"He volunteered as a counselor at a boot camp for young offenders, and sixty percent of the kids he advised managed to stay out of trouble." *Wow, what a guy! By the way, would you like me to explain how he let a fifteen-year-old kid take the rap for a murder he committed?*

She was working herself up to the point where she was at risk of doing something dangerous, as opposed to merely foolish. She knew she ought to leave the reception with no further delay, but she couldn't drag herself away. Pain, she discovered, was an addictive sensation after years of emotional numbness.

St. Anthony's was second only to the cathedral in size. It was located in Bexley, one of the city's most upscale suburbs, so there were plenty of refreshments provided by the affluent parishioners. Maggie was getting seriously short of money and she tried to justify her decision to linger at the reception by eating enough food that she wouldn't have to buy herself dinner. Unfortunately, every time she looked across the room at Archbishop Grunewald, her throat closed up and she couldn't swallow. He was masterful at working the crowd, chatting informally to groups of parishioners, joking and laughing and being so modest and charming that the mood in the room soon shifted from friendly to outright adoring.

Maggie's mood shifted, too, from hostile to near homicidal rage. Why didn't people ever realize what a fraud this man was? Wasn't it supposed to be impossible to fool all of the people all of the time? There was no answer to that, of course, and for the sake of her sanity she was on the point of putting down her paper plate and leaving when a gravelly voice spoke her name.

"Hi, Christine. So this is how your spend your time off. Guess I can't complain that you're out lookin' for trouble, huh?"

Maggie drew in a couple of deep breaths and swung around to greet her boss. "Hello, Dorothy. What a small world. How are you?"

"Hot and sweatin'. If I ever meet the man who invented panty hose, I'm going to strangle him with his own invention."

Maggie's smile was only a little forced. "If you need an accomplice, I'm your woman."

"At least you were smart enough to wear slacks. You look cool as a cucumber." Dorothy took a sip of punch, grimaced, then put the plastic cup down. "This is way too sweet for my taste. Man, I could use an ice-cold beer right about now."

"Mmm. Me, too." Maggie was glad to find an excuse to put down her cup and plate of uneaten tidbits.

Dorothy nodded toward the archbishop. "He's an impressive guy, don't you think?"

"Very impressive." Maggie didn't trust herself to look at the archbishop and keep her smile, although she pretended to glance in his direction. "He's an excellent speaker, isn't he?"

"Sure is. And I hear he's a man of action, not just a guy who's great with words. He really wants to get out and make the world a better place for everyone, especially kids."

Everyone except the innocent young girl who'd been

locked away for a murder she didn't commit. Or did he consider a scholarship to college full and total repayment for letting her take the fall? "I'm sure he'll be a great asset to Columbus," Maggie said, trying not to choke.

"I'm real hopeful." Dorothy sent her a look that was hard to interpret. "I volunteer at our local battered women's shelter, and the director there told me the archbishop took the initiative when he was in Phoenix and got a new shelter built on the south side, then raised the funds for a full-time counselor for the kids living there."

"How wonderful."

"At least it's an improvement over the last archbishop we had here. He thought women who got beaten up should stop sassing their husbands and then the problem would vanish."

"It's amazing how people can say really stupid things and get away with it if they happen to have the right job title." Maggie barely managed to keep the bitterness from her voice. When she saw the archbishop and his entourage heading in their direction, her stomach threatened to throw up the few mouthfuls of food she'd actually eaten and she knew it was past time to leave. "Dorothy, will you excuse me? I really have to be going."

"I need to get goin', too." They walked together toward the exit from the parish hall, but it was crowded and their pace was slow. "So, how are you likin' Columbus? Have you found a decent place to live?"

"Yes, thank you, I moved in yesterday." To a rundown apartment with nothing much in its favor except the low rent. But she'd lived in a lot of places that were worse, including an eight-by-ten prison cell that she'd shared with a woman in jail for killing her baby. "I'll give you my new phone number as soon as I have one. The phone company is supposed to turn on the service tomorrow."

"No rush." Dorothy fanned herself as they finally stepped outside. "Jeez, it's hot enough for midsummer. Makes me wish I didn't have so much paperwork to catch up on this afternoon. Those IRS forms are real sons of bitches. I'd like to sit on the porch and do nothing except watch the world go by."

"Even IRS paperwork sounds more appealing than scrubbing floors, which is what I have waiting for me." Maggie glanced pointedly at her watch. "Good grief, look at the time. I've got to run or I'll never get my place cleaned up before bedtime. It's been nice talking to you Dorothy. See you tomorrow."

Dorothy blocked her path before she could move more than a couple of steps. "Christine, before you go, we need to talk some business. I won't keep you more than a couple of minutes. Let's step back under the awning, where we have some shade."

Maggie reluctantly complied. "Yes?"

"I called both those references you gave me."

"Yes, you said you would." Maggie produced a confident smile. Amazing how she could do that when her heart was hammering like a bongo drum and her legs were shaking like aspen leaves. "I hope they both said real nice things about me."

"They didn't say anything at all," Dorothy said. "The

Cove changed hands six months ago, and the new managers had no records that went back to last year. And Landmark Steak House filed for bankruptcy last month. So nobody could give you a reference there, either."

"Gee, I'm sorry you went to so much trouble for nothing. And that's awful about Landmark. I can't believe they've gone out of business. They seemed to be doing fine when I worked there."

"Don't bullshit me, Christine. You're smart, but I'm smart, too, and I know when I'm being fed a load of garbage."

"Garbage? What do you mean?"

Dorothy made an exasperated sound. "Garbage means giving me two references where I'm not going to be able to find out a thing about you because—by amazing coincidence—neither of the places exists anymore. Let me tell you, I don't believe in coincidences."

"You should. They happen all the time."

"Yeah, but I don't think this is one of those times. You're lying about your past, and I'm pretty sure I know why. You're on the run and you're scared out of your mind. You don't know who to trust, so you don't trust anybody."

Maggie wondered if she'd really turned white or whether it only felt that way. "That's plain crazy—"

Dorothy interrupted with an impatient exclamation. "Look, I only want to help, not add to your problems. I'm not goin' to tell anyone where you are."

Maggie eyed her boss warily, keeping silent because she didn't know what to say. Dorothy's offer of help made no sense. If she suspected that Maggie was on the run, why would she offer to keep quiet about her suspicions?

Dorothy sighed. "It's okay, Christine. I understand why you find it hard to trust me, but you have to believe I'm on your side. When you came into my office, I guessed right off the bat that you were running away from something, and it didn't take me long to figure out your ex-husband was the maggot in the woodpile. That's why I offered you a job. I figured you'd been through enough and you deserved the chance to start over."

Maggie let out the breath she'd been holding. Of course! How could she have been so slow on the uptake? Dorothy thought she was an abused wife, trying to hide from a violent husband.

Dorothy laid her hand on Maggie's arm, her touch gentle. "I realize what kind of hell you're going through. I had a husband who was a drunk and a mean, lying bastard to boot. He also happened to be president of the local bank and a respected member of the community, whereas I was just a pretty girl with a sexy body from the wrong side of the tracks. I kept hopin' that if I only educated myself a bit more, learned to be a more suitable wife for such an important man, then he'd quit knockin' me around. But I soon realized that the better educated I got, the more he resented me. When we first got married, he only beat me up on the weekends. By the time I dragged myself out of his house after five rotten years of marriage, it had reached the point where the fool beat me damn near every time he saw me."

Her boss was a truly generous woman to share her

story, Maggie reflected. But she had no right to accept Dorothy's friendship under false pretenses, so she responded the only way she could—by lying. "Dorothy, I appreciate your offer of help, but you've got it all wrong. I had a lousy marriage, but my husband didn't beat me. Honestly. I don't know where you got that idea—"

"I told you—I recognize a woman on the run when I see one. Take some advice from a woman who's been right where you are. I went through all the same rationalizations you're going through. You're tellin' yourself that if you don't talk about what happened with your ex, then people won't despise you. If people respect you, then you're hopin' you'll learn to respect yourself. And so on and so on. But I found out the hard way that you can never run far enough or fast enough to wipe out the memories. In the end, if you want to start your life over, you have to acknowledge what's happened and accept that your husband's brutality wasn't your fault. As long as you deny that it happened, you're still in his power. When you accept the past, you'll be able to move on without feelin' like you're always lookin' over your shoulder, wonderin' when he's going to catch up and beat the crap out of you again."

Dorothy had completely misunderstood the details of her plight, and yet Maggie felt a sudden intense yearning to confide in her, to lay down the burden of years on the run without any real friends. Maggie had come to Columbus because she was no longer willing to deny the injustice that had been done to her in the past. She was fighting demons and forcing herself to confront the reality of her own past, even if the demons she fought weren't the ones Dorothy imagined. But aiding an escaped convict was a crime and she had no right to involve Dorothy in the horrific details of her past, so Maggie reluctantly resisted the longing to ask for help.

Some hint of her struggle must have shown in her face, however, because Dorothy reached out and took her hand. "Let me put you in touch with a support group, Christine. If you don't want to talk to me, there are some good people here in town who could help you through the rough times."

Maggie discovered that she was close to tears, but she refused to succumb to them. "You're mistaken, Dorothy," she said, making her voice cold and repelling. "I appreciate your generous offer of help, but my ex-husband isn't a brute or a bully. He's just a typical idiotic man who couldn't keep his fly zippered. I'm angry at him and his new wife, but I'm not scared of him."

"If you say so." Dorothy was nothing if not persistent. She reached into her purse and pulled out a business card. "If you need help, you can always call that number night or day. In the meantime, since I've seen for myself that you're a damn good waitress, I'll not embarrass either of us by asking you to provide another reference."

Maggie took the card and stuffed it into her purse. "Thanks, Dorothy," she said stiffly. "I do appreciate all your advice and your concern."

"Yeah, sure." Dorothy sent her a sharp, assessing look. "And just so I know how to handle the staff scheduling, are you going to come in tomorrow or are you going to run again?"

With anyone less kind, Maggie would have lied without a second's pause. As it was, she hesitated for a moment, weighing the severity of her financial need against the risk of continuing to work for a woman who was as perceptive as Dorothy. She quickly realized that honesty was a luxury she couldn't afford. There was only one possible answer she could give, even though she would have to go home and think long and hard about what she really planned to do.

"Of course I'll be coming in tomorrow," she said. "The Buckeye is a great place to work, and you know how much I want to get started on saving some money."

Dorothy obviously sensed the insincerity of Maggie's response and the warmth of her gaze finally chilled. "Sure you do. Have a good night's rest, Christine. And here's a final word of advice. Get a strong lock for your door." She started to walk away, but her progress was slowed by a sudden exodus of people leaving the parish hall.

Maggie didn't want to turn tail and run while her boss could still see her. But when she realized that Archbishop Grunewald was at the center of the crowd emerging from the reception and that he would pass within a couple of feet of her as he headed toward his limo, she discovered that self-discipline would only take her so far. Mesmerized as she was by the man's fake charm, she wasn't yet ready to put herself in such close proximity to her mother's murderer. Edging away from the crowd as rapidly as she could without breaking into a run, she backed up toward the corner of the building.

"Excuse me," she muttered, squeezing sideways between two priests and three older women. "Excuse me, please."

The priests obligingly stood aside to make way for her, closing ranks again as soon as she'd passed. Which meant, thank goodness, that she was finally screened from Dorothy's view. Maggie turned and ran.

Straight into the outstretched arms of Sean McLeod.

Seven

Maggie opened her mouth to scream, but shock had sucked all the air out of her lungs and no sound emerged. When Sean grabbed her, she collapsed against his chest, limp and unresisting.

He immediately pushed her away, forcing her to stand under her own power but keeping her wrists shackled within his grip. "Oh, no, you don't, sugar. Even a dumb ol' cop like me doesn't fall for the same trick twice."

She fought to calm the panic racing through her. "No trick," she said tiredly. "I'm fresh out of tricks. What do you want with me, Sean?"

"That should be obvious. Margaret Juliana Slade, you're a fugitive felon, there's a federal warrant outstanding against you, and you're under arrest. That about sums it up."

He spoke softly, but each word exploded against Maggie's ears like a detonating land mine. It was all over, then. Done. Finished. Sean McLeod was aware of her true identity and he was taking her back to jail.

She knew that a cop from Colorado had no authority to arrest anyone in Columbus, Ohio, not even an escaped felon. Sean must be aware of that, too, and he hadn't bothered to explain her right to keep silent or her right to the advice of a lawyer, essential steps in a legal arrest. But they both knew his lack of official status was a mere technicality and that it would be child's play for him to tidy things up. He would haul her off to the nearest police station, where he would swear out a complaint, and the local cops would trump up some reason to hold her. Within hours, the Colorado authorities would fax full details of her criminal record to Ohio, including the fact that there was a federal warrant out for her arrest. At which point, nobody was going to give a damn that she'd been captured by an out-of-jurisdiction detective, least of all the judge signing papers for her extradition back to Colorado.

So when Sean clamped her arms behind her back and frog-marched her toward the parking lot, Maggie didn't attempt to struggle. What was the point? There was nowhere to run, nowhere to hide, nowhere to go except back to prison. If she fought Sean, he would overpower her. He was faster and stronger than she was, and now that he'd realized who she was, he'd be relentless in his pursuit. If she cried out for help, he'd tell everyone she was a convicted murderer and he was a police officer. After that, nobody was going to come rushing to her aid. In the current law-and-order mood of the country, convicted murderers ranked right up there with the Ebola virus in terms of popular appeal.

A middle-aged couple approached from the opposite direction. "Don't speak and keep walking," Sean said into her ear, propelling her past the couple on the narrow sidewalk.

She would have spoken in a flash if she could have thought of anything to say that might win her freedom, but nothing came to mind. She'd given up expecting miracles. In the distance, she heard the cheerful noises that marked the departure of Archbishop Grunewald's limo. Somehow it seemed appropriate that her mother's murderer was gliding off to a life of comfort and public honor while she—his victim—was being escorted back to jail.

At the thought of thirty or forty years confined within the bleak concrete walls of the Colorado state prison, Maggie's resignation mutated into rage. Dammit, she wouldn't return meekly to Cañon City! She couldn't bear it. Belatedly, she started to struggle to break free of Sean's hold, trying to bite his arm and aiming a vicious kick at his groin.

She might as well have fought against a two-ton steel robot. Sean sidestepped her puny kick, evaded her bite and had her back under control again without breaking a sweat.

"Don't fight me, Maggie. You'll only end up getting hurt."

She'd heard those words so many times before. From sympathetic guards in prison, from other inmates, from guidance counselors and well-meaning volunteers determined to redeem her. In the past, their advice had only made her all the more anxious to stand up for herself against the power of the system, to force people to pay attention to what she was trying to tell them: that she didn't need redeeming; she needed justice. But at a certain point, you had to put aside teenage fantasies and accept that life didn't often deliver justice.

Time to face reality, Maggie. Sean McLeod is taking you back to prison, and you'll probably die there.

Her body started to shut down system by system, sending her into the semicatatonic state that had enabled her to endure the worst abuses of her captivity. The colors around her faded to gray; the sound of laughter and happy voices receded far into the distance....

Then awareness snapped back, and she realized Sean was forcing her head down toward her knees. "Don't faint on me," he said.

"Why not? Is fainting a crime, too?"

"With a rap sheet as long as yours, the D.A. could probably make it sound like one to a jury."

"I won't get a jury," she said. "I'm an escaped felon, so the penal system can impose whatever punishment it wants."

"Yup, it sure can. They're gonna lock you up and throw away the key. Count on it." She stumbled and his arm tightened around her waist. To curb her, not to comfort or support. "Forget it, Maggie. After the trick you pulled back in Tampa, if you had a full-scale heart attack right here in the parking lot, I'd assume you were faking it until the paramedics officially declared you dead."

"I'm surprised you'd bother to call the paramedics," she said bitterly. "Why not pretend I resisted arrest?

That way, you could shoot me and save the taxpayers a bunch of money."

"It's a real tempting thought. Luckily for you, I don't have my gun."

They arrived at what was presumably his car, a rented white Ford Taurus, parked in the empty far corner of the church lot. He pushed her up against the Taurus, pinning her there with his body while he opened the door on the driver's side.

"Okay, Maggie, here's the deal. I didn't expect to meet up with you today, so I'm not carrying any handcuffs. But since I don't want you attempting to hijack the car while I'm driving, I have to restrain you."

"You could trust me not to run."

He laughed without a trace of mirth. "Yeah. And for my next comic routine, I'll ask Timothy McVeigh to take charge of the FBI's supply of dynamite."

He tugged off his tie as he spoke. Then he swung Maggie around, pulling her hands behind her back in order to bind her wrists.

Her resistance was instinctive, a visceral reaction to years of being cuffed and chained. Sean's response was probably equally instinctive after more than fifteen years as a cop. He put his knee against her spine and jerked her backward until struggling was impossible and the pain made her cry out.

He ignored her yelp of pain and spoke from behind her, his voice cool. "Your choice, Maggie. You can let me tie your hands behind your back or we can fight about it, and I get an excuse to knock you out. Personally, I'd say you'd be real smart to choose the restraints.

The way I'm feeling right now, you don't want me to start throwing punches anywhere in your direction."

There was no way she was ever going to tell a cop that he had permission to tie her up, so she didn't reply, but she stopped fighting, which was a tacit surrender, and he started to lash her wrists together with his tie. Maggie stared into space as she felt the bonds tighten. She focused on an old brick building across the street, refusing to let any coherent thoughts form. When things got really bad, taking yourself to another place was the best way to survive.

"What do you think you're doing? What's going on here?" an angry voice demanded.

"Shit!" Sean pulled her back against his body, trapping her half-bound wrists between them.

Maggie jerked out of her trance. "Dorothy!" she exclaimed, blinking as she refocused on the reality of her surroundings. "Wh-what are you doing here? I thought you'd left ages ago." She hadn't succeeded in numbing her feelings as well as she'd hoped, and she felt a deep wave of shame that Dorothy should see her in such a humiliating situation. Instead of struggling, Maggie cringed against Sean, helping him to hide her bound wrists. In the brief time they'd known each other, she'd come to admire and like her feisty, tenderhearted boss and dreaded the thought of Dorothy's finding out she was a convicted murderer.

"I saw this man stalking you, so I hung around." Dorothy directed a withering glare at Sean. "He's your ex-husband, right?"

"Er, no, no, actually he's not my husband—"

Dorothy gave an impatient and disbelieving snort. "Christine, don't let him do this to you. If you don't want to go with him, just say so. Whatever bullshit he's pushin' on you, he has no right to force you to go with him even if you're not legally separated." She held out her hand. "Just say the word, honey, and I'll take you home with me. You'll be safe there, I promise."

The lump in her throat was so big that Maggie couldn't have answered even if she'd known what to say. Kindness was a commodity in short supply in her life, and Dorothy's generosity overwhelmed her. As it was, Sean took the problem of finding a reply out of her hands.

"Excuse me, ma'am," he said to Dorothy, locking his arms around Maggie's waist as if he was giving her a hug, but in reality holding her completely immobile. "It looks like there's been a misunderstanding here—"

"You're damn right there's been a misunderstandin'." Dorothy turned on him, her cheeks scarlet with indignation. "And the misunderstandin' is all yours, mister. Come on, Christine. Buck up your courage and just walk away. When are you gonna realize that this man has no power over you that you don't give him?"

Sean was beginning to look frazzled. "Ma'am, believe me, you have no idea what's going on here."

"Then explain it to me. Are you Christine's husband?"

"Christine?" Sean shot Maggie a glance that was more quizzical than anything else. Holding her breath, Maggie waited for him to explain that she was a murderer and he was a cop. Instead, to her amazement, he hesitated. "It's way too complicated to explain," he said finally. "Ma'am, I apologize, but you need to let go of this young woman's arm. She isn't going to come with you. I can't allow that."

As he spoke, he wrested Maggie's upper arm free of Dorothy's clasp, tugging hard enough that Dorothy tottered backward on her high-heeled sandals and almost fell over. While Dorothy was still tottering, Sean put his hand on top of Maggie's head and shoved her down into the car. "Get in," he said through gritted teeth. "Get in, dammit!"

Dorothy wasn't a woman to be deterred by a simple warning and a near spill. She righted herself, straightened her jacket, tugged on her cuffs and came roaring back, fists clenched and chest heaving in righteous indignation. "You're a real macho man, aren't you? Makes you feel good to push women around, does it?"

"No, ma'am." Sean's expression had gone from frazzled to hunted. As another woman approached from across the parking lot, he seemed to decide that this was an argument he couldn't win. "Sorry, ma'am, but we have to go!" He jumped into the car, slammed the door and turned on the ignition.

"I'm calling the police!" Dorothy yelled. "This is kidnapping, you hear me?"

For answer, Sean reversed out of the parking lot at breakneck speed, leaving Dorothy and the other woman staring after them in evident frustration.

For the first couple of minutes as they screeched around corners and whipped through yellow lights, Maggie was so consumed with self-pity that she didn't attempt to analyze what had just happened. But as they turned the corner onto Sawmill Road, it dawned on her that Sean's behavior was beyond strange for a police officer taking an escaped convict into custody. Why hadn't he informed Dorothy that he was a detective? Why hadn't he simply announced that Maggie was a murderer and an escaped felon? What possible motive could he have for keeping quiet about her criminal status?

The possible answers that she came up with were all horrible. Maggie shivered. Oh, God! Bad as it was to know that she'd been recaptured and was destined for jail, it would be even worse if Sean turned out to be some sort of rogue cop who liked to torture and abuse his prisoners before turning them over to official justice.

"Where are you taking me?" she asked.

He shot her a quick, sideways glance. "To my motel room."

Her heart plummeted. "If you don't mind, I'd prefer to go straight to the nearest police station."

"That could be arranged, of course. On the other hand, I thought you might like to put off your return to jail for a few hours while you tell me exactly why you're so interested in Archbishop Grunewald."

She concealed her surprise at his mention of the archbishop's name, then realized it no longer mattered if she reacted spontaneously. Ironically, in losing her freedom, she'd won back the right to be Maggie Slade, whatever being Maggie Slade might mean. Still, after years of keeping secrets, denial was almost reflexive.

"We don't need a motel room to talk about the archbishop," she said. "I'm not interested in him, and there's nothing for us to discuss."

"Do you ever tell the truth, Maggie?" Sean sounded genuinely frustrated. "Don't you worry sometimes that you might forget what the truth really is?"

"No," she said. And realized she was lying.

"Try telling the truth occasionally," Sean said. "It'll be a whole new experience for you. You might even discover that people are more willing to offer their help if you don't lie to them."

The only help she needed was to prove that Archbishop Grunewald had murdered her mother, and nobody was going to provide that sort of help. They stopped at a traffic light and Maggie watched a young woman wipe melted ice cream from her toddler's chin. They were both laughing, caught up in the delight of the moment, and she quickly turned away. Of all the things she regretted about her life on the run, the fact that she could never have a home and a family was what she regretted most.

She spoke brusquely because she felt like crying and she never, *ever* allowed herself to cry. "Has it occurred to you, Detective, that I might not lie so often if the people in my life had been more trustworthy?"

"My name's Sean, not Detective, and of course it's occurred to me." He slowed the car to turn into the forecourt of a Hampden Inn. "I realize a lot of people have let you down, Maggie. I won't."

She was smart enough not to respond to that obvious attempt to win her over. If there was one type of cop she'd learned to distrust more than any other, it was the supposedly sympathetic one. Tell a cop anything, and you could count on hearing it read back to you at your trial.

"I know you don't have any reason to trust me or any other officer of the law," Sean said, reading her thoughts with disconcerting accuracy. "But couldn't we agree on a compromise? You stop lying, and I'll try to earn your trust."

"What a deal!" she said, the sarcasm intended as much to hide her confusion as anything else. "Forgive me for mentioning that it sounds just a tad one-sided."

"Stick around. I guess time's the only thing that will convince you I'm not the enemy."

Sean's attitude was making her very nervous. Maggie's gaze darted around as she assessed her surroundings and weighed her chances of getting away from him when he finally parked the car. Slim to none seemed the realistic answer since she couldn't even release the latch on her seat belt without his help. But once they were inside the hotel room… He couldn't be on his guard every second of every minute. Surely some opportunity for escape would present itself. She felt better that even such a tiny sliver of hope had reappeared on the horizon.

Sean parked the car by the side entrance to the motel. "You can stop working on your escape plan. No way I'm going to let you get away." Once again he had read her thoughts with chilling precision. He reached into his pocket and pulled out a key card. "I'm not going to provide you with any chance to run away, Maggie. And if you don't trust anything else I say, you can trust me on that one. It's time for the running to stop."

She stared out of the window, refusing to look at him, as if that somehow would negate the unwelcome accuracy of his statement. The truth was, she'd come to Ohio precisely because she'd finally realized that she couldn't spend the rest of her life as a fugitive from the law. At a certain point, real prison bars had begun to seem less horrific than the phantom ones imposed by her lifestyle.

"Sulk all you please," Sean said, "but it won't change your choices. You can come with me to my room and we'll talk about Archbishop Grunewald and what you were hoping to achieve by following him here to Columbus. Or I can drive straight to the nearest police station and get them to book you. What's it to be, Maggie?"

"Why do you want to talk to me about the archbishop? What do you want to know about him? And why have you brought me here instead of taking me to the police station? What's in it for you?"

He pulled a wry face. "A whole heap of trouble would be my guess. But from your point of view, what have you got to lose if you come with me? And before you answer, remember that once you're in the hands of the authorities, there'll be no turning back for either of us. When the official wheels start turning, it's all over. The system will swallow you whole and spit you out when you're an old, old woman."

He was entirely right. When you got down to it, she had nothing left to lose except her life and she couldn't bring herself to believe that Sean McLeod was actually a threat to her life.

She brought her gaze back from the scraggly bushes surrounding the parking lot and turned to look at him, trying to detect subtle signs of latent violence or sexual perversion in his features. He met her gaze steadily, his eyes brooding and his mouth stern, but without any hint of sadism or cruelty.

Having looked into his eyes, she found it oddly difficult to look away. When she continued to search his features, his gaze flickered just for a second before becoming steady again. A faint flush darkened his cheekbones and Maggie realized that she was blushing, too. Incredibly, despite all the reasons they had to dislike one another, it seemed the sexual attraction that had sparked between them at the Pink Parrot still had the power to generate heat.

Sean spoke into the silence thrumming between them. "You know that I find you attractive, Maggie, so let me spell out exactly what I want from you. I'm not asking you to come to my room to have sex. I'm asking you to come to my room so you can tell me what happened the night your mother was murdered."

"You already know what happened that night," she said, the mention of her mother's murder dousing any hint of sexual desire with brutal efficiency. "It's all on record. I shot my mother in a fit of drug-induced rage. Oh, and don't forget that although the prosecution claimed I was high, they also managed to convince the jury the killing was premeditated. Quite a feat to be drugged out of your mind and yet capable of premeditation."

"It happens. People decide to commit a crime, they lay plans and then pump themselves up with drugs to find the courage to go through with it. But, for what it's worth, I disagreed with the decision to try you as an adult and I didn't think the D.A.'s office presented any valid evidence of premeditation on your part."

"Don't expect me to thank you for your limp suggestion that maybe my trial wasn't a perfect model of the legal system at its shining best."

"Your trial showed the legal system at its worst."

"For God's sake, you were the system. You're the cop who found the murder weapon! You testified in court that I'd tried to hide the gun behind the nightstand in my mother's bedroom."

"No," he said. "I never said that. I testified, in response to a question from the prosecuting attorney, that if you'd tried to hide the gun, then it was a very clumsy attempt on your part."

She shrugged, not wanting to resurrect dire memories of the fiasco that had been her trial. "Whatever."

The look he directed at her seemed genuinely sympathetic. "There's obviously a lot we need to talk about and it's hotter than hell in this car. I need to know your decision, Maggie. What's it to be? My room and lots of questions, or the police station, where they won't bother you with any questions at all after they establish your identity and read your rap sheet?"

She hesitated only another few seconds. "Your room," she said. She didn't know what she hoped to achieve by going along with Sean, but she did know that turning herself in to the police meant the end of hope as well as the end of freedom.

"Smart decision." He unfastened his seat belt and pocketed the car keys. "Let's go."

"Okay, but you'd better be quite clear on what I'm agreeing to. I'm agreeing to talk, that's all. I'm not feeling in the mood to put out for anyone right now, least of all a cop, and if you're planning on enjoying a quickie before you take me in, forget it. If you so much as touch me, I swear I'll kill you. I'm already facing life in prison, so I haven't got a damn thing to lose."

"That's true," he said. "In fact, even if I behave like a perfect gentleman, once we're inside that room, you could kill me, rob me, steal this rental car and be five hundred miles from here before anyone discovers my body. So it seems to me that I'm the person who should be worried about taking you to my room."

"You're stronger, taller and heavier than I am. If you stay alert, I can't overpower you." It was the simple truth and she'd be foolish to pretend otherwise.

"Yeah, I'm counting on that, but don't sound so regretful." He checked to make sure her wrists were still tightly bound before unlatching her seat belt and dragging her out of the car. They were only yards from the side entrance to the motel and he walked behind her, holding her pinned against his body, allowing no chance for her to escape. Sean might be acting strangely for a cop, but he wasn't giving her any opportunity to escape.

His room was five doors down from the entrance, a typical midprice motel room with dark blue carpeting, imitation-oak furniture, and two queen-size beds, which

were placed beneath cheap prints of Japanese-style flo-
ral arrangements. Maggie sat on the end of one bed,
waiting while Sean closed the curtains, switched on a
couple of lights, then cleared a space on the table between the room-service menu and a plastic bucket containing a can of soda set into melting ice. He put a
soft-sided briefcase on the table in the space he'd
cleared and unzipped it without lifting the cover or taking anything out.

Satisfied with his arrangements, he pulled one of the
chairs next to the bed and sat down, careful to avoid
touching her, which she considered a vaguely optimistic
sign. Maybe he was taking her threats of retribution seriously. He leaned forward, and she was surprised to see
something that might almost have been a rueful sort of
admiration in the depths of his eyes.

"Okay, Maggie, I'm going to untie your wrists and
I'd be real appreciative if you'd agree not to steal my
car keys the minute your hands are free. In exchange,
I'd like you to believe that I've brought you here because I have your best interests at heart."

It had been so long since she'd believed anyone had
her interests at heart that Maggie could no longer imagine what such trust would feel like. But in return for
having her hands free, she was willing to say whatever
was necessary. "You can trust me to behave. I won't try
to escape."

She was sure he understood the emptiness of her
promise, but he chose to accept it without comment. "I
don't have any scissors so it's going to take a while to
untie all these knots," he said, sitting behind her on the

bed. "If you wriggle, there's a good chance that I'll accidentally touch you. If I do, I'd take it as a personal favor if you'd refrain from killing me and/or slicing off my balls."

His attitude was making her more nervous by the minute. The cops she'd met—and it sometimes seemed as if she'd met a million—had been universally devoid of even the slightest sense of humor. She cleared her throat. "I won't wriggle," she said.

She kept her word and didn't move although he worked in silence for three or four minutes before he finally succeeded in loosening the bindings enough for her to free her hands. He kept his word, too, and never once touched any part of her anatomy except her wrists.

The instant he finished, she sprang up from the bed, anxious to get away from the enforced closeness. He lunged after her, grabbing her by the belt of her slacks and dragging her backward. Because her own motives had been entirely innocent, his lightning-fast reaction was a surprise. Not expecting to be tackled, she lost her balance and sent both of them toppling onto the bed.

"Dammit, Maggie, can't you stop trying to escape long enough to hear what I have to say? Until you listen to me, how do you know I can't help you?" Breathing hard, Sean rolled on top of her. He pinned her to the mattress and held her hands spread-eagled above her head so that her breasts were crushed against his chest and their legs tangled together in a parody of sexual intimacy.

"I wasn't trying to escape!" She squirmed and twisted to no avail. "Get off me, you stupid, moronic oaf!"

He sprang up from the bed even faster than he'd reached out to grab her. But not quite fast enough to prevent her feeling the thrust of his erection against her pelvis. He walked over to the table, keeping his back toward her. "If you really weren't trying to escape, I apologize."

"Apology accepted." For some reason, she chose not to mention that brief, betraying moment of arousal.

Sean tossed his ruined tie into the garbage. "It'll probably take a couple of minutes for the circulation in your wrists to come back. We'll talk whenever you say you're ready."

He sat down at the table, his back still toward her, and opened his briefcase, pulling out a file folder and a notebook and starting to read.

Maggie glared at his unresponsive back, determined to be furious with him because that was a lot easier than analyzing the flash of regret she'd felt when he'd rolled away from her. When she realized that she was half hoping that he'd turn around so she could see his face, she swung quickly away and strode up and down the room, rubbing her wrists, trying to get the circulation back into her hands. In no time at all, she'd worked herself into a fine lather of indignation at what a brute he was and how needlessly tight he'd bound her wrists.

"Put your hands under running water," Sean said without looking up from his reading. "Alternate hot and cold. It'll help to ease the stinging."

"Stop doing that," she said angrily. "It won't work."

"Stop doing what?" he asked mildly.

"Pretending to feel concern for my well-being. Behaving like a regular human being instead of a cop!"

"Cops are regular human beings," he said. "That's why there are good cops and lousy cops and all the range in between."

"Oh great," she muttered. "I'm locked up in a motel room with a burned-out cop who thinks he's a philosopher. It's enough to make me wonder if a prison cell can be all that bad."

Sean looked up, his face totally void of expression— the only reaction he displayed to being called a burned-out cop. Refusing to feel guilty at using information she'd gleaned from Don against him, Maggie made her way to the bathroom.

Sean followed, watching her as she let the streams of hot and cold water flow over her wrists. "I'm sorry I had to make the knots so tight, but I couldn't afford to let you run away, Maggie."

She shrugged. "When you've been cuffed and chained at the ankles so you can only shuffle when you walk, having your wrists lashed together with a silk tie is no big deal."

"You hated being tied up and we both know it." She said nothing and Sean handed her a clean towel. "How long is it going to take before you say one damn thing to me that's actually the truth?"

"I don't know." Suddenly, to her amazement, she realized she was smiling. "That was the truth, so I guess it didn't take very long."

"No, I guess it didn't." His gaze lingered on her face.

"You know, this is the first time I've seen you really smile. You should do it more often."

She turned away to hang up the towel. "I smile all the time, Detective. It's one of my trademarks."

"No. You curve your lips upward because that makes people think you're friendly and earns you big tips, but that's got nothing to do with smiling. And my name's Sean."

She fussed with the towel to give herself an excuse to ignore him. Being alone with him in a small motel room was creating a sense of connection that she didn't want, so she diffused the intimacy by sending him a cold, aggressive look. "I needed to earn big tips," she said. "It costs a lot of money to hide from the law."

"Yes, I'm sure it does. Changing your identity on a regular basis doesn't come cheap." He stood aside to let her walk back into the bedroom. "And that was the second time you told me the truth in the space of a few seconds. I'd say our relationship is progressing by leaps and bounds."

Ignoring his effort to reestablish the connection she'd broken, Maggie sat down on the bed, relieved when Sean positioned his chair at a considerable distance. "Well, what happens now?" she asked.

"Nothing very dramatic. We talk."

"What about?"

"Lots of things. The past, mostly. But first, the present. You know what surprises me more than anything about what's happened this afternoon? You haven't asked me how I found you."

"I know how you found me," Maggie said. "I made

a stupid mistake. That's how all escaped convicts get caught."

Sean's eyes narrowed. "Then you've already realized that you left behind a folder of notes and clippings about Archbishop Grunewald?"

She'd left her file on the archbishop someplace where it could be found? But she couldn't have. Maggie shook her head in disbelief. She simply couldn't have made a mistake that elementary or that enormous. Besides, she distinctly remembered checking her Tampa apartment from end to end and she hadn't left behind so much as a worn-out toothbrush, much less a stack of incriminating papers.

"I know I collected all my trash from the apartment and I chose the Dumpster where I got rid of it at random. Are you telling me that with all the Dumpsters there must be in Tampa, you somehow found my trash?"

"No, I'm a detective, not a magician."

"Then exactly where did you find those papers?"

"You left the file in the trunk of your Chevy."

"In my Chevy? In my *car?*" Maggie's emotions had spun through so many cycles in the past couple of hours that she seemed to have developed a diminished capacity to react. She ought to have been distraught—hysterical—to learn that she'd finally been caught by the sort of slipshod error she'd struggled for years to avoid. Instead, she just felt numb.

Sean spread the magazine articles and newspaper clippings over the table. She'd hurriedly torn up the contents of the file before she left Tampa, but Sean had painstakingly pieced and taped them together again.

The collection was quite substantial, and yet it didn't seem much to Maggie when she considered that this was all the information she'd accumulated on Archbishop Grunewald after years of diligent searching. Even more disturbing from her point of view, the articles were almost universally complimentary. A few conservative commentators in church quarterlies suggested that the archbishop's theology was too liberal to be acceptable, but otherwise she'd never managed to find a negative article about the man who'd killed her mother. After years of studying him from a distance, she had no clue as to what his secret vices might be or what weak points could be exploited.

Maggie stared down at the crumpled pages, resisting the evidence of her own eyes. Even though she'd been in a frantic hurry to leave Tampa, it defied reason to acknowledge that she'd forgotten to dispose of such an incriminating collection. And yet she obviously had left the papers behind, otherwise Sean couldn't have found them.

"You really found these in the trunk of my car?" she asked, still not able to accept the magnitude of her mistake.

"Yes, in a plastic shopping bag. The bag was gray and so is the interior of the trunk. Plus it had slipped down the side, near the housing for the spare tire, and it wasn't easy to see."

She had been so careful, so damn clever, ever since she escaped from Cañon City. It was almost funny to realize that she'd tripped up in such an elementary way. Funny—or frightening.

"You were in such a hurry to transfer your stuff from the Chevy to Don's Pontiac that you were bound to leave something behind." Sean sounded almost as if he wanted to reassure her. "And you were unlucky that I managed to check out your car before the landlord had it towed away."

Yes, she'd been unlucky, but she'd been careless, too. So careless that she could no longer deny that there had been an element of fatalism in her actions. Her life on the run had become so unmanageable that she'd subconsciously allowed herself to make a terrible mistake. A mistake that would force her to risk everything on one giant spin of the wheel of fate. How else could she explain that she'd run off to Columbus, leaving a file on Archbishop Grunewald in a place where Sean McLeod was quite likely to find it? She'd even highlighted with a yellow marker the parts of the newspaper article that announced his promotion to archbishop and his transfer to the diocese of central Ohio.

She'd run away, changed her name, covered her tracks and zigzagged across country as if she was determined to remain hidden. And yet she'd left an arrow that would point Sean McLeod straight to Columbus and the archbishop.

The fact that her own motives weren't entirely clear didn't make her any more ready to accept that Sean's intervention might be to her advantage. It was infuriating that he'd obviously found her today by sheer good luck, and she pounced on the rage, one of the few emotions it seemed safe to feel right now.

"My God, you had absolutely no clue where to find

me, did you? And if I hadn't gone to that service today, you'd never have found me. You didn't even know what name I'm using here!"

"I know it now. Christine, according to your feisty friend."

"You still don't know my last name."

"That's true, but irrelevant. And although I wasn't expecting to track you down quite this fast, I'd already requested an interview with the archbishop, so as soon as you contacted him, I'd have been informed."

"Maybe. That's if I ever contacted him and if he recognized me. The bottom line is, you found me this afternoon through sheer dumb luck."

"Luck maybe, but not dumb luck. And any successful police investigation owes something to luck. Often more than we want to admit."

"If that's supposed to make me feel better about being caught, it's not working."

Sean leaned forward in his chair. "You can't rewrite the past, Maggie. The fact is, I've found you, and now we have to move on from here."

Her skin felt clammy and hot at the same time. "Move on to where?" she asked. "That's what I don't understand. Where is all this leading? Why am I here? Why aren't we down at the local precinct, with you showing me off to all your colleagues, explaining how brilliantly you tracked me down? Why aren't you basking in the glow of having brought in one of America's most wanted female criminals?"

"Before we analyze my motives, let's get back to yours. Why are you so obsessed with the archbishop that you risked following him here? Are you hoping that he'll take up your cause and fight to get you a new trial?"

She laughed. "No, I have absolutely no hope or expectation that the archbishop will do anything to help me."

"That's good. That's very good. Because the truth is, Maggie, I don't believe there's a single thing the archbishop can do for you except pray."

"Thank you, but I'd prefer not to be on the receiving end of Archbishop Grunewald's prayers."

Sean sent her a searching look. "He's a decent man."

"You're wrong," she said, and despite her best efforts to control herself, she heard how her voice shook. Not with fear or anger, but with the passion of justice too long denied. "Everyone is wrong about the archbishop. He's an evil man, and I don't want his prayers or his charity. All I want is for him to tell the truth."

"About what?" Sean asked.

"About my mother." Maggie swung around.

"He knew your mother?"

"Intimately."

Sean's gaze locked with hers. "How intimately?"

"Very."

"Maggie, say what you're trying to say. Don't drop hints. Spell it out for me."

Should she spell it out for him? She recognized that she'd reached a major turning point in her life.

She could either trust Sean enough to tell him the truth, or she could accept that the rest of her life was going to be spent locked up in a prison cell. He couldn't keep her in this motel room forever, and if she refused to cooperate, eventually he'd have no choice other than to bring her in.

Expressed in those stark terms, her decision should have been easy, but it wasn't. Since the day of her mother's death, every time she risked giving someone her trust, she had been betrayed. The fact that she was even considering telling Sean the truth terrified her. This was crazy! Her choices weren't limited to going back to prison or trusting Sean. What about her faithful old standby of running away? She ought to be looking for a makeshift weapon and plotting ways to escape. Sean himself had said it. She could knock him unconscious, steal his money and his car keys and be in another state before anyone even realized she was gone.

Don't trust a cop. Never trust a cop. You're making a huge mistake if you tell him anything.

Sean still held her gaze. "I want to help. But I can't help if you won't talk to me."

She shivered with the enormity of what she was about to do. "All right!" The words broke out of her, spilling over the barriers she'd kept fortified and unbreached for almost a decade. "All right, I'll tell you why I came here! I'm here because fifteen years of silence and cover-up is long enough and I plan to force Archbishop Grunewald to admit what he's done. I'm finally going to make him confess to the whole world that he killed my mother."

Eight

The archbishop's reputation was so sterling that Sean wondered why he didn't dismiss Maggie's accusation either as sheer malice or as the fantasy of a sick mind. Perhaps because nothing about her behavior suggested that she was insane or that she was the sort of criminal who got her kicks from accusing respected public figures of obscene secret vices. Still, he was an officer of the law—although you'd never know it from the way he was acting right now—and the professional habits of a lifetime screamed at him to remain skeptical. Maggie might sincerely believe that the archbishop was a murderer, but that didn't mean she was right.

"You must admit that's an astonishing claim," he said.

Maggie kept her back turned to him. "Astonishing, perhaps, but also true. Father Tobias—he was just a parish priest in those days—killed my mother and then stood back without a qualm while I took the fall."

"You sound very confident of what you're saying. Did you see the archbishop murder your mother?"

"Not…exactly."

"If you didn't see him commit the murder, then why do you suspect him? Help me out here, Maggie. Help me to understand what grounds you have for accusing the archbishop of something so terrible."

She stopped pacing and turned to smile at him. Not the warm smile he'd glimpsed earlier on, but the sardonic, world-weary smile he'd seen too many times before. "There's no need for you to sound so carefully calm and sympathetic. I'm not going to turn psychotic and rip out your tongue if you tell me you don't believe my accusations."

She sounded cynical, but he didn't think she was, and her pretense of indifference got to him in a way that tears and appeals for sympathy never could. Forgetting that he was supposed to be handling her with at least some degree of professional detachment, Sean strode across the room and grabbed her by the arms. "I'm not the enemy, Maggie! When are you going to realize that I'm on your side, dammit?"

She directed a cool, pointed glance at his hands. "You're a police officer. Of course you're the enemy. Back off, Detective, or a certain cherished part of your anatomy is going to be in serious danger."

"To hell with your threats. I'm not backing off. Not until you stop reacting like some preprogrammed robot and start thinking for a change. Ask yourself this. If I'm the enemy, if I'm nothing to you except the cop who found the murder weapon in your mother's bedroom, then why did you confide in me? A few minutes ago, you trusted me."

"I shouldn't have. That was a mistake."

"So you're going to cover up your mistake by pretending there's nothing happening between us?"

"There isn't anything happening between us."

He reached out and touched her arm with his finger. She jumped back as if she'd been shot. He looked at her, not needing to say anything to make his point.

She flushed. "That doesn't mean anything. There's nothing between us except the natural tension between the hunter and his prey."

"I'm not hunting you anymore. I've caught you."

"Yes, you have." She paced up and down the small room, so full of nervous tension that the air around her almost visibly crackled. "And do you expect me to believe that now you have me tied up in your net, you're going to cut the mesh and help me get free?"

"We're both caught in the same net, Maggie. I can't free myself unless I take you with me."

"I can't stand this! Why are we talking in stupid metaphors?" She walked away from him, hugging her arms around her waist. "I don't understand what you want from me, Detective. Spell it out."

"I've told you a dozen times already. I want the truth about what happened the night your mother was murdered."

"Okay, I'll spell it out for you. Someone shot her. I came home and found her bleeding from multiple gunshot wounds. Minutes later, she died. End of story."

"No, that's barely the beginning." He was getting

mighty tired of taking one small step forward and then watching her run three giant steps back. "I've put my career on the line to bring you here. Doesn't that earn me the right to a few straightforward answers?"

"It doesn't earn you the right to a single damn thing! I was crazy to trust you! Do you think I'm stupid enough to fall for this phony friendship stuff?" She lunged for his throat, grabbing the collar of his shirt and ripping it open, her rage so fierce that buttons popped and scattered all over the room. She tore the shirt from his shoulders and reached beneath his undershirt, patting her hands feverishly over his chest. "Where's the wire, Detective? What's the game we're playing here? Are you hoping I'm so starved for friendship that a few minutes of sympathy will have me confessing to my mother's murder? Is that it? Or have you and your fellow cops found a few more unsolved murders you'd like to pin on me?"

"Maggie, calm down! There's no wire, and I'm not playing any kind of game."

She paid him no attention. Her hands moved down toward his belt, fumbling feverishly with the buckle, and he shoved them away. "Jesus Christ, Maggie, there's no wire!"

She stepped back, panting as she leaned against the wall. "Then what's this all about? You're right, if this isn't some sort of setup, you shouldn't have brought me here. So why did you?"

Sean drew in a long, deep breath. "Because I owe you something," he said.

Her eyes were dark with suspicion. "Why?"

"Because the investigation into your mother's death was mishandled. I knew it, but I made no attempt to put things right. Last week when I realized who you were, I decided maybe I was being given a chance to do things over. Second chances don't come around all that often, and I didn't want to blow this one."

"What do you mean mishandled?"

"Lots of ways. Too many ways." He paused for a moment. "For example, nobody believed your story about slipping out of the house that night, so nobody tried very hard to find the guy you said had tried to rape you. Then there was the bar where you claimed to have been drinking. The owner denied seeing you, of course. Why wouldn't he? His liquor license would have been pulled if he'd admitted serving beer to a bunch of underage kids. Not to mention that you said marijuana was being bought and sold on his premises. But his denial fitted right in with what we wanted to hear, so nobody put pressure on him to see if he was lying. And then there were those neighbors of yours, the ones who were supposedly driving home at the same time you claimed to be sneaking back into the house—"

"The Jacksons," Maggie said. "But they didn't see me because I hid behind a clump of aspens in Tiffany's front yard."

"The Jacksons insisted they hadn't seen you," Sean agreed. "But there was something about Mrs. Jackson's attitude…somehow I didn't believe her. So I went back to their house when I knew her husband wouldn't be there. And it turned out she had seen you dodge behind those trees, just like you claimed."

Maggie's head jerked up. "But why didn't she come forward and speak out? Surely she must have known how important her testimony would be. I was on trial for killing my own mother, for God's sake!"

Sean shook his head. "She saw you right around two in the morning. You put in a call to emergency services at 2:20, and your mother was alive then. You said so yourself. I guess Mrs. Jackson squared her conscience by telling herself that what you were doing at two o'clock had nothing to do with whether you killed your mother twenty minutes later."

"But at least it would have shown I was telling the truth about being out of the house! And how would it have hurt her to come forward and back up my story?" Maggie suddenly sounded younger and a lot more vulnerable. Sean heard bewilderment in her voice, as if she was reliving old feelings of abandonment.

"Mrs. Jackson wanted to protect her own reputation," Sean said. "The reason she and her husband were out so late was because Mr. Jackson had just hauled her out of a motel room where she and her boss—also married—had apparently been indulging in some pretty kinky sex. When I told her that in a criminal case she didn't have any choice about testifying if the prosecution subpoenaed her, she immediately changed her story. Suddenly, she wasn't sure that she'd seen anyone, and even if she had seen somebody, she couldn't possibly testify that you were the person she'd seen. In fact, the more she thought about it, the more she wondered if she'd even seen a person at all. Maybe it had been a deer, or a dog, or a bull moose."

Sean felt a return of long-forgotten anger. "Hell, by the time she'd finished backtracking and covering her ass, I didn't see any way your defense counsel would have been able to persuade her to testify to anything. And I was too much of a rookie to realize that there were all sorts of pressure I could have applied to scare her, or shame her, into admitting the truth."

Although the room was warm, Maggie rubbed her arms as if she felt chilled. "When absolutely nobody came forward to support my version of events, I began to wonder if I was going crazy. It would have helped to know about Mrs. Jackson."

"It would have helped even more if we'd made a real effort to find Cobra."

"My attorney should have hired a private investigator," Maggie said. "Although in the long run, I doubt if anything would have mattered after the prosecution played the 911 tape over and over again so the jury could listen to me sobbing into the phone and apologizing to my mother for having hurt her. In the face of that sort of evidence, proving that Cobra tried to rape me probably wouldn't have helped my case."

It was true that the 911 tape and Maggie's fingerprints all over the murder weapon were the two main reasons that the jury had convicted her, but Sean wasn't about to let himself off the hook, not that easily. "The point is, your attorney should have been made aware that Mrs. Jackson was a potential witness who could have corroborated at least some of your story. He wasn't. Detective Sergeant Garda buried my report about the Jacksons so your attorney wouldn't suddenly get energized by the belief that maybe you were telling the truth after all. And I let him do it."

"Was there some special reason why you and your buddies were determined to convict me?" Maggie's face had turned white. "Or did the police officers in your department make a habit of selecting the culprit first and manipulating the evidence afterward to suit their convenience?"

"Garda was an old-timer who thought criminals were cosseted too much and their victims ignored, but he was usually fair."

"It never occurred to him that maybe he was putting me into the wrong category?" she asked.

"Your case came along at a bad time, Maggie. We were smarting because we'd failed to get a conviction against a serial rapist named Nathan Brookings, who'd mutilated at least three women, including a sixty-year-old woman who lost one of her eyes as a result of his attack. We had two psychologists who testified that Nathan was capable of homicidal violence, as well as two eyewitness identifications. But Nathan spoke softly and dressed real nice, and his daddy paid for the best defense lawyer in town. Together they managed to sucker the jury. When he walked out of that courtroom a free man, everyone in the department knew we were watching a ticking time bomb. And we were right. Less than a year later, Nathan was back in court, charged with the murder of one young woman and the rape and attempted murder of another."

"I'm sorry for those women, but I don't see what any of this has to do with my case."

"It has everything to do with your case. Tom Garda was convinced you shot your mother and he wasn't willing to let another spoiled, psychopathic teenager make a mockery out of the justice system."

"Three cheers for Sergeant Garda." Maggie gave a harsh laugh. "He made his point, and I ended up with a life sentence for a murder I didn't commit."

"Yes," Sean said. Deliberately, he added, "I'm afraid that's exactly what happened."

It took a moment for the significance of his words to sink in, and even then she reacted with typical wariness. "If I'm supposed to be full of gratitude that you're finally admitting I'm innocent and my trial was a travesty of justice, then I'm afraid you're fresh out of luck. My lifetime supply of gratitude ran out about ten years ago."

"You don't owe me gratitude or anything else. What I owe you is my best efforts to get the guilty verdict overturned and your sentence dismissed. What I need in order to achieve that is your cooperation."

She was still pale as a ghost, but she was rapidly recovering her composure and she laughed, sounding genuinely amused. "When a cop talks to me about cooperation, I start running as fast and as far as I can. Are you expecting me to hold out my hands for the cuffs and trot off back to jail—simply because you're promising to help me? If so, revise your plans."

"That would be the only legal way for us to handle this situation."

"Even if I accept that you're sincere, there's no way for you to root around in fifteen-year-old files and drum up enough evidence of police misconduct to give me grounds for an appeal. Thanks, Detective, but no thanks."

He spoke through teeth clenched so hard his jaws ached. "My name, as I keep reminding you, is Sean. Just once, could you bring yourself to say it?"

"I don't believe so. I like to remind myself what our respective roles are, *Detective.*"

He knew she was purposely baiting him and he even understood why. After she'd spent years being on the run, desperate to avoid attention, there had to be an intoxicating sense of power to the realization that she no longer needed to act humble and keep a low profile. He knew who she was, and that gave her the freedom to taunt him as much as she pleased. Sean understood what she was doing, but his emotions were running two steps ahead of his reason, and frustration at her unwillingness to cooperate slammed headlong into the simmering sexual tension with explosive results.

He pushed her against the wall, taking her face between his hands and forcing her to look straight at him. "My name is Sean. Sean McLeod. Say it, damn you!"

He had her pinned so she couldn't move, but she stared up at him, her gaze deadly. "You know something, Detective? From where I'm standing right now, you look amazingly like Beau and Cobra and all the other men who think that when persuasion fails, they can always rape the annoying little bitch into submission."

Her accusation briefly stunned him. Then his hands fell to his sides, and he backed away from her as fast as his feet would carry him. "Jesus, Maggie, I'm sorry. I was way out of line."

"Yes, you were." She walked over to the table, popped the top on the lukewarm can of soda and took a long sip.

He squared his shoulders. "Look, we seem to have gotten badly offtrack here."

"I've never been sure what track you're on, Detec—" She stopped abruptly. "I'm still not clear what you want from me, Sean."

It was a major concession on her part, and they both knew it. "I want you to provide me with the information I need to help prove your innocence," he said.

He saw tension flood back into her body, sparking around her like an energy field juiced up with bursts of electricity. "I don't have the sort of information that you'd find useful," she said.

"You must have some reason for accusing the archbishop of murder. Share it with me."

She sent him a wary, sideways glance. "I can't provide corroborating evidence for anything. If I could, I'd have brought it to the attention of the police already. There's no compelling reason for you or anyone else to believe me."

"Try me," he said.

"All right." She looked almost as shocked as he felt when she agreed. A torrent of words tumbled out of her. It seemed as if she'd given herself permission to tell her story and suddenly couldn't get the details out fast enough.

"About eighteen months after my father died, I realized my mother was having an affair. Almost right away, I knew there was something not quite right about the relationship. I was fifteen years old and pretty naive, but I had plenty of friends with stepparents and I knew what the ritual was supposed to be. After my mother and her boyfriend had been dating for a while, if things were getting serious between the two of them, she was supposed to make a big deal out of introducing him to me, and then we were all supposed to go out on a date. To the movies, maybe, and then to some really great pizza place for dinner. The kids I knew who'd gone through it said the evening was always dreadful, but it was an important rite of passage and you just had to grit your teeth and get it over with.

"So I waited and waited, but nothing happened. Mom was still seeing this guy, but the introduction never came. Instead, there were all these strange phone conversations that ended the second I walked into the room. And then there were times when her boyfriend would let himself into the house in the middle of the night, and they'd sit downstairs talking for hours before they finally went up to bed. I hated that this guy whose name I didn't even know had a key so he could walk into our house—my dad's house—any time he wanted, without even needing to knock on the door."

She paused to draw breath, then fell silent, and Sean was afraid to inject a question in case he put a halt to the flow of her memories. Fortunately, she started to speak again without any prompting from him.

"I liked to ski and I often went up to Breckenridge with Tiffany and her parents. They had a condo up there, and we'd spend the whole weekend on the slopes. But this one weekend, Tiffie's grandfather got taken to the hospital, so we came down from Breckenridge late on Saturday night. It was after midnight when I got home, and I let myself in real quietly because I expected my mother to be in bed."

This time, Maggie fell silent for so long that Sean decided to risk prompting her. "But your mother wasn't in bed?"

"No." Maggie's cheeks flushed as if the memory embarrassed her even at a distance of fifteen years. "Mom was lying on the sofa in the living room, and there was a man with her, although I couldn't see him very well because his back was turned toward me. They'd lit a fire, but the lights were out and I couldn't see too clearly. But I realized the man was undressing my mother, that they were kissing and he was fondling her breasts...." She cleared her throat. "Well, you get the picture."

"Yes, I do." Sean spoke softly. "What did you do, Maggie?"

"I didn't do anything. I turned to go upstairs. But Mom must have heard me because she sort of sat up on one elbow and looked around. Of course, she saw me right away. She didn't say anything, just stared at me. Then the man who was with her threw an afghan over her and moved away just a bit so that she could sit up properly. He kept his head turned away, but he misjudged the angle, I think, and from where I was standing, I had a pretty good view of his profile. I got this vivid sort of freeze-frame image of the man."

"And you recognized him?"

Maggie shook her head. "No, the lights were dim and I was embarrassed. I could hardly bear to look at him. Remember, I was fifteen and going through that stage when you can't think of anything more gross in the entire universe than accepting your parents as passionate and sexual. When my mother started to get up, I ran as fast as I could into my room and slammed the door. I stayed in there the whole of the next day and didn't come out until it was time for school on Monday."

Her mother had been waiting for her when she came back from school on Monday afternoon. Maggie had arrived home late since she'd deliberately hung out at Tiffie's house and hadn't called because she was so mad and embarrassed and confused.

She tossed her book bag under the hall table and walked toward the stairs without acknowledging that she'd even seen her mother. Rowena had moved quickly to block the stairs.

"Maggie, please, we have to talk. Come into the kitchen and I'll fix you some milk and cookies. I baked frosted raisin oatmeal this afternoon, your favorites."

She wanted her mother to hurt as much as she was hurting, so she jerked her arm, tossing off her mom's hand. "No thanks." Since her mother wasn't going to let her lock herself in her room, Maggie turned and walked back to the door. "I'll see you later, Mom."

"You know the rules, Maggie. You're not allowed out without telling me where you're going."

"It seems to me it's the rules about when I come home that you should worry about."

"That, too. Where are you going and when are you coming home?"

"Don't worry," Maggie sneered. "I'll make sure to call and give you warning so that your lover can slip out of the back door before I come in the front. That's what's been happening for the past three months, isn't it, Mom? He slips out as I slip in. I guess I should apologize for Saturday. I'm real sorry I fucked up and came home from Breckenridge without giving you proper warning, but Tiffie's grandfather had a heart attack."

Her mother turned white. "Maggie, I know you're shocked by what you saw that night and I know you're hurting. That doesn't excuse the language you just used and the rude way you're speaking to me. Your father and I always respected you and taught you to respect oth—"

"How dare you even mention my father?" Maggie yelled. "He was a hero and he only died eighteen months ago, and now you're…now you're…" She burst into tears, great gulping sobs that were part grief for her father and part grief because her mother wasn't the perfect woman she'd always believed.

Rowena hesitated for a moment before putting her arms around Maggie, tentatively at first, then with more assurance when Maggie didn't push her away. She stroked Maggie's hair, making soft shushing sounds of comfort until Maggie's explosion of grief ended and she struggled to get out of her mother's embrace.

Rowena let her go. "Honey, I'd give almost anything for you not to have seen what you saw last night, but you did, and now I have to ask you to please try to understand something that will be very hard for you. I loved your father more than anyone in the world except you, and when he died I was quite sure that there was nobody who could ever take his place. And I was right. Your father was unique. But what I've learned recently is that there are different ways of loving, and that although nobody will ever take your father's place, there is a man I can love, a man I very much want to marry—"

"You're going to get married again?" Maggie was appalled. "But I've never even met this guy! How can you consider bringing someone into our family without even asking me to meet him? Doesn't he like kids or something?"

"He loves kids and he's wonderful with them." Rowena paused. "Maggie, it's a very complicated situation. We want to get married, but there are problems, obstacles, that you shouldn't have to deal with and—"

"Oh my God!" Maggie stared at her mother in dawning horror. "He's married, isn't he? You're having an affair with a married man!"

Her mother hesitated a fraction of a second too long for her denial to be convincing. "No, he isn't married. But there are problems, difficulties...."

"He's married," Maggie stated flatly. "Is he one of our neighbors? Is that it? You're having an affair with one of the neighbors?"

"Maggie, I've never lied to you and I'm not lying to you now. I promise that the man I'm involved with isn't married. In fact, he's never been married. But there are reasons why we have to wait, why we can't rush into marriage. There are steps he has to take, procedures he has to follow, or a very important part of his life will be ruined."

Again Rowena stopped abruptly. "Maggie, I don't want to lie to you or fill your head with half-truths and promises I might not be able to keep. I'm just asking you to trust me for a little while longer and then I'll be free to tell you everything. And when you do know everything, I hope you'll understand why I couldn't be more open with you."

Maggie had done her best to pretend that she didn't care who her mother was involved with or what the big secret was. But when the clandestine meetings went on and her mother became more and more evasive, Maggie's schoolwork started to suffer. If her mother could screw around with some guy who was hiding a secret so terrible that he could never arrive at the house in daylight, then she saw no reason to carry on striving to be little Miss Perfect. Except for Tiffany, she cut loose from the crowd of overachievers she'd previously hung out with and started to make friends with the Red Raiders and the kids who smoked pot and drank. Her grades slipped, and she felt a strange mixture of guilt and satisfaction when she handed her mother a report card full of C's and D's instead of her usual A's.

Ms. Dowd, the guidance counselor at school, called her mother in for a conference. Maggie sat through it in sullen silence, ignoring the looks of appeal her mother was sending her and refusing to feel worried when the counselor pointed out that she could be ruining her chances for getting accepted by a top-notch college if she continued to allow her grades to slip.

When the two adults had finished talking, Ms. Dowd

directed a disapproving look at her. "You've been very silent, Maggie, and you used to be so cheerful and talkative. Don't you have anything you want to tell us?"

"Yes," Maggie said, "I need a cigarette. Can I go now?"

"Ms. Dowd was the guidance counselor who testified at your trial to your hostile, out-of-control behavior, wasn't she?" Sean asked when Maggie fell silent.

"Yes." Maggie laughed without amusement. "It's ironic, you know. I'd never smoked a cigarette in my life when I made that stupid remark. I just said it because it seemed like the best way to show my mother how furious I was because she still hadn't let me meet the guy she was dating. But by the time Ms. Dowd and the D.A. had finished analyzing my attitude, you'd have thought I was shooting up in the middle of class and having wild sex in the kindergarten playground."

"Did you ever meet your mother's lover?" Sean asked.

"No, never." Maggie's voice was flat. "My mother was murdered less than a week after we had that meeting with Ms. Dowd."

"But you know now who your mother's lover was, don't you?"

"Yes."

"Who was it, Maggie?"

"You know the answer to that," she said. "It was Father Tobias."

Nine

Maggie didn't expect Sean to believe her and she steeled herself to answer a barrage of hostile questions. As so often happened, Sean surprised her. Instead of commenting on what she'd just said, he completely changed the subject.

"This room's beginning to feel claustrophobic," he said, throwing back the drapes and exposing the dreary view of the parking lot. "When I was out jogging this morning, I discovered a park a couple of blocks from here. Would you like to take a walk over there? We could sit on a bench, watch the ducks and the kids, and talk for a while."

She eyed him warily, distrustful of a suggestion she didn't understand. "Aren't you afraid I'll try to run away?"

"Will you?"

It was one of the hardest things she'd ever done, but she made the promise she knew he wanted. "No."

"Then let's go." He picked up the room key, then took the car keys and tossed them in the air, letting them fall onto the center of the bed nearer to her. She stared at them, heart pounding. Oh, God, it would be so easy to grab them and make a run for it. She shoved her hands into her pockets and scurried toward the door.

A grin flicked across Sean's hard mouth. "Good girl," he said softly.

Her heart turned over at the sight of his smile, so she scowled at him. "Don't make too big a deal out of it. You'd have caught me before I could get to the car."

"True, but that's not why you left the keys on the bed. You left them because you promised me not to run away."

It was infuriating to know that he was right. Scary, too. An escaped felon didn't stand much chance against a law enforcement officer if she started playing fair and sticking to the rules.

Outside, the sun was still high in the sky, but a slight breeze delivered occasional puffs of cool air that made walking pleasant even on the hot sidewalks. She didn't want to talk and Sean seemed content with the silence until they were in the park and passing a concession stand.

He came to an immediate halt. "Food!" he exclaimed, rocking back on his heels to read the overhead menu, which included such delicacies as Polish sausage for 2.99 and chili cheese dogs for 3.20. "I'm going to splurge and order a large hot dog with extra everything. How about you? Would you like something?"

Maggie forgot she was mad at him. She laughed. "Is

this another example of your skill at finding gourmet eating establishments, Detective?"

The minute she spoke, she cursed herself for being a brainless idiot. Good grief, the last thing she needed was to remind Sean of the disastrous morning when he'd taken her to breakfast and she'd stolen his car. But to her relief, Sean simply grinned. "Hey, babe, I've told you before, if you want the best in fine dining, you can count on me."

They ordered lemonade and two "SuperSize" hot dogs, which Sean rendered invisible beneath layers of ketchup and mustard. Armed with a lifetime supply of paper napkins, they found a bench shaded by a horse chestnut tree and sat down to eat. From their vantage point, they could see children clambering over yellow and purple play equipment, two fathers gleefully racing model sailboats across the pond, and an old woman feeding stale bread to the ducks. It was a clichéd picture of Norman Rockwell happiness, but Maggie felt a pang of bittersweet pleasure that she could be part of it, however briefly.

"This hot dog is fantastic," she said, tilting her head to catch a shred of ketchup-soaked sauerkraut that was falling out of her bun. "Have you ever noticed that food always tastes twice as good if you eat it outdoors?"

Sean grinned. "I've noticed. Of course, for concession-stand food, it also helps if you have a cast-iron lining to your stomach. Fortunately, being a cop will do that for you."

And eating prison food would do it even quicker. That reminder should have dampened her mood, but

Maggie didn't have time to feel gloomy because a Frisbee struck her on the knee and bounced off to land at her feet. A little girl came running up, closely followed by her father and a lop-eared dog of dubious parentage.

"Sorry," the man said. "Heather and I were trying to teach Rocket to play Frisbee."

"Rocket's a real slow learner," the little girl said. "He doesn't understand he has to jump up to catch it."

Rocket, despite his name, looked as if his entire approach to life was on the slow side. When Maggie handed over the Frisbee, the man held it out to the dog and made encouraging noises. Rocket eyed the Frisbee and the man with equal boredom, then collapsed at the girl's feet, panting. His huge eyes rolled yearningly in the direction of Sean's hot dog.

"Don't even think of it," the man warned. "Get up you lazy hound." He prodded Rocket affectionately, and the dog lumbered to its feet.

Heather ran off, laughing. "Come on, Rocket. Throw it to me, Dad. Do it high, okay?"

"Okay, pumpkin." The man jogged away. "Sorry to have bothered you," he called over his shoulder. "Here it comes, sweetie. A real high one."

There were some forms of torture you didn't need to put yourself through, and Maggie usually tried to avoid being around families with young children. But this afternoon, Heather and her dad just seemed part of the Norman Rockwell scenery, people whose antics she could watch and enjoy without inflicting pain on herself. Belatedly, she realized that Sean was watching the

Frisbee players, too, but without any of her enjoyment. She understood at once what was bothering him.

"Your daughter's name is Heather, isn't it?" she asked.

"Yes. I guess it's a real popular name these days."

He swirled the melting ice cubes in his lemonade, but Maggie could see that his attention was really fixed on the little girl. When Rocket failed to catch the Frisbee for the umpteenth time, she dissolved into giggles, rolling around on the grass with her dog.

"It's at moments like this that I miss my daughter the most," Sean said.

"I can see how it would be hard. Did you often take her to the park?"

"No, I hardly ever took her anywhere." He aimed his plastic cup at a distant trash can and scored a basket. "The truth is, I was an ambitious, workaholic asshole who didn't know how incredibly lucky I was to have such a wonderful daughter."

"At least you understand now. Some men never learn."

"Yeah, I've learned my lesson, but it's too late. Heather's not living with me anymore, and my ex-wife gets to approve the time and place of every visit." He stared down at the napkins wadded in his hands. "Trust me, she's not approving many."

It was odd to think that she would feel a need to comfort Sean McLeod of all people, but she did. "Have you and your ex-wife been divorced for long?"

"Three months. But we've been separated for a lot longer."

Maggie resisted the urge to reach out and stroke Sean's tightly clenched hands. She never wanted to touch anyone, least of all a man who was a cop, and she couldn't understand where her feelings of sympathy came from. "I expect things will get better when everyone's emotions aren't so raw," she said.

"Maybe."

Her hand was in the air, halfway toward him, before she realized what she was doing and pulled it back. She locked her fingers together in her lap. "Don't let it eat at you, Sean. You'll find some way to play a meaningful role in Heather's life. It may take a couple of years, but eventually you'll find the way."

He sent her a quizzical glance. "You sound very authoritative, Maggie."

"I am," she said quietly. "In a woman's prison, you learn everything there is to know about the heartbreak of long-distance parenting."

Sean drew in a harsh breath and sent a ball of napkins scudding after his lemonade cup into the trash. "Tell me how you came to discover that Father Tobias was your mother's lover," he said.

So they'd finally returned to the subject of Archbishop Grunewald. Maggie wiped mustard from her fingertips with meticulous care before replying, "It's a long story."

"We have lots of time," Sean said.

"Do we? I keep wondering when you're going to remember that you're a cop and I'm a convict."

"Trust me, there isn't a second that goes by that I don't remember. I'm not just breaking the law, I'm acting against every rule and principle I've ever laid down for myself."

"Why *are* you breaking all the rules for me?"

"Because some time between your stealing my brother's car and my finding you here in Ohio, I realized that I never believed you killed your mother."

"You really do believe I'm innocent." It was such a novel concept that she couldn't absorb all the ramifications. Sean didn't believe she'd killed her mother. The cop who'd discovered the murder weapon believed she was innocent. The statements jiggled around in her head, too slippery and startling to be grasped.

Sean tossed bits of the hot-dog bun toward the pond. "I don't think you murdered your mother and I want to help you stay out of prison, but you know as well as I do that my opinion counts for absolutely nothing in a court of law. There's only one way you're going to win a legal release from prison, Maggie, and that's by handing the authorities incontrovertible proof that somebody else killed your mother. And we're never going to get that kind of proof unless you open up and start trusting me with the truth about what you know."

A battle erupted inside her, a knock-down-drag-out fight between experience and instinct. His words were beguiling, but ever since the night her mother died, every time she'd trusted anyone, she'd ended up getting shafted. Sean sounded sincere, and yet the more she yearned to trust him, the more her instincts yelled at her to step back from the brink.

"Maggie, you've been out of prison for almost seven years and you haven't managed to find a shred of evidence you can take to the authorities." Sean put his hand over hers, and she pretended she didn't notice so she wouldn't have to pull away from the comfort of his touch. "Maybe, if you let me work with you, we'd have better luck. I have access to a lot of sources that you don't. There's information on the archbishop that I could dig up in a couple of hours that you might never be able to find."

"I've been too busy staying out of jail to have time to find proof that Archbishop Grunewald isn't the saint everyone imagines," she said defensively.

"My point exactly."

He'd turned her hand over and linked his fingers with hers so that they weren't just touching, they were actually holding hands. Maggie blinked quickly several times and looked away from the sun, which was so bright it was making her eyes water. At least she told herself that the sudden moisture in her eyes was caused by sunlight. She swallowed a gulp of air, then another.

"Tell me how you first came to suspect the archbishop, Maggie. I really want to hear the basis for your suspicions."

It was as if he had flipped on a switch, giving her permission to voice her suspicions and the memories spewed out of her with volcanic speed and intensity. "When my trial started, I had no idea who my mother's lover had been. In fact, I didn't realize who he was until long after I was convicted. I'd already served eighteen months of my time when I was sent for a routine psych test with a new counselor. It turned out to be someone I knew. Ms. Dowd, my high school guidance counselor."

* * *

Maggie tapped on the door of the medical center. She was early for her appointment, but she'd read all one hundred and thirty-seven books in the so-called library a gazillion times and she was bored out of her mind. Even an appointment with a geeky psychologist was better than another morning hanging around the rec room, waiting for the high point of the day: the hour she was allowed to spend working out in the gym.

She was surprised to see her former high school guidance counselor seated at the other side of the big desk, but until Ms. Dowd indicated that she remembered Maggie, Maggie wasn't going to say a thing.

"Come in, Margaret." Ms. Dowd looked up from the notes she was writing as Maggie took two steps into the room and then stopped. These days, breathing was about the only thing Maggie did without waiting first for permission.

"You can sit down, Margaret." Ms. Dowd spoke quite kindly, but Maggie didn't let down her guard even for a second. She'd already discovered that the appearance of kindness meant jack shit. Teachers, guards, doctors and counselors were all equally likely to turn on you if the mood took them.

She sat in the chair, legs neatly together, hands clasped in her lap, the picture of docile obedience. Most of the other girls at the center delighted in lounging around, being insolent to everyone in authority and defying the system every way they could. But most of the other girls weren't facing transfer to an adult prison the day they turned eighteen. Maggie had already discovered that, within the surreal world of the criminal justice system, the squeaky wheel didn't get greased, it got smashed, and the absolute last thing she needed was to get sent off to the state prison already tagged as a troublemaker.

Ms. Dowd leaned back in her chair and took off her reading glasses. The look she directed at Maggie was assessing, but not hostile. "I've been reading your file, Margaret, and I'm glad to see that you've taken advantage of the educational opportunities available here. You must have studied hard to get such good grades on your GED. It's quite an accomplishment to pass the test when you're only seventeen and with the limited instruction you were able to get here."

"Thank you, ma'am. I did my best."

"You have many years of incarceration still ahead of you," Ms. Dowd said. She stopped for a moment and pulled Maggie's file toward her, apparently not finding the information she wanted. "Remind me. How long a sentence are you serving?"

"Fifteen years to life, ma'am, with a chance of parole after eight years." She could say the words without choking now.

"That's a long time, Margaret."

"Yes, ma'am."

Ms. Dowd's expression warmed slightly. "Margaret, it's not for me to judge what brought you here, but I've known you for several years and I'd like to help if I can. You have an intelligent mind, and I think you might be motivated to put it to good use. You're a baptized and confirmed Catholic, aren't you?"

Since her mother's death, she'd been a baptized and confirmed atheist, but she wasn't dumb enough to admit that. The warden was very keen on inmates going to church, so Maggie made sure she went faithfully to mass whenever she was given the opportunity. Besides, being in chapel was marginally less boring than staring at the walls of her locked eight-by-nine-foot room, which was the alternative.

So she permitted herself a small, polite smile. "Yes, ma'am. I'm a Catholic."

"That's good." Ms. Dowd chuckled, looking almost friendly for a moment. "I'm not just saying that because I'm a Catholic myself, but because I know the Catholic church has a college scholarship fund for young people who are incarcerated."

She paused, seeming to expect some response, so Maggie said politely, "Yes, ma'am?"

"I don't want you to get your hopes up too high, Margaret, because there's a lot of red tape to go through before you're admitted to the program, but with your GED scores and your grade point average from high school being so good, I believe you have an excellent chance of being accepted as a scholarship recipient."

Maggie held her breath, refusing to let hope or excitement get ahold of her. Hope and excitement were very dangerous emotions when you were serving a possible life sentence. Still, she couldn't help showing just a little bit of interest. "Excuse me, ma'am, but I don't understand how I could go to college when I'm locked up in here, waiting for transfer to prison when I'm eighteen."

"Well, you wouldn't actually attend classes on campus, of course. But we would find you a few sympathetic professors who are willing to work with you by mail and we'd arrange for all the course lectures to be videotaped." Ms. Dowd's voice softened. "It's not the best way to go to college, Margaret, we both know that, but it does offer you a way to occupy your time and fill your mind with something beyond the activities within the walls of this institution."

In comparison to the utter boredom she'd resigned herself to facing, four years of college courses sounded like heaven. Maggie usually tried to show no emotion at all, but for once she couldn't help herself. She could feel her face light up with eager anticipation. "If you could arrange for me to go to college, ma'am, I'd be really, really grateful."

"I'll do my best, Margaret. Whatever the crime, I like to think nobody is beyond redemption. I'll set the wheels in motion for you."

Any change in routine, especially if it involved special privileges, normally took months to get approved. But it was only a week later when one of the security guards came into the rec room where Maggie was playing solitaire with a grimy deck of cards. The other inmates resented Maggie's obviously middle-class background and the fact that she was so quiet and well-behaved, so she spent a lot of time sitting by herself in a corner of the rec room, playing cards. On good days, nobody got bored and picked a fight with her. On bad days, she found herself in lockup over fights she hadn't started and couldn't control.

"You have a visitor," the guard said.

"A visitor?" Maggie never got visitors. Tiffany's parents had come to see her once, but Mrs. Albers had cried the whole time, and they'd never come back. Tiffany managed to send her the occasional package along with a stiff little note saying that she hoped Maggie would find the contents useful. Pride urged Maggie to send the packages back since the Alberses had obviously moved into the camp of those who believed she'd murdered her mom. But pride wasn't a very useful attribute in a detention center and common sense dictated that she should hang on to the goodies for dear life. Shampoo, deodorant and chocolate were valuable enough to make the stiff notes that accompanied them completely irrelevant.

"Come on, I'm not waiting all night for you to get your ass in gear." Officer Teasdale grabbed her by the arm, deliberately letting her nightstick crack painfully against Maggie's legs. Most of the guards were surly and indifferent. A couple were genuinely kind. Teasdale was a sadist. She slapped cuffs onto Maggie's wrists, making the procedure as rough as possible. This was a juvenile facility, but it was designed for serious offenders, and the rules made it more like a jail than a reform school. "Get a move on, will you? We don't want to keep the bishop waiting."

The bishop? With any of the other guards, Maggie would have asked why a bishop was coming to see her. With Teasdale, she kept silent, hurrying along the corridors to the room that was usually reserved for meetings with lawyers, probation officers and other officials.

The guard knocked before throwing open the door. "Margaret Slade is here to see you, Your Excellency."

A tall man stood at the window, watching the sun set. He turned around at the sound of the guard's voice, and Maggie saw he was wearing a clerical collar, with a plain silver crucifix hanging over his purple shirtfront. She gave a tiny gasp of surprise and pleasure when she recognized Father Tobias Grunewald, the priest who'd come to St. Jude's about a year after her father died. In her other life, before her mother's murder, Mass on Sundays had always seemed like a total drag, something she did for no other reason than to please her parents. After her father died, she'd been so mad at God, she'd refused to take communion or join any of the youth groups, but she'd occasionally sat at the back of the church and dozed through the service just to make her mom happy.

Now, even though she no longer believed in God, she sometimes thought wistfully of those peaceful Sunday morning sessions in church. Of Christmas, when the church had been filled with the smell of pine and cinnamon and the joyous sound of carols, or of Easter, when the flowers on the altar had been a riot of spring color. In retrospect, she realized just how anchored she'd felt by the rituals of the church calendar even though she'd tried to ignore them.

Her nostalgia bubbled over into a quick laugh of sheer pleasure. "Father Toby! What are you doing here?"

"I came to see you, of course." He smiled warmly. "Maggie, my dear, how are you?"

"Very well, thank you, Father." She recovered her protective poise and answered him woodenly although her mind was racing. Priests and ministers were usually chosen by the powers-that-be to pass on bad news about family members. Except that her mother and father were dead and her grandparents had already disowned her, so there weren't many family members left for her to worry about. What bad news could he be bringing?

Father Tobias turned to the guard. "The warden has given me permission to speak to Maggie in private. I'd appreciate it if you could leave the two of us alone for a few minutes."

"Yes, sir." Officer Teasdale directed a venomous look toward Maggie. She clearly didn't approve of anyone as unworthy as Maggie being allowed to spend time in the company of a bishop. "I'll be outside if you need me, Your Excellency."

"Whew, that's better," Father Tobias said as soon as they were alone. He gave Maggie a friendly grin, as if they were co-conspirators in getting rid of the guard. "Let's sit down, shall we?"

Maggie sat down, automatically adjusting the heavy metal cuffs so they didn't cut into her wrists. Father Tobias looked at the cuffs and then at her, and there was no mistaking the sadness in his gaze.

He shook his head, turning his hands palm up in a gesture of helplessness. "Maggie, I've been trying all day to find the right words and I guess I haven't been able to come up with them. My dear, this is a terrible situation, and I want you to know that you're in my prayers every day."

"Thank you, Father."

"I'm especially sorry that it's taken me so long to come and see you."

"That's all right, Father. I never expected you to come."

"You should have." For some reason, his voice sounded grim, almost as if he was angry with himself. "I was your priest, and you had every right to expect my help and comfort. Unfortunately, I've been in Rome and I only came back to Colorado two months ago."

"Officer Teasdale said you're a bishop now. Congratulations."

"Yes, I was recently appointed bishop of Pueblo." He grimaced, looking embarrassed. "The truth is, I've done very little to deserve the promotion, but I guess that just means I'll have to work twice as hard in the future." He smiled ruefully. "Try to earn my stripes after the fact, so to speak."

It was so outside the norm of her current lifestyle to have someone expressing doubts about their worthiness—to her, of all people—that Maggie had no idea what to say. She wriggled on the chair, and the handcuffs made a clinking noise. Father Tobias—she guessed she should call him Bishop Grunewald now—reached out and took her hands, folding them into his clasp and squeezing gently.

"Maggie, we don't have too much time, so we need to get right to the point. I want you to know that I'm your friend, and you can count on me to help you in any way I can. I know how easy it is to make mistakes, to commit sins that we would despise in other people, and end up hurting the people we love. If you have any problems, share them with me and I'll do my very best to help you find solutions. If you have anything you want to confess, I'll always be ready to hear your confession. And you know that the seal of the confessional is absolute. Nothing you tell me during the sacrament of confession would ever be repeated to anyone, whatever you said."

Was he expecting her to confess to her mother's murder? Maggie didn't know how to answer him, so she didn't say anything. After eighteen months in custody, she'd learned that when you weren't sure what to say, silence was a real good option.

The bishop leaned forward, his crucifix jangling against her handcuffs. He circled it with his hands, holding the cross so tightly that his knuckles turned white. "As you know, I didn't start at St. Jude's until after your father's accident, so I never had the pleasure of meeting him. But I knew your mother...well." He hesitated, then started again. "Your mother often talked to me about you and your dad. She told me how close the two of you had been."

Maggie could feel a lump forming in her throat, but she swallowed hard, refusing to let the tears start to fall.

The bishop seemed to guess how close she was to crying, and his voice became even more gentle. "Maggie, I understand how devastated you were at losing your father and I know you and your mother were having a few problems in your relationship. Could you please try to help me understand what happened the night she died?"

He turned away, and Maggie realized to her amazement that he was fighting some pretty heavy-duty emotions of his own.

"I really need to know how this terrible tragedy came about, Maggie. Was it an accident? Were you arguing and the gun just went off? I keep trying to understand what might have happened and nothing makes sense. All I do know is that nothing will ever convince me you deliberately and cold-bloodedly plotted to kill your own mother."

She had survived all these months without telling anyone how alone she felt or how depressing it was to be an orphan with grandparents who hated you. She'd never tried to convince anyone in authority that she was innocent or that her trial had been a travesty. She'd gritted her teeth, hunkered down and learned to endure. But the bishop's sympathy shattered the wall she'd built around her emotions, and the lump in her throat grew until it was big enough to choke her. The grief she'd never before allowed herself to express exploded in a cascade of scalding tears.

The bishop coped admirably with her sudden sobs. He patted her shoulder and rubbed his thumb soothingly across her knuckles, murmuring quiet words of comfort, letting the tears flow until she was all cried out. Then he silently handed her a stack of tissues and crooked his finger under her chin, tilting her face up to blot away the final tears.

"Ah, Maggie, I can see how much you're hurting," he said softly. "But I promise you, there's no sadness that's too great for God to heal, and there is no sin you've committed, however terrible, that God can't forgive. All it takes is for you to ask God for His help and for His forgiveness and He'll open His arms and pour out the comfort of His love. I know that's true because I've felt grief that I thought was too terrible to bear and I've committed sins that I thought God could never forgive. And I was wrong on both counts. God is a lot more generous with us than we are with Him."

The bishop's words provided comfort even though Maggie wanted to resist his message, and for the first time since her mother's death, she felt a flicker of hope. Hope that perhaps her life wasn't totally screwed up. Hope that she might have a future that would be worth something. But before she could speak, the door opened and Officer Teasdale poked her head into the room. "Everything okay in here, Your Excellency?"

The bishop didn't attempt to conceal his annoyance at the intrusion. "Everything's fine," he said curtly. "We need another few minutes of privacy, please."

"It's evening roll call in fifteen minutes, sir."

"We'll be through in ten." The bishop shut the door and swung around to face Maggie again. As he walked back toward the center of the room, he was silhouetted against the window, and for a moment, his head obscured the setting sun. For a second or two while he blocked the light, the room was cast into shadow, making it difficult to see anything except his head, which was circled by a halo of red light from the sun. Against the surrounding darkness, his profiled features stood out with stark clarity.

Transfixed, Maggie gazed at the bishop while her

world fell apart. She held her breath, afraid that she would shatter into a billion disconnected dust particles if she moved anything, even her lungs. Her sense of taste and smell vanished. She forgot how to hear. Only her eyes still functioned. She stared at the bishop with an intensity so fierce and focused she wouldn't have been surprised if he'd burst into flame.

Once before, she'd seen the bishop silhouetted against a source of light in a darkened room and she could visualize that earlier scene with shocking, laser-sharp clarity. On that earlier occasion, her mother had been lying on the sofa, sighing with pleasure as a man made love to her. A man whose back had been turned toward the hallway. A man who'd turned and looked at Maggie, his head haloed by a revealing circle of fire-light, his features etching themselves into her memory, before he grabbed an afghan and threw it over her mother's naked breasts.

That man, she now realized, had been Father Tobias Grunewald. Her parish priest, supposedly sworn to a life of celibacy and service to God, had been her mother's lover.

There wasn't a trace of doubt in Maggie's mind that her mother's lover and Bishop Grunewald were one and the same man, but the implications were so mind-boggling that for a moment she couldn't quite accept the truth of her own discovery. But the more she thought back, the more clearly she realized that the identification of Father Tobias as her mother's lover was the key that solved so many puzzles. She remembered how Rowena had explained that there were problems to be overcome before Maggie could meet the man her mother wanted to marry. There were complicated steps to be taken, procedures to follow, obstacles to be overcome, Rowena had said. At the time, Maggie had thought only about married men or friends in the neighborhood. In retrospect, it was clear that her mother had been referring to the fact that her lover was a priest who needed permission to be released from his vows. She recalled her mother's dying words, when Rowena had clearly been trying to tell Maggie something. She'd choked, unable to complete what she was saying, but the sounds she'd made were carved in acid into Maggie's memory, and now she was sure that the name her mother was trying to say had been Toby.

Looking at the bishop, she almost gagged. The revulsion she was feeling must have shown in her face because he returned her gaze rather anxiously. "Maggie, what is it? What's wrong? Please tell me."

She would more willingly have poured out her troubles to Officer Teasdale, and that was saying something. She sent him a mocking glance, too distraught to weigh the consequences of deliberate insolence. "What do you think is wrong, Your Excellency? Nothing much, I guess, except that I'm fucking locked up in jail for the rest of my life."

It felt so good to spit out the words that she didn't care what punishment they handed out to her afterward. She turned away so she wouldn't have to look at him, her whole body vibrating with hatred.

For reasons Maggie couldn't begin to guess, he didn't summon the guard and report her. "I'll ignore your rudeness this time," he said. "But one free ride is all you get, Maggie."

She didn't thank him, but she pulled her emotions sufficiently under control that at least she didn't toss any more insulting remarks at him. No point in getting herself punished because Bishop Grunewald was a lying son of a bitch.

The bishop sighed. "All right, Maggie, since you obviously don't want to confide in me, I can't force you. So let's get down to the business that brought me here before Officer Teasdale intrudes on us again. I understand from your counselor that you want to apply for a church-sponsored scholarship to attend Georgetown University, which happens to be my alma mater. I've reviewed your academic records, and they certainly suggest that you have the IQ to succeed. Georgetown University has worked with young people within the prison system before, and I'm willing to recommend you for inclusion in their program on one condition."

She hated him all the more because he had the power to give her the thing she wanted so desperately: a window to the world outside this prison. She wanted to scream insults at him and fling her defiance in his face, and yet, if she did, he wouldn't suffer and she would lose all chance of going to college. Right at this moment, she was so confused she hardly knew which way was up, but she dimly understood that if she was to survive the next fifteen years with her sanity intact, she needed to have something to do besides read a hundred and thirty-seven books over and over again.

The effort to answer him politely almost choked

her, but she did it. "What is that one condition, Your Excellency?"

"That you study hard and strive to do the very best work you can. Open your mind to all the experiences that your professors will offer you."

She shrugged. "There's nothing else for me to do in this place except study."

"I take it that's your version of a promise to do your best," the bishop said dryly.

"Yes." She forced herself to expand her answer. "I'll do my best with my studies, Your Excellency."

He didn't say anything more for quite a while. She couldn't bring herself to look at him, so she had no idea what he was doing or thinking. Finally, he spoke from behind her. "Maggie… What happened just now when the guard interrupted us? Why are you suddenly so angry with me that you won't even look at me?"

Because I found out your dirty little secret, Bishop. The truth trembled on the tip of her tongue, but in the end she didn't reveal what she knew. Knowledge was power, and she had no intention of tipping the scales any further in the bishop's favor.

Since she had to give him some sort of an answer, she forced herself to turn around and face him. He was really quite good-looking for a middle-aged man, although she still couldn't understand how her mother could have fallen for a creepy jerk in a dog collar when she'd once been married to a man as wonderful as Maggie's father. What happened the first time her mother had had sex with him? she wondered. Had he been wearing a cassock and taken it off? Had his crucifix brushed against her mother's naked skin?

Maggie hated what she was thinking, hated that she had these images of her mother that wouldn't go out of her mind. The confused and angry feelings threatened to swamp her again, so she spoke quickly.

"I'm not angry with you," she lied. "How could I be? It's just that things sometimes get to me in here. I'm sorry I was rude to you, sir. Really sorry."

For some unfathomable reason, her answer seemed to depress the bishop. His shoulders slumped, and for a moment he looked almost defeated. Then he gave a tiny shrug and walked over to the desk.

"So be it." He picked up a bright red file folder and handed it to her. "Here you are, Maggie. These are the application forms for admission to the Georgetown University Special Degree Program. They're rather long and complicated, but it will be a good test of whether you have the powers of concentration you need to complete a degree course successfully. When you've filled them out, make an appointment to see your counselor, and she'll make sure that the application is sent to the right place. Ms. Dowd and I are working together on this, and with any luck, we should be able to get everything approved and have you enrolled for the spring semester."

"Thank you, Your Excellency. That would be wonderful."

"We've known each other for a long time, Maggie. I don't think you need to call me Your Excellency every time you open your mouth."

"If you say so, sir."

"Bishop will do, Maggie." He came and stood in

front of her, tracing the sign of the cross on her forehead. She tried not to cringe, and it was at that precise moment the full, horrifying truth dawned on her. If the bishop had been her mother's lover, he was also the man who had a key to their house. Which meant that Bishop Grunewald was the man she must have heard letting himself out of the back door the night her mother was shot.

Which meant that Bishop Grunewald was the man who had murdered her mother.

The room started to spin around her. The bishop put his hand beneath her elbow and steadied her. "Maggie, are you sure you're okay? You don't seem well and you're worrying me."

You bet your ass she was worrying him. The slimy slug was probably peeing in his pants with fright in case she knew more than she was letting on. Well, let him worry. One day—maybe—she'd give him a real fright and tell him that his dirty little secret wasn't quite as secret as he hoped.

She disengaged her arm from his supporting hold and managed, somehow, not to throw a punch straight at his hypocritical nose. "I'm fine, thank you, sir. Your Excellency. I mean, Bishop."

He stepped away from her, the sad expression back on his face again. "Well, if you're sure there's no way I can help you." He turned and placed his hand lightly on top of her head. "God bless you and keep you safe, Maggie."

She squirmed out from under his hand. "Thank you, Bishop. You, too." If there was a God, surely he'd strike the lying creep with a bolt of lightning and rid the world of such a terrible, evil person.

No lightning bolt came, and the bishop walked unscathed to the door, proof positive of God's utter indifference to the world he'd supposedly created. But Maggie didn't care. Her life now had a purpose. She was a woman with a mission, a recruit on a crusade.

Somehow she was going to escape and prove to the world not just that she was innocent, but also that Bishop Grunewald was the monster who'd murdered her mother. It might take a lifetime, but she'd do it. One day, his excellency the bishop would be made to pay for his crimes.

Ten

Sean had been hoping against hope that Maggie would provide him with some solid evidence against the archbishop—something that he'd be able to grab and run with. But she'd given him nothing. Not a shred of evidence that would stand up in a court of law, not even a hint of where he might start looking in order to uncover such evidence. Her accusations against the archbishop amounted to nothing more than her own instincts based on a flimsy, long-after-the-fact identification.

The truly bizarre thing was that he believed her. In a horrible way, the murder of Rowena Slade finally made sense to him, which it had never done when Maggie was the supposed killer. Piecing his own memories together with Maggie's account, he could visualize the night of her mother's death with almost uncomfortable clarity.

Archbishop Grunewald—in those days just a handsome and ambitious parish priest—meets Rowena

Slade at a church function and starts an illicit and secret affair with her. After a few months of red-hot passion, Father Toby learns that the big honchos in the Catholic hierarchy are getting ready to approve his appointment as bishop of Pueblo. His sexual fervor dies a sudden and total death as his ambition reasserts itself. He tries to end the affair.

Unfortunately, Rowena doesn't share Toby's ambition. She's still in love and she isn't willing to let him go. She clings to the hope that she can persuade Toby to renounce his vows and marry her.

Sean's imagination provided a vivid mental picture of the couple's final hours together. He could all too easily envision Rowena pleading for their love and being spurned by Father Toby. And when he insists that their affair is over, she becomes angry and threatens to tell the whole world that he's broken his vows and betrayed his promises to marry her.

Of course, the world wouldn't exactly have been shocked to discover that a handsome Catholic priest was having an affair with one of his parishioners. The scandal would barely have rated a column in the local weekly newspaper. But a sexual scandal would have doomed Father Toby's prospects of promotion to the important and powerful position of bishop, and the more Rowena begged and threatened, the faster he would have seen his once-prestigious career heading directly for the sewer.

Toby's rage must have boiled over into violence when Rowena had stubbornly refused to keep silent about their affair. They'd been lovers for months and

Toby had been in her bedroom many times, so he already knew about her husband's gun, kept in the drawer of her nightstand. In the fury of the moment, before he had time to second-guess himself, Toby had grabbed the gun and squeezed the trigger. And Rowena Slade was dead.

There was a sickening authenticity to the scenario, Sean reflected, an almost tragic sense of inevitability, culminating in the wrongful conviction of Rowena Slade's daughter. When he considered all Maggie had endured since the night she came home and found her mother dying, his stomach roiled. She'd been fifteen years old and newly orphaned when she'd been accused of murder—and he'd done nothing to help her. He'd stood back, brownnosed his superiors and let the weight of the criminal justice system collapse on top of an innocent child.

Nobody ever said that life had to be fair, but when fate was handing out tokens of good fortune, Maggie Slade seemed to have come up seriously short. Sean wanted to take her into his arms and promise that he'd work a miracle for her—that he'd find the evidence that would simultaneously indict the archbishop and set her free. Unfortunately, if there ever had been such evidence, time had long since destroyed it. He knew it, and Maggie knew it, so he couldn't even offer her the false coin of temporary comfort.

He'd taken too long to respond, and she turned to smile at him although there was weariness in her eyes, a resignation that tied his gut in knots. "You don't have to be polite and pretend to believe me, Sean. I've lived for years with the knowledge that Grunewald is getting away with murder. I realize I don't have anything concrete to offer as evidence against him—that's why I've spent almost seven years running and hiding instead of trying to bring him to justice."

"You have one thing now that you didn't have before," Sean said.

"What's that?"

"A cop who believes your story."

Her bottom lip quivered slightly, and he wasn't sure whether to give her an admiring hug or yell in frustration when she turned the betraying tremor into a wry, self-mocking smile. "Thanks, Sean. I'm truly grateful for the moral support. But until I can come up with solid proof to back up my accusations, you'd better keep your beliefs to yourself or you're going to be in big trouble."

He didn't point out that he was already hip-deep in trouble, and that if word of his activities over the past few days ever leaked back to Denver, the best he could hope for was dismissal from the force. At worst, he was looking at serious jail time.

Since he had no intention of turning Maggie in, it was useless to worry about what he was risking by aiding and abetting her escape. "Was today the first time you'd seen the archbishop since the day he offered his help in getting you a scholarship?" he asked.

"No." She shook her head. "I saw him once again after I left juvenile hall, plus he wrote to me each semester, congratulating me on my grades and always enclosing a gift."

"He sent you gifts?" Sean was surprised. "What did he send? Prayer books? Rosaries?"

"No, he sent useful gifts," she admitted grudgingly. "A typewriter, stationery, a dictionary. I wanted to toss the stuff straight into the garbage but…"

"But you couldn't because you needed it."

"Yes." She seemed grateful that he understood what it had cost her to utilize those tainted supplies. "Then he came to visit me again right after I finished my final exams. I was in the women's prison in Cañon City by that time and I got summoned to the warden's office. Bishop Grunewald was waiting there, all fake smiles and warm encouragement. He'd brought me a copy of my final transcript and a letter from the dean of students at Georgetown, congratulating me on graduating with honors. He also brought me another present."

"Something worthy, I'll bet."

She rolled her eyes. "Very worthy. A two-volume leather-bound set of the complete works of Shakespeare. He said he hoped Shakespeare would provide me with enough food for thought to keep my mind nourished until I was eligible for parole."

"And that was the last you heard of him?"

"Not quite. He promised to do everything in his power to get me released at the earliest possible moment, and the warden told me how lucky I was to have such a wonderful, caring man as my mentor and chaplain."

She fell silent, her expression so blank that Sean knew there had to be a giant stew pot of emotions bubbling away beneath it. "I guess the bishop didn't follow through on his promises."

She shrugged. "Who knows? A month later, he sent me a copy of a letter he claimed to have written to the parole board, singing my praises, but even if he really sent it—which I doubt—his comments turned out to be irrelevant."

"It's hard to imagine a parole board ignoring a favorable letter from a bishop."

"Usually I'm sure that's true. But in my case, the psychological evaluation outweighed everything else. When I was transferred from juvenile hall to the women's prison in Cañon City, the warden told me that Ms. Dowd had written a report claiming that I was in acute denial, refusing to accept responsibility for my actions, and that until I was ready to admit that I'd killed my mother, the state would be taking an enormous risk in setting me free."

"Ms. Dowd!" Sean exclaimed. "But wasn't she the counselor who'd helped to get you enrolled in the Georgetown degree program in the first place?"

Maggie nodded. "The very same. I guess she was disappointed when none of the college courses I took convinced me to publicly repent my sins and admit I was guilty."

Sean winced at the pain in her voice, barely disguised by her pretense of cynicism. "Okay, but you're a smart woman, Maggie. You should have seen your way around that obstacle. Ms. Dowd worked with juveniles. She had nothing to do with the adult prison system. So when you went for your mental-status evaluation in Cañon City, you should have lied. The system required you to repent, so you should have become the most penitent criminal in the entire universe. You should have told the prison psychologist that you'd finally seen the error of your ways, that you were guilty, and that although you'd never meant to kill your mother, you accepted full responsibility for her death even though the gun had gone off accidentally."

Maggie gave a rueful laugh. "It sounds like you read a transcript of my session with Dr. Agnelli—that's almost exactly what I told her. Unfortunately, she was much too smart to be fooled and she twigged to that ploy right away. Even more unfortunately, she was so conscientious that she conferred with Ms. Dowd about my case before writing up her report. How many prison doctors do you know who'd have bothered to do that?"

"None," he conceded.

She pulled a face. "Just my luck to get assigned to the most dedicated prison psychologist in the state of Colorado. In the end, Agnelli and Dowd submitted a joint report to the parole board saying that, in their considered professional opinion, not only did I still refuse to accept responsibility for what I'd done, but I also had a mind with a dangerously cunning and criminal bent and I represented a real threat to society. Honestly, Sean, if you'd read their final report, you'd have been convinced that the world was no longer safe for democracy if the parole board set me free." For a moment, Maggie stared unseeingly across the pond. "That's when I decided that if I ever wanted to see the outside world again, I had no choice except to escape."

Sean could certainly understand why she'd reached the conclusion that playing by the rules wasn't getting her anyplace she wanted to go, but he also knew that the life she'd lived for the past few years couldn't have been much better than life behind bars. "The parole board wouldn't have denied your freedom forever, Maggie."

"Why not?" she asked coolly. "Innocent people aren't supposed to go to jail, but I did. Fifteen-year-old kids never got tried as adults back in 1982, but I did, mainly because the cop in charge of my case was annoyed that a guilty rich kid had just gotten off. Forensic evidence is supposed to set innocent people free, but in my case, it convicted me. The gun had my fingerprints on it and nobody else's, except a blurred print that was my mother's. Besides, call me paranoid, but I couldn't shake the feeling that the bishop was never going to let a parole board set me free as long as he was alive—he had way too much to hide."

"But you said yourself that the bishop had nothing to do with the fact that the board denied you parole."

"That's not exactly what I said. Even though it was the psychologists who seemingly caused me so much grief, something about their reports never felt right to me. I was getting pretty good at faking out psychologists by the time Dr. Agnelli interviewed me. Why was she so suspicious of my answers? Had somebody warned her? And why did she confer with Ms. Dowd when communication between the adult and the juvenile systems is usually so lousy? Don't you think it's probable that the bishop was somehow pulling strings behind the scenes?"

After all that she'd gone through, Sean didn't think

Maggie was in the least paranoid, but he couldn't think of any reason why Bishop Grunewald would have wasted time pulling strings and manipulating prison psych reports. That would only have drawn unwelcome attention to his interest in Maggie, something he would be anxious to avoid. Personally, he suspected that the bishop's attentions to Maggie stemmed more from a guilty conscience than anything else and he suggested as much to her.

"Bishop Grunewald can be a murderer without being a total villain, you know. It's at least possible that his efforts to help you survive life in prison were well-meant."

"A pathetic attempt on his part to compensate for his failure to confess his crime, you mean?"

"It's possible," Sean said. "People are rarely all good or all bad. The archbishop probably has a few redeeming features tucked away in an obscure corner of his soul."

She shook her head. "You're giving him way too much credit. I think he kept tabs on me so he'd be one of the first to know if it ever seemed likely that I was going to be released from custody."

"If all he wanted was to keep tabs on you, why did he send you presents and intervene with Georgetown University to get you enrolled in their special-degree program?"

"To impress the authorities with how kind and noble he was?" she conjectured. "He needed to provide some explanation for his interest in my case, and the George-town program was a very plausible excuse to get access to my official records. Or maybe he got a perverted thrill out of his contacts with me. I can imagine him sending off his care packages and then sitting back in his study, gloating because I was too stupid to know the gifts came from the very man who'd killed my mother."

The picture she'd conjured up was compelling, but for some reason, Sean couldn't accept it. "I still think it's possible that he might simply have been trying to appease his guilty conscience."

She laughed at that. "Paying me off for the murder of my mother with a two-volume set of Shakespeare and a leather wallet? Surely even Bishop Grunewald would realize that's not exactly a fair trade."

No, it wasn't a fair trade and he couldn't blame her for being bitter. Maggie might be unwilling to acknowledge even a trace of goodness in the archbishop, but, given the circumstances, it was incredible that she'd managed to retain such a relatively sane and balanced view of the world. Watching her as she made cooing noises at a battered pigeon, apologizing because she had no more bread, Sean felt an urgent need to give her back the life that had been snatched away when she was fifteen. He wanted to make everything perfect for her, to compensate her for too many years when everything had gone wrong.

The hell of it was, he couldn't think of a damn thing he could do to make her life even marginally better, let alone perfect. In fact, as far as he could see, about the only way he could be of any practical use right now was to drive her as fast as he could to Mexico and show her a few insider tricks on how to get lost there.

And, God help him, he was seriously thinking of throwing away his entire career and offering to do just that.

"It's getting dark," he said, propelled to his feet by the discomforting trend of his thoughts. "I have a proposition for you. Why don't we stop obsessing about the archbishop of Columbus for a couple of hours and find a place to drown our sorrows?"

"A bar, you mean?"

"I was thinking more along the lines of someplace that's famous for its decadent desserts."

"Hey, I'm a pushover. You've persuaded me." She stood up, finding a last crumb on her lap for the ever hopeful pigeon. "Hmm, let's see. You've already treated me to Denny's and a hot-dog stand. Yup, I do believe I can see a Dunkin' Donuts in our future."

He had a sudden, almost irresistible urge to kiss her. "You seriously underestimate my flair for finding great eating establishments, Maggie."

"Well, let me think. If it's not Dunkin' Donuts…I know, it must be Dairy Queen! Wow, what class!"

He grinned and shook his head. "Not even close."

"Where, then?"

He hadn't the faintest idea. "Somewhere very fancy," he said. Heck, there had to be someone back at the motel who could point him in the direction of a gourmet coffeehouse or an expensive pastry shop.

She looked down at her slacks and grimaced. "I'm not dressed for very fancy."

"You look great," he said. "Perfect for the place I have in mind."

She raised an eyebrow at that but didn't push him any further. When they got back to the room, to his relief she said that she felt hot and sticky and wanted a shower. He encouraged her to take as long as she needed and hurriedly phoned the front desk. He was in luck. The woman who answered the phone had lived in Columbus all her life, and he got directions from her to a café that she guaranteed served the best cheesecake and the best espresso in the entire city.

The Coffee Mill was located in a converted house that dated from the 1920s. The original backyard had been paved over, and since it was such a fine night, they were able to sit outside and enjoy the fresh air. Sean had noticed that, like most people who had been imprisoned, Maggie disliked cramped spaces and instinctively moved toward a door or a window whenever she was inside a room. She gave a tiny sigh of pleasure as the hostess led them to a small table in the courtyard, set near a waist-high stone flowerpot overflowing with geraniums and petunias.

"The waitress will be right over to take your orders," the hostess said, handing them each a menu.

"This is lovely." Maggie studied the menu for only a minute or two, then put it down.

"Did you decide already?" Sean asked.

"Mmm, it was easy. I just searched for the dessert that packs the most chocolate per square inch. The double fudge chocolate torte looks perfect."

"And I'm going to have the cheesecake. Do you want coffee?"

"A cappuccino would be great."

Sean managed to attract the attention of their waitress and Maggie leaned back in her chair, looking
around the courtyard while he gave their orders. The
darkness concealed some of the tension that was as
much a part of her as the smoky blue-gray of her eyes
or the soft silkiness of her hair. But now that he knew
her better, he could see a hundred small, betraying signs
of stress, from the restless movements of her hands to
the utter stillness that she imposed on herself when she
realized that she was fidgeting.

He'd never seen her truly relaxed, Sean thought.
There was always an element of wariness in her posture, a subtle stiffness that suggested she was steeling
herself to dodge the next blow fate aimed in her direction. He wondered if that wariness ever left her, even
when she was making love. He suddenly wanted very
much to find out the answer to that question.

The waitress returned with unexpected speed, bringing their cups of cappuccino. "I'll be right back with
your desserts," she said.

Maggie scooped up a spoonful of foamed milk and
tasted it appreciatively. "Delicious," she said. "This is
such a great place, Sean."

He laughed. "You're easy to please."

"Maybe I am," she said quietly. She took her spoon
and drew a pattern in the frothy milk. "Anyway, I'm
glad we came somewhere nice because today's kind of
a special day for me." She glanced up at him, hesitat-
ing for a moment. "It's my birthday," she confided, her
voice a little breathless. "I'm thirty years old today."

Her birthday! Sean wished he had an extravagant

present to give her, something totally frivolous—a quart bottle of her favorite perfume, huge diamond earrings, or a satin robe trimmed with swan's down—something to make up for all the birthdays, like today, when he suspected she'd received nothing.

"Happy birthday," he said softly, saluting her with his coffee cup. "We should have ordered champagne."

"The cappuccino's wonderful enough." She smiled, her expression almost shy. "I guess today didn't start out too well, but it's turning out to be a great birthday. Thank you."

"Here you are, folks. Enjoy your desserts." The waitress returned, carrying generous portions of chocolate torte and cheesecake. "Would you like more coffee?"

Maggie shook her head. "Not for me, thanks. Just some ice water when you have a minute."

"Same for me," Sean said. He waited for the waitress to leave, then pushed a fat candle in a hurricane glass across the table toward Maggie. "Since we don't have a birthday cake, this will have to do. Make a wish, then blow it out."

"We probably shouldn't. Someone might see me...."

He put his hand over hers. "Even if everyone sees you, blowing out a restaurant candle isn't an indictable offense."

"Are you sure?" she asked wryly. "With my luck, it'll turn out that the city of Columbus just passed an ordinance."

He pushed the candle closer and spoke commandingly. "Make a wish, Maggie."

"Okay, here goes." She squeezed her eyes tightly shut, then opened them again to blow out the flame.

He pushed the unlit candle out of their way. "Your wish is going to come true," he said. "I saw a falling star right at the moment you blew out the candle."

"Did you? What a coincidence."

She avoided his gaze, and it didn't take a genius to work out what she'd wished for.

Sean experienced a sudden, nearly uncontrollable urge to throw a punch at someone, preferably Archbishop Grunewald, but since that wasn't possible, he took a fork and scooped up a small mouthful of chocolate torte.

"Tell me if it's as good as it looks," he said, directing the fork toward her mouth.

She swallowed obediently. "It's delicious," she said, licking a crumb from the corner of her mouth. "Would you like a taste?"

He was damn near dying for a taste—of her mouth. Using her fork, he helped himself to a small piece of the cake. "Definitely delicious," he said, his gaze fixed on her lips.

A faint wave of color heated her cheeks and she spoke quickly. "Since you ordered cheesecake, I guess that means you're not a chocoholic like me."

"I'm an equal opportunity dessert freak. Cheesecake, chocolate, apple pie, ice cream—you name it, and I'll inhale it with the greatest of pleasure."

She smiled. "How do you stay in shape, Sean? You certainly don't look as if you spend much time inhaling cheesecake."

"I have a fast metabolism," he said. "When I was a teenager, I couldn't put on weight even though I wanted to. I started playing football in high school partly because I was desperate to build some muscles to disguise how skinny I was."

"Sure, and impressing the cute cheerleaders had nothing to do with your choice of sporting activity, of course."

He grinned. "Well, there was that."

She smiled at him, another one of her smiles that made his heart skip a beat. "Do you still play any team sports?" she asked.

"Nothing serious or organized. I like to spend time out of doors, so I mostly keep fit by doing a lot of mountain climbing in summer, and in winter I ski whenever I can get away."

"I used to love skiing. Where's your favorite place to go?"

He didn't need to think. "The back bowls in Vail."

"Mine, too. On a sunny day, with fresh powder, early in the season when there aren't many people around." She sighed. "Pure bliss."

He realized that this was probably the first time in years that Maggie had even talked about going skiing. God knew how long it had been since she actually soared down a mountain with the sun beating on her head and a spray of crisp, dry snow spewing out from her skis. "We should go skiing together sometime," he said. "I'd like that."

She looked at him rather wistfully. "Let's not stretch the fantasy too far, Sean. We both know we can't continue this pretense for much longer. At some point quite soon, you're going to have to turn a blind eye and let me escape or you're going to have to turn me in. There are no other choices for us."

Maggie was absolutely right, but Sean wasn't willing to abandon their fantasy world just yet. "It's your birthday," he said. "For tonight, let's pretend that impossible dreams will come true."

She agreed quickly enough, but Sean could see that somewhere along the line, Maggie had lost the capacity to dream at all. He suspected that the only way she would be able to enjoy her birthday night was if they lived strictly in the moment, so he encouraged her to talk about books and movies, and he swapped cute stories about Heather's antics in exchange for Maggie's amusing anecdotes about people she'd worked with.

She was great company, intelligent and witty, and time flew by. When he'd first seen Maggie at the Pink Parrot, he'd noticed what a flair she had for entertaining customers and making them laugh. Tonight, she played along with him so well that it took him the best part of an hour to recognize that the way she was treating him was simply a modified version of the way she'd treated her customers.

"Maggie, stop." He reached across the table and took her hand. "You're not on the job and there's no tip waiting at the end of this. You don't have to laugh politely when I tell you a lousy joke."

"You don't tell lousy jokes. Most of them were pretty good."

"Then relax and stop trying to please me. Just be yourself for once."

"You know I can't do that," she said quietly. "It's much too dangerous."

For one terrible moment, Sean looked into her eyes and saw the isolation caused by years of lies and secrets with such appalling clarity that he felt her loneliness as a physical pain.

It was in that same moment he realized the truth. There was only one way he could possibly help Maggie, and it wasn't by sending her fleeing to Mexico. Somehow, in some way, the man who'd murdered her mother had to be brought to justice.

Somehow they were going to have to find the key that would force Archbishop Grunewald to confess to his crime. Without that confession, whether Maggie was behind bars or on the run, she was going to spend the rest of her life imprisoned in the chains of her mother's brutal death.

Eleven

Sean suggested that they stop at an all-night drugstore on the way back to the motel so Maggie could buy a toothbrush and other essentials, but his real purpose in stopping was to get her a birthday present. While she searched for toiletries, he hurried over to the cosmetics aisle and picked out the biggest and most expensive gift pack of body lotion and bath oil he could find, along with a sheet of fancy wrapping paper and a giant pink satin bow. It was only as he sneaked to the counter to pay that he realized he'd left Maggie completely alone for over ten minutes.

He quickly scanned the store, but he couldn't see her anywhere. She wasn't in the aisle with all the toilet articles, and she wasn't waiting to pay since he was standing at the only cash register that was open. Sean cursed long and hard. Jesus, she was probably on a bus to Cleveland by now! What a fool he'd been to believe that he could trust her. He snatched the bag and his change from the cashier and rushed toward the exit.

He almost crashed into Maggie as she stepped out from behind a tall revolving rack of books. "Hi," she said, giving him one of her quick, uncertain smiles.

"Hi." Sean hoped she wouldn't notice he was panting. "Sorry, did I keep you waiting?"

She shook her head. "I haven't even paid for my stuff yet. I can never resist checking out the latest paperbacks. I love the bright covers and the new smell, not like the used books in—" She stopped abruptly. "Anyway, I'll just pay for this and be right back."

"No rush. We have all night. Do you have money?"

"Yes, thanks." She scurried to the checkout.

Sean watched her, his heart thumping. Maggie put the items she'd selected on the counter without looking at the clerk. Then pretending to search in her purse, she ducked her head when the clerk handed back her change. Dammit! He hated to see how she instinctively avoided eye contact with everyone, and how she walked hunched over as if her primary goal was to fade into the woodwork. When he'd first seen her at the Pink Parrot, she'd seemed overflowing with confidence. He recognized now what an act that had been, her breezy manners every bit as false as her bouncy blond curls and thick layers of makeup. In retrospect, he could only guess what it must have cost her to maintain the illusion of brash self-confidence for hours and hours at a stretch.

Once they were back at the motel, he used the time she spent in the bathroom to wrap up the gift pack of lotion and bath oil. He'd forgotten to buy any sticky tape, so the package was lopsided, to put it mildly, but he hoped Maggie would appreciate the thought and overlook the artistic deficiencies. At least the pink satin bow was cute.

She emerged from the bathroom wearing the T-shirt he'd loaned her to sleep in. Her hair was piled on top of her head and fastened with a clip that left damp auburn tendrils clinging to her neck. She'd scrubbed her face bare of makeup, and the sun had turned her cheekbones and the bridge of her nose pink.

She was beautiful enough to take his breath away.

Sean took a few steps toward her, then stopped at a safe distance, knowing how much she disliked any physical contact she didn't initiate. He held out his gift at arm's length. The package was already falling apart for lack of tape, but he hoped she would understand.

He cleared his throat. "Happy birthday."

Maggie stared at the package as if she couldn't quite believe he expected her to open it.

"Sorry about the tacky gift wrap," he said hurriedly. "Lynn always used to wrap all the presents and so I haven't done this very often." *Way to go, Sean. Mention your ex-wife's name as you hand Maggie her present.*

"It's…lovely." She reached tentatively toward the package. "You did a…great job."

He grinned ruefully. "Hey, let's not stretch the truth too far."

She still didn't take the box, so he put it into her hands. "Here. I'm sorry it couldn't be anything more exciting, but my shopping options were limited."

She finally took the present, looking at it for several seconds more before she carefully removed the bow.

Then she unfolded the wrapping paper and slowly smoothed it out, putting it next to the bow on the dresser before opening the display box and stroking the tips of her fingers over the two bottles. She didn't take either of them out of the package, just stared at them without a trace of a smile or a glimmer of emotion. Abruptly, without speaking, she turned her back to him.

Even from that angle, Sean could see that her whole body was rigid with tension. He came up behind her, certain that somehow he'd offended her, although he couldn't imagine how. She must have understood that the drugstore didn't offer much in the way of choices. "Maggie? I'm sorry if you don't like the—"

"Don't touch me!" Her voice was thick and unsteady.

Suddenly, he understood. Sweet Jesus! Maggie wasn't offended; she was dumbfounded and desperately struggling not to cry. Ignoring her command, which he realized was actually a plea not to threaten her precarious self-possession, he fastened his arms loosely around her waist. "Maggie," he said softly, "Please look at me."

"I...can't."

She was trembling, so he held her and waited for her to regain her poise. Her hair tickled his face and he longed to bury his face in it, but he resisted the temptation. He understood how important it was to her pride not to break down in front of anyone. Especially in front of him, perhaps, since he was one of the cops associated with the night when her life had changed so terribly. After a couple of minutes, she stopped shaking and turned around, but it was obvious that she was hanging on to her control by the thinnest and most fragile of threads.

"I hope you enjoy smelling like an ocean breeze," he said, wanting to give her some extra time. "It was that or tropical fruit passion."

"Yes, you made the right choice…." Her voice broke and she had to clear her throat a few times before she could go on. "It's always a real treat to take a long, hot bath, especially a scented one. It's a truly wonderful present, Sean. Thank you."

"You're welcome." She didn't need to explain that in jail there were no hot, scented baths, only quick showers, observed by guards. He cradled her face in his hands and gazed down at her, his whole body aching with tenderness. He brushed his thumbs gently across her eyelids and they came away wet, although he suspected she'd die a thousand deaths before she'd expose her vulnerability and let the tears escape in his presence. "How long is it since anybody gave you a birthday present, Maggie?"

"I—I don't remember."

Fifteen years, Sean thought. *It's fifteen goddamn years. Nobody's given her a birthday present since her mother died.*

His arms tightened around her. She was still clutching his gift, and he reached between them, taking the box and tossing it onto the bed near the window. She murmured in protest when the lid fell off, and he crushed the sound with his kiss, unable to bear any more reminders of how bleak and lonely her life had been, how overwhelmed she'd been by a gift that was nothing more than twenty bucks' worth of drugstore goodies. For a second or two, she didn't respond in any way, either with pleasure or with rejection. Then her lips opened and she returned his kiss with a deep, hungry passion.

Despite the fact that he'd been sexually attracted to Maggie almost from the first moment he glimpsed her across the Pink Parrot's crowded dance floor, Sean's kiss had been prompted more by feelings of tenderness and compassion than anything else. But when her mouth opened beneath his, tenderness and compassion both fled on a bolt of desire that left him instantly hard and fully aroused. He hadn't had sex since the night Art had been killed and he'd been shot, but his sudden need for Maggie was caused by much more than a backlog of sexual abstinence. Something about her vulnerability gave a sharp and powerful edge to his desire, an edge that cut through the emotional barriers he'd constructed and exposed the raw intensity of his feelings. He wanted Maggie. He wanted her despite all the reasons why he knew that making love to her was a seriously lousy idea.

He kissed her again, his hands all over her, and she returned his caresses with an awkward shyness that he found oddly endearing. But she gave a strangled gasp when he unzipped his slacks and tugged off his shirt, although she didn't resist when he removed her T-shirt and pulled her naked body against his.

Her skin was hot and smooth, her breasts unbearably soft and sexy, her mouth the most enticing he'd ever tasted, and he didn't want to wait a moment longer before sinking himself deep inside her. Putting his arm around her waist, he led her over to the bed, tossed back the covers and lay beside her, his hands urgently possessive, his kisses hot, his breathing harsh and strained. Maggie didn't protest when he reached down to part her thighs, but he felt her instinctively stiffen before she forced herself to relax again.

A warning bell sounded in the passion-hazed recesses of Sean's brain. Belatedly, he recognized that apart from those first few awkward caresses, Maggie had merely been accepting what he was doing to her, not participating. He already knew that at least two men had tried to rape her and he could make a pretty good guess that her other sexual experiences hadn't exactly been textbook examples of slow and tender seduction. Now he was getting ready to assault her with yet another slam-dunk performance that was all about his needs rather than hers.

Sean realized the last thing he wanted was to add this night to Maggie's list of grim sexual memories. Pulling away from her, he rested his forehead against hers, fighting a lingering urge to plunge into her, take what he wanted and worry about everything else later.

After a few moments of listening to his heavy breathing, Maggie sat up, her expression uncertain. "Is something wrong, Sean?"

"Yes, I think so. I was having a great time, but you weren't. We need to slow down some so you can catch up with me."

"I was enjoying myself." She wrapped her arms around her knees, drawing them up to her chin. "Anyway, it doesn't matter—"

"Like hell it doesn't matter. No way you're faking it, babe, not with me."

She raised an eyebrow at that. "Your masculine ego was offended? I'm sorry I didn't instantly go up in flames at the first touch of your expert hands."

"This has nothing to do with my ego or my expertise. I'm just not into virgin sacrifices."

She stared at her kneecaps as if she'd never seen them before. "I'm not a virgin."

"Hey, what a coincidence—neither am I!"

That coaxed a tiny laugh out of her. He was surprised at how wonderful it made him feel each time Maggie laughed or gave him one of her shy smiles. She turned toward him, leaning back so that her cheek rested briefly against the palm of his hand, and he wondered why such a fleeting gesture should strike him as so incredibly erotic.

Wanting to touch her again without being too aggressive, he reached across the bed to pull out the clip she'd used to pin up her hair. He ran his fingers through the straight, silky strands and spread them out across her shoulders. Her laughter faded, but her eyes stayed on his, clear at first, then gradually turning smoky as his hands strayed lower.

Sean resisted the urge to instantly turn up the heat. Whatever happened between them tonight, he wanted to be sure it was by Maggie's choice. And if they ended up not making love…well, he guessed he would survive. Possibly. Maybe.

Maggie glanced at him with equal parts embarrassment and wry amusement. "My move, huh?"

"Your move," he agreed.

She trailed her hand across his chest, pressing her palm flat on his rib cage so he could feel the thud of his heartbeat vibrating against her fingertips. "Tonight, at the restaurant, when I blew out my birthday candle, do you know what I wished for, Sean?"

Her freedom? A terrible punishment for Archbishop Grunewald? He shook his head. "No, I can't guess. And you're not supposed to tell what you asked for or it won't come true."

"In this case, maybe it will. I hope it will." She sent him a slightly quizzical glance. "I wished that you would make love to me."

He gave a strained laugh. "I have to tell you, Maggie Slade, you wasted a wish. You didn't need to use any birthday magic for that one—all you had to do was ask."

"Then I'm asking," she said huskily. She turned and lifted her mouth to his. "Make love to me, Sean."

He was suddenly having a hell of a time remembering how to breathe. But this time when he took her into his arms, everything felt right. This time when they kissed, there was no hesitation on her part, no ambivalence on his. He leaned across to the other bed and found his birthday gift. Uncapping the bottle of body lotion, he poured some of the cool blue liquid onto his hands.

Maggie shivered—but not from the cold—as he smoothed the lotion over the top of her breasts, around her nipples and down the flat plane of her stomach. He moved in slow, expanding circles toward her thighs, his touch so light that it was scarcely more than a tantalizing hint of what might lie ahead for them when she was ready. In a very short while, the coolness of the lotion changed to heat, and the sweat from their bodies became slick on his palms. The heat of their lovemaking flushed her entire body, and with every breath he inhaled the erotic scent of the lotion, subtly changed by contact with her skin. With every stroke of his fingers, he could see her climb closer to her peak. With every thrust of his hips, he could see her surrender a little more of herself to his keeping.

Just when he thought he wouldn't be able to hold out a moment longer, Maggie gave a stunned, strangled gasp, and he felt her shatter around him, totally vulnerable, totally exposed. She held nothing back, hid nothing, guarded nothing. The waves of her pleasure swept over him, pushing him to his own urgent and tumultuous climax.

Sated and exhausted, Sean collapsed alongside her, agreeably aware of Maggie curled half-beneath him, her hands splayed trustingly against his chest. It was several long and exhilarating moments before he could think again, and then his euphoria dissipated with lightning speed.

He had just created one hell of a problem for himself, Sean realized. Maggie had finally abandoned her defenses and offered him her trust. But now that she'd surrendered, how in the world was he supposed to avoid betraying her?

Maggie came slowly back to earth, although her body still felt as if it were floating blissfully in outer space. Sean was lying beside her, his legs twined with hers, and the intimacy felt wonderful, not threatening as she would have expected. There was an amazing difference between making love and having sex, she decided. Tonight, she'd made love to Sean, whereas in the past she'd simply had sex, and her other partners—all two of them—had aroused no complex feelings, nothing beyond a vague bewilderment that people made such a fuss about an activity she'd ranked somewhere between tedious and faintly comic.

Her body was just beginning to feel as if all the parts belonged to her again and she stretched, aware of a tremendous sense of well-being even as she slid delightfully toward sleep. "Thank you, Sean," she murmured. "You've given me the best birthday I can ever remember. It was a wonderful day."

"You're welcome." He stared down at her, his eyes dark and unreadable. "Tomorrow we have to—" He broke off.

"Tomorrow we have to what?"

He kissed her very lightly on the lips. "Tomorrow we have to make love to each other at least twice before breakfast."

For some reason, his good humor sounded forced, but Maggie was too sated and drowsy to analyze subtle nuances of expression. "Sounds like a great plan," she said sleepily.

"Then it's a deal." His arms tightened around her, and she yawned and snuggled more closely against him, resting one of her hands on his hip just because it felt so wonderful to indulge in such a casually intimate gesture. She wanted to tell Sean that she'd never before experienced such a sense of completion or such closeness to another human being, but her eyelids were too heavy to keep open, and she drifted into sleep while she was still trying to find the words she needed.

She had no idea how much time passed before she woke up, jolted out of sleep by a terrifying nightmare. She couldn't remember why the dream had scared her, but her heart was pounding, her breath coming in fast, jerky gasps, and although she soon realized that she was safe in the motel room, her panic didn't seem to diminish in the least.

She looked across to the other side of the bed. Untroubled by bad dreams, Sean slept peacefully. While she watched, he turned over, his hand flopping around until it encountered her thigh. He half opened one eye, gave a little grunt of satisfaction and immediately fell deeply asleep again.

Maggie's panic increased as she looked at him. Nightmares were a fact of life where she was concerned, and she'd learned to live with them. Usually, the fear began to fade as soon as she woke up. But tonight, instead of feeling better, the more removed from sleep she became, the more her foreboding increased until the knowledge of danger close at hand became physically painful.

Her gaze swept around the darkened room, skittering from object to object, then finally came to rest on the small table where Sean had put her files about Archbishop Grunewald.

The instant she saw the files, Maggie realized why she was so panicked. Sean.

Yesterday, for a few hours, she'd genuinely forgotten the harsh facts of her life. Starting with their trip to the park, Sean had created a fantasy that was so appealing, she'd entered into it with scarcely more than a few token murmurs of protest. But Sean's world, enchanting as it was, could never survive even a passing brush with reality. If she stayed with him, the ugliness of her life would soon explode with terrible consequences, not just for her, but also for him. And Maggie had no desire to drag Sean down into the cesspool of lies and deceptions that made up her life.

Her stomach churned with the realization that there was only one possible solution to the problem. If she had any genuine concern for Sean, she had to be out of this motel room and miles away to somewhere—anywhere—before he woke up. It was tempting to tell herself that Sean was a cop and that he understood what he was getting into, but Maggie couldn't allow herself to be seduced by that beguiling half-truth. Nobody could understand what life on the run was like until they'd lived it. How would Sean feel when he realized that by staying with her even for a night or two, he was risking the chance that he'd never again get to see his daughter? It wasn't just Sean's career that was at stake here; it was his entire life.

She'd run so many times before, quit jobs she'd enjoyed, ducked out on tentative friendships and scuttled her two brief sexual relationships, but she'd never felt this wrenching sense of tearing herself loose from her last best hope of happiness. Worst of all, she'd given Sean her word that she wouldn't try to escape, and now she had to break that promise.

Looking back, it seemed that she must have told a million lies in the years since she'd escaped from jail, but through it all, she'd liked to kid herself that there was some basic core of integrity buried deep inside her that remained untouched by her dishonesty. When she'd promised Sean not to run out on him, she'd been drawing on those reserves of integrity, and it hurt terribly to realize that she had been drawing on an illusion.

She wasn't going to keep her promise. The pain was so fierce that Maggie could only handle it by turning off all her feelings. Carefully and deliberately, she closed her emotions down, shutting off hope and joy along with a bitter sense of loss. The bedside clock, screwed down to the nightstand, told her that it was 2:47 in the morning. Fortunately, her car was still parked near St. Anthony's Church, and Sean didn't know the address of her apartment, so once she got outside this room, escape shouldn't be too difficult. God knew the routines of packing up and making a fast getaway were mind-numbingly familiar to her.

As always, it was the little things that made escape difficult. Sean's hand was still resting possessively on her thigh, and she very carefully lifted it off and tucked it under the sheet. He stirred again, and for a moment she was sure he was going to wake up. But then he rolled over onto his side and his breathing became soft and regular.

Maggie didn't feel relief because she wasn't allowing herself to feel anything. She sat on the edge of the bed, waiting for three minutes by the clock to be sure that Sean was fully asleep again. When he didn't stir, she inched out of the bed, stood up and waited yet again. He didn't move, and she silently scooped up her clothes and her birthday present before creeping into the bathroom and quietly shutting the door. She didn't risk switching on the light, just dressed hurriedly and tugged a comb through her hair to avoid looking untidy enough to attract attention. Her purse, with her money and her identification, was hanging on the hook behind the bathroom door. She put the bottles of bath oil and body lotion into her purse, concentrating on checking to make sure that both the caps were securely tightened and refusing to remember how she'd felt when Sean had given them to her.

She now had everything she needed to escape—except the keys to Sean's rental car. St. Anthony's was at least five miles from here, only a few minutes by car, but too far to walk when she was operating under acute time pressure. She had to be out of Columbus before Sean woke up and came looking for her. What did it matter if she stole his car again when she'd already broken her promise not to try to escape?

But where were the keys? Sean had tossed them onto the bed just before they left to go to the park and that was the last time Maggie remembered seeing them.

The drapes were thick and heavily lined, but they weren't tightly closed, and a narrow beam of light from the parking lot shone into the bedroom, making her search easier. She couldn't see the keys on the bed, but she patted her hands all over the coverlet just to be sure they hadn't slipped into a crease. They weren't there and they weren't on the table, either. They weren't inside

Sean's briefcase. They weren't on the nightstand. She even checked in the pockets of his discarded slacks. No keys. The only other possibility seemed to be that they'd fallen off the bed and were somewhere on the floor, probably under one of the beds.

It was taking her way too long to find the damn keys. She glanced at Sean to make sure he was still sleeping. He was. She stared at him a few seconds longer than was necessary, unable to tear her gaze away. He'd rolled over again, and the sheet had slipped down to his waist. When they made love, she'd been so caught up in the amazing sensations he evoked in her that she hadn't realized what a gorgeous body he had. Her stomach lurched, then tightened with a sensation that would have been desire if she'd been allowing herself to feel anything. Turning abruptly away, she went down on her hands and knees and began silently patting the carpet near the beds.

A hand came down on the scruff of her neck and hauled her to her feet. Before she could draw breath to scream, Sean threw her onto the bed, straddled her and held up a set of car keys. His expression was somewhere between savage and ferocious. "Is this what you're looking for?"

Twelve

Maggie didn't attempt to hide her despair. "Let me go, Sean," she pleaded. "It's the only realistic solution for us."

"You promised me that you wouldn't try to escape. I trusted you."

"Did you?" she asked sadly. "If you trusted me, why did you hide the car keys? If you trusted me, why were you pretending to be asleep when you obviously weren't?"

Abruptly, he released his grip on her wrists and rolled away from her. "You haven't given me much reason to trust you," he muttered.

"I know. And the way my life is going, you'll never be able to trust me. That's the bottom line. My life doesn't allow me to be trustworthy."

"Give me the chance to help you change your situation."

"We both know that's not possible." Maggie sat up,

rubbing her wrists, wishing there was some miraculous way to make everything come out right and knowing there wasn't. "Sean, making love to you was one of the most wonderful experiences of my life, and I wish it could be the start of a real relationship for us, but it can't be. We have to split up now, right this minute, before I ruin everything for you."

He took her hands in his and stroked his thumbs over her wrists. "I didn't mean to grab you so hard. I'm sorry, Maggie."

"It's okay." She closed her eyes so she wouldn't be weakened by looking at him. "Sean, I need to go—"

"Where to? Do you have money? New documentation? What about your boss here? She doesn't strike me as the sort of woman who's going to let you disappear without kicking up one hell of a fuss. If you're not at work on schedule, what will she do?"

Maggie was worried about Dorothy, too. Her boss was more than capable of accusing Sean of assault and launching an investigation that would draw just the sort of attention Maggie was desperate to avoid. But she couldn't allow potential problems with her boss to prevent her from doing what she knew was right. She had to leave town.

"It's better if you don't know anything about my plans. If you really want to help me, drive me back to St. Anthony's so I can pick up my car. Once I have transportation, I promise you I'll be out of Columbus before noon."

"Running blind again?"

"There are no better choices," she said flatly.

"And what am I supposed to do once you've gone? Fly back to Denver and forget you exist?"

Maggie drew in a deep breath. "Yes, that's exactly what you're supposed to do."

"Not a chance," he said softly, and bent his head to kiss her.

Desire rekindled between them with shocking speed and intensity, and Maggie didn't even try to resist. Just once more, she told herself. She could allow herself the gift of making love to Sean one more time before she disappeared from his life forever. She reached out and took him into her arms, then he pressed his body full-length against hers, moving in a way that already felt comfortingly familiar as well as exciting. The bed cocooned them, dark and warm and safe, an oasis that was theirs to enjoy, created out of a desert filled with cruelly hard choices.

They didn't speak because that might have brought the real world crashing in on them. This time, there was no hesitation on her part, no long, slow seduction on his. They came together with an elemental need that stunned Maggie by its fierceness and dazed her by its breathtaking conclusion. But in the aftermath, when she could think coherently again, she discovered that the world was still waiting for them and that nothing had changed.

Sean seemed to be feeling some of the same pressure from the stark forces of reality. He got off the bed and rummaged in the chest of drawers to find sweatpants and a T-shirt. "Okay, it's past time for some serious discussion here," he said, pulling on the pants and sitting at the foot of the bed, just out of touching range. "Bottom line. You've been running for almost seven years, and it's time for the running to stop."

"I agree," Maggie said quietly. "But I have to run once more before I call it quits. I won't have it on my conscience that your life was destroyed because of me. I have enough to keep me sleepless at night without adding that."

Sean tugged on the T-shirt, impatiently poking his arms into the sleeves. "Instead of making a martyr of yourself, how about working with me on finding a way to establish that Grunewald's guilty of murdering your mother?"

"That's impossible, Sean. There is no way to prove his guilt. Not at this late stage."

"I don't believe you. Why are you here if you're convinced there's no hope of proving your innocence?"

Maggie was only just beginning to understand herself why she'd come to Columbus when she had no realistic hope of forcing the archbishop to admit his guilt and no hope at all of finding evidence to convict him without his cooperation. "In an odd sort of way, I came here because of you," she said finally.

"Me?" Sean looked startled.

Maggie tried to find the words to make him understand. "You were the cop who discovered the gun that killed my mother, and the prosecution used that gun as their prime piece of evidence to get me convicted of murder. When you walked into the Pink Parrot with your brother, it was as if the wheel had turned full circle and fate was sending me a message. 'Give up, Maggie. You'll never be able to outrun your past.'"

"So you stopped trying to outrun your past and came to Columbus to confront it."

"Yes," she said. "I wasn't hoping to uncover miraculous proof of my innocence. I was simply planning to confront the archbishop and force him to listen while I told him that I knew what he'd done to my mother. After that, I didn't much care what happened to me."

"Grunewald's going to deny everything. If he's lived with his guilty conscience for fifteen years, he's not going to crack and pour out a confession just because you accuse him of murder."

"Maybe not, although he'd have to lie to my face and that might be harder for him than simply keeping silent. But to a certain extent, the archbishop's reaction is irrelevant. I've regretted for a long time that I didn't confront him years ago, when I first recognized him as the man who'd been my mother's lover. I want him to realize that I know the truth about him. I want him to sweat for a few hours, wondering if I'm going to accuse him of fornication and murder in front of every TV camera and print journalist who's willing to listen."

"It's not much of a payoff. You risk everything, and Grunewald gets to find out that somebody else besides God knows that he's a scumbag. He won't even sweat much about your threat to go public with your accusations. If you manage to tell your story to the media before you're arrested, the archbishop's reputation is so stellar that the public will dismiss you as crazy. Or worse—vicious and perverted."

"Maybe, but it doesn't matter anymore if it was a lousy plan because I'm not going through with it."

Maggie got off the bed and crossed over to the window. She drew back the drapes enough to see the first pale hints of dawn lighting the sky. She and Sean needed to part company before anyone else saw them together. And she needed to get on the road, although the prospect of driving to yet another city and searching for yet another dead-end job left her weary to the marrow of her bones.

She shook off her depression and swung around, squaring her shoulders. "I'm thirty years old, Sean, and I've quit believing in fairy tales. I've reached the point in my life where it doesn't make much difference whether I'm behind bars or not. To all intents and purposes, I've been a prisoner ever since the night my mother died and I have nothing much left to lose if I'm sent back to jail. But I've waited this long to stage my showdown with the archbishop and I can wait a few months longer to make sure you don't get caught in the cross fire."

"I appreciate your concern, honey, but it seems to me you should spend a bit more time worrying about yourself and a lot less time worrying about me. Right now, you need to concentrate on how you're going to expose the archbishop without getting captured and sent back to jail."

"I've told you, I don't care about staying out of jail anymore." Maggie slumped against the window ledge, aware that she was uncomfortably close to tears. "I'm tired. Tired of running, tired of hiding, tired of lying. I want to start telling the truth even if that lands me back in jail and even if nobody ever believes me."

"I believe you."

The tears were pressing closer and closer. To stop them falling, Maggie took refuge in sarcasm. "Gee, thanks, now I feel a lot better. With you on my side, I guess a presidential pardon is just around the corner."

He actually smiled. "Yeah, I guess it is. I pride myself on always getting my man. Or my woman." He came and stood next to her, cupping her face with his hands so she was forced to look at him. His gaze was tender and admiring. She couldn't imagine where the tenderness came from or what there was about her that he found worthy of admiration. He kissed her on the nose, then on the mouth, very lightly. "We're going to nail the bastard, Maggie. Trust me."

It was his offer of hope that was her undoing. The tears she'd kept bottled up for so long refused to stay inside where they belonged. They squeezed out of her eyes and trickled down her cheeks. Sean brushed the drops away with the tips of his fingers, which only made the tears come faster.

He folded her into his arms, holding her steady while the tears changed to sobs and the sobs to shuddering gasps of anguish. She cried because she was never going to make love to Sean again. She cried for her parents, for her lost youth, for the fact that the last time she'd cried this hard, Bishop Grunewald had been the man who pretended to comfort her. She cried for all the indignities she'd suffered in jail and for all the fear and hopelessness of her life on the run. Above all, she cried because she couldn't accept Sean's offer of help. And when there were no more tears left to cry, she stood within the circle of his arms and wondered how in the world she was going to find the strength to move out of them.

But she could only delay the inevitable for so long. As soon as she had herself under a semblance of control, she forced herself to meet his eyes squarely and speak the words that wanted to remain stuck in the back of her throat. "Sean, it means a lot to me that you're willing to help, more than you can imagine, but I can't accept your offer. Now, would you please drive me to St. Anthony's before they open the church for early-morning mass? Too many people have already seen us together, and I need to be on my way."

"No."

She stared at him. "What does that mean?"

"I always thought *no* was a real simple word to understand, honey. No means no, I don't plan to drop you off at St. Anthony's and disappear from your life. Now that we have that out of the way, why don't we start working on our plan to force a confession out of the archbishop?"

She wasn't sure whether to feel exasperation or exhilaration. "Did you listen to anything I said? I can't let you throw away your life on a totally lost cause."

"You're right, you can't. Fortunately, the choice isn't yours to make. It's mine. And my decision is to stay here in Columbus and do my damnedest to help you prove your innocence."

"But this is my fight—"

"And mine. My mother always tells me I'm a sucker for lost causes. But quite apart from the injustice you've suffered, it bugs the hell out of me that Archbishop Grunewald is thumbing his nose at the world and getting away with murder. No more arguments. I'm staying to help."

She tried to summon the moral fiber to argue with him some more, but she couldn't. He was offering unconditional support when she'd been starved even for a few crumbs of friendship, and that made his offer doubly irresistible. She swallowed over a lump in her throat the size of a grapefruit. "Thanks, Sean."

"You're welcome. Now, let's get started on a game plan."

"If we're going to do any serious planning, we should go back to my apartment," Maggie said. "We'll have more privacy there."

"A good idea," Sean agreed.

"I need to pick up my car first," Maggie said. "If we leave it in the parking lot too long, it may get towed and then the police will come looking for me, which we definitely want to avoid. I'll drive my car, and you can follow me home."

Sean sent her a long, steady look, and she knew he was thinking that if she wanted to give him the slip, she was setting up the perfect opportunity. She didn't say anything, silently challenging him to accept her words at face value. After a couple of seconds, he got up and started to pack his belongings into a small suitcase. "You're right. We need to pick up your car. What name are you using here? I better remember not to call you Maggie except when we're alone."

She felt a momentary glow of sheer happiness at the

trust that was implicit in his response. She didn't realize she'd smiled at him until he smiled back, his gaze faintly rueful. "I nearly blew the test, huh?"

"Nearly." Her smile widened into a grin. "But you redeemed yourself in the nick of time. My new name is Christine Williamson, by the way. Christine's from Pittsburgh and she's moved here to get away from an unhappy marriage and a messy divorce."

He raised an eyebrow. "That sounds very much like the story you were telling about Maggie Stevens in Tampa."

She shrugged. "It works well, even if it's a bit shopworn. There are so many wives escaping from unhappy marriages that nobody really questions me about the details."

"Except your boss."

Maggie grimaced. "Unfortunately, Dorothy has a heart of pure gold and a personal interest in women who've been abused by their husbands. For some reason, nothing will convince her that I'm not escaping from a nightmare of physical and emotional abuse."

"Because that's what you *are* escaping from," Sean said. "It just wasn't a husband who inflicted the abuse. You're an amazing woman, Maggie. There aren't many people who'd be able to go through everything you have and survive. Dorothy recognizes that quality in you and responds to it."

Maggie mulled over Sean's comment as she drove her rattletrap car from St. Anthony's back to her one-room walk-up apartment near the university. She was glad he found her amazing, although that wasn't a word she would ever have used to describe herself. She had always been content simply to count herself a survivor.

Her new apartment had once been the top floor of a house built right after World War II. In its heyday it might have been reasonably attractive, but these days it was showing serious signs of wear and tear after ten years as a rooming house for Ohio State students. Maggie escorted Sean up the dusty stairs, wishing she had somewhere nicer to take him. She hoped he'd notice that her apartment was spotlessly clean, even if it was shabby and filled with cheap, ugly furniture.

"Come in," she said, unlocking the door. "I'll make us some coffee while you unpack your suitcase. The bathroom's through there, and that other door leads to the closet if you want to hang up any of your clothes."

She hung her purse on the hook behind the front door, automatically tidy because she was so accustomed to living in cramped spaces. She went into the kitchen, which was really no more than a stove, a sink and an ancient fridge set against a wall and divided from the living/sleeping area by a harvest yellow counter, marred by multiple cigarette burns.

"I'm sorry, I can only make instant coffee," she said, setting a kettle to boil. "I don't have a percolator."

"Hey, you're talking to a cop. If it doesn't dissolve the cup, I can drink it." Sean prowled around the small room, stopping by the sofa to examine two photographs she had in a double frame. "Are these your parents?" he asked.

"Yes. I taped those to my stomach when I escaped, otherwise I wouldn't have any pictures of them at all."

For a moment, his lips tightened and he appeared almost angry, but he said only, "You look a lot like your mother."

"Everyone always commented on that when I was a kid. Except my mother was very blond with bright blue eyes and a pale complexion. She could never go out in the sun without burning. My coloring is darker, more like my father's."

"He was in the air force, wasn't he?"

"Yes, he was a fighter pilot in Vietnam and he decided to stay on and make a career of it. It's ironic to think that he survived three years of combat duty, with two planes shot out from under him, only to die during a routine training flight."

"How old were you when he died?"

"Fourteen. I guess that was better than losing him when I was still a baby, with no memories of him, but it was tough for me and my mom to lose him that way because it was so unexpected. When Dad got assigned to the Air Force Academy as senior instructor, my mom was ecstatic that he'd finally been given a safe, cushy post to make up for all the hardship tours he'd been sent on."

Sean put his arm around her waist, hugging her. "And then, just when you were getting over your father's death, your mother was murdered."

"Yes." The coffee mugs rattled as Maggie set them on the counter. "It was a rough couple of years."

"That's a slight understatement." He dropped a light kiss on the top of her head, his arms tightening around her in wordless consolation.

The kettle whistled, and Maggie poured boiling water onto the coffee crystals, thinking how strange it felt to talk about her parents after all those years of enforced silence. It was even stranger, although wonderful, to lean back into the circle of Sean's arms and soak up the balm of his sympathy.

"Do you take milk or sugar in your coffee?" she asked him.

"Just milk, thanks. Is it in the fridge?"

"I'll get it. Why don't you clear a space on the table so we can spread out the papers I've collected about Archbishop Grunewald."

She carried the mugs over to the table, which was fake walnut, circa 1965. Sean had taken out the file on the archbishop, but he didn't seem in any rush to open it.

Maggie, on the other hand, could barely contain her impatience. Now that she had an ally, it suddenly seemed as if a whole new world of possibilities was arrayed in front of her. "We need to read through every document," she said, sitting down and simultaneously reaching for the file folder. "If we're going to find a starting point to build a case against him, it's going to be in these papers. I think I have copies of every article that's been written about him."

Sean put down his mug and took her hand. "Maggie, I've been over those documents twice already, and you've probably combed through them a hundred times. We both know there's absolutely nothing in this file that would get the archbishop convicted of anything. On the contrary. If the guy died tomorrow, you could send these clippings to the Vatican and use them as evidence to get him declared a saint."

Maggie went cold. "Then what are we doing here? How are we going to show the world the kind of man he really is if you're so sure there's nothing in my file that's going to damage his reputation?"

"If the evidence isn't here, we have to find it some other place."

"There is no other place. Unless you know a way to scan the inside of the archbishop's head."

"Not quite," Sean said. "But once we've eliminated everything that's impossible, we have to go with what's left, however difficult that might be. So what's possible? At this stage of the game, we're not going to find any physical evidence that would link Grunewald to the crime, and as you've pointed out, we can't tunnel inside his head to get a printout of his thoughts. So we're left with only one remaining option. We have to make the archbishop tell us what's inside his head. In other words, we have to force him to confess."

Maggie fought back bitter disappointment that Sean hadn't been able to wave a magic wand and come up with a solution that she had somehow overlooked. "To force a confession, we need a weapon, a threat. We don't have one."

"Sure we do," Sean said. "We have a real powerful weapon, and you were the person who suggested it, at least indirectly. Blackmail."

"Blackmail?" Maggie frowned. After all that the archbishop had done, she had no moral objections to the idea, but she couldn't imagine the man she knew succumbing to threats unless those threats came packed with mighty sharp teeth. "I don't see how we'd make blackmail work. No matter what we threaten to reveal, the archbishop will just ignore us. You were the one who pointed out that if we go to the media with my story, we'll simply be considered lunatics with a grudge."

"We'd have to play it just right, but I think—with careful timing—we can blackmail him into doing something stupid."

"How stupid? Stupid enough to get him into real trouble?"

Sean nodded. "I think so. We've decided that Grunewald's ambitious, right? After all, isn't that the reason he killed your mother? So she wouldn't reveal their affair and screw up his appointment as bishop of Pueblo?"

"Yes, but I don't see—"

"Wait. You will. First he was bishop of a small diocese. Then he was promoted to bishop of a bigger, more important diocese. Now he's climbed all the way up to archbishop. But archbishop still isn't the top of the ladder. Cardinals are the top men on the totem pole. And a couple of articles in your collection suggest that Grunewald is considered by insiders to be a shoo-in for appointment as a cardinal sometime very soon. I'm not very religious, but from what I remember, getting to be a cardinal is a really big deal."

"It's a huge deal," Maggie agreed. "Cardinals are chosen by the pope to serve as his advisers, which means that they're the governing body for the Catholic Church throughout the world. In the old days, they used to be called princes of the church and lots of them were richer and far more powerful than real princes, or even kings."

"Sounds to me like getting appointed cardinal would be real power trip for our friend the archbishop and something he probably wants *real* bad. But, fortunately for us and unfortunately for him, I'm guessing that the pope doesn't appoint cardinals who are embroiled in the thick of a media scandal."

It would be great to think that she could derail the archbishop's ambitions even if it was less than the total humiliation Maggie would have liked him to suffer. But was it possible? Too tense to sit still, she got up from the table and paced across the threadbare, mud brown carpet. "If I go to a regular newspaper or TV network with my story, they're going to hand me straight over to the police and they may not even print my accusations against the archbishop. What if I went to the tabloids? They're always willing to bend the rules and they might actually print what I tell them before they turn me in to the cops."

"But what good does it do us if the *National Reporter* or a similar junk tabloid prints your accusations? The story will probably appear right next to a headline that claims Elvis and Bigfoot are jointly running a Boy Scout camp in California. And the likely consequence of that sort of garbage is that the church bigwigs will be more sympathetic to the archbishop, not less."

"Then what can we do? If we can't go to the tabloids, there's nothing—"

"Yes, there is." Sean got up and joined her in pacing.

"You don't want to take your story to the media. The opposite, in fact. You need to keep your information top secret. This is one of those situations where keeping a secret gives you more power than revealing it, and the threat of taking action is a whole lot more powerful than actually doing it."

Maggie asked doubtfully, "You mean we have to threaten Grunewald with exposure and make him nervous enough that eventually he overreacts and incriminates himself?"

"Exactly." Sean shot her an approving glance. "The fear that something bad will happen is often far more nerve-racking than the actual event. We have to build up a blackmail campaign that will set the archbishop so much on edge that he reacts impulsively. The buildup of tension is the key. It's important to start out with some threat that's kind of tame—"

"We could send him a note that nobody else would understand, but one he'd recognize right away as a threat."

"Yes, that's it." Sean grabbed his mug as he passed by the table and gulped down the cold dregs of his coffee. "We need some mild message like… I don't know. Help me out here."

"How about asking him if he remembers Rowena Slade?" Maggie suggested, beginning to absorb just a little of Sean's confidence that the archbishop could be made vulnerable.

"Perfect." He grinned in approval. "We should slip the note to him in a public place so he'll read it while people are watching him, thinking it's a regular message, and then he has to cover up and carry on as if nothing's happened. We could follow up a day later with something more specific."

Excitement bloomed inside Maggie. "How's this? 'I know all about your affair with Rowena Slade.'"

"That's good, and we mustn't let him know the note comes from you. It's the not knowing that'll drive him crazy. He'll be wondering who's making the threats. Wondering how he can neutralize the danger when he doesn't know who's behind it."

Ideas were tumbling through Maggie's head at such lightning speed that she could scarcely sort them out. "If we're really going to scare him, we need to make the threats more concrete. We know we have no proof of anything we're saying, but the archbishop doesn't. Instead of just writing 'I know about your affair with Rowena Slade,' we could add a sentence that says 'I have her diary and her letters.'"

"Yes!" Sean punched his clenched fist into the air. "That should give the ol' bishop a sleepless night or two."

For a moment, Maggie felt almost euphoric. Then she calmed down a little. "The trouble is at a certain point he's going to realize that our threats are toothless. He's worried, he's anxious, but he ignores us—and then what do we do?"

"Then we come in with the real hard-core blackmail," Sean said. "We send him a note demanding money in exchange for our silence."

The last of Maggie's euphoria vanished at the speed of light. "That's extortion," she said. "Sean, if this doesn't work out, you could go to jail. I can't let you be involved in this."

"We already had this conversation," he said. "And I pointed out that it isn't your choice. It's mine."

She'd allowed herself to be persuaded once, but she wasn't going to ignore her conscience a second time. "You're wrong," she said quietly. "This is my problem, not yours, and I have the right to decide how to solve it. I appreciate your help and advice, you've given me some insights to work with that I'd never have come up with on my own, and I'm deeply grateful. But you have no reason to put your entire life on the line for a scheme that has only a slim chance of success."

"I'm not putting my life on the line for a scheme. I'm planning to put it on the line for you."

Maggie's heart seemed to stop beating before rushing on again twice as fast as normal. "Sean, please don't tempt me. I'm struggling to do what's right...."

He wasn't listening, she could tell. His gaze was fixed on her mouth, his expression a mixture of tenderness and wry amusement. "You know what your problem is, Maggie? For an escaped felon, you have an infuriatingly delicate conscience."

"Don't change the subject."

"I'm not. Did I happen to mention last night that I believe I've fallen in love with you?"

Maggie's mouth opened, then shut again without any sound emerging.

"Apparently not," Sean said.

It had been so long since Maggie had allowed herself even to think about falling in love that she had no parameters for handling the concept. She could only stare at Sean in a blank, stupefied bewilderment, wondering how she was supposed to respond to a statement that was so far outside her experience that he might as well have told her that he was an alien from a distant galaxy and that she could beam aboard his spaceship any time she wanted.

Love. She tried to work out what it might mean if Sean really loved her. She let the word roll around inside her head, but that scared her and she quickly stopped. Love, she realized, was an emotion packed with terrifying power, and whenever she'd loved anyone in the past, the result had been agonizing pain.

Sean gave her a rueful grin and squished the end of her nose with his finger. "Don't look so stunned, Maggie. Does it make you any more willing to accept my help now you know that I'm in love with you?"

She finally recovered her voice. "No," she croaked. "It simply convinces me you're crazy."

"Then you'll have to take care of me," Sean said promptly.

Maggie drew in a long, unsteady breath. "You're right. Since you're not capable of making sensible decisions, I'll have to make them for you. Go home. That's an order."

He bent his head slowly toward her mouth. "That's the trouble with us crazy people," he said, kissing her. "We can't understand simple English."

"Sean... Help me, please. Let me do the right thing for once in my life."

He stepped back from her, his expression suddenly

sober. "The right thing is for you to accept my help. It's freely offered, with no payback required. Don't keep fighting me on this, because I won't let you win."

She was torn between gratitude and fear. Gratitude because when Sean was making plans, she had moments when she thought they might actually manage to bring the archbishop to justice. Fear because she realized that her chances of getting Sean through this escapade without a jail sentence were close to zero. And if she was sent back to prison knowing that she'd condemned Sean to the same fate, she wasn't sure she'd be able to survive.

But he was already walking away as if the matter was settled and no longer worthy of discussion. "I'm going to buy a couple of newspapers," he said. "I'll pick up some bagels for breakfast and be right back."

She didn't ask why he wanted the newspapers. She knew. He needed them for the anonymous letters they were going to write to Archbishop Grunewald. She hoped he'd remember to buy rubber gloves while he was out. They didn't want to leave fingerprints.

God forgive her, she was going to accept Sean's help.

Thirteen

Maggie forced herself to concentrate on taking an order from the customers seated at table five. It was almost two in the afternoon, and she was anxious to get home so that she could devote a hundred percent of her attention to obsessing about Sean's upcoming attempt to pass the first blackmail note to the archbishop. They'd spent yesterday evening searching through local newspapers and they'd discovered that tonight the archbishop was scheduled to deliver the keynote speech at a ceremony honoring Ohio's parochial school Teacher of the Year. Maggie felt sick with mingled excitement and fear every time she visualized Sean slipping their note into the archbishop's hands. After years of waiting patiently to exact even the most minor revenge, things were suddenly moving too fast for comfort.

The two couples she was waiting on had taken five minutes to decide what they wanted to drink. It looked like they were going to take twice that long to select their food. "What about the guacamole burger?" one of the men asked. He'd complained about everything from the moment he walked into the Buckeye, and now he was scowling at the menu like Godzilla with an attack of hemorrhoids. "Does your chef know how to cook a burger and do it right?"

Did he think she was going to tell them their cooks were incompetent and the burgers were lousy? Maggie pasted on a smile. "The guacamole burger is one of our most popular items," she said. "We serve that with French fries, and our chef's special garnish of red onion, tomato and green peppers. It's a touch spicy, but not really hot."

The man grunted as if she'd just confirmed his worst suspicions. Maggie resisted the urge to upend a glass of ice water over his head and took orders for shrimp salad from the two women and a tuna melt on rye from the other man. "Maybe you'd like a few extra minutes to make your selection," she said, giving Godzilla another bright smile. "I'll get your beverage orders and be right back."

Dorothy came out of her office and into the main body of the restaurant just as Maggie arrived at the soda machine. Maggie gave her boss what she hoped was a carefree wave and pretended to be busy pouring drinks. So far, Dorothy hadn't mentioned Sean or what had happened in St. Anthony's parking lot on Sunday, but Maggie had an uneasy feeling that it was just a matter of time. With any other boss, she'd have quit her job in a heartbeat and avoided the problem of too much interest in her personal affairs. With Dorothy, she was afraid that quitting would only make the problem worse. Dorothy was smart enough to have scented a mystery in Maggie's life and kindhearted enough to be determined to solve it, possibly even to the extent of filing a missing persons report with the police if "Christine" disappeared.

Maggie's sense of foreboding seemed justified when her boss came up to her. "I need to talk with you before you go home," Dorothy said. "Come to my office when you're finished with table five, will you?"

Maggie saw no way to refuse. If she claimed that she needed to get home without delay, Dorothy would conclude that Sean was acting the tyrant. Insisting that Sean wasn't her ex-husband wouldn't help with the basic problem, which was that Dorothy had seen Sean strong-arming Maggie with her own eyes, and there was no way for Maggie to explain that, in this case, appearances were totally deceiving.

Maggie tried to sound cheerful as she accepted the inevitable. "Sure, Dorothy, I'll be there as soon as I'm through with cleanup. Oops, my customers are signaling to me. I'd better go. That guy sitting by the window has been complaining about every darn thing since the moment he walked in."

It was after three by the time Maggie had cleaned off table five, pocketed Godzilla's one-dollar tip and collected her purse from her locker. Sighing, she knocked on Dorothy's office door. In normal circumstances, she'd have appreciated her boss's concern for her welfare, but the circumstances weren't normal, and right now, Dorothy's concern was causing nothing but trouble.

"Hi, Christine, I need your help," Dorothy said as soon as she entered the office. "The Women's Crisis Center is holding its annual meeting on Saturday morning at ten, and I've volunteered to cater brunch for everyone before we get started with the business sessions. I can handle the food preparation myself, no problem. But Jan usually serves for me and she has to go to her daughter's gymnastics contest that day, so she isn't available. Would you be able to help out? I'm not asking you to donate your time. I pay servers twelve bucks an hour for events like this since there won't be any tips."

Dorothy was trying to find yet another subtle way to introduce "Christine" to the help she supposedly needed, Maggie realized, feeling a surge of reluctant affection for her boss. She wished with sudden fervor that she could stop lying and tell her boss the simple truth. Except, of course, that the truth wasn't simple and she had no right to involve Dorothy in her affairs.

It was all very confusing, and Maggie wasn't used to feeling confused. In fact, she wasn't used to feeling at all, but over the past twenty-four hours she'd been deluged with unfamiliar sensations. When Sean had made love to her, it seemed as if he'd thrown the defrost switch on the freezer where she stored her emotions. Now she was floundering in a puddle of emotions that were too soggy to identify, but too powerful to ignore.

Dorothy tapped her pencil on the desk. "Christine, hello? I'd appreciate an answer before we both take root."

"Sorry," Maggie said hurriedly. "Yes, of course I'd

be happy to help you out, Dorothy. How long do you expect the brunch to last?"

"Not more than three hours, start to finish, including prep and cleanup time. But you're scheduled to work your regular hours here that night, so it'll be a long day for you."

"No big deal. I could use the extra thirty-six bucks and it's a worthy cause."

"Yes, it is, and you'll meet some interesting people. Kathleen Younger will be there. She's planning to run for senator next election and she's surprisingly sane for a politician. Also Moira Povitch. She's the director of the local child welfare association and a real supporter of the Crisis Center. And Archbishop Grunewald is going to try to fit in a visit, and you already know what an inspiring speaker he is."

"Yes, I sure do." Maggie managed to keep all trace of excitement out of her voice. What an unexpected bonus! She'd found out where the archbishop might be on Saturday morning!

"And even if the archbishop can't make it, his sister will be there. She played a real active role in her brother's efforts to establish a new safe house for battered women in the Phoenix area, and she's already volunteered to fill one of the vacancies on our board. She has an impressive résumé, so we're pleased about that."

"The archbishop's sister is here in Columbus?" Maggie said. "I didn't know that."

Dorothy sent her a curious glance. "Why would you?"

"No reason." Maggie discovered, as always, that once she started to react spontaneously, she was doomed to make mistakes. In her research on the archbishop's family background, she'd learned that he was the youngest of three children born to farmers turned small-store owners in South Dakota, and that he had two sisters, both married to doctors in Rapid City. But, of course, families moved all the time so there was no significance to the fact that one of the archbishop's sisters now happened to be here in Ohio. Aware that her boss was looking at her, she brightened her smile. "Anyway, if you'll excuse me, Dorothy, I need to get going. I have a real busy schedule tonight."

"Sure." Dorothy scribbled a note on her calendar. "Okay, I've penciled you in for Saturday. I'll need you around nine-fifteen to help with the brunch setup at the Center. Do you know how to get there?"

Maggie shook her head. "No, I still get lost all the time even though Columbus isn't that big. Can you write me out some directions?"

"Why don't you meet me here at eight forty-five, and I'll drive you? That way you can't get lost."

"That would be great."

"Thanks for helping out, Christine. I really appreciate it."

"You're welcome."

Maggie could hardly wait to get out of the door and back home to tell Sean her news. They couldn't post their blackmail notes to the archbishop since most of his mail was probably opened by a staffer, and the whole point of their scheme was to keep their threats totally private. That decision meant the most difficult part of their planning process so far had been finding out where the archbishop was going to be so they could devise ways to slip him the notes. Now it seemed that she'd been handed one vital snippet of information on a platter.

"Guess what!" She burst into her apartment, feeling an odd constriction in her lungs when she saw Sean sitting on the battered couch, his feet up on the equally battered coffee table, reading a copy of *Newsweek*. She'd never before come home to find a man waiting for her, and the experience was novel enough to stop her in midstride.

"I can't guess." Sean put aside the magazine and patted the sofa cushion. "Come sit next to me and tell me what's so exciting." He smiled at her in a way that did absolutely nothing to improve her breathing problems.

She sat down because she wanted to be close to him, although she could barely sit still for excitement. "I know where the archbishop is going to be on Saturday morning!"

Sean gave her a high five. "Great going, honey. Where?"

"Well, it's not a hundred percent confirmed yet, but he's almost definitely going to attend the annual meeting of the Women's Crisis Center—you know, the safe house for abused women that Dorothy's so interested in. And not only is Dorothy doing the catering, she's asked me to help her serve! So I'll be in the perfect position to slip the archbishop one of our blackmail notes. Isn't that fantastic?"

Sean stared at her. "You're joking, right?"

She pulled away from him, hurt by his reaction. "No, of course I'm not joking. When Dorothy asked me to help out, she hit some of the high notes on the guest list, and the archbishop was one of them. There aren't going to be more than fifty people at the meeting, and if he does show up, I'll be able to walk right up to him—"

"You sure will," Sean said. "And how many seconds do you think it will take Grunewald to recognize you? One? Three? Ten?"

For a few moments, there was total silence in the room. Then the refrigerator motor switched on and its rasping hum broke Maggie's trance. "Oh my God," she whispered. "I must be losing my mind. I completely forgot that he could recognize me."

She felt the blood drain from her head, and Sean pulled he down to rest against his shoulder. "Maggie, don't overreact," he said. "You have a lot on your mind and it's easy to lose track of one of the threads."

"But I can't afford to lose track of anything, let alone something so important."

"No, you can't, but it happens, and that's one of the reasons you need me for backup. I've been a cop for sixteen years, and you'd be surprised how many times we've set up a sting or an undercover operation, and then a detective who hasn't been directly involved points out a hole in our plans that's big enough to drive a squad car through. Just be grateful we caught this particular mistake in time."

Maggie luxuriated in the sensation of being soothed for no more than a couple of seconds before a new problem occurred to her. "We're still in trouble, Sean. I've told Dorothy that I'll help her serve brunch at the Crisis Center. I can't go, obviously, but what excuse am I going to give for not turning up? I don't want to wait until the last minute and call in sick. That wouldn't be fair."

"Call in the day before so Dorothy has time to find a substitute," Sean suggested.

"That's possible, I guess, but I'd prefer to come up with something better. Dorothy's the type to come around with a pot of chicken soup if I tell her I have a cold."

Sean glanced down at his watch, then kissed her on the end of her nose. "See if you can come up with a better excuse while I'm gone," he said. "I'm off to Holy Innocents High School to deliver our first blackmail note to the archbishop."

"You got a ticket for the award ceremony tonight?" Maggie breathed. "How did you manage that?"

"Brilliant, insightful detective work. What else?"

She was beginning to realize when he was teasing her. "Hah! Let me guess. They're handing out tickets at the door to anyone who wants one."

He grinned. "It's not even that tough. I found out that you don't need a ticket except for the reception after the ceremony. So, I'm off. See you later, babe."

"Wait!" Maggie grabbed his hand. "Did you remember a glove so you won't leave prints on the envelope?"

Sean reached into his hip pocket and produced a neatly rolled, disposable latex glove. "It's the same type we used yesterday. Surgical quality, already dusted with talcum powder for easy fit."

Without speaking, Maggie watched him return the glove to his pocket. His imminent departure to the award ceremony invested their blackmail plan with a reality it had previously lacked. Yesterday morning, she'd been almost lighthearted as the two of them created a series of blackmail notes by cutting and pasting words and letters onto sheets of untraceable white bond computer paper. Perhaps she'd deliberately blocked the significance of what they were doing from her mind. Or perhaps she'd been genuinely oblivious because, in many ways, piecing together the blackmail notes hadn't felt all that different from the hundreds of other hours she'd wasted over the years, sitting around in the privacy of her apartment and fantasizing about revenge.

Creating the blackmail notes hadn't been criminal, only potentially criminal. But now they were moving on to a new level of danger. The instant Sean put one of those anonymous notes into the archbishop's hands, there would be no turning back.

Her lips were so dry she needed to lick them before she could speak. "I should be the one to hand over the note, Sean, not you. I can't let you put yourself at risk." They'd been over that ground so many times already that he didn't even bother to respond. Wrapping her arms around her waist in a vain attempt to stop her stomach from swooping up and down, she abandoned that concern for another. "Just going to the award ceremony isn't going to be enough. If you can't wheedle a ticket to get into the reception, how are you going to get close enough to Grunewald to hand over the note?"

"I don't know yet." He took her hands and pulled he closer so that he could hug her. "Don't worry, Maggie. I've worked under cover a lot and I'm damn good at improvising."

She felt another surge of strong emotion that she couldn't name, although she knew that fear for Sean's safety was a major component. "We're rushing too much, Sean. Let's give ourselves time to think this through. We don't need to hand over the first note tonight."

"Yes, we do, honey. This has already dragged on fifteen years too long."

Maggie realized it had been a lot easier to hate the archbishop at a distance—to hate him and not do anything about it. "Promise me you won't try to hand over the note unless you're sure you won't be caught."

He tilted her head up and kissed her swiftly on the mouth. "I promise," he said.

Looking around the crowded auditorium, Sean decided that unless he figured out some way to make a move real soon, he would have no problem keeping his promise to Maggie. It looked as if he wasn't going to get within a hundred feet of his target. The archbishop and his entourage had entered the auditorium by a side door that led directly onto the stage and it was highly likely that he would leave by the same route.

In addition to the teacher of the year, five other educators were being honored for various acts of dedication, and the congratulatory speeches droned on endlessly. Only the archbishop managed to be both witty and succinct as he handed over each plaque and statue. Sean repeatedly found himself starting to laugh at one of the archbishop's jokes, and if he hadn't known better, he would have sworn that Archbishop Grunewald was sincere in his heartfelt praise for the teachers who were creating a better future for everyone because of their devoted care for their students.

Sean began to feel more and more uncomfortable each time the archbishop spoke. After Grunewald made an especially moving presentation to an elderly teacher who seemed to have achieved miracles working with children previously considered unteachable, he realized what was bothering him. He was beginning to question the man's guilt.

Grunewald seemed so totally sincere, so warm in his praise for others, so unaware of his own achievements. Could Maggie be mistaken in her identification of him as the one who killed her mother? Sean wondered. Everything the archbishop said suggested he was a man with an exceptionally generous spirit. His words breathed compassion and humility. It was literally sickening to believe that this appearance of goodness was no more than a cynical facade, hiding a soul that was tainted to its core.

Sean joined in a thunderous round of applause as the teacher of the year walked up onto the stage to accept her award. Doubting Maggie's identification of Grunewald didn't mean that he was questioning her innocence, Sean reflected. He believed with every fiber of his being that Maggie had been wrongfully found guilty of her mother's murder. He was also convinced that she was a hundred percent sincere in her identification of Tobias Grunewald as the man she'd seen making love to her mother.

But the detective in him demanded—belatedly—that he should consider the possibility that Maggie and the archbishop might both be innocent: Maggie wrongly condemned by the state, Grunewald wrongly condemned by Maggie. In fact, when he thought about it with his head instead of his gut, Sean realized there was a major flaw in Maggie's story. If Grunewald had been Rowena Slade's lover, why hadn't Maggie immediately recognized him the night she came home early from the mountains and discovered them making love on the living-room sofa? Father Tobias had been her parish priest for almost a year before Rowena Slade was killed, and although Maggie didn't like to go to church, she'd accompanied her mother often enough that she must have watched the priest say mass at least a dozen times. Even if she'd goofed off with her friends after services and hadn't stopped to shake his hand or chat, why hadn't she recognized him when she caught him lying naked in her mother's arms? Why did it take her almost two years before recognition clicked in?

Maggie's answer, of course, would be that recognition had only dawned when she'd seen the archbishop's profile silhouetted twice in virtually identical conditions—once when he was making love to her mother, and the second time when he visited her in prison. As for why she hadn't recognized Father Tobias when she found him with Rowena, Maggie would probably claim that the idea of her mother being sexually involved with their parish priest was so far outside the boundaries of her experience that she simply couldn't make the mental connection.

And those were both valid points, Sean acknowledged. But in his desire to exonerate Maggie, he hadn't stopped to work out that her innocence didn't prove Grunewald's guilt. It was perfectly possible to imagine that some other man, not Grunewald, had been Rowena's lover and murderer. Maggie herself had originally believed that her mother's lover was a neighbor who lived in the Pineview subdivision and walked to Rowena's house at night under cover of darkness. There was no mystery as to why this neighborhood lover would have needed to keep his visits secret. He was a married man. Maggie had worked that one out for herself when she was only fifteen. As for this neighbor's motive for murder…well, that wasn't difficult to fathom. He either had a rich wife or a bitchy wife who threatened to take the kids if he divorced her. And when Rowena threatened to tell the world about their affair, the neighbor lost his temper and killed her. Police files were full to overflowing with murders that had been committed for no better reason.

When you got right down to brass tacks, Maggie's identification of the archbishop was the only piece of firm evidence tying him to the crime, and she could easily be wrong. Losing both her parents to violent deaths within the space of twenty-three months and then being wrongly convicted of killing your own mother could twist the mind and memories of even a woman as strong as Maggie.

Dismayed by the trend of his thoughts, Sean began to feel oppressed by the stuffy heat of the auditorium. He was seated in the back at the end of a row, which made it fairly easy for him to slip out of the auditorium into the hallway and make his way outside to the parking lot. The blackmail note he and Maggie had prepared seemed to be burning a hole in his pocket and he paced the lot, trying to decide what the hell he was going to do.

The sounds of a choir singing "Ave Maria" drifted through the closed doors, poignantly beautiful. Halfway through the hymn, Sean felt a weight lift from his shoulders and he realized that he was worrying needlessly. He could deliver the blackmail notes to Grunewald with a clear conscience. If the archbishop was innocent, if he'd never been Rowena Slade's lover, if he'd never committed a brutal murder and allowed a fifteen-year-old orphan to pay for his crime, then he would read the blackmail notes and feel only bewilderment. His most likely reaction would be to ignore them.

The first blackmail note, the one in Sean's pocket, was especially innocuous. It simply asked, "Remember Rowena Slade?" If Maggie had made a terrible mistake and the archbishop wasn't the monster she imagined, then that question would cause him no more than a moment's sadness as he remembered a long-ago parishioner and a young girl in prison who hadn't shown appropriate gratitude for the helping hand he'd extended her. Even if Grunewald was guilty, a note this vague might produce no visible reaction. But by the time they found a way to hand over the third note, demanding a meeting and a payoff, it should be easier to judge the archbishop's guilt or innocence. An innocent man would surely turn the note over to the police. A guilty man was far more likely to keep quiet and come to the meeting.

The choir was almost finished with "Ave Maria." Sean acted before he could second-guess himself again. He went back into the school, cut through the auditorium and came out into the corridor just as the archbishop and the other dignitaries exited the stage to a final round of applause. In the corridor, there were at least a dozen people milling around the archbishop and another dozen trying to congratulate the teacher of the year. The people in the archbishop's group clearly didn't know the people congratulating the teacher, or vice versa. To add to the confusion, a couple of journalists were asking questions, and a large woman wearing a corsage of pink carnations kept trying unsuccessfully to shepherd her flock of VIPs in the direction of the faculty lounge.

He was never going to have a better moment than this, Sean decided. Shrinking into the shadows, he stuck on a pair of oversize glasses that covered the top half of his face and shoved two wads of cotton into his cheeks, making his face appear round and puffy. Not much of a disguise, but enough to give him momentary protection. Walking briskly toward the cluster of people gathered around the archbishop, he pulled on the plastic glove and removed the blackmail note from the breast pocket of his shirt.

In honor of the ceremonial nature of the occasion, Archbishop Grunewald was wearing a purple cassock, with the traditional fringed sash tied around his waist. As the archbishop reached out to shake the hand of a well-wisher, Sean slipped behind him and tucked the single folded sheet of paper between his cassock and his sash.

Leaning close, he spoke tersely, in a harsh monotone. "Special delivery for you, Father Toby." He melted back, edging swiftly into the crowd of people clustered around the teacher of the year, aware from years of investigative work that he would be far less readily noticed if he didn't try to run away.

The archbishop spun around quickly, but not quickly enough to spot Sean. He pulled the note out of his sash, opened the single fold and read the three-word message. For a split second, he went utterly still. Then he crumpled the note and made to throw it away. At the last moment, he changed his mind and unobtrusively pushed the note into a concealed pocket in the side of his cassock. His face, normally so expressive, had not betrayed a hint of emotion. Not surprise, not puzzlement. Nothing. But Sean noticed that he looked immediately toward the door to see if he could spot anyone running away.

Even though they'd all seen him read the note, nobody in the archbishop's entourage seemed to realize that anything was wrong, but Sean was shocked by the completeness of Grunewald's self-betrayal. An innocent man would never have reacted with such revealing self-control. An innocent man would have shown the note to the priest standing next to him and asked if anyone had noticed who had given it to him. Only a man with a lot to hide would have hidden the note and spoken not a word about it.

The woman with the pink carnations was becoming more determined in her efforts to get everyone into the faculty lounge, where, she promised them, chilled fruit punch, coffee and delicious home-baked brownies were waiting for them. The archbishop expressed delight, and once he started to move, the rest of the crowd followed.

Sean ducked backward into the auditorium, which was rapidly emptying. He wasn't sure to feel elated or depressed. It was certainly a relief to know that he and Maggie were on the right track. On the other hand, it was depressing to know that the archbishop was a first-class fraud rather than the wonderful man he appeared to be.

If total silence could ever count as a confession, Sean would say that tonight, Archbishop Grunewald had just confessed to murder.

Fourteen

Maggie bounded up the stairs to her apartment, full of energy even though she'd just worked a hectic five-hour lunch shift. For the second time in two days, she burst into the apartment on a wave of enthusiasm.

"We're saved!" she exclaimed, beaming from ear to ear. "Dorothy is totally bummed and I'm ecstatic. Archbishop Grunewald has sent word that he can't come to the annual meeting at the Crisis Center on Saturday. It's definite. He's sending his sister instead, so I can serve at the brunch, no problem. Whew, what a relief!"

"That's great, honey." Sean closed the fridge door with his elbow and held up two frosted cans of soda. "That calls for a double celebration because, while you were at work, I just passed the archbishop our second note."

"Terrific!" Maggie flung her arms around Sean and kissed him. "What a man! How did you manage that?"

He handed her a soda. "It was surprisingly easy, in fact."

She walked over to the sofa, rubbing the chilled can over her forehead before popping the tab. Columbus was experiencing an early heat wave, and her apartment was hot since the air-conditioning unit in her apartment was more noisy than functional. "I get *real* worried when you claim something was easy. How come it was so easy? When I left home this morning, we had no idea where Grunewald was going to be today."

Sean hesitated. Maggie, who was getting to be quite good at interpreting his silences, realized he was debating whether or not to tell her the truth. She put down her soda and glared at him. "Don't you dare lie to me," she said fiercely. "What did you do that was so risky you're afraid to tell me about it?"

"I had a meeting with the archbishop," Sean said. "In his offices at the cathedral."

"A *meeting?*" Maggie screeched, jumping to her feet. "As in face-to-face, pleased to meet you, I'm Sean McLeod?"

"Well, face-to-face and pleased to meet you, but I didn't introduce myself as Sean McLeod. I gave a false name. Grunewald thinks I'm a private investigator."

"Are you nuts? Have you gone totally and completely wacko?" In the circumstances, Maggie was quite impressed that she was merely screeching as opposed to developing immediate, full-blown hysterics.

"Maggie, the meeting was already set up before I ever left Florida."

"Oh well, excuse me, I guess that makes everything just fine and dandy!" She stormed up and down the room. "Besides, how could it have been all set up? Why would have arranged an interview with the archbishop under a phony name before you even left Florida?"

Sean spoke quietly. "Because I'd already decided that I wasn't going to turn you in to the authorities without hearing your side of the story. And that meant I couldn't tell the archbishop my real name or occupation because it would have compromised my freedom."

Maggie spun around to look at him. "You'd already decided that I might be innocent before you left Florida?"

"Why are you sounding surprised? If I'd been convinced you were guilty, I'd have arrived here with a squad of federal marshals in tow. You know that." Sean took her hands and held them so that she was forced to stop pacing and look at him. "Remember when I caught up with you at St. Anthony's and you asked how I'd managed to find you so quickly?"

"Yes." Maggie scowled at him as they sat down. It was infuriating how completely Sean had disarmed her just by saying that he'd believed she was innocent before he left Florida. It wasn't *safe* for her to care this much about somebody else's opinion of her. "You explained that you'd found my file on the archbishop and you played a hunch that I was coming to Ohio to see him."

"If you remember that, you should also remember that I told you the archbishop had agreed to meet with me."

"But I never expected you to keep the appointment," Maggie protested. "Not when we're actively plotting to coerce the man into making a confession, for heaven's sake!" She leaned back against the lumpy sofa cushions, then shot up again, too tense to sit still. "Good grief, Sean, what did you say to him? Come to that, what excuse did you give that persuaded him to meet with you in the first place?"

"When I requested the interview, I was expecting to ask for the archbishop's help in tracking *you* down. Of course, I had to change my story to fit our new circumstances, but that wasn't difficult."

"Oh, no, I'm sure it was a breeze," Maggie said sarcastically.

"Pretty much." He actually had the audacity to grin. "After we exchanged a few pleasantries about scuba diving in the Florida Keys, I told the archbishop that I'd been hired a couple of months ago by a young woman called Mary Karakas who wanted me to collect a complete dossier of information on him. I pretended that I'd agreed—there's nothing illegal about collecting published information—but I told Grunewald that I'd become nervous about the mental stability of my client—"

"Somebody around here is mentally unstable, that's for sure," Maggie muttered.

"Honey, you're overreacting. It was a good cover story. I explained to the archbishop that my client had disappeared from Florida and I had reason to believe she intended to come to Ohio and stalk him. I warned him to take the threat seriously and also gave him a detailed description of you—"

"Have you totally lost it?" Maggie was back to screeching again. "Great going, hotshot, that's two for one. Now the archbishop not only knows what *you* look

like, but he's also been warned that a woman who looks just like Maggie Slade has flipped and is out to get him."

"But it's all for the good if he suspects that you're on his tail, especially if he thinks you're mentally unstable. As for recognizing me, the archbishop has no idea what I really look like." Sean got up and went into the bathroom. He emerged ten seconds later with a shaggy blond wig perched on top of his head a mustache stuck crookedly over his top lip. "I wore a disguise."

He looked so completely ridiculous that Maggie's anger dissolved into reluctant laughter, but her fear remained. "Sean, you're trying to make light of this, but I don't understand what you've accomplished except to make things more difficult for us. Why do we want him to suspect that I'm on his tail—and probably unstable?"

"It increases the menace of the notes we're passing to him," Sean said, tossing the wig and mustache onto the coffee table. "You were always the most likely person to have written them, so we're not really giving much away by dropping another clue that you're in Ohio. But now, in addition to worrying about you, Grunewald has to worry about my role in all of this. Who am I? What do I know? What am I hoping to achieve? Am I a co-conspirator, or have you tricked me in some way?"

Sean was right, Maggie acknowledged silently. By meeting with the archbishop, he'd diffused the focus of Grunewald's attention. Unfortunately, he'd also increased his own exposure to a dangerous level. If their scheme to incriminate the archbishop failed, Sean was going to fall hard and deep—right into a prison cell.

But there was nothing to be gained by pointing that out to him yet again. He was a cop, she was a convict, and they both knew precisely what dangers they were facing at the hands of the law. She tacitly acknowledged the validity of his arguments by changing the subject. "Where did you put the second blackmail note?"

Sean took a swig of soda. "I slipped the note into Grunewald's in-tray when his attention was distracted. I left it sticking out so he'd be sure to notice it."

Maggie swallowed a gasp. "How can the archbishop avoid putting two and two together and concluding that you're the person who passed him the note?"

Sean looked momentarily grim. "I don't think he can."

Maggie's fear was so acute she expressed it as anger. "My God, Sean, suppose he'd seen you hiding the note? He'd have called the police on the spot! You had no right to take such a big risk."

"I disagree. Anyway, he didn't catch me passing the note, so we don't need to worry about what might have happened. All the archbishop knows is that a private investigator from Florida came to his office this morning and told him a story about a crazy client who looks like Maggie Slade. And then the archbishop found another blackmail note on his desk. So what? The man who came visiting was called Scott Schmidt, and he was blond with a mustache. Even if the archbishop tries to track me down, he'll get precisely nowhere."

"What about fingerprints? You can't have worn gloves—"

"I wrapped the note in a tissue. I didn't leave prints." Sean gripped her shoulders, twisting her toward him. "Maggie, the archbishop is a sophisticated man, accustomed to operating in the public arena under quite a bit of media scrutiny. He's not going to crack just because he receives a couple of mildly worrying anonymous letters. He's got to feel threatened at the deepest levels, so that when we pass him our final note, he'll come to the meeting ready to make the payoff or at least ready to bargain for your silence. Getting him to say something incriminating on tape is the only way we're going to persuade the D.A.'s office that he might be guilty."

"I agree he isn't going to be easy to break—"

"Look, in my judgment, it was worth taking a calculated risk this morning to show the archbishop that he's vulnerable, that we can get to him even in the sanctuary of his own office." Sean drew in a ragged breath. "I should have told you what I was planning, but I knew you'd try to stop me and I couldn't afford to waste time arguing with you. We're operating under intense time pressure, Maggie. Have you forgotten that I have to report back to work in Denver less than two weeks from today?"

"No, I hadn't forgotten." Maggie picked up their empty soda cans and carried them into the kitchen as an excuse for moving.

Sean wasn't deceived. He followed her into the kitchen and refused to let her fuss with tidying as a ploy to avoid his scrutiny. "Maggie, when I go back to Denver, I want you to come with me. You know that, don't you?"

She tried to imagine going back to Colorado with Sean as a free woman and couldn't. For fifteen years, she'd survived by living only for the day at hand, drawing what pleasure that she could from passing moments. Even though Sean had increased her happiness quotient by a thousand percent, even though it made her almost unbearably sad to imagine parting from him, she'd lost the ability to visualize a future where she wouldn't wake up each morning with a knot of fear in her stomach in case this was the day when she'd end up back in jail. The past cast a shadow that blacked out her future.

"I can't think about what might happen if we ever manage to prove Archbishop Grunewald is guilty," she said finally. "The truth is, even the wildest flights of my imagination just come to a dead stop at that point."

"We'll have to work on that," he said, cradling her head against his chest and caressing her gently on the cheek. "In the meantime, why don't we forget about the archbishop for the rest of the day and go to the movies? I think Bruce Willis is saving Dallas at the local multiplex. Does that appeal to you?"

"Sounds like a great idea," she said. "I love Bruce Willis."

Sean sent her a glance full of wry humor. "Lucky man," he said.

Despite the fact that Maggie kept expecting disaster to strike as a result of Sean's encounter with the archbishop, the most nerve-racking event during the next few days was her realization of how dependent she'd become on Sean's company. The first few nights they had slept together, she'd woken up clinging to the edge of the bed as if some barrier in her subconscious compelled her to preserve her sense of space and privacy even during sleep. But for the past two mornings, she'd woken up to find her legs tangled with Sean's and her hand resting with casual intimacy on his thigh. Her subconscious, it seemed, had already abandoned the pretense of not needing him and was waiting patiently for her waking mind to acknowledge the truth.

But Maggie wasn't yet ready to admit to full-blown dependency. The most she would concede was that she'd grown accustomed to seeing Sean on the other side of the rickety table, and that she looked forward to coming home in the afternoon and sharing the day's gossip with him over a glass of iced tea or a can of soda.

As for the nights, Maggie had no frame of reference in which to put what happened to her each night when she and Sean made love. Sean had shown her a whole new world of sensual pleasure, a pleasure so intense that she would sometimes find herself holding her breath when she looked at him or trembling when he touched her because the memories she was conjuring up were so erotic. She told herself that if you didn't discover sex until you were older, it wasn't surprising if it hit you with the force of a two-by-four applied straight to the skull. If what happened in bed with Sean was just sex, she didn't have to worry. People could live without sex if they had to. She tried to consider the possibility that it wasn't sex that she'd discovered with Sean, but something a lot more frightening. Like maybe love.

"You're lookin' real dreamy-eyed this morning," Dorothy said, reversing her minivan out of the Buckeye Brewery parking lot where Maggie had met up with her. "I guess that man of yours is treatin' you all right, at least for now."

"He's treating me fine," Maggie said. "He's a good man, Dorothy, a real friend."

Her boss jabbed her finger into the steering wheel, setting her armful of bracelets jangling. "Don't you take any nonsense from him, Christine. That's the secret to trainin' a man so he's housebroken and fit to live with. When he steps out of line, you stomp on his foot real hard and slap him back between the traces quick as you can get him there."

Maggie laughed. "I'll be sure to remember your advice. It sounds very wise."

"Based on hard experience. It took me three attempts before I got it right. Pay attention to me, and you might make it work in two."

"Trust me, I'm listening to every word."

"Don't just listen, kid. Act. Now, about this morning's brunch." Dorothy was suddenly all business. "I kept it simple. I've got fresh fruit all prepared and cut up. We just have to set it out on platters. Then I've got individual containers of yogurt and plenty of muffins and Danish pastries. Orange juice, of course, and I brought a gallon of skim milk for the health-nut crowd. We can ice that and serve it in jugs. First thing you need to do once we've carried in the supplies is set the coffee going. They have two forty-cup percolators at the Center, and we'll need them both."

"Eighty cups in total. That should be enough, although people tend to drink more coffee in the morning. What was the final number count? Yesterday you said forty-five."

"It's still forty-five," Dorothy said. "Not counting Archbishop Grunewald, but counting his sister."

Maggie's heart felt as if it slammed against the wall of her chest. "Why would we even consider counting the archbishop?" she asked. "You told me a couple of days ago that he definitely wasn't coming."

"I know, but we got lucky and he changed his mind. He called the president last night and said he's real interested in the work of the Center, so he's goin' to squeeze us in, but he doesn't expect to arrive in time to eat. Nobody thought to ask whether his sister's still coming at ten or whether she'll miss the brunch, too. Not that one or two extra people make all that much difference one way or the other."

Maggie stared blindly ahead. "Did he give you any idea of when he might arrive?"

"Ten-thirty or so, which would be just in time for the start of the business meeting. We're all delighted. If he decides we're doing good work and recommends us to Catholic Charities, we could get a real boost to next year's operating budget. Who knows, we might even be able to repaint the lounge or buy a few new picture books for the kids. What a dream, huh?"

Maggie tried to get her panic under control. It was amazing how even a few days of Sean's company had taken the edge off her self-protective skills. Instead of reacting with adrenaline-induced sharpness, her wits felt slow and sluggish.

The archbishop was coming to the Center. What was she going to do? Short of throwing herself out of the van, she had to go with Dorothy as far as the Center, that much was clear. She glanced at her watch. Five minutes past nine. Was it safe to assume he wouldn't be there until ten-thirty? No. Maggie shook her head. The risk was too great; she couldn't assume anything except the worst.

So, assume Grunewald might arrive as early as ten o'clock, the official starting time for the brunch. That gave her a maximum of forty minutes at the Center before she needed to be out of there. She could help Dorothy carry the food and equipment from the van into the Center, then she would have to stage an accident to give herself an excuse to leave.

But what sort of an accident? Something that required immediate medical attention, obviously. Not a burn—that was easy to stage but impossible to fake, and she didn't want to be hospitalized with a genuine injury. What about a broken ankle, arm, wrist? It was doubtful that she could fake any of them well enough to deceive Dorothy and the other board members. In an organization dedicated to helping women who'd been physically abused, she had to assume there would be plenty of people milling around who could tell when bones were broken and when they weren't. How about a fainting spell? That wasn't much easier to fake than a broken bone. She'd seen women in prison try to pull that stunt, and it was damned hard. People who were genuinely fainting turned white. If you were acting and therefore nervous, you were more likely to flush than turn pale.

She was still wrestling with the problem when they arrived at the unmarked doors of the Women's Crisis Center. Normally, Maggie would have been interested in seeing the facilities of the Center, but this morning it was taking every ounce of willpower she possessed just to carry on a coherent conversation and respond to Dorothy's directions about where to take equipment and supplies. In jail, she'd met plenty of women whose lives had been one long round of abuse from childhood on, and she was sure the Crisis Center provided an invaluable resource to many frightened women and children. Right now, though, she wasn't in the least interested in meeting staffers or seeing the nursery and the small room they'd converted into a library and resource center. She just wished Dorothy would keep quiet and allow her two minutes of silence to think up an escape plan.

Maggie worked at a feverish pace, setting the coffee to brew, arranging food on the serving platters, putting out plates and cutlery and arranging cups and saucers on a separate table, along with jugs of creamer and containers of sugar and artificial sweetener. Bad enough that she was going to quit early, but she didn't want to leave Dorothy totally in the lurch.

Nine-forty. A couple of board members had arrived early and were checking the printed agenda that had been set up on a table next to the podium at the oppo-

site end of the lounge. Maggie was terrifyingly aware
that time was running out. Suppose the archbishop and
his sister arrived before ten? It wasn't impossible. How
could anyone know for sure when they would turn up
since they'd changed their minds twice already?

The room was air-conditioned to within an in inch
of its life, but Maggie had to use a paper napkin to wipe
beads of sweat from her forehead. The oven pinged to
indicate it had reached the desired temperature, and
Dorothy slid a giant tray of Danish pastries and mini-
croissants into the oven. Preoccupied with manipulating the heavy tray, she stopped chattering for a moment,
giving Maggie a precious moment of quiet.

Nine forty-five. Either the quiet or the rapid count-
down toward ten o'clock brought Maggie the inspira-
tion she needed, although the excuse wasn't one she was
happy to use. "Dorothy?" She stuck her head over the
counter into the kitchen area. "Can you point me in the
direction of a rest room?"

Dorothy closed the oven door and tipped her head
over her left shoulder. "Down the corridor there. First
door you come to."

"Thanks. I'll be right back."

Dorothy straightened up so she could look at Maggie, her attention caught by the genuine worry she must
have heard in Maggie's voice. "Are you okay, Christine?"

"Yes, sure. At least I guess so." Maggie hurried away
in the direction of the rest room before Dorothy could
ask any more questions. She didn't want her boss to
offer assistance at this crucial point in time. She stood

in the rest room, staring dazedly into the mirror, and waited for five agonizingly long minutes before coming out again. That should be long enough to convince her boss she'd been coping with a medical crisis.

Nine-fifty. Maggie drew in a deep breath. Time was running out and this had to work.

She approached her boss. "Dorothy." She was distressed enough about what she was doing that she had no problem sounding upset and scared.

"What's up?" Dorothy was wrapping forks inside paper napkins, but she stopped at once, her forehead wrinkling in concern. "Jeez, Christine, you don't look too good."

"I don't feel too good, either." Maggie smiled weakly. "I'm bleeding," she said, her voice husky with the lie. "Dorothy, I didn't tell you, but I'm pregnant and I think I'm having a miscarriage." She pressed her knuckles to her mouth and was astonished to discover that she was choking back a real sob. "Oh, God, Dorothy, I didn't want this to happen."

Dorothy was immediately all concern, and the worst of it was that Maggie had no choice other than to exploit her boss's kindness. Dorothy insisted on finding her an armchair to sit in, with her feet propped up on an empty cardboard carton. She brought Maggie ice water to drink and offered to find someone to drive her to the hospital, but Maggie refused to go to the emergency room, pretending that she'd prefer to see her regular doctor. Sick to her stomach at her own deception, she refused to consider accepting a ride from any of the people arriving for the board meeting. Sounding distraught, which was no act at all, she said that what she wanted was to call Sean and have him drive her to the doctor as quickly as possible.

Dorothy helped her up from the armchair and hovered over her as she placed a call to Sean. Maggie prayed that he would be home and that he'd pick up the phone. Some time this morning, he planned to check out a store that specialized in security equipment for small businesses, where he hoped to buy a microrecording device. He picked up the phone on the second ring. Thank God he either hadn't yet left or was already back at the apartment.

"Sean?" she said quickly. "This is Christine. I need you to come and get me right away. There's a problem and you have to come right now, okay?"

"Honey, of course I'll come. What is it? What's wrong?"

"I'm bleeding," she said baldly. "I think maybe I'm having a miscarriage. Sean, you have to come right now and take me to the doctor. I can't stay here."

"I understand, honey. I'm on my way. Hold on, and I'll be right there. Can you give me directions to the Center?"

"No. I'll put you on to Dorothy. But you have to come fast. This is an emergency." She dropped her voice. "I need to leave right away. There's no time to lose."

"Don't worry, honey, I understand. Put me on to Dorothy quickly, okay?"

"Yes." Maggie turned to her boss, holding out the phone. "He needs directions," she said, and collapsed back in the chair, weak with relief that Sean was coming for her.

Nine fifty-seven. She'd managed to provide herself with a valid excuse to leave the Center, but her problems had barely begun. She still had to get away before the archbishop arrived. Fortunately, Dorothy had her hands full coping with the final setup of the buffet now that she'd lost her assistant, and Maggie was relishing the luxury of being alone when a kindly, middle-aged woman came up and introduced herself.

"Hi, I'm Natalie Carpenter, and I'm one of the board members here at the Center. Dorothy told me I should keep an eye on you—make sure you sit still until your friend arrives to pick you up."

"Thanks, but I'm doing much better now."

"Do you think you're still bleeding?" Natalie asked sympathetically.

Maggie had no choice except to say yes.

"It's always horrible when you're afraid you might lose your baby," Natalie said, trying to offer some comfort. "But I had a miscarriage the first time I got pregnant and then I went on to have two sets of twins. And I wasn't using fertility drugs, either!"

Maggie gave a wan smile and forced herself to make conversation. "Were your twins identical?" she asked.

"Yes, they were. Two sets of identical twin boys. Little monsters, all four of them. But the two oldest are in college now and they're beginning to turn into normal human beings. Finally!"

Maggie managed another smile. Natalie seemed such a kind woman, whereas she was being such a rotten hypocrite. "How long before the younger twins leave for college?"

"Three years. If they make it through high school, which seems unlikely right at this moment. They're real smart kids, but they just won't do the work, you know?"

"That must be very frustrating for you," Maggie said.

Ten-ten. At least thirty people had already arrived, almost all women. A flurry of noise greeted a new arrival, a tall man with silver hair, and Maggie's stomach jumped so hard she thought she might genuinely faint.

"Well, would you take a look at who's decided to honor us with his presence," Natalie said.

"I don't recognize him." Maggie was so relieved her voice shook.

"It's our esteemed mayor." Natalie's sarcasm was thick enough to cut with a blunt knife. "Well, you can safely bet he'd never have honored us with his presence if Archbishop Grunewald hadn't shamed him into it."

Chalk up yet another public relations coup to the archbishop, Maggie thought bitterly.

Ten-thirteen. At least another six or seven minutes before there was any hope of Sean getting here. Maggie was so tense her jaw ached from clenching her teeth. "Natalie, I have to go to the bathroom again," she said, stumbling to her feet. Any excuse to escape for a few minutes.

Natalie gave her a sympathetic glance. "Would you like me to come with you?"

No, leave me alone! Maggie forced her mouth to shape into a smile. "Thanks, but I'll be fine. I'd prefer to go alone, honestly."

"Well, if you're sure you don't need help…"

"I'm sure."

But it was worse being shut up in the ladies' room than it had been waiting outside. At least out there in the main lounge she could see everyone who arrived, whereas here she was cut off from any view of what was happening. The archbishop could arrive at any second and she wouldn't know. Maggie realized she'd put herself into a trap of her own contriving. What if she opened the door and he was right outside?

Maggie opened the door a little way and squinted through the crack. The corridor was still empty, so she scurried out. Heart pounding, she made her way back into the lounge, expecting to see Archbishop Grunewald pop out from behind every group of people she passed.

Natalie grabbed her hand and almost pushed her into the chair. "Is the bleeding worse?" she asked. "You're not hemorrhaging, are you?"

"No, but I'm anxious to get to the doctor's." Maggie turned toward the door just in time to see Sean arrive, and she sprang to her feet, weaving and dodging her way across the room to get to him.

"Sean." She almost fell into his arms. "Thank goodness you made it."

"It's okay, honey, it's okay." He brushed his thumbs across her cheeks and she realized she was crying. Having scarcely shed a tear in the entire fifteen years since her mother's death, from the moment she met Sean, it seemed as if she cried at the drop of a hat, for no reason at all. It wasn't as if she was really having a miscarriage, for heaven's sake!

Sean handed her a tissue. "Come on, honey, let's get you out of here and into the car."

"Mind you take her straight to the doctor," Natalie warned from behind her. "A miscarriage isn't something to fool around with."

"We'll go straight there," Sean promised. "Fortunately, her doctor sees patients until noon on Saturday mornings." He turned to Maggie and swung her up into his arms. "Okay, honey, here we go."

"Sean, put me down! I can walk!"

"Don't tell him that," Natalie said, smiling her approval. "Let him take care of you for a couple of days."

"Tell Dorothy I'm sorry to leave her to do all the work," Maggie said. "I'll call her at the Buckeye tonight."

"I'll tell her," Natalie promised. "Take care of yourself, Christine."

"I'll make sure she does," Sean said, then carried her outside.

Maggie rubbed her eyes with the heel of her hand, feeling like a complete idiot for crying and a worthless fraud for deceiving so many caring women. "Sean, nobody can see us anymore. You can let me walk to the car. We need to hurry."

Sean didn't put her down. "You aren't really have a miscarriage, then? I wasn't absolutely sure."

"No, I just needed an excuse to leave, and a miscarriage was the only disaster I could think of where nobody was likely to check up on my symptoms."

"Smart thinking," he said approvingly. "But let's be safe. You never know who might be watching." He elbowed his way out of the door onto the sidewalk, still holding her. "My car's parked right across the street," he said, waiting for a red light so that they could make the crossing. "So what happened? Why did you need to get out of there so urgently?"

"The worst happened. Archbishop Grunewald had another last-minute change of plans and he's scheduled to arrive at the Center by ten-thirty."

Sean let out a low whistle. "Hot damn! You must have had a few bad moments when you heard he was coming."

"A few bad moments? Good grief, Sean, I damn near had a heart attack!"

He grinned, finally setting her on her feet as he reached into his pocket for his car keys. "But you coped brilliantly, as always, and we're making our escape with—" he checked his watch "—six minutes to spare."

"That's way too close for comfort," she said, getting into the car.

"You're right. Let's get out of here." He latched his seat belt and turned on the ignition. "Why don't we celebrate our narrow escape by visiting the security store on the way back to the apartment? They told me over the phone that they have all the very latest electronic monitoring equipment."

"Great idea. Let's do it." Maggie leaned back against the headrest, finally allowing herself to relax as they pulled out from the curb. Disaster had once more been averted.

Archbishop Tobias Grunewald drew his unremark-able gray Chrysler to a halt and slipped into the parking spot left vacant only seconds earlier by a white Toyota. "Did you notice that couple who just drove away?" he asked his sister.

Bernadette looked up from the pamphlet on domestic violence that she'd been reading. "No, I wasn't paying any attention, Toby. Was there something special about them that I should have noticed?"

Archbishop Grunewald hesitated, uncertain how much to confide in his sister. "Probably not. The woman looked familiar, that's all."

"Who did you think she was?"

"It's not important."

His sister was not an easy woman to deceive and she scrutinized him intently. "Toby, is something worrying you? You've seemed unusually tense and distracted lately."

It was unfair to weigh her down with the consequences of his past sins, and yet the temptation to unload some of the burden was overwhelming. Should he tell her about the anonymous notes? But how could he explain why they affected him so deeply without telling her everything else? As always, when trying to talk about Rowena, he fell back on a half-truth. "Do you remember Maggie Slade?" he asked, switching off the engine.

"Of course I remember her!" Bernadette unlatched her seat belt and smoothed a crease out of the skirt of her neatly tailored dress. "How could I forget a girl who committed such a horrible crime and at such a young age, too? Especially since you devoted so much time to trying to help her when she was in prison."

"You helped her, too. Besides, she was very bright and she worked exceptionally hard. It seemed worth making a special effort."

Bernadette huffed angrily, waiting for him to lock the car. "And then she rewarded you by breaking out of jail and throwing away everything you'd worked to achieve on her behalf. Though that was only to be expected, I suppose, given that she'd shot her own mother."

"Do you think so? She always struck me as a young woman who had a lot of potential good in her," the archbishop said as they walked across the hot sidewalk toward the Center.

Bernadette chuckled ruefully. "Toby, my dear, you believe there's a lot of potential good in every person you meet. That doesn't mean you're right. It just means you're such a good person yourself that you don't recognize evil in others, even when it's blatantly obvious to everyone else."

He winced, painfully aware of how wrong she was, particularly in relation to Maggie Slade. His sins in that direction were manifold and became more oppressive with the passing of each year. Sometimes he thought that God couldn't have devised a better punishment than to keep elevating him to positions of ever more power and dignity in the church. The more respect and honor he received, the more he was forced to confront the reality of his own unworthiness.

"You vastly overestimate my virtues," he said, holding the door open for his sister. "You always have, Bernie. And I'm not as blindly naive as you seem to think. In fact, I have a thoroughly old-fashioned belief in the frailty of human nature and the power of evil."

Bernadette stopped suddenly, just inside the door. "Wait, I must be a bit slow on the uptake this morning! Why did you mention Maggie Slade just now? Are you telling me that the woman you noticed getting into that car might have been Maggie Slade? Good heavens, Toby, what an extraordinary coincidence that would be."

"The woman getting into the car definitely looked familiar, although her hair color was different." He decided not to mention that he didn't think there was anything in the least coincidental about Maggie's presence in Columbus—if she was here.

"But why would Maggie Slade be in Ohio?" Bernadette asked.

"She has to be somewhere," he pointed out, not exactly lying.

"Would you recognize her if you saw her?" His sister sounded doubtful. "It must be five or six years since she escaped from jail and she's probably changed a lot."

"It will be seven years this October since she escaped," the archbishop said. "And yes, I believe I would recognize her. The FBI issued that computerized update of how she might look nowadays, remember?"

"Vaguely. But even that must have been two years ago."

"You're right." The archbishop wondered what his sister would say if he told her that he had every reason in the world to remember Maggie Slade. Quite apart from the photo update, every detail of her trial and subsequent history was etched into his memory, along with a razor-sharp image of her features on the day he'd last seen her. "I guess this isn't the time or place to go into details, Bernie, but I have good reason to suspect that Maggie Slade might be right here in Columbus."

Fortunately, his sister didn't ask what reason. Why would she? Maggie Slade wasn't an obsession for her as she was for him. "Then you have to notify the police that you might have seen her," she said. "She's an escaped felon, and it's your duty, Toby."

"Yes, I suppose it is. I'll call someone appropriate on Monday." Maybe.

The buzz of voices grew louder as they approached the room where the reception was being held. "Just a thought, Toby, but since you saw this young woman here, you should ask around and see if anyone knows her. Maybe she works for the Center? Or perhaps she's a client? It would be very helpful if we could give the police a clue as to where they should go looking for her."

"We can't be certain it was Maggie Slade that I saw," he pointed out, wanting an excuse to back away. "I could easily have been mistaken."

"Well, of course. Personally, I think it's most unlikely that she's here in town. But if the young woman you saw *wasn't* Maggie, then no harm will have been done if you make a few inquiries, will it?"

He wished that moral choices could seem as simple to him as they always were to Bernie. He wished that he could be more sure that he wanted to see Maggie

Slade back in prison. He wished there was some way to take care of the problem created by those anonymous notes without sending her back to jail. Besides, notifying the police wasn't as easy a decision for him as his sister naively assumed. How could he explain his interest in Maggie Slade and his conviction that she was here in Ohio, stalking him, without mentioning the notes and that strange visit from Scott Schmidt, the private investigator who didn't exist, according to Florida's State Licensing Board?

Whatever he ultimately decided to do, he needed more information, the archbishop decided. It couldn't hurt to ask a few discreet questions and find out if anyone knew who the young woman was that he'd seen driving away. After that, he'd go home and pray for a while. Maybe God was telling him that the time had finally arrived when he would have to pay a public price for Rowena Slade's death. He had a suspicion that one day very soon, he was going to receive a note demanding a meeting. In which case, he might actually go. In some ways, it would be a relief to look Maggie Slade in the eye and acknowledge the truth at last.

Fifteen years was much too long to live in the bitterly cold shadow of a mortal sin.

Fifteen

The Brite Security Store was stocked with a wide selection of gadgets and gizmos that looked as if they belonged in the latest James Bond movie. New and improved voice-distortion devices promised to change the sound of a caller's voice on the telephone, making a man sound like a woman and vice versa. If desired, the distorted voice could speak English with a range of three different foreign accents. For five thousand dollars, it was possible to buy a briefcase already fitted with a concealed surveillance camera, a voice-activated recording device, a sensor that detected the presence of other electronic equipment within a twenty-five-foot radius, and a security lock that squirted dye over the hands and body of anybody who attempted to open the case without keying in the correct code. For eight thousand dollars, a customer could buy all of the above, plus a night-vision-enhancement feature that enabled the camera to record in almost pitch-darkness.

In a store like this, Maggie and Sean's desire to purchase an electronic recording device, voice activated and designed to be worn concealed, didn't raise so much as an eyebrow, much less a demand to know why they needed it. When Maggie expressed astonishment at the size of the store and the number of customers, their sales assistant pointed out that Columbus was the state capital as well as being a university town and major research center, so there were lots of valuable secrets to protect and to steal, both commercial and political. Business at the store was clearly booming, and Maggie had a strong feeling that their salesman didn't much care whether he sold his goodies to customers trying to protect valuable secrets or to steal them.

A mind-numbing variety of recorders was produced for their inspection, and the sales assistant patiently described the advantages and disadvantages of each system—one recorded longer, another was shielded and couldn't be detected by scanning devices until it was actually in operation, and yet another was the smallest on the market. Maggie was soon hopelessly confused, but Sean had plenty of experience with undercover surveillance and asked several questions that seemed to impress the sales assistant, who congratulated them on having made an excellent choice when Sean finally picked a device no larger than a silver dollar. This one could be programmed to record nonstop for sixty minutes at the touch of a remote control or at a preassigned time.

"Very reliable technology at a decent price," the clerk said, nodding in approval. "I think you'll be happy with your purchase, sir. Will that be cash or charge?"

They paid cash and left the store without ever having been asked their names or why they wanted the recorder. Considering that she'd nearly met disaster doing something as innocent as serving brunch that morning, Maggie found it ironic that they'd been able to purchase an electronic eavesdropping device with no difficulty at all.

"When you see a store like that, you can understand why the police have such a hard time keeping up with criminals," Sean said as they drove away. "The annual equipment budget in many police departments would barely be enough to buy a couple of those fancy night-vision cameras, but a thief can use a fraction of the profits from his last crime and buy everything he needs to steal an industrial secret that will net him millions of dollars on the international market. And he'll probably get away with it, too. Half the time, nobody knows the crime's been committed, and the other half, we sure as hell can't prove it."

"I realized when I was in prison that educated, big-time criminals almost never get caught," Maggie said. "The few high-profile cases that do come to trial all get a lot of coverage in the media, but they're the exception. Eighty percent of the women in jail with me had been arrested for crimes related to drug use, and the whole time I was incarcerated, I only met three other women who'd been to college, and none of them had actually graduated."

After a quick lunch, they drove to St. Joseph's Cathedral, which was on East Broad Street in the heart of downtown Columbus. The cathedral was almost a hundred years old and had been built in an elaborate nineteenth-century Gothic Revival style, with plenty of nooks and crannies to counter the nave with its soaring high arches. It took them three hours before they were comfortable that they'd fully explored both inside and out and were familiar enough with the surroundings to set up an effective plan for Maggie's confrontation with the archbishop—and her getaway afterward.

Back at the apartment, the heat wave had finally broken in a summer storm, and they made their plans to the accompaniment of rolling thunder and flashes of lightning. "How long do you think it will be before we can pass the final note to the archbishop?" Maggie asked. "We haven't a clue about where he's going to be next week, and the brochures we found at the cathedral were no help at all."

"I'm not going to pass him any more written notes," Sean said. "I'm going to phone him."

A huge crash of thunder punctuated his announcement and Maggie gave a wry glance heavenward. "My opinion exactly," she said.

Sean shoved his hands into the pockets of his jeans. "At this stage, a phone call is less dangerous than risking another physical encounter."

"Perhaps, but how will you get through to him? I'm sure he has secretaries and assistants who screen every incoming call. You'll have to state your name and business before they connect you, and presumably most people get palmed off on a staffer."

"I'm sure they do," Sean agreed. "But if I tell the secretaries that Scott Schmidt is calling on an urgent personal matter, I'm guessing that Grunewald will agree to speak to me. And, hopefully, he's already primed to expect the worst when he hears that name."

Maggie glanced down at the shiny new tape recorder she and Sean had just bought and wondered if the chancery phone calls were automatically recorded like customer-service calls to many businesses. Unlikely, she decided. The expense of such a system wouldn't be justified for a church. "You'll call from a public phone?" she asked.

"Of course. And I'll be real concise. How does this sound?" Sean paced the worn carpet. "This is Scott Schmidt, Your Excellency. I'd like to arrange a meeting with you for my client, the young woman we spoke about last Thursday. She's asked me to inform you that she has documented proof of your relationship with Rowena Slade that she's willing to sell to you for... twenty thousand dollars?"

"That's too much," Maggie said quickly. "We don't want him to be scared off by a blackmail demand that's too high for him to pay."

"Good point," Sean said. "Okay, ten thousand dollars. How about that?"

She considered for a moment. "Better. That's just enough to sound as if we're serious, but not so much that he couldn't raise it on short notice."

"Although we don't really care whether he brings the money or not. In fact, he might say something more incriminating if he doesn't bring the money and feels obligated to negotiate a deal with you."

"That's true," Maggie acknowledged. "I guess the

crucial thing is to set up the meeting in such a way that he'll feel more at risk if he stays away than if he comes. So when are you going to make the call? Now?"

Sean shook his head. "Wish I could, but we can't do anything until Monday. The chancery offices are closed for the weekend and there's no way we can find out Grunewald's private phone number."

Maggie tried not to feel frustrated. The morning's near disaster at the Crisis Center had left her more on edge than she would have expected, and she didn't relish the prospect of waiting almost forty-eight hours to find out if Grunewald would walk into their trap. "If you manage to get through to the archbishop on Monday, when will you schedule our meeting?"

"It needs to be as soon as possible after I make the call, don't you think? Unfortunately, there's no guarantee that Grunewald will be in his office on Monday morning, but if I do get through to him, I plan to suggest five o'clock that afternoon."

"Five o'clock on the same day that you call him? That's kind of short notice, isn't it?"

"We're not issuing an invitation to speak at a church luncheon, Maggie. We want this to sound like a non-negotiable demand. And the fact is, either those two earlier notes have worked, or they haven't. Either he's already scared enough to come to the meeting, or our scheme hasn't worked. So from our point of view, there's nothing to be gained by waiting, especially since we don't care whether he has time to get the payoff money or not."

Five o'clock Monday afternoon. For years, Maggie

had fantasized about forcing a showdown with Grunewald. Now there was an actual time and place tethering her fantasies to reality, and she was terrified. She held no hidden aces in her hand, and the archbishop wouldn't be an easy man to bluff. Sean had been her lifeline so far—without him she wouldn't even have had the money to buy the recorder—but on Monday, when she finally faced the archbishop, she would be alone. Everything was going to come down to her ability to trick Grunewald into a confession.

She walked over to the window, watching the downpour of rain without really seeing it. The rain was seeping in around the air-conditioning unit, leaving a rusty brown stain as it trickled down the wall. She went to get a towel and padded the leak, thinking how odd it was to be bothering about such mundane details when her whole future hung in the balance. She turned around to look at Sean, trying to smile, hiding her hands in the damp towel so that he couldn't see the way they were shaking. "If I told anyone that I'm planning to trap the sainted Archbishop Grunewald into a confession of murder with your help, they'd conclude that I was stark, raving mad."

He tossed the towel onto the floor and took her hands. "Then we won't tell anyone," he said. "Not until we can say that I'm the cop who proved your innocence as well as the cop who found the gun that killed your mother."

"Tell me the truth, Sean. Is this going to work?"

He didn't insult her with facile reassurances. "I don't know, honey, but we're sure going to give it our best damn shot."

As he spoke, lightning flashed, followed by a crash of thunder so close that it rattled the window glass. Simultaneously, the lights flickered and went out.

Maggie hoped very much it wasn't an omen.

Bernadette tapped on the door to the library, where her brother was working on his speeches for the following week. "Don't you know that the Sabbath is supposed to be a day of rest?" she asked, only half-teasing. "I've set a tea table in the parlor. Will you join me? I'd enjoy your company."

Her brother looked up, setting aside his reading glasses and giving her a warm smile, although he looked tired. "A cup of tea sounds wonderful," he said, smothering a yawn. "I'm writing gobbledygook, so it's time to quit anyway."

He was wearing himself out, Bernadette thought worriedly. He kept up a pace that would have exhausted a thirty-year-old, let alone a man who would soon be sixty-one. "You should slow down, Toby. I'm really looking forward to going to Rome one day soon and seeing you installed as a cardinal." She gave him an affectionate smile. "I'll be a very frustrated old lady if you up and die on me from overwork before I get there."

Toby looked down at her, his gaze sober. "You've wanted to make a pilgrimage to Rome ever since you retired," he said. "You should go, Bernie, not wait for me to become a cardinal. That's probably never going to happen."

"Nonsense. You're the ideal candidate, and I'm not the only person who says so. Why, only the other day,

Bishop Burnham mentioned to me that he thought you were the most impressive young man serving the church in North America."

Toby chuckled. "The fact that Burnham calls me a young man should tell you a lot, Bernie. He's eighty-seven and he's been officially retired for fifteen years. He's a dear, sweet man, but he's totally out of the political loop."

"Being appointed a cardinal isn't only about politics, Toby. It's about God's will at work in the world."

"I don't wish to sound irreverent, but that merely reinforces my opinion that you should purchase your ticket to Rome without delay! If my appointment depended on politics, I might have a chance. But God is much too smart to choose me."

Bernadette smiled. "I beg to differ." She poured tea into the delicate china cups that had once belonged to her deceased husband's mother. She loved their fragile beauty and the fact that they were finally being used in a setting worthy of that beauty. Her parents had owned a gas station and feed store in Rapid City, South Dakota, and there had never been much money to spare when Bernadette and Toby were growing up with their sister Loretta. Beauty had been in desperately short supply in the Grunewald household.

Toby, perceptive as ever, noticed her give a quick, sentimental stroke to the sugar bowl, and he flashed her a sympathetic look. "You're thinking about Tom and the old days in Rapid City, aren't you? Do you still miss him, Bernie?"

She added lemon and a lump of sugar to Toby's tea

and handed him the cup before answering. "No," she said finally. "I think of him often, of course, but there isn't any pain attached to the memories, not anymore. After all, it's almost thirty years since he died."

Tom had been one of the most respected doctors in Rapid City, and his family had been from a very different social class than the Grunewalds, whose ancestors had been peasant farmers in southern Germany. Everyone had been thrilled for her when she'd married Tom, and their life together had played out like a fairy tale until a tragic accident killed him and her whole life changed course. Left a childless widow at the young age of thirty-three, she'd discovered that her husband had been a much better doctor than he had been a businessman and that she'd inherited very little money.

Many women of her generation would have been at a loss as to how they could support themselves, but Bernadette was rather proud of the fact that she hadn't wasted any time lamenting her woes. She'd spent her inheritance to support herself through four years of college and two intense years of graduate studies and then, a newly qualified forty-year-old, she'd found a job near her brother, who was working as an assistant parish priest in Chicago. A year later, he'd been given his own parish in Denver, and she'd transferred to Colorado with him.

By the time he was assigned to the sprawling parish of St. Jude's in Colorado Springs, it had been a foregone conclusion that she'd go, too, and keep house for him as she had been doing for the previous five years. Rumors were already circulating that Toby was on the fast track to advancement, and the magic word "bishop" had begun to be heard. Bernadette felt a special glow of pride in his achievements since she didn't have a husband and children. She'd always known that Toby was destined to go far in his chosen career and she liked to think that by helping his household run smoothly, she'd contributed to his success.

"What's your schedule like for next week?" she asked, refilling his cup. "I used to think you worked yourself to a frazzle in Phoenix, but it's been simply amazing since we arrived in Columbus. Your fame has definitely preceded you, Toby. They seem to want you on every committee in the city."

He pulled a face. "I'm going to try to keep out of the limelight for a while. The media is a very hungry monster, I've discovered, and a fickle one, too. After they've spent a few months showering you with praise you don't deserve, they turn around and indulge in an orgy of criticism, which is often no more deserved than the praise. I'm going to spike their guns and retreat from the battlefield before they get so bored with saying nice things about me that they say nasty ones instead."

"That's probably a wise decision." Bernadette smiled. "But, then, you're a wise man, Toby. And don't scowl at me like that. You won't allow anyone else to pay you compliments, so I'm going to claim sisterly privilege."

Toby returned his cup to the tray and leaned back in his chair. "Thank you for making me take a break, Bernie. I hadn't realized how tired I was."

"I suppose it's useless for me to suggest that you

might cancel a few appointments tomorrow and just sit in the back garden with a good book?"

"Yes," he said, "it's useless. I have a particularly difficult meeting scheduled for tomorrow morning. The principal of Holy Trinity High School has been accused of having an affair with one of the teachers. She's denying it, and now a group of parents have got wind of the scandal—"

"And they want her dismissed," Bernadette finished.

"No," Toby said. "They say she's a wonderful person and they want her to stay. And one of the parents supporting the principal happens to be a reporter for the local ABC affiliate. She's threatening a full-scale on-camera exposé of the quote 'tyranny of parochial school disciplinary procedures' unquote."

"What nonsense! She clearly doesn't know what she's talking about."

"Maybe not. Unfortunately, ignorance rarely seems to stop a reporter from expounding at length in front of the camera. I'm supposed to sort out that little problem by lunchtime, or we're going to be the lead feature on the five o'clock news. And in the afternoon, I'm scheduled to conduct a midyear budget review." He gave a slightly weary shrug. "Unless I can find a way to turn into Solomon overnight, I predict major squalls ahead."

"There's one problem I can take from your shoulders," Bernadette said. "I can notify the police that Maggie Slade may well be in Columbus, going under the assumed name of Christine Williamson."

Her brother got up and walked over to the French doors that led out from the parlor onto a small stone patio. "That might be jumping the gun. I'm not at all sure I even saw Maggie Slade, and we have absolutely no proof that she's living here under an assumed name."

"Well, she certainly wouldn't be living here under her own name, would she? And we know from the inquiries you made yesterday that this Christine person has only just arrived in town and nobody really knows anything about her background. Doesn't it strike you as more than mere coincidence that Christine Williamson, who looks astonishingly like Maggie Slade, arrived in town less than three weeks after you?"

"Life is full of coincidences," Toby said.

"You'd never have mentioned seeing Maggie Slade unless you were pretty certain of your identification." Bernadette crossed to her brother's side, laying her hand on his arm and wishing that he wasn't quite so determined to think the best of everyone, even a convicted murderer. "Toby, be reasonable. You've always had a protective urge where Maggie is concerned, but this goes beyond the reasonable."

"I knew her mother. She was one of my parishioners." Toby's voice was thin. "It's only natural that I should care about her daughter."

Bernadette barely refrained from snorting. "Toby, this is a moment to put individual compassion aside and think about the greater good of society. We're talking about a young woman who shot her own mother at point-blank range, escaped from a tough prison and has managed to stay on the run for almost seven years. Why has she come to Columbus? How many people might she injure if she came after you with a gun—and murder on her mind?"

Toby pinched the bridge of his nose as if kneading away a headache. "You're right," he said, and this time the weariness in his voice was unmistakable. "We need to tell the police what we suspect. And, of course, if Christine Williamson turns out to be a young woman who simply happens to look like Maggie Slade, then no harm will have been done."

"Exactly." Bernadette was relieved that her brother was finally seeing reason. He was the type of man who would believe in a person's good intentions right up until the moment that the hatchet was buried six inches in his skull. "You needn't worry that I'm going to make a mountain out of a molehill, Toby. I'll simply call Captain McNally and let him know that Maggie Slade might be in the area. I'm sure the captain will respond appropriately. After all, it would be quite a feather in his cap if he recaptured a dangerous murderer who's been on the run for so long."

"Yes, you're right. We have a responsibility to notify the police. Although I wish that, as a society, we were more willing to concentrate on rehabilitation and leave punishment to God, where it belongs."

"Dear Toby." Bernadette gave her brother an affectionate hug. "Sometimes you sound like a totally unreconstructed sixties liberal."

Toby finally returned her smile. "Don't tell anyone, Bernie, but I believe that's exactly what I am."

Sixteen

Sean called the chancery offices at 9:05 on Monday morning from a phone in the neighborhood drugstore. He was told that Archbishop Grunewald was in meetings all morning and couldn't be disturbed. He called back at noon, using the phone in a crowded pizza parlor, and once again almost failed to make it through the barrier of assistants. In the end, he got lucky and managed to cajole his way past a dragon lady who seemed to feel she was guarding access to the heavenly gates rather than a mere archbishop. After so much difficulty in getting connected, when he finally presented his demands to Grunewald, Sean was disconcerted by the ease with which the archbishop surrendered. After a few token protests and with only mild arm-twisting on Sean's part, the archbishop agreed to meet with Scott Schmidt's "client" at five that afternoon.

"My client will wait for you to enter the confessional that's located on the north side of the chapel dedicated to St. Joseph," Sean said, keeping to his script even though Grunewald wasn't playing his part as anticipated. "When you enter the confessional and switch on the light to indicate that you're ready to hear confessions, she will immediately approach you. At that time, she will give you further instructions in regard to the exchange of your money for her documents."

"I understand. Tell your client not to worry, Mr. Schmidt. I'll be at the appointed place at five o'clock. I believe this meeting has been a long time coming, for both of us." The archbishop's voice sounded crisp and decisive rather than nervous.

Sean's sense of foreboding was increasing by leaps and bounds, but he attempted to impart a suitable degree of menace as he delivered his parting shot. "Don't imagine that you can double-cross us, Grunewald. That would be a real bad mistake on your part." He hung up before the archbishop could reply, determined to reap what psychological benefit he could from having gotten in the last word.

After years of undercover work, Sean considered himself pretty good at hiding his feelings, but Maggie took one look at him when he walked back to the table, and her eyes darkened with anxiety. "What's up?" she asked, keeping her voice low. "Didn't you get through?"

"I got through and I made our demands and arranged the time and place for the payoff."

"So why are you looking as if somebody just popped your birthday balloon," she said. "What went wrong?"

"Nothing," he said, sitting opposite her. "Not a damn thing. And that's what's worrying the hell out of me,

Maggie. It was too easy. Grunewald agreed with hardly a murmur of protest. I squeezed and he didn't even squeak before he gave up."

Maggie pushed aside an untouched slice of pizza, her expression grim. "You think he's planning to set us up, don't you?"

"We have to consider that possibility," Sean said.

She didn't say anything, just stared into the distance, silently assessing the gaping hole that had appeared in their plans. Sean could almost see her rebuilding the protective armor that she'd gradually been shedding over the past few days and he cursed himself for having screwed up on what amounted to the most important sting operation he'd ever worked on. He'd scarcely given Denver and the looming interview with the department's psychologist a thought since coming to Ohio, but now the nagging doubts about his competence returned to plague him. Was he losing it?

For years, he'd had the reputation of being the cop who never fucked up, who had a sixth sense that warned when danger lurked behind a closed door or around a corner. But he'd heard on the street that Art had been fingered and he'd failed to find his partner in time to warn him. Art had died and he'd been shot for the second time. Now it seemed likely that he'd totally misread the archbishop, putting Maggie's freedom at risk and her whole future in danger.

"I'm sorry," he said. "I've screwed up, Maggie. I guessed that Grunewald would rather make a payoff than face a scandal, but it looks like I may have guessed wrong. He's gotten away with murder for fifteen years, so maybe he figured he could call in the cops, get you locked away again, and the world would ignore any accusations you might try to make."

She frowned, thinking. "And then again, maybe we're both reading too much into the way the archbishop sounded on the phone."

"Maggie, the guy basically said thanks for calling, I'll look forward to seeing you this afternoon."

"But we have no way of guessing why he gave in so easily." Maggie made a tight ball of the paper napkin she'd just shredded. "Maybe somebody was standing right next to him when he took the call and he didn't dare protest. Maybe he'd already anticipated a demand for money and was relieved we didn't want more. After all, he thinks I have documents that prove he was having an affair with my mother. He's an archbishop with a genuine shot at becoming a cardinal. Think about it, Sean. How can he afford to call the cops? If he does, he's risking a scandal that's almost guaranteed to wreck his career. That's what we were counting on when we made this plan, and I don't see what's changed."

Grunewald's career was vitally important to him, Sean reflected. It was why he'd murdered Rowena Slade in the first place—to protect his appointment as bishop of Pueblo. Feeling marginally more cheerful, he nibbled a slice of cold pizza and considered ways to protect Maggie so that it would be safe for her to keep her appointment with the archbishop. He had to strike a balance between reasonable caution and knee-jerk panic. Maybe Grunewald had sounded so cooperative because he was already terrified into compliance. And maybe he'd sounded so cooperative because he'd already alerted the cops. How the hell could they find out which?

"I need a disguise," Maggie said, breaking into his thoughts. "You've described me to Grunewald as a redhead, five foot seven, slender build. I can't do anything about my height, but I could dye my hair blond and tie a cushion in front of me so I look pregnant. That should change my appearance enough to throw the cops off my tail."

She had the most amazing resilience of anyone he'd ever met, Sean thought. No wonder she'd managed to evade capture for nearly seven years. However many times she was knocked down, she picked herself up, dusted herself off and came out fighting. "Yes, a disguise would help a lot in terms of getting you inside the cathedral," he agreed. "But you'd only be safe until the moment you walk across the aisle to the confessional, and then a cushion ain't gonna save you, no way. Trust me, Maggie, I've worked operations like this and I know how the cops will behave. If the archbishop has alerted them to the possibility of blackmail by an escaped felon, once it gets to five o'clock, they're going to swarm all over anybody who approaches the designated meeting place, even if that person appears to be the wrong age, height, weight, sex, you name it."

Maggie started shredding another napkin, the only sign of her inner tension. "Realistically, how many cops might be sent to the cathedral?"

"It's short notice, so it depends on how many officers they can round up. On the other hand, the archbishop is an important public figure, and they're going to take him seriously if he says he's being menaced by a felon. They'll call in off-duty cops if they need to. I'd say they could decide to send in as many as a dozen cops."

The napkin was shredded into confetti, but Maggie's hands and voice were both steady when she finally lifted her head and looked straight into his eyes. "Okay, the bottom line is that we can't possibly find out whether the archbishop has called in the cops. We can only hope that he hasn't. So now I have to decide whether I should meet with the archbishop this afternoon or not."

"*You* don't have to decide. *We* have to decide."

"No," she said coolly. "This decision is mine to make and I've made it. I'm going to meet with the archbishop, but I don't want you to come with me."

He returned her gaze as implacably determined as she was. "No way that's going to happen, Maggie. If you go to meet with Grunewald, I go, too."

"Don't play the hero," she said, her voice hard and cold. "This is a no-win situation for you, and it's time for us to stop pretending otherwise. If you want to do me a final favor, drive me back to the apartment and help me get wired up. Then I want you to pack your suitcase and get the hell out of Ohio. At five o'clock this afternoon, you need to be as far away from Columbus as you can get. Preferably on a plane so you'll have an unbreakable alibi."

"If you want me to stop playing the hero, you need to stop playing the martyr. I'm not interested in waving goodbye, then watching you on the evening news as you're marched back to jail. I want you free, living in my house, sleeping in my bed, waking up with me in the mornings. And that means I have to help you nail the archbishop's sanctimonious hide to the wall."

"If the cops are surrounding the cathedral, it isn't the archbishop who's going to get his hide nailed anywhere."

"So if the cops are there, we won't go in." Sean got to his feet, energized by the realization that they weren't doomed to walk into the situation blind. "If we get to the cathedral early enough, we'll be able to see if any cops arrive to stake the place out. We've told Grunewald we'll meet him at five. Take it from me, we can count on the fact that the Columbus Police Department doesn't have the manpower to start surveillance more than an hour in advance."

For the first time since he'd called the archbishop, Maggie's face showed a gleam of hope. "Which means that if we get to the cathedral by three, we can see whether or not any cops actually arrive."

"Yes, ma'am, that's exactly what we can do. When we arrive, we'll check out the interior first. Once we're sure the place is clean and that no cops are inside, we'll go outside and keep watch. If no cops show up, when Grunewald makes an appearance, you can follow him into the cathedral. If the cops do show up, then we'll simply fade away and not make contact with him."

"Then we'd have to start all over again with a new plan to trap him."

"That's right." Sean didn't want to give her time to

brood, so he tugged her to her feet and urged her toward
the door. "Honey, I know it's hard when we've gotten
this close to nailing him, but if he's notified the cops,
it's better to retreat and live to fight again another day."

"It's just that I've waited so long, and for the first
time I allowed myself to hope…"

"I know," he said. He kissed her forehead. "And now
we've got to get you home in a hurry so you can dye
your hair while I go back to the security store and buy
us a nifty miniversion of a two-way radio. One that al-
lows us to communicate with each other. That way I can
keep watch outside the cathedral when you're inside
with the archbishop. And if we're going to get to the
cathedral by three, we need to haul ass."

Maggie was blow-drying her newly blond hair when
she realized that the phone was ringing. So few people
knew her phone number that she felt sure it would be
Sean, and she hurried out of the bathroom to grab the
phone.

"Hello."

"Christine? Or should I say Maggie Slade? This is
Dorothy. How's your miscarriage or shouldn't I ask?"

Maggie would have slammed down the phone, but
her fingers were locked around the receiver in a death
grip. "D-Dorothy…" she stuttered.

"Don't say anything. It'll only make me madder than
hell. I don't know why I'm doin' this, except I must have
some crazy idea at the back of my head that you're innocent. I'm callin' to let you know the cops were here
at the Buckeye, askin' after you. They showed us pic-

tures of a woman called Maggie Slade. Told us she'd murdered her mother and then escaped from prison in Colorado. Asked us if we'd ever seen you, and when two of the staff said yes, they'd seen you, you were working here under the name of Christine Williamson, the cops asked me for your home address. I gave it to 'em."

Maggie struggled to find her voice. "I didn't kill my mother, Dorothy, I swear it."

"I hope you didn't, kid, for your sake as well as mine. That's a hell of a thing to have to live with." Dorothy slammed down the phone.

For ten seconds or so, Maggie stood listening to the dial tone and then she realized exactly what it was that her boss had just told her. The police had been checking out the possibility that Christine Williamson and Maggie Slade were one and the same person, and Dorothy had given them Christine's home address. Which meant that the cops could be knocking on her door in no time flat.

Maggie felt one quick stab of searing frustration, then her brain shifted into escape mode. She grabbed her oversize purse from behind the door and shoved into it the recording device that she and Sean had bought on Saturday, adding a travel pack of toilet articles that she always stored already packed in the bathroom. Personal hygiene was important when you were on the run because cops tended to be suspicious of anyone who looked like a vagrant. All the money she possessed in the world was already tucked deep into a zippered pocket inside the purse, but she ripped the photos of her parents from their frame while she engaged in a split-second mental debate about stuffing a cushion down the front of her jeans. She decided against it since the advantage of a fake pregnancy in terms of a disguise was more than offset by the way it would impede her movements if she needed to run.

She wondered what Sean would think when he came home from his trip to the Brite Security Store and found her gone, but the thought was too painful to hold for more than a moment and she pushed it aside. When Sean returned to the apartment, he would notice that the pictures of her parents were missing, but that was the only message she could leave him. She hoped to God he wouldn't come home while the police were still hanging around, or if he did, that he would see their squad car outside the door. If the cops did manage to corner him, Sean would be in big trouble. His only defense would have to be that he had no idea that Maggie Slade and Christine Williamson were one and the same person, not a very credible story for a cop who'd been present the night of Rowena Slade's murder.

But she couldn't worry about Sean, couldn't afford to waste any more time thinking about him. Two minutes after hanging up the phone, Maggie was running down the stairs, making a dash for the corner drugstore so she could use the pay phone to call a cab. She saw a police cruiser approaching just as she got to the drugstore entrance and, in the distance, heard the wail of a siren that might well come from a second squad car summoned to give backup.

Instead of ducking inside the drugstore, where she

might find herself trapped, she kept on walking steadily until she got to the corner of the block. Breathing hard, forcing herself to keep a sedate pace, she made a left turn and walked a few yards more. The second she was out of sight of the police car, she broke into a run. Fortunately, a bus drove past her, heading toward a stop halfway down the block, providing her with a perfect excuse to be running. As an unexpected bonus, the driver waited the extra few seconds she needed to reach the stop, and she hopped on, not caring where the bus was going just so long as it carried her safely out of the vicinity of the cops.

She slumped into a seat by the window, hot and sweating, her heart pounding from stress rather than physical exertion. She'd made it! She was still free, and it was only two-thirty. She had the recorder in her purse and absolutely nothing to lose, Maggie decided. She got out of the bus on a circular plaza somewhere on the vast campus of Ohio State University and hailed a cab to take her to the cathedral.

"What is your opinion about that, Your Excellency? Our health costs this year have risen at a rate fifteen percent higher than we budgeted for, and the projection for the next six months looks even more alarming."

Archbishop Grunewald came to with a start and realized that a dozen heads were turned in his direction, waiting for him to speak. He also realized that he hadn't the faintest notion what he was supposed to be giving an opinion about. "My opinion is that I'm brain-dead," he said, forcing a smile. "I suggest that we take a twenty-minute break and get back to this when we've had some refreshments. I know that Ginny has iced tea and her famous fresh lemonade already set up for us in the dining room. Shall we adjourn, gentlemen?"

With everyone milling around the refreshment table, he managed to evade both the director of education and the diocesan accountant, sneaked out of the chancery offices and made his way into the private residence. He desperately needed a few minutes of solitude if he was going to make it through the rest of the afternoon's meeting without embarrassing himself. He instinctively made his way into the library, which already felt like home after a mere four weeks of living in Columbus. He sank into the wing chair beside the empty fireplace and closed his eyes, luxuriating in the blissful quiet, breathing in the smell of leather-bound books and old wood, lovingly polished.

The peace was refreshing but brought him no answers. After five minutes of meditation, he was left wrestling with the problem of what he was going to do about Maggie Slade. Agreeing to meet with her had been the easy part. Deciding whether to inform the police of their upcoming meeting was a lot more difficult. The decision should have been easy, a no-brainer, but he'd harbored a terrible guilt about Rowena's daughter for fifteen years, and he couldn't bring himself to pick up the phone and make the call that would send her back to jail.

It seemed that the echoes of old sin reverberated down the hallways of time, still loud enough to drown out the voice of justice. He pulled a face, mocking his high-flown rhetoric. What it all boiled down to was that he wanted to save himself from public humiliation. Once a coward, always a coward, it seemed.

He glanced at his watch. Five more minutes and he'd have to go back and devote his undivided attention to the budget discussions. He walked over to the desk and picked up the phone. He stared at it for a few seconds, then returned it to its cradle. Who was he kidding? He wasn't going to call the police and he'd known that from the moment he'd agreed to the meeting. After all these years, he was still a hypocrite at heart.

He was just about to return to the chancery offices when his sister came out of the parlor. "Toby, I didn't know you were here. What a pleasant surprise! Have you stopped by for afternoon tea?"

"I'm afraid not. I was just stealing a few minutes of downtime before I get back to work on our diocesan budget."

"Oh, yes, you told me about that yesterday. What time do you expect the meeting to be over?"

He smiled ruefully. "At the moment, it seems unlikely that we'll finish any time this side of eternity, but I have to call a halt in a couple of hours whether we're through or not. I've arranged to meet someone else at five o'clock."

"Oh, Toby, you're hopeless! You've been up since dawn. Don't you ever quit?"

He hesitated for a moment. "This is an important meeting, Bernie, but it won't keep me long, I don't suppose. I'll try to be home at six."

Bernadette looked at him anxiously. "This meeting—I hope you don't have to go tearing all over town to get there?"

"No, it's right here in the cathedral, in fact. Now I really have to get back to the budget discussions or I'll be keeping everyone waiting. For some reason, they all expect me to produce answers to their problems despite the fact that I obviously can't read a flowchart, much less come up with brilliant new ways to make a nickel do the work of a dime."

"They look to you because they know God is guiding your decisions, Toby."

The archbishop grimaced. His sister had a frighteningly exaggerated opinion of his spiritual worth. "God is much too smart to use me as an intermediary for any decision that involves money or accounts," he said dryly, bending to kiss his sister's cheek. "I'll see you this evening, Bernie."

There were no cops inside the cathedral, Maggie was sure of it.

She'd checked everywhere with extreme care, opening every door in the building, including several bearing signs that said No Admittance. As far as she could tell, there were no more than half a dozen people in the building, and none of them seemed likely to be cops in disguise.

Two elderly women knelt in the chapel dedicated to Our Lady, and she'd crept up close enough to each of them to be quite sure that they were genuinely elderly, not young women in disguise. An old man had lit a candle and placed it in a holder in front of the statue of St.

Joseph before resuming his seat. In the twenty minutes she'd been in the cathedral, Maggie hadn't yet seen him move or switch his gaze from the candle flame. She was sure no undercover cop would have sat that still for that long. He'd have been shifting on his seat, walking up to check on his candle—anything that gave him an excuse to get up and look around for his quarry.

It was four o'clock, so she had at least fifty-five minutes to wait before the archbishop would arrive. During the years she'd been imprisoned, she'd had a lot of dead time to endure when the lights were out and she wasn't tired enough to sleep. She'd trained herself to tune out her surroundings and let her mind float free, but she couldn't utilize those techniques this afternoon because she needed to remain alert and intensely aware of what was happening around her. If the police did arrive, it was vital that she notice them at once.

The minutes dragged by with agonizing slowness. The two elderly women left. A couple in their forties with a pair of teenage daughters came in and made a brief tour of the cathedral. The daughters looked bored, the parents tired, and they left within ten minutes. The old man's candle burned out, and he finally got up and left. Maggie saw that there were tears streaming down his cheeks and she wondered what grief he'd been trying to assuage and whether the candle had helped. Another elderly woman came in and lit a candle to the Virgin. The sun moved lower in the sky, striking the stained-glass windows and sending colored light dancing across the walls and floor. At a quarter to five, moving as soundlessly as she could, Maggie made a final tour of the cathedral, partly to stretch her stiff muscles, but mostly to reassure herself that she hadn't overlooked any potential threats. Two more worshipers came and went, both elderly, chatting to each other about someone called Father Patrick as they passed Maggie.

At five minutes to five, she found a seat that was hidden behind a pillar but still gave her a clear view of the confessional located on the north side of St. Joseph's shrine. Her heart began to pound, her breathing became shallow, and her palms turned slick with sweat as she counted down the seconds until the moment when she could anticipate the archbishop's arrival.

Five o'clock came and went. Maggie's stomach lurched through a series of somersaults. One minute past five. Two minutes past five. What if he didn't come?

She heard the sound of footsteps behind her and knew it was the archbishop long before he appeared in her line of sight. He'd come alone and he walked quickly to the designated confessional, pausing to unlock the door. He stepped inside without stopping to look around.

The door of the confessional closed behind him and the light came on. Maggie rose to her feet. She wished that she remembered how to pray. This would have been a good place to ask God for help if only she thought he would listen. She walked over to the confessional, but instead of kneeling in the space provided for penitents, she went around to the same side that the archbishop had used and pulled open the door.

The archbishop looked up. "Hello, Maggie," he said. "I'm very glad to see you again."

Seventeen

Traffic on the roads had been heavy due to summer construction work, and it had taken Sean longer than he'd expected to get to the security store to buy a two-way communicator. He was satisfied with his purchase, however, and didn't regret the slight delay in his schedule. Provided he and Maggie didn't meet with more traffic delays getting downtown, they should arrive at the cathedral no later than a few minutes after three. Later than he would have liked, but well before any law enforcement personnel would turn up.

He took the last flight of stairs two at a time and let himself into the apartment. "Honey, I'm home!"

His smile faded as he stepped into the living room. Maggie wasn't there, and the place had an empty feel to it. He tapped on the bathroom door, the only other place she could be in the tiny apartment, and the door swung open at his touch. No Maggie. He frowned when he saw the hair dryer resting on the counter, switched off but still plugged in. Feeling a sudden chill, he went back into the living room and looked behind the door. Maggie's purse was gone.

Grimly, he began a methodical search of the closet and chest of drawers. With only two places to search, it didn't take long, and as far as he could tell, she'd left the apartment taking nothing with her except her purse and the tape recorder they'd bought on Saturday. Even as he reached that conclusion, his eyes were drawn to the end table beside the sofa where the pictures of her parents always stood. The frame was empty.

He rejected the idea that Maggie had deliberately run out on him almost before it formed. Over the past few days, she'd had dozens of opportunities to leave him and she never had. Besides, he could only imagine one set of circumstances that would have induced Maggie to flee less than three hours before her appointed meeting with Archbishop Grunewald: something had happened that scared her into running at a moment's notice, presumably some warning that the police were closing in on her. But did the missing tape recorder mean that she still hoped to meet with the archbishop this afternoon? If so, Sean decided, his smartest move would be to drive straight to the cathedral and hope to meet up with her there.

He returned to the bathroom and made a swift, final survey to make sure he wasn't missing anything. He didn't want to go storming off to the cathedral without checking every possibility. Maggie's emergency kit of toilet articles was gone, which was exactly what he'd have expected if she left in a big hurry. More puzzling was the disappearance of the package of hair dye they'd bought on their way home this morning. The fact that the hair dryer was on the counter and the old towel tossed into the plastic laundry basket with splotches of hair dye on it suggested that she'd finished coloring her hair and was blowing it dry when she got spooked and decided to run. So where was the empty dye package? Not in the bathroom wastebasket. And not in the kitchen trash, either. The conclusion was obvious, but puzzling. Either Maggie had taken the time to wrap up the empty package and take it with her, or someone had been in the apartment after she'd left, and taken the package.

The lock on the front door wasn't broken, which meant that thieves couldn't be responsible. It made no sense to think that Maggie had let someone in and they'd kidnapped her, along with pictures of her parents and a bottle of hair dye, so he could think of only one scenario that fitted all the facts. Sean started to sweat. Law enforcement officers of one sort or another must have come calling, presumably armed with a search warrant. That was bad news in and of itself since it meant they'd persuaded a judge to agree that there was probable cause for believing that "Christine Williamson" was guilty of a crime. Maggie most likely had no more than a couple of minutes warning that they were coming—he couldn't imagine how or what—and she'd made an immediate run for it.

When the police arrived and found the apartment empty, they must have shown the search warrant to the landlady, who lived downstairs, and she must have agreed to let them into the apartment. Law enforcement officers were the only people Sean could think of who might collect a package of hair dye and take it away. It would be invaluable to them since it was bound to be covered with Maggie's fingerprints. If he was correct, and the police had taken the dye, then it would be a matter of minutes for them to compare the prints from the package with official FBI records of Maggie Slade's prints. He had to work on the assumption that any minute now the Columbus police would have a confirmed ID. They would know that Maggie Slade was in Columbus, they would know the alias she was using, and they would know exactly what she looked like, right down to the latest color of her hair. Which, if he remembered correctly, was Moonbeam Gold.

Sean couldn't begin to imagine how the police had come to suspect that Christine Williamson was Maggie Slade, but the source of their information didn't matter right now. What mattered was that Maggie had probably gone tearing out of here to keep her appointment with Archbishop Grunewald—and the chances were better than excellent that Grunewald planned to hand her straight over to the police.

Sean swore briefly and violently, already heading for the door. He'd known the archbishop was up to something ever since their phone call. He should have refused point-blank to let Maggie go ahead with the meeting. And if she'd given him crap about the decision being hers to make—well, there was a time for sweet reason and there was a time for action. He should have tied her up, slung her over his shoulder and driven her at high speed out of the state of Ohio.

He was halfway down the stairs with nowhere to run and no way to hide when he saw two uniformed police officers coming up the stairs toward him, weapons drawn, moving fast. In the split second that he had to assess the situation, he saw that one of them looked young and very nervous. Definitely not good news.

"Police! Put your hands above your head and don't move." The older cop barked out the command, his voice and his gun steady.

So this is what it felt like on the other side of the badge, Sean thought, dropping the plastic bag that contained his two-way communicator and holding his hands high so that the nervous young cop could see that he wasn't carrying a weapon.

"Turn around real slow and walk back upstairs to your apartment."

Smart move on the older cop's part, Sean decided. A good way to avoid accidents if the rookie was really as nervous as he looked. Get the suspect off the narrow staircase before asking any questions. Ascertain if there's sufficient cause to make an arrest, then get the cuffs on in an area where there's enough light and space to see what you're doing. Nobody bumps into anyone else by mistake. Nobody's finger accidentally squeezes the trigger.

He wondered how he could keep his brain split into two parts, with one half making a detached, professional analysis and the other half in a whirl of terror on Maggie's behalf. What had happened to her? Was she in custody after all? Or was she still free, about to meet with the archbishop—and about to walk into a trap that could end in a hail of bullets?

Because a shoot-out that ended Maggie's life was now his greatest fear. The arrival of the cops had focused his mind completely, and Sean wondered why in the world it had taken him so long to realize that Maggie's death was the only way Archbishop Grunewald was going to guarantee preserving everything that was important to him. To keep his reputation pristine, he not only had to let the police know that crazy Maggie Slade was stalking him, but he also had to be sure she died before she could make any accusations that might—just possibly—be taken seriously.

The cathedral wasn't an easy place to ambush; that's why he and Maggie had chosen it. But with the police determined not to let a notorious felon escape, the fact that they were working in a difficult environment didn't protect Maggie. It merely added to the risks from her point of view. The archbishop could easily call out that she had a gun.

Maggie would quickly realize he was setting a trap. She'd try to run. The police would scream at her to stop. Panicked, she probably wouldn't obey. Shots would be fired. The end. The archbishop would be overcome with remorse when he realized—too late—that Maggie wasn't actually carrying a weapon.

Sean drew in a shaky breath, visualizing the tragedy with painful clarity. Christ, there had to be some way he could stop this from happening. They reached the front door and the older cop approached cautiously. "Anyone inside?" he asked.

"No." Sean spoke for the first time.

The cop didn't take his word for it. He banged on the

door. "Police, open up!" He waited for a couple of seconds, repeated the procedure, then turned to Sean. "Do you have keys?" he asked.

"Yes."

"Where are they?"

"In the back pocket of my jeans."

"Get them." The older cop nodded to the rookie.

The rookie patted him down. "He's clean," he said, pulling out Sean's wallet along with the keys. "His driver's license is from Colorado. Identifies him as Sean McLeod, with a residence on Alameda."

The older cop grunted as if this bland information confirmed his worst suspicions. "Stand aside," he said to Sean. "Mike, you unlock the door. I want to take another look inside that apartment."

They all trooped into the apartment. Sean stood in the middle of the bare living room, waiting with the older cop's gun pointed squarely at his heart while Mike searched to confirm that nobody else was there. At this distance, he could read the guy's name tag. Officer Richard Russo.

Mike returned to the living room. "There's nobody here," he confirmed.

Officer Russo gestured with his gun. "You want to tell me what you know about the woman who lived here?" he asked Sean. "We could start with her name."

"Christine Williamson," Sean said. "What's this all about, Officer? I've been gone from here less than two hours and I come back to find my girlfriend has vanished and that the police are ready to blow me away if I look at them cross-eyed."

"We have reason to believe that your girlfriend is an escaped convict," Russo said.

"Christine?" Sean managed a laugh. "You're kidding, right?"

"This is no joke, Mr. McLeod. We believe Christine Williamson is the alias currently being used by a very dangerous escaped felon. Name of Maggie Slade. Convicted of murdering her mother way back in 1982. If you know anything at all about her whereabouts, I strongly advise you to share that information with us. Unless you want to risk being charged with aiding and abetting a felon, that is."

Sean weighed his various options at lightning speed. He could continue to lie, in which case the police would be stymied. But, unfortunately, even though Officer Russo had no grounds for making an arrest, he did have sufficient grounds to take Sean into temporary custody and demand answers to some sticky questions. It wasn't the questioning that worried Sean. Provided he kept to his story that he knew nothing about Christine Williamson except that she worked as a waitress and that he found her attractive, there wasn't a damn thing they could charge him with. But while he was down at the police station, refusing to answer questions, what would happen to Maggie? The fear that she was already at St. Joseph's Cathedral and that the archbishop didn't plan for her to leave there alive gnawed at his gut.

"Okay, Russo, I'm going to offer you a deal," he said. "I'll tell you everything I know about Christine Williamson on one condition. You have to tell me if Archbishop Grunewald has been in communication with the police about a possible meeting Christine may have set up with him."

The cops exchanged glances. "We don't do deals," Russo said after a brief hesitation. "If you have information, Mr. McLeod, you'd better give it to us."

"Of course you do deals," Sean said. "Hell, I'm a cop. I know. Without deals, none of us would be able to get a dog convicted of pooping on the sidewalk."

"You're a cop?" Russo was too smart to lower his weapon. "Show me your badge."

Sean decided not to mention that he was on compulsory leave, awaiting certification that he wasn't stressed out to the point of being wacko. "I'm on vacation. I don't have my badge with me. But I am a detective sergeant with the Denver Police Department. What's more, I happen to be the detective who found the murder weapon that killed Rowena Slade, Maggie Slade's mother, way back in 1982."

Russo finally lowered his gun, although he didn't holster it. "Okay, Sergeant McLeod, I'm listening. You like to revise your earlier statement that you don't know anything about Christine Williamson except her name and current occupation?"

"I'll tell you that I know for a fact that Maggie Slade has arranged a meeting with Archbishop Grunewald. I won't tell you where or when, at least not yet. All I want to know right now is whether your department has been informed of that meeting, and if so, whether there are any plans being developed to ambush the meeting place."

"Not as far as I know," Russo said, his gaze watchful. "If we'd known Maggie Slade had arranged to meet the archbishop, we wouldn't have been sent out here for a second time to check and see if she'd returned to her apartment."

That made sense, Sean decided. The fact that Russo and Mike were poking around in this neighborhood probably meant that their captain hadn't been warned that Maggie was planning to be at the cathedral. He glanced at his watch. Three o'clock. It seemed as if days had passed since his phone call to the archbishop this morning, but in reality it was little less than three hours.

"How long since you checked in with headquarters?" he asked.

"An hour," Mike said.

Then it definitely wasn't safe to assume that the archbishop hadn't informed the police about his meeting just because Russo and his partner knew nothing about it. Sean held out the phone, realizing that the balance of power in the interrogation had shifted the moment he identified himself as a police officer. He was now the person running the show. "Do me a favor," he said. "Call your desk sergeant and find out the latest information on Maggie Slade, will you?"

Still holding his gun in his right hand, Russo took the phone with his left. "If you're working under cover, McLeod, you're way out of jurisdiction, and claiming to be on vacation isn't going to make you one bit more popular with the captain."

"I'm not working under cover. I'm not claiming any official standing in this case whatsoever."

"Then what's your interest in it?"

There was no point in saying he was in love with Maggie. Even less in suggesting that Maggie had been wrongly convicted and that Archbishop Grunewald was the person who'd really murdered Rowena Slade. The most likely result of a claim like that was to get him escorted to the nearest mental health facility. Sean compromised by telling Russo the truth, but not the whole truth.

"If your department is about to mount an operation designed to capture Maggie Slade, I want to help you bring her in alive, with no fatalities on any side. Trust me, Russo, your captain needs to talk to me before he sends in his troops or the situation will end in the sort of shoot-out that's every police department's nightmare."

Russo looked at Sean silently for a full minute. Then he holstered his gun and made the call.

Eighteen

How did he dare to say that he was pleased to see her again? Maggie looked straight at the archbishop, so full of anger that she saw him through a mist that blurred his features. "You know why I'm here," she said as soon as she could control herself enough to speak.

"Yes, I believe I do. You want me to pay you money for your silence. Ten thousand dollars, to be precise." The archbishop returned her gaze, his expression unexpectedly mild. "Extortion is a crime, you know."

"It will hardly be noticed in the long list of crimes I've supposedly committed. Besides, this isn't about money, Your Excellency." She spoke his title with mocking emphasis. "What I want from you is a confession. I've chosen a very appropriate place, wouldn't you agree?"

"Perhaps, although the sacrament of confession promises us forgiveness along with penance, and I'm not sure either of us knows how to offer that."

"I'll never forgive you. Never in a hundred lifetimes."

"I probably don't deserve your forgiveness even if you could bring yourself to offer it."

The archbishop seemed more sorrowful than anything else, and Maggie felt a shiver of revulsion. This man gave new and nauseating meaning to the word "hypocrisy."

"What do you want to hear me say, Maggie?" His voice was low and husky with remorse. "That I loved your mother more than I've ever loved anyone else in my life? That I wanted to marry her, and to this day, I can't bring myself to regret the fact that I broke my vows, betrayed the rules of my church and became her lover? Do you want me to confess that if a miracle occurred and Rowena walked into the cathedral right this minute, my first impulse would be to take her into my arms and beg her to marry me? Do you want me to say that I find it bittersweet to look at you and see so much of Rowena's beauty recaptured in your features? If that's what you're waiting to hear, then I admit it freely. I was your mother's lover for five of the happiest and most anguished months of my life. I'm sorry if it offends you, but I'm not willing to say that I regret having loved her. Rowena was a truly remarkable woman and loving her has been one of the defining facts of my life."

Maggie almost choked on her anger. "How dare you pretend that you loved my mother! You don't have any concept of what the word 'love' means."

The archbishop reached out as if to console her, and

Maggie jumped back, sickened at the thought of being touched by him.

"I guess you have every right to be angry with me," he said, letting his hand drop. "I should have found the courage to admit the truth long before now. You deserved better from me both as your priest and as the man who loved your mother."

Maggie fought to draw breath, barely able to stand still, she was so furious. "If you loved her a tenth as much as you claim, you would never have hidden your relationship with her."

"The decision to keep our love secret wasn't entirely mine. It was your mother's wish, too." For the first time, the archbishop sounded a little defensive. "And your well-being was a major factor in our decision. Rowena and I both recognized that you were very idealistic beneath your rebellion, and we didn't want to thrust you into the ambiguities of the adult world any sooner than was necessary—"

"So you encouraged my mother to live a lie! Sure, I can see how that would protect my idealism." Maggie's voice dripped sarcasm.

"In retrospect, it's easy to see we made bad choices. But the process for releasing a priest from his vows is long and difficult, and Rowena wanted to protect you from the mudslinging and the gossip for as long as possible. You were her daughter, not mine, and I felt she was the person who had to make that choice."

"And after my mother died, Your Excellency? When I was arrested, did you keep silent then because of my well-being and my mother's right to choose?"

The archbishop flushed. "No. I kept quiet because I was in Rome and didn't know you'd been arrested until your trial was almost due to begin. And then I kept quiet because I was angry with you. The woman I loved was dead, and I convinced myself that no purpose would be served by coming forward—except to dishonor the reputation of the church and the priesthood to which I'd renewed my dedication."

Maggie stared at him in incredulous silence as he rushed on. "Eventually, I realized that I had no right to sit in judgment on you. God helped me to understand that if I truly loved Rowena, the very best way I could honor her memory was to help her daughter. That was what prompted me to visit you in prison and offer my assistance so that you could acquire the skills and the education you would need to lead a productive, meaningful life once you were released from jail."

God helped him to understand! How could he dare to link his vile behavior to God's will? Maggie's mind reeled under the weight of her rage. "You're truly despicable! You let me go to prison for killing my mother and then you lulled any faint remnants of your guilty conscience by helping me get a college degree. It's sick how twisted you are, how self-righteous."

"You can't blame me any more than I blame myself. I'm willing to accept my full share of responsibility for the tragedy of your mother's death. Do you think I haven't tortured myself for years, wondering to what extent your discovery of our affair may have pushed you toward violence—"

"*Stop!*" Maggie barely managed to prevent herself

screaming. "Listen, I don't care what sort of perverted feelings you had for my mother or how sorry you felt for me. I only care about the fact that you murdered her."

"Murdered her?"

"*Yes!* And I want to hear you admit it, just once. Stop dancing around the truth and say it, damn you! Tell me how you shot my mother and left her wounded and bleeding, gasping for every breath she tried to drag into her lungs. The lungs you ripped apart with the shot you fired! Then tell me how you let yourself out of the house and crept to whatever secret spot you'd parked your car. Tell me how you drove back to your comfortable presbytery and offered up a pious prayer or two for my mother's soul while I held her in my arms and watched her die."

"Maggie, no! Wait…"

"I've already waited far too long," she said harshly. "Now it's your turn to speak up. I want to hear you explain why you stood back for fifteen years and let me pay for your crime! I was fifteen years old, I was alone in the world, and you left me to suffer for the murder you'd committed. I can't imagine how you've lived with yourself all these years, except that you're a monster, a devil hiding behind a mask of virtue."

The archbishop stared at her as if he no longer understood the English language. Her words dissolved into sobs. She realized she was pummeling his chest and crying hot tears of bitter anguish, but she didn't care. She pounded him with the force of fifteen years' accumulated anger and the bitter frustration of knowing that she had no future.

She had no idea how long the archbishop let her hit him without attempting to defend himself, but it was a long time. Then he stood up, moving out of the confessional and grabbing her wrists with unexpected strength. He marched her over to the window and held her at arm's length, staring at her as if he'd never seen her before.

The archbishop curved his hands around her cheeks, and she simply stood there. "Dear God in heaven," he murmured. "You didn't kill your mother."

The rage that had sustained her vanished, replaced by grief. Grief as consuming and overwhelming as the night she'd come home and discovered her mother dying. Her body went limp, and if the archbishop hadn't been holding her, she would have fallen. "Of course I didn't kill my mother," she said wearily, not even caring that he was holding her, touching her, supporting her. "What a ridiculous thing to say. I didn't kill her. You killed her. We both know that."

The archbishop's face turned whiter than the candles burning in front of the statue of St. Joseph. He spoke with slow and heavy deliberation. "As God is my witness, Maggie, I didn't kill your mother."

"Yes, you did. Of course you did."

"Maggie, until this very moment, I've always believed that you were the person who killed Rowena."

"That's impossible...."

He shook his head, staring at her as if he still couldn't believe what he was seeing. "I often wondered if you knew that I was your mother's lover. It never once occurred to me that you might have reason to believe I was also her murderer. I simply assumed that the police version of what happened was the truth. You killed your mother, and your story of hearing a man leave the house by the kitchen door was simply an attempt to divert attention from your guilt. Today is the first time it's ever occurred to me that you really did hear someone leave the house."

She didn't answer him because she couldn't make sense of his words, and yet, at some dimly perceived level of her subconscious, she understood what he was claiming. That he hadn't killed her mother. That he'd always thought she was guilty.

At some even more deeply buried level, she recognized the incredible fact that he was telling the truth.

But the habit of so many years was hard to shake, and it gave her the energy to wrest her arms out of his grip. "Don't lie to me," she said. "There have been too many lies and I can't stand any more."

"You're absolutely right," he said quietly. "And I'm not lying. I've never lied to you except by omission. But you don't have to take my word on trust, Maggie. I can give you proof that I didn't kill your mother. The night she died, I was in Chicago, a thousand miles away from the scene of the crime."

This time, his words sank in a little further, penetrating years of hatred, but she was still having difficulty grasping the full meaning of what he said. "You were in Chicago when my mother was killed?"

"Yes. By the most ironic of coincidences, I'd gone there to ask an old friend of mine for his help in leaving the priesthood. Bishop Burnham had recently retired, but he'd always been my mentor in the church, and he was the wisest, kindest man I knew. A week before she was killed, Rowena and I had decided to get married as soon as possible, but we wanted to be married with the blessing of the church, so I asked Bishop Burnham for his advice on the best way to set about getting an official dispensation from my vows of celibacy. We stayed up talking until well after midnight and then started our discussions again first thing in the morning. Finally, we went for a long walk to blow away the cobwebs. We'd just returned from that walk when my sister phoned to tell me the shocking news about your mother."

Enough of her old suspicion remained for Maggie to think how convenient it was that the archbishop's alibi for the night of the murder depended on a church dignitary who was most likely dead. "Is this Bishop Burnham still alive?" she asked.

"Very much alive, and active in the community. He's eighty-seven now, but he has an excellent memory. Ask him if what I've just told you is true and I promise you he'll confirm it."

Maggie was disoriented to the point of feeling dizzy. The man she'd considered her archenemy was simply a man who had loved her mother. When he'd visited her in jail, he hadn't been gloating over the fact she was paying for his crime. On the contrary, because of his love for her mother, he'd extended a helping hand—even though he believed she was guilty of murder.

"You didn't kill my mother." She spoke out loud, clothing the incredible concept in the reality of words.

"No, I didn't. And it seems that you didn't kill her, either." The archbishop's expression was bleak. "I have to ask myself why it is that I committed the sin, and yet your mother died and you were imprisoned, while my only punishment has been to receive one undeserved promotion after another."

Maggie had no answer for him although she doubted he expected one. Her thoughts were like a river in flood, too tumultuous and fast moving to halt or direct. Questions popped up and vanished unspoken like pieces of flotsam smashed by the force of the water. Finally, she realized that there was one question that kept whizzing by, waiting for her to seize it. She turned to look at the archbishop, so consumed by her question that she wasn't even shocked when she realized that he had his arm around her shoulders and was patting her arm in an awkward effort to provide comfort.

"Who killed my mother?" she asked. "You didn't. I didn't. Do you realize we have absolutely no idea who killed her?"

The archbishop hugged her a little tighter. "Yes, I've just realized that myself."

"But how are we going to find her murderer?"

"I think, unfortunately, we may never know the truth of what happened that night."

Maggie shook her head. "No, I can't accept that. I won't accept it. How can you bear to know that somebody took the life of the woman you loved and has gone totally unpunished? Don't you want to know why she was killed? How she was killed?"

"We can guess at the answers to those questions, my

dear. Probably a burglar woke your mother while in the process of robbing her. He lost his cool. He had a gun. He was scared, ignorant, very likely high on drugs. He pulled the trigger." She shuddered and the archbishop took her hand, squeezing it gently. "Maggie, let it go. If knowing the name of her murderer would bring Rowena back to life, then I would care very much about finding him. But I've learned over the years that the quest for vengeance exacts a high toll and has consequences we rarely expect. I've found that it's usually much wiser to leave justice to God. That's not the answer you want to hear, I'm sure. But at this late stage, how could we possibly hope to discover the perpetrator? If we're correct in assuming it was committed during the course of a robbery that went wrong, where would we start to look for clues? There won't be any physical evidence left—"

"I don't believe she was killed by a thief. If she'd been shot by an intruder, he'd have run the moment he killed her. But he didn't. Whoever killed her stayed long enough to be sure he hadn't left any trace of his presence—"

"How can you know that?"

"I didn't hear any shots or any sound of running," Maggie said. "I was in the house at least two or three minutes before I heard someone opening the kitchen door and quietly letting himself out. That's not the way a burglar would behave. Besides, nothing was stolen. What kind of a burglar shoots someone before he manages to steal a single item?"

"A burglar who's stoned?" the archbishop suggested.

"But even if Rowena wasn't shot by a thief, everything I said before still applies. We have no crime scene to examine, no witnesses to question. The trail is cold, Maggie. We have to move on with our lives and trust that God will make everything come right in the end."

"You seem to be forgetting something rather important, Your Excellency. I can't afford to leave justice to God. Unless I can find out who killed my mother, I'm destined to spend the rest of my life either in jail or running from the authorities."

The archbishop stared at her in consternation. "How stupid of me," he said. "I had completely forgotten that you're an escaped felon."

"In which case, you've probably forgotten another problem of more immediate concern to yourself. What are you going to do about me now that you've met with me? You may believe I'm innocent, but the law says I'm guilty. Which means that you're guilty of a crime yourself unless you walk out of here right now and notify the police that you've seen me in this area. You're obliged, by law, to give them every scrap of information that will help them to track me down."

"Fortunately, that problem seems rather easy to resolve in comparison to some of the others we've encountered today. I suggest that you come home with me and I'll call the church's lawyer—"

"If you tell any reputable lawyer why you need him, he'll advise you to turn me straight over to the police. He has to give you that advice unless he wants to be disbarred."

"Hmm, scrap that idea, then. We won't call my

lawyer. Let's move on to plan B. You'll come home with me and we'll discuss what we might do next over dinner and a glass of wine. My sister's a great cook—"

"I can't meet your sister," Maggie said flatly. "I can't meet anyone. Think about it, Excellency. It's bad enough that you're already guilty of hiding me from the police. We can't ask your sister to break the law, too."

The archbishop sighed. "You're probably right on that one. Bernadette is such a law-abiding citizen that she would undoubtedly say that you should turn yourself in and trust in our legal system to exonerate you." The archbishop gave a rueful grimace. "I have to say that her confidence in our judicial system seems entirely misplaced in your case."

Maggie had never felt less like running away in her entire life, but she didn't see what other choice she had. "If you would like to turn your back on me, Excellency—maybe walk over to the high altar and pray for guidance—I think you'd find that all your problems would be solved."

"You're going to make a run for it while my back's turned?"

"It's for the best," she said, exhausted even thinking about making her way to the bus station and starting the laborious process of establishing herself in a new state with yet another new identity. She was so tired of having to wake up each morning and remind herself of her name.

As for Sean... She couldn't even think about leaving Sean or the pain would be so great that she would simply collapse onto the floor of the cathedral and howl like a wounded coyote. She turned away, wrapping her arms around her waist, searching for reserves of inner strength that seemed to have vanished.

"I can't let you run away," the archbishop said. "Maggie, I'm not going to turn my back on you twice in one lifetime. I did it after Rowena died and I'm not doing it again tonight. We can't stay here because the cathedral is due to close, and anyway, my sister expects me home for dinner. But I should be able to smuggle you into the residence without anyone catching a glimpse of you. The staff have already left the chancery offices, my sister is almost certainly busy in the kitchen at this hour of the evening, and the cleaning people don't come in until nine tomorrow morning. You'll be safe for a few hours at least."

"Even if you manage to sneak me inside, how can I avoid meeting your sister?"

"Well, actually, I thought you might hide in my bedroom. It's the only room I can think of that she definitely won't enter. It's only a temporary solution, I know, but at least we would have somewhere safe from scrutiny where we could continue our discussion. If we think things through together, I know there has to be some solution to this truly frightful dilemma."

After only a moment of hesitation, Maggie accepted the archbishop's invitation. She shared none of his confidence regarding possible solutions, but she couldn't help allowing a tiny sliver of hope to wriggle its way back into her heart. At the very least, if she went with the archbishop, she would be able to ask him to contact Sean and explain what had happened. It wasn't much, but there was some consolation in knowing that she wouldn't have to exit from Sean's life leaving nothing but questions and uncertainty.

Walking at the side of the archbishop certainly provided her with great protective cover, Maggie discovered. They encountered half a dozen people as they left the cathedral. Everyone nodded respectfully to her and exchanged polite, murmured greetings with the archbishop. They made their way to the official residence, and he successfully smuggled her through the hallway and up the imposing oak-banistered staircase to his bedroom.

"My sister and I usually eat dinner at seven if we're alone," the archbishop said after pointing out the room's only chair and offering her a supply of books and church journals as reading material during his absence. "I'm sorry I can't offer you anything to eat," he said. "But my sister goes to bed early and I'll raid the refrigerator as soon as she's safely out of the way."

"Thank you, but I'm not hungry and I can get water from the bathroom if I'm thirsty."

"I should be able to get back up here by eight-thirty or so. After we've eaten dinner, my sister and I usually spend fifteen minutes or so over coffee, discussing what's happened during the day. It's something of a ritual, and Bernadette would find it odd if I made excuses to avoid it."

"I understand." Maggie felt no sense of urgency to start her discussions with the archbishop. He still had the gung ho optimism of a person presented with a fresh problem to solve. She'd been nursing the dilemma of how to prove her innocence for fifteen years and she no longer believed there were any solutions to be found. Sooner or later, the archbishop was going to come to the conclusion that there was nothing for him to do except turn his back and let her run.

He seemed to sense something of what she was thinking because he walked over to her and laid his hands gently on her head. "Don't despair, my dear. With God's help, we'll find a way to set you free."

Maggie wished she could believe him.

Nineteen

Her brother was worried about something, very worried. After years of loving observation, Bernadette was aware of every nuance of Toby's behavior, and although he had tried to appear cheerful throughout dinner, she hadn't been deceived.

"You seem troubled," she said, handing him a cup of coffee, served strong and black the way he liked it. A very masculine way to drink coffee, she thought approvingly, adding skim milk and artificial sweetener to dilute her own serving into a weaker, more feminine brew. "Is the problem something you can share?"

"And here I thought I was doing such a terrific job of maintaining appearances." Toby smiled ruefully. "You know me too well, Bernie. I'm sorry, have I been brooding?"

"Not at all. You've been great company—just a tad distracted, that's all."

"I'm sorry. I'm chewing on a problem that doesn't want to be solved."

"Let me guess. The high school principal who had an affair with one of her teachers is refusing to resign."

"No, she was quite cooperative, thank goodness, and we worked out a compromise everyone seems willing to live with. This is something a little more personal."

"Anything I can help with?"

"Thanks for offering, but no. I have to resolve this by myself."

"Just so long as you remember that I'm always here if you need a shoulder to lean on."

"I know you are, Bernie. You're a rock." He gave her an affectionate smile. "In fact, I often wonder how I'd have managed all these years if you hadn't been doing such a great job of taking care of all the domestic details of my life. You've spoiled me rotten, and I'm deeply grateful."

"It's the least I could do," she said lightly, although her heart swelled with pride and pleasure at his praise. "I always knew that you were destined to rise to great heights in the church, Toby, and I'm glad that I was here to smooth your path."

He answered her politely enough, but she could see that his attention was already drifting back to his problem, whatever that was. If it had been an ecclesiastical problem he was wrestling with, Bernadette wouldn't have cared. Toby's professional judgment was impeccable, the perfect blend of efficiency, decisiveness and compassion. Since it was a personal problem, Bernadette cared a lot. She debated pressing him for more details, but in the end, she decided to let events take their course. She would find out eventually what was bothering him. She always did.

"By the way, I mustn't forget," she said—as if she could possibly forget. She'd been waiting all night for the best moment to slip a seemingly casual comment into their conversation. "Captain McNally called earlier this evening. His men were at Christine Williamson's apartment this afternoon. She'd already flown the coop, unfortunately, but the police were able to get several excellent fingerprints, and when they ran a check against the FBI records of Maggie Slade's prints, it was a perfect match. Christine Williamson and Maggie Slade are one and the same woman."

Toby looked up immediately, focusing on her with sudden laser-sharp intensity. Why was she surprised? Bernadette thought bitterly. After all these years, anything to do with Rowena Slade still had the power to command a hundred percent of her brother's attention. "Are the police keeping her apartment under surveillance?" he asked.

"No, because they're fairly sure she won't go back. Captain McNally did seem to feel that you should take precautions for your safety. He asked me to remind you that this woman could be armed, and she's certainly dangerous."

Toby nodded. "Thanks, I'll bear that in mind. What steps is the captain taking to recapture her?"

"Naturally, he didn't confide the details to me, but I believe that tomorrow he plans to hold a press conference to ask for the public's help in apprehending her.

He hopes to get her picture circulated to as many media outlets as possible. If she's still in Columbus, that should flush her out into the open."

"Do you think so? I can't imagine that an old mug shot would be a very good likeness."

"The police aren't working with an old mug shot. They have a computer-generated photo that shows how Maggie Slade probably looks today."

"Oh, yes. Of course, I remember. They circulated one a couple of years ago. I was very impressed with the technology."

Bernadette shook her head. "Captain McNally has one that's even more recent. The FBI produced it, to show how Maggie Slade might have changed over the past couple of years, and to give people an idea of how she'd look with different hair styles and colors."

"It's amazing what the FBI can do these days." Toby cleared his throat. "However, one would assume that Maggie Slade's halfway to California by now. She hasn't avoided capture all these years by hanging around town once she knows the police are on her tail."

Bernadette forced a laugh. "You sound almost as if you hope she gets away, Toby."

Her brother hesitated. "She never struck me as a vicious killer, Bernie. Has it never occurred to you that she might have been telling the truth all these years? That perhaps she didn't murder her mother?"

"No, it never occurred to me." Bernadette refused to feel alarm.

She got up and walked across to Toby's side, putting her arm around his shoulders and kissing his cheek. She closed her eyes, relishing the sensation of closeness. She loved the combination of masculine beard stubble and the faint scent of incense that clung to him. It gave her a strange sensation of spiritual ecstasy just to be near him.

He moved away from her embrace and she released him reluctantly, looking at him with a playful smile. "Dear Toby! This sudden doubt about Maggie Slade's guilt has to be the ultimate example of your determination to think good of all the world. Maggie was a troubled teen. She was violent, rebellious, sexually promiscuous and she smoked pot, even if she wasn't doing more dangerous drugs. It's not in the least difficult to imagine a girl like that losing her temper and shooting her mother."

"Fortunately, there's a big difference between being a rebellious teen and being capable of killing your parents," Toby said dryly. "Otherwise the world would be facing an epidemic of murdered parents."

"I'm a trained psychologist," Bernadette reminded him. "My judgment was always that Maggie Slade's behavior passed far beyond the normal boundaries of teenage rebellion."

"I know." Toby frowned. "And yet Rowena certainly never felt that she had any major problems with Maggie—just that she'd been acting up and hanging with the wrong crowd. When you wrote to tell me that Maggie had been arrested and was about to go to trial for Rowena's murder, I remember that my first instinct was to dismiss the idea as completely ridiculous." He shook his head. "I should have stuck by that first instinct and not

allowed you to convince me that the police had conclusive evidence of her guilt."

Bernadette felt a chill of foreboding. It had been
many years since Toby had mentioned Rowena Slade's
name, and she'd allowed herself to be lulled into believing he'd stopped thinking about her. If his behavior
over the past couple of days was any indication, that had
been a major misjudgment on her part. Toby had
glimpsed Maggie outside the Crisis Center and he'd
been in the strangest of moods ever since. In retrospect,
it seemed obvious that Maggie Slade was at the heart
of the problem that had kept her brother struggling to
maintain a conversation during dinner. In fact, she
wouldn't be in the least surprised to discover that his
five o'clock meeting this afternoon had somehow been
connected to Maggie's presence in Columbus.

Bernadette compressed her lips, guarding against
any unwise outburst. Trust Maggie Slade to turn up
now, just when Toby's name was being seriously can-
vassed as a potential candidate for cardinal. Rowena and
Maggie both seemed to have a special talent for arriving on the scene at the precise moment when they could
wreak the most havoc with God's plan for Toby's great-
ness. Bernadette had no doubt that the pair of them
were instruments of Satan.

Knowing her brother as well as she did, she realized
that it would be counterproductive to trot out all the reasons why Maggie Slade had been convicted of murder.
She resisted the temptation to remind him that Maggie's
fingerprints had been all over the murder weapon and
that Maggie had condemned herself by sobbing into the

phone during her 911 call, begging her mother to forgive her for having hurt her. She'd even been smart enough to wash away telltale evidence from her skin, pretending to feel sick and dashing into the bathroom to scrub herself repeatedly with scalding hot water, drenching her sweatshirt in the process and ruining the hope of conclusive forensic testing. It was quite amazing how it had all worked out, really.

She picked up her brother's coffee cup and returned it to the tray. She took care not to betray any nerves by letting the spoons rattle in the saucers. It was her remarkable self-control, her ability to think before speaking even in the most trying circumstances, that had kept everyone in Rapid City believing that she and Tom were happily married, when the reality was that she had barely been able to tolerate her husband's touch. Released from the torment of marriage, she'd perfected her skills at dissembling for the even more important task of grooming Toby to meet his great destiny.

She carefully aligned the creamer with the bowl of sweeteners. "All I can say is that Maggie Slade does her own cause no good by running away like this. If she's innocent, she should turn herself in to the authorities and work with them to find evidence that will convict the person who's truly guilty."

Toby's smile was wry. "Somehow, Bernie, I was quite sure that was how you would feel."

Dear God, that meant he'd been considering what her reaction might be to the possibility of Maggie Slade's innocence. She returned to her seat on the opposite side of the empty fireplace and hurriedly sought for a way to change the topic of conversation. She needed solitude to assess what she'd heard tonight. She would have to decide whether there was anything truly worrying in what Toby had revealed, anything that required action on her part beyond keeping on top of the police and making sure that they captured the scheming vixen with all possible speed.

"This talk about Maggie Slade reminds me that I heard from Norma Paglino today."

Toby cocked his head inquiringly. "I'm sorry, I missed what you said."

Of course he'd missed what she said. His attention had switched off the moment she stopped talking about Maggie Slade. Bernadette repeated her remark with every appearance of placidity. "I heard from Norma Paglino today. She's the executive director of the Women's Crisis Center. We met her on Saturday morning, remember?"

"Yes, of course I remember. I was very impressed by her. What did she have to say?"

"She wanted to thank you for your wonderful speech. It seems that you inspired a change of heart in the mayor, and he's promised to campaign for stricter enforcement of domestic violence laws. Apparently, he was even heard to mumble something indistinct about the possibility of a few city dollars being allocated to the Center for a youth health program."

"That's great news!" Toby visibly perked up. Finding ways to prevent domestic violence and rebuild shattered families was one of his most actively pursued goals. "If we can get the funds for a full-time nurse-practitioner at the center, those kids are going to be so much better off." He pulled a notebook out of his pocket and scribbled a note to himself. "I'll give the mayor a phone call tomorrow and reinforce his good intentions. Getting him firmly on our side would be a big step in the right direction."

"I agree. Although it's a pleasant change to be in a city where they've already done so much to educate the community about the problem of domestic violence." Bernadette got to her feet, allowing a ladylike yawn to escape. "Well, on that somewhat optimistic note, I believe I'm going to bed. I have an early start in the morning and I've been tired all day for some reason."

"Good idea." Her brother barely managed to conceal his relief at her early departure for bed. He picked up the tray of coffee things. "I'll take this to the kitchen, Bernie, and then I guess I'm going to turn in for the night myself."

His eagerness to be alone both hurt and intrigued her. Why did he need solitude? Simply to continue gnawing on his problem? Or maybe for some more practical reason—like making phone calls from the privacy of his bedroom? "You'd better let me take the tray out to the kitchen," she said. "I don't suppose you have any idea what to do with those coffee cups."

"Sure I do." He grinned. "I'm going to put the milk in the fridge and leave everything else for the cleaning women in the morning. You go to bed, Bernie."

His desire to be rid of her was so urgent as to be almost tangible, but she didn't comment on it. "Good night, Toby. I'll see you in the morning."

"Good night, my dear. God bless."

Bernadette went up to her room and sat on the edge of her bed, trembling. Her brother was nearly sixty-one years old, she'd been his helpmate and companion for more than a quarter of a century, and yet she still felt that he remained elusive, the core and essence of him closed off from her possession. She realized that God was testing her, forcing her to be strong so that she would be worthy of her destiny as the woman who stood at his side when he was acclaimed as the first-ever American pope. But sometimes it was hard not to feel resentment, not to question why God insisted that women should always stand in the shadow of their men-folk, never in the full radiant sun of their own achieve-ments.

And men were such weak creatures, even the best of them, like Toby. Rowena Slade had no achievements to boast of, nothing to offer except her body, and yet she had possessed him, physically, spiritually and mentally. In order to sleep in the bed of that sly, simpering widow, Toby had been ready and willing to throw away every-thing that Bernadette had worked so hard to achieve.

The memory of those awful times still had the power to make her weep.

Fifteen years ago, Toby had received word that he was about to be appointed bishop of Pueblo. For five days, Bernadette had been almost delirious with joy, her ambitions finally on the way to fulfillment. Somebody had to become the first American pope in the history of the pontificate, and she was determined that Toby—her glorious, handsome brother—should be that man.

And then Toby sounded the death knell of her hopes. He'd come home, glowing with happiness, but not because he was so excited about his forthcoming appointment as bishop. He'd taken her to one side and shared with her his big secret. He was in love with a woman called Rowena Slade—a nobody, a parishioner—and they were going to be married.

Bernadette had stood in the center of the presbytery living room and seen her exciting dreams transformed into instant nightmares. "You can't possibly get married," she said, breathless with horror. It was unthinkable that her chaste, pure brother was contemplating indulging in the sordid, degrading activities of the marriage bed. "Toby, think what you're saying! You've taken lifelong vows of chastity! You can't possibly have thought through the consequences of what you're contemplating. You're about to throw away everything you've worked so hard to achieve."

"I'm not throwing my life away," he said. "I'm just changing directions. Bernie, you were married, you loved Tom. You must understand what I'm going through right now. I love Rowena. I love her physically as well as every other way. We want to be together."

"You must have been sexually tempted before." She hated—*hated!*—that she was being forced to discuss sex with her brother. "You overcame those temptations. You'll overcome this one, too."

"But Rowena isn't a temptation," he said quietly. "She's the woman I love." He seized her hands. "Bernie, don't look so worried. We've been considering what to do for five months and we're both absolutely certain that this is what we want. Please be happy for us."

She couldn't believe that for five months he'd been consorting with another woman and she hadn't known. Bernadette could barely stop herself from screaming. "But you have a vocation," she said. "You've known you wanted to be a priest ever since you were in high school."

"There are other ways for me to fulfill my vocation," he said, his eyes shining as he contemplated a future in which she knew she would play only the most peripheral of roles. "I already have a degree in family counseling and I'm sure I can get a job somewhere."

"But you have a job waiting for you," she wailed. "Think of what you're rejecting, Toby. You're about to be appointed the bishop of Pueblo and you're the perfect man for the position."

"You're wrong," he said, flushing. "I'm a million miles from perfect. The truth is, Bernie, that I've already broken my vows of chastity. Marrying Rowena is not just what I *want* to do, it's the *only* honorable thing for me to do."

Bernadette shut off the appalling, horrible memory. She'd prayed long and hard to make sure God understood that this had been a one-time slip on her brother's part, and that if God promised to get Toby elected pope, she would personally make sure that he never again gave way to the temptations of carnal lust. Once Rowena had been removed from the picture, her brother had never again shown the smallest sign of falling for the sins of the flesh. But Bernadette was taking no chances. Maggie Slade looked like her mother and she no doubt shared many of the same wiles. Bernadette needed to be on guard since it was common knowledge that Satan most often chose to present himself in the form of a beautiful woman.

She opened her door a crack and listened carefully. She heard Toby climbing up the stairs and going into his bedroom. She waited a few minutes to be sure he didn't plan to come out again, then she crept along the corridor in her stocking feet and pressed her ear to his bedroom door.

She heard his voice, although it was frustratingly difficult to distinguish individual words. So she'd been correct in her assumption that he wanted to get her out of the way in order to make a private phone call. He was calling a woman. She could even hear her answering him.

Bernadette froze in horror, all her energy radiating toward the one spot where her ear was pressed against the door. It had been sheer stupidity to imagine she was hearing a woman speaking on the other end of a telephone and yet she could definitely hear a woman's voice. But if she could hear a woman talking on the other side of this door, there was only one possible conclusion to be drawn. Her brother had a woman in his bedroom.

Bernadette pressed her hand to her heart, which was palpitating so fast she feared she might suffer a heart attack and die. She prayed for God to keep her alive and strong so she could prevent the disaster she sensed unfolding inside her brother's bedroom. As always, when she prayed, God answered, ordering her to save her brother from himself. Her heartbeat slowed, the red haze in front of her eyes lifted, and reason returned. The implications of her brother having a woman in his bedroom were so enormous that she could barely grasp them. She craned her head against the door, trying to catch some words that would provide a clue as to who the woman might be and what her brother was talking about.

"Captain McNally...composite photo...press conference." That was her brother speaking. His voice was low, really hard to hear, but he seemed to be repeating the information she'd given him just a few minutes ago over coffee.

"Sean McLeod...apartment...Denver Police Department...career at risk if he helps..." That was the woman speaking. Her voice was higher, softer, making it easier to distinguish words and even short phrases.

Bernadette fought to draw breath. She had every detail of Maggie Slade's trial memorized and she recognized the name Sean McLeod immediately. He was the young police officer who had discovered the gun behind the nightstand next to Rowena's bed. The infamous bed where Rowena had lured Toby to indulge his low, carnal appetites. The bed where she had met her God-appointed end.

Bernadette knew she couldn't afford to drift off into memories of the past. *Focus*, she ordered herself. *Listen. Think.*

The woman spoke again, her voice suddenly lower and much harder to hear. "Christine...police...escape...Sean...love...prison. I can't go back to prison."

It was Maggie Slade on the other side of this door.

Bernadette accepted the knowledge with a sense of resignation, almost inevitability. When Maggie Slade first escaped, she'd hoped against hope that she would be shot by an overeager police officer trying to recapture her. Years went by and Maggie remained free, so she concluded this was simply God's way of reminding her to be alert and vigilant, always ready to protect her brother. Now she realized that God wasn't going to be satisfied that she and Toby were truly worthy of supreme power until Maggie was dead. Fifteen years ago, Rowena Slade had almost destroyed God's plan for Toby. Rowena's daughter was obviously infected with the same Satanic powers.

It was going to be an easy death to arrange, Bernadette decided, walking quickly and silently back to her bedroom. She had the story she would tell the police concocted within seconds. Maggie Slade, desperate and deranged felon, had burst into the archbishop's bedroom while he was on his knees, praying. Bernadette—who'd been on her way down to the kitchen for some hot milk—had heard his cries and the sounds of a struggle. Rushing back to her bedroom, she removed her gun from the nightstand where she kept it, then ran to her brother's aid. Demented, Maggie Slade refused to back off or stop slashing at her brother— she'd have to remember to filch a knife from the kitchen—and eventually, she actually rushed at Bernadette, attacking wildly. Tragically, the gun went off and Maggie Slade was dead.

Far and away the most difficult part of this scenario was going to be convincing her brother to go along with her story, Bernadette recognized. Still, she'd tackle that problem later. First things first. Right now, she needed to take care of Maggie Slade.

She took the gun from her nightstand. It had once been Tom's gun, and she'd kept it as a happy memento of the ending of their marriage. No need to worry about fingerprints. It was okay this time to have her prints on the weapon. She paused outside Toby's bedroom door and listened again. She couldn't hear the sound of voices anymore and panic washed over her in a gigantic wave. Why weren't they talking? What might they be doing? If Maggie Slade had already tempted her brother into breaking his vow of chastity, then God would never allow him to become a cardinal.

She burst into the bedroom without knocking, and her worst fears were realized. Maggie Slade was seated on a chair and Toby was leaning toward her, his hands clasped around hers. He turned toward the door, his face filled with dismay when he saw her. *"Bernadette!"*

Maggie sprang to her feet, speaking at the same time. "Ms. Dowd? *Ms. Dowd!* What are you doing here?"

It was the last straw for Bernadette. Years of iron self-control snapped at that question. "What am I doing here?" she demanded, advancing into the room, her arms waving wildly. "I live here. This is my home. The question is, what are *you* doing here? The daughter of a whore has no business invading the sanctity of my brother's bedroom."

"Bernadette, you don't know what you're saying." Toby approached her with obvious wariness, and she suddenly remembered that she was holding a gun. She brought her arms down and took aim at Maggie's heart.

"Stand aside, Toby. She's in league with Satan to tempt you, and it's my duty to protect you."

She watched as Maggie and her brother exchanged glances. The silent language of lovers. Wasn't that what the poets called it? Then Maggie spoke, so softly that Bernadette had to strain to hear. "This is your sister?"

"Yes."

"She was my guidance counselor, first in high school, then in the juvenile detention center. Did you know that?"

"No, I had no idea. I knew she volunteered at the local juvenile detention center, but she never told me she'd taken on any official role."

"Of course I didn't tell you, I knew you'd disapprove," Bernadette said. "But somebody had to keep an eye on her in prison. Who knows what trouble she might have caused if I hadn't been there to stop her getting out on parole like they wanted her to."

"*Oh my God,*" Maggie breathed. "You lied to the parole board and convinced them they needed to keep me locked up."

"You have no God," Bernadette shouted. "Satan wants to prevent my brother becoming Supreme Pontiff, and you are his chosen instrument."

Toby was chalk white, and Bernadette felt a sudden fear that he might have a stroke or succumb to some other medical disaster. Then all her magnificent plans would be ruined.

"Don't worry, Toby," she said. "I'll make sure that everything goes smoothly for you. I always have, ever since you were a little boy. You were the cutest toddler, you know, and the best-looking boy in high school. All the girls were in love with you, but I knew you were going to be a priest, so that meant you would always be mine."

"You've been a wonderful sister," Toby said as he walked toward her, hands outstretched. "Bernie, my dear, you're not well. Give me the gun. Please."

"Not until I've killed Maggie Slade. She's a terrible threat to us, Toby. You've no idea how hard I had to work to convince everyone that she'd murdered Rowena."

Toby's expression suggested that he wasn't in the least pleased to learn of her frantic efforts on his behalf. But that was always the way. Women did all the work and men reaped all the rewards. Still, when Toby was the first American pope, she would live in a palace in Rome and be one of the most powerful women in the world. The pope's sister. What a beautiful title. She would finally be in a position to influence decisions that would affect the lives of a billion people all over the world. Not bad for a girl whose parents had been too poor to pay for a dress so that she could go to the prom.

"You killed my mother!"

Her daydream had been so pleasant that Bernadette had almost forgotten about Maggie Slade. Maggie's angry voice pulled her back to reality with an unpleasant jerk.

"Your brother had gone to Chicago, so you stole the key to my mother's house. And then you drove over in the middle of the night and killed her! It was cold-blooded, premeditated murder!"

"Nonsense. I never planned to kill your mother. I simply told her that she had a duty to leave my brother alone, that he was destined for far greater things than to marry some little nobody and mow his lawn every Saturday morning. I told Rowena that God intended for Toby to be the first American-born pope and she laughed at me. Told me I was crazy." She sneaked a sideways glance at her brother, hoping finally to see approval. "So I shot her," she said.

Her brother wasn't looking at her with the approval she craved. He made a funny little sound deep in his throat and then he turned on her, his eyes black with fury, his face drawn into an expression of disgust and horror the likes of which she'd never seen before.

"You killed Rowena," he said. "You killed the woman I loved and deliberately conspired to get a fifteen-year-old child convicted of your crime. Dear God, Bernadette, I'm not sure I'll ever be able to forgive you."

"But you must! I did it for you, Toby. It was all for you. Don't you know how much I love you?" Crying, she made to launch herself into his arms, but he recoiled, looking sick, and her tears gave way to anger. She aimed the gun at her brother and pulled the trigger before she could allow herself to have second thoughts. Blood spurted from his chest, scarlet as the cardinal's robe he would never wear. "I've sacrificed my whole life for you, Toby, and you didn't come through for me. God intended for you to be pope, and I am his instrument—"

Her words were cut off in a strangled gasp as an arm

went around her neck and choked off her breath, then squeezed so hard that her hands lost control and she dropped the gun. She'd been too busy trying to explain the facts to Toby and she'd lost track of what Maggie Slade was up to.

Bernadette gave a great cry of despair. She cried because Satan had won. She cried because, without her help, Toby would never become pope. And she cried because Maggie Slade had won. Rowena Slade, the evil temptress, was dead, but her daughter would live on.

Maggie pushed Bernadette to the floor, giving her a solid punch to the jaw for good measure. She ran to the archbishop's side, kicking aside the gun as she went. Blood made a dark stain on the purple of his clerical shirt, and she was terrified of what she would see when she got closer. She knelt beside him, cradling his head in her lap, memories of another terrible night jostling for space with her present fears.

The archbishop's eyes were closed, but she could see that he was breathing. He had a pulse, strong enough for her to feel with her fingers. She hoped that was as promising a sign as she thought. She grabbed a pillow from the bed and held it against his chest, pressing on the point near his shoulder where she could see blood seeping out onto his shirtfront. She reached for the phone and dialed 911, bitterly aware of all the ironic parallels to the night of her mother's death. If the archbishop died, was she going to find herself accused of another murder?

"Emergency services."

"I need help fast! I'm calling from the official residence of Archbishop Grunewald, on Broad Street, next to St. Joseph's Cathedral. The archbishop's been shot. He's bleeding and he's unconscious. You need to send police and an ambulance."

"And what's your name, caller? Are you injured, too?"

"No, I'm fine." She paused for a minute, realizing the amazing truth. "No, I'm absolutely fine," she repeated. "And my name is Maggie Slade."

Epilogue

Denver, Colorado
September, 1997—

He hadn't seen her for almost ten weeks, unless you counted endless images in newspapers and on TV, but today she was finally coming. By three, she'd said, and it was already twenty past. Sean paced the front yard, pretending to clip bushes, but smart enough to realize that if he actually applied shears to foliage he was likely to terminate the existence of any shrub unlucky enough to come under his blade.

The weeks since the arrest of Bernadette Dowd had only made him more sure than ever that he wanted to spend the rest of his life with Maggie, but her silence suggested that she wasn't anywhere near as certain about her own feelings. There was no way to overcome the unpleasant fact that he would always be linked in her mind with the death of her mother and her incarceration for a crime she didn't commit. Was that going to be too big a hurdle for them to jump over?

A green Ford Escort drew up at the curb and Maggie got out. He saw only that she had her own light brown hair again and that she was beautiful. The other details were lost in a blur of desire and longing.

"Hi. Sorry I'm late. The plane sat on the runway for half an hour before taking off." She stood on the sidewalk, squinting against the brilliant Colorado sun, smiling. "You look…lethal."

"What?" He glanced down and saw that he had the garden shears pointed straight at her stomach. He grinned. "That's to scare off any lurking journalists."

She glanced down the deserted street. "It's worked. We're not being watched."

"Great." He tossed the shears into the empty wheelbarrow and gestured toward the front door. "Let's go inside. It's hot out here."

"The heat is wonderful. So dry and bright. I didn't realize how much I missed Colorado until I came back. Although it's amazing how much it's been built up in the past fifteen years. The new airport's almost the least of the changes." They walked through the house, bypassing the living room to sit at the kitchen table, which looked out onto the backyard. "I like your house," Maggie said. "It's light and airy, a good place to make a fresh start."

Sean allowed himself to feel a small stir of hope. "That's what I thought, too. The whole street's new, so all the neighbors have to get to know each other right from scratch." He reached across the table, covering her hand with his, unable to keep from touching her any longer. "How've you been, Maggie?"

"Stressed. Ecstatically happy. Busy. Sometimes all of those things at the same time. Between the lawyers negotiating deals with the D.A.'s office, the TV interviews and the Hollywood agents trying to buy the movie rights to my life story, I've scarcely had time to sit back and realize that it's finally over and I'm free. Legally free, morally free—the whole ball of wax."

"How did your visit with your grandparents go?"

For a moment, she looked sad. "It was difficult for all of us, I guess. They feel guilty, and I felt…distant. I'm not a saint like the archbishop. I'm a regular human being and I can't help resenting the fact that they were so ready to believe the worst about me."

"It's going to take time to sort out all your relationships."

"I know, but I'm impatient. My life has been on hold for fifteen years, and I have this urge to reach out and grab every new experience without a moment's delay."

Sean got up and pulled two Cokes from the fridge. He handed one to Maggie. "That isn't what you did about our relationship. You refused to see me and limited our phone calls to one conversation a week."

"That's because I had just enough sense left to realize that our relationship was too important to reach out and grab." She stood up and leaned against the window, arms crossed in front of her. "I'm thirty years old, Sean, and I want to be married, with my own home and children to love and care for, more than I want anything else in the world. I know you love me, and it was really tempting to fall into your arms and let you take care of everything. When the police in Columbus said that I was free to go, I fantasized about flying home with you, letting you tuck me into your house and take care of all the fallout from Bernadette Dowd's arrest. I wanted you to get me pregnant before either of us had a moment to think."

"Sounds like a great plan to me," Sean said wryly.

Maggie shook her head. "It would have been disastrous. We shared something really special, and you deserved better from our relationship than my using you as a shortcut to my fantasy future. We both needed to be sure that I wasn't just using you to provide me with an instant home and family."

"And are you sure now? Is that why you finally agreed to come and stay with me?" He held his breath while he waited for her reply.

"Yes."

His mouth broke into a grin. "That's it? Just *yes?* No passionate declarations of undying love?"

"I'm saving those for later."

He took her into his arms. "How much later?"

She tipped her head back, laughing, her eyes dancing, relishing her freedom to make choices. "I don't know. When you make love to me and I'm crazy with desire. How's that?"

"I think it's a fine decision, honey." He put his hand on the small of her back and guided her to the stairs. "So let's get started. The bedroom's this way."

She followed him willingly, then paused on the first step so that he swung around to face her. She linked her hands behind his head, drawing him closer. "I do love you, Sean, and not just because you saved my life."

"Honey, you saved your own life, and the archbishop's, too. I wasn't even there when that crazy Dowd woman started shooting. I was at police headquarters, miles away from the action."

"That's not what I meant," she said. "You saved my life when you gave me the courage to stop running and to stand and fight. Thank you."

"I'm happy to take the credit, but the courage was all yours, Maggie." He leaned forward, intending to keep his kiss light, but she responded fiercely, with a passion that ignited his own, and he pulled her hard against him, pouring all of his love and his promises for their future into the embrace.

Hands linked, they walked upstairs together.

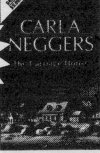

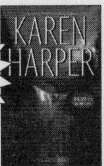